HIS ASSISTANT

Sarah L. Pauper

Contents

Connor Meyers, Vice President and COO of Meyers Motors, has always been focused on his job and doing it well. As he is currently working on planning the biggest business meeting of his life, one that will merge his company with one in Japan and earn him the title of CEO, he has no desire for distractions. He only has a few months before his meeting and nothing will make him happier than single-handedly managing this and finally getting his father to retire.

Greyson Lewis, on the other hand, is a young college student who enjoys her care-free life in Miami, Florida. Her talkative nature surprisingly managed to land her a job in Meyers Motors, and not just any nine to five. She is told she will gain the title of COO, as partner to the current one. She has no idea what the title means, but her need for a summer gig means she won't pass this up.

To say Connor is unhappy about this development is an understatement. If his father believes he will partner up with some random college student, he has truly gone insane. Greyson, on the other hand, has no intention of quitting just because her partner is an absolute ass.

With their obvious clash, is a merger even possible?

Chapter One

Chapter 1- She's Unprofessional (Connor's Perspective)

It was how it always was at Meyers Motors. Walking into the building I've known for years now, seeing people walk back and forth, hearing the phones buzzing with any number of important people, the sweet sound of keyboards clicking and the hushed greetings to be expected in the lobby.

"How was your lunch, Mr. Meyers?" One of the few female workers in the building greeted me. She took her place in the elevator I always used to ride up to the fifteenth floor where my office was.

"Good." I replied absentmindedly. I had hardly ever seen this woman who, judging by the floor button she pressed, apparently worked on the sixth floor. Like most other people, however, she recognized my power and sanctified the shoes I walked in. When the doors opened to reveal her stop, the woman scurried out to do whatever job she was in charge of and I was happy to be departed from her presence.

After the elevator opened up to my floor, I took a sip of my coffee, ready to work for the rest of the afternoon. The men who worked on my floor didn't spend time greeting me like those in other departments, which I preferred since it wasted too much time. They knew to get out of my way and work on whatever they were to do, it made for what I truly believed was the most efficient floor in the company and that's the way it was going to stay.

I finally sat down looking over what Adam, my best friend and closest advisor, had sent to my email to look over for the Tokyo merger in a few months. I was in my element, calmed with the orderly chaos that was my job. With how efficient my work habit had become, I was confident I'd be completely ready for the meeting in only five weeks, four weeks if I worked overtime. Once I proved to Jonathan that I could successfully pull off something this major, he'd finally retire happily and I'd finally be the CEO.

Jonathan, my father and boss, was in his 60's now with salt-and-pepper hair and an aura that demanded respect from all of those he came in contact with. Though this company was founded by his father, Jonathan took it from the tiny business it once was and flipped it into a multi-million dollar company that, once this merger goes the way I wanted it to, would be worth more money than ever.

There was a soft knock at my door before Samantha, my personal assistant, walked in with a wicked smile on her face. "I have some news for you, Connor!" She was the only person I allowed to walk in without so much of a knock, probably due to our 'coworkers with benefits' status. Probably not the most ethical decisions on my part, but that would remain the extent of that relationship.

Sam generally wore her thick red hair pulled back into a tight ponytail that helped maintain her professional aura. Though lacking in both hips and height she had a decent chest that she kept tucked away behind tight button up blouse. Her personality was that of a high school gossip. It was no secret to anyone that I used her to relieve some of the stress of my job, but where was the shame in that? She enjoyed it, and I allowed her to continue to work for me despite the way she annoyingly gossiped throughout the department all the time. A win-win situation if you asked me.

"I only have time for good news or news that can easily be fixed." I paid her no mind, knowing how she was.

"Never mind then." She turned on her heel and began to walk out.

Even when I tried to tell myself this red head wasn't completely annoying she always seemed to prove me wrong, "Sam," I warned, most of my attention still on my computer and what I was typing.

"Well," She spun around and stood above me from across my desk, "rumor has it that we are getting a new employee," She paused, waiting for me to give her my full attention, which did not happen. "It's going to be a girl." Sam said, and although it was usually male in my specific line of work it wasn't all that noteworthy.

"Get on with it." My fingers typed faster, tired of my time being wasted.

"Okay, okay, you buzzkill. Apparently she's still in college, about twenty-one years old and most importantly your father is holding her interview. Today." My eyes quickly darted up to meet Sam's eyes. She smiled, knowing she finally had my full attention and I frowned forcefully back.

One thing to know about my father is that he very rarely does interviews himself. If he did, that person would have to have the potential to hold a major part in the company. He also had a personal policy of not hiring anyone not yet finished with college. Not to mention, the last time he hired a higher up that was female was when he just wanted a booty call. Considering this girl literally defied all his exceptions was concerning. It was starting to seem that he just wanted to leave me with a mess to clean up when he finally retired.

"Oh yeah and one more thing," Sam said with a smile so wide you'd think she'd pull a damn muscle, "The position she's being hired for is COO."

"Sam if you're trying to be funny right now I will seriously fucking fire you." My index finger found itself only a centimeter from the tip of her nose, really wanting to strangle her neck rather than give her a gentle poke on the face. Her expression turned grim and that was all I needed to walk myself over to Jonathan's office.

The office space became deathly quiet as I walked out of my room. There was no question they had already heard of the absurd news. My jaw clenched and unclenched as I rode the five stories to the top of the building where Jonathan's office was. Whoever was behind this rumor better hope they were already out of the country or risk my wrath for raising my blood pressure and wasting my time. I just needed Jonathan to say he never heard of this or that the details of this interview had been terribly misconstrued and I could rest easy.

However, who would start something so aggravating? If this was Sam's sick joke, she'd better be fine with never working in Florida again unless it was for a McDonald's. The elevator opened up and I was welcomed with many confused glances. There were very few times that I'd come to this floor. I had no business here and if I needed to speak to Jonathan he'd either see me or we'd speak through some sort of technology. For me to come up here, we'd have to have very specific business together. If this news was even remotely true, it would appear we would have very specific business together.

I walked straight into his office, only to see him laying leisurely in his La-Z-Boy, reading some book. His professionalism seemed to decline with age and with his slightly insane brother whose advice he took way too seriously. He was definitely way past due for his retirement.

"My son! It's been some time since you've visited me. What do I owe the pleasure?" He stood up from the recliner to give me a handshake and take his seat at his grand Cherry Oak wood desk. I couldn't help to think that this desk, along with the office, would soon be mine and there was much interior design work to be done on the space yet.

I remained standing, eyeing him warily for any signs of knowledge on the current buzz. "I hear you are interviewing a probable female employee today." I spoke slowly, making sure he caught the gravity of each word.

"Ah yes! In fact, she should be arriving here any moment now. You should stay and meet her." He smiled so warmly you'd think he was the noblest man to ever walk the face of the Earth.

"I hear she is to be the COO." I said frankly, not liking how he treated me as someone unworthy of knowing what was going on with the business.

"Indeed." His smug look faded and he finally regained his professional mannerism.

"Does this mean I am to become CEO? Or are you legitimately firing me for a girl still in college?"

"Don't disrespect me, Connor," Jonathan pointed his index finger in my face, causing me to clench down on my teeth tightly. "This girl, as you should care to know, is to become COO as a partner to you, the current COO. She's not here to take your job or bring your status up, she's merely here to learn about how the company works and be present at my merger." He stated frankly, as if that explanation was enough to finalize our conversation. It wasn't.

"Are you being serious? The merger is only a few months away and if you haven't realized, I can handle it. Giving me a child to babysit while I'm supposed to be working on my job is insane. Not to mention the fact that you're giving this child the title of COO, when there are so many more capable people working who could fill that position as a partner to me, which again I do not need!"

"Listen to me carefully. Jackson believes she's the key to a successful merger, and I didn't build my empire so widely just by a freak accident," He started and my composure was swiftly declining. Jackson, his brother and closest adviser, was borderline insane and was seen as a good luck charm to Jonathan. Most, actually all, of Jackson's advice was not successful and required someone to fix up before it became a fiasco. "My business continues to grow because no matter how unorthodox my methods may seem, they always work."

"Yeah, they work when I step in because Jackson doesn't know what the hell he's talking about!" My voice was rising dangerously, there was no way I was leaving this office with him thinking so absurdly. Maybe it was time to put him and his brother in a hospital.

"Watch your mouth Connor! I'm a second away from-" Jonathan smashed his fists into his desks as he stood up swiftly, getting cut off by the sound of his double doors being thrown open.

"Good afternoon Mr. Meyers!" I turned my head around to find a person no words could describe appear.

"Greyson! What a pleasure to see you again." Jonathan sat down with a goofy smile on his face, completely ignoring my presence as if we'd never spoken.

"Yeah, sorry I'm kind of late. I took a weird way to get here and after taking multiple wrong turns I stopped to figure out the GPS on my phone. When I was parked I saw this homeless man singing and you will never believe what the song was! It turns out, he was singing Differences from Ginuwine! Now you know I had to get out of my car and donate some money to that man, his voice was absolutely heavenly. Not to mention how I haven't heard that song in a minute. He was a very nice person to and his wife had left him!"She rambled on and on.

You've got to be kidding me.

"Anyways he ended the song and he looks at me and he's like, 'Girl where you going in that cute outfit? If I'd had known we were going on a date I would have worn my best shoes.' He was absolutely hilarious. Then he sang me another song, one he'd come up with, and that's how I got here."

You've got to be fucking kidding me.

Jonathan just laughed and offered her a seat. He started saying something, and my attention shifted straight to her. First off, her attire was more runway than business. It could probably pass for a more formal business look if you were only looking at her bright pink skater skirt and matching blazer. However the black 'belly' shirt, studded stilettos, chunky gold chain necklace, and, oh, the studded snapback cap with the word 'hater'across the front kind of offset the look. It was as horrible a look as you could imagine.

"That sounds like fun." She spoke, snapping me out of my full body interrogation. She never looked at me once, nor had my father since she arrived, and I was starting to wonder if I'd turned invisible.

I gathered that she was pretty tall right when she walked in, especially in her heels. Her hair was long and coiled, almost mane-like flowing from her hat, and her chocolate brown complexion was very even throughout.

"So tell me something about yourself." Jonathan spoke up, his eyes crinkled on the outer edges as he continuously smiled at the girl.

"Umm, I don't know?" She questioned, sounding like an immature idiot who has never had a job interview in her life, "Oh! I like to dance." There was no possible way anyone could be so moronic. What the hell does that help with in a car company?

Jonathan laughed for the umpteenth time. Is it actually possible that he only fancied this girl and wanted her for sex? But why would he make her work with me of all people? "What do you believe you can contribute to this specific office environment?" Part of me really wanted to just walk out and pretend none of this was real, but the other part of me was so baffled as to if this was really my reality that my Bettanin & Venturi shoes stayed glued to floor.

"Well, y'all don't really have many girls working here so there's that. Also, I'm loads of fun so I can hopefully liven up this place and I'm confident in my ability to get you your Japanese thing. I like learning and always try my hardest to do my best on whatever I set my mind to so yeah. I'm also really easy to get along with, and all of my past bosses would probably recommend me." She spoke using her hands to make motions in the air and even bobbed her head and swayed her body with every word, her grammar and focus were all over the place. A complete freak show.

"Well I think you are definitely the woman I want for the job," Jonathan said, and they both stood up, "I'll get you someone to show you around the building for now. Oh and that's Connor, the one who'll be your partner. We'll start getting you a desk set up in his office so that you can spend today getting acquainted with the place." Wait, wait, wait. Back the hell up.

"There's no way you're putting her in my office- Oh I get it! I finally get it! This is a prank! Sam put you up to this, didn't she?" I laughed, turning towards the door so the camera crew could walk on in and everyone could get a good laugh, "You got me good, I'll give you that."

"That's not seriously your son is he? He is such a negative Nancy! He completely contradicts your cool and laid back persona! He's been standing there, staring at me, with that bad mood cloud over his head for the past ten minutes! Please tell me you have another son, Meyers." This girl did not seriously disrespect me. What the actual fuck.

"Who the hell do you think you're talking about? If you knew better, which your small brain obviously doesn't, you'd respect me as your elder and get the hell out of this office." I spoke, and she finally looked directly at me with the brightest green eyes I'd ever seen.

"Umm, excuse you?" Her face contorted nastily at me, bringing her eyes up and down my body, sizing me up.

"Connor that's enough! I am your boss. You will obey whatever I decide or get the hell out of my office for the rest of your damned life." My eyes slowly shifted to my idiotic father and I eyed him for a long moment, before I realized I could not win. I looked back to the only person to disrespect me so openly in nine years, and shot metaphoric daggers at her.

Fine, if Jonathan was going to do this to me, I'd just get her to quit. That wouldn't be too hard with a dimwit. I've done it before.

With a slight smirk, I turned on my heel and decided to let myself out, "Have it your way, boss." I said, sarcastically.

"I'll see you in our office later...Partner." I looked back to see the girl smirking wickedly at me.

Oh, she knew how to push my buttons, I'd give her that. I guess this meant war. I smiled friendly back, and with a wave went on my way.

Game on.

Chapter Two

Chapter 2- He's Uptight (Greyson's Perspective)

It was how it never was before! I scurried up to the huge modern looking building and watched the expensive looking cars drive all around it. I was about to get a job at a multi-million dollar company, after meeting the frickin' owner at a frickin' alumni event I waitressed at. It was hard to believe. I know.

I stared up at the multiple stories trying to picture myself actually working there. I probably had the most ridiculous smile on my face, but I didn't care, this was awesome! My entire body felt like it was floating in space, but luckily my bubblegum pink pumps assured me that I was grounded.

"May I help you?" Some fancily dressed up guy approached me. He had a ridiculous vest on over his shirt so naturally I assumed he was the company butler.

"No thanks Alfred, I got this." I walked passed him and finally through the very expensive doors. It honestly looked wild, with so many dudes in tuxes walking all around. I was sure all of their suits and watches combined could pay my college tuition fees for ten years or more! "This is heaven."

"Ma'am, you can't leave your car parked out front. I can move it for you, or if you'd prefer you can, but it has to go nonetheless."

"Okay, okay. Jeez." I fumbled through my non-designer purse for the keys and tossed it to the butler. A lot more snappy than I'd thought he'd be.

I took another moment to behold the beautiful men in front of me, to which I'd love to advocate a shirtless day for, and sped-walked up to the elevators.

"Hello! I'm Greyson, I'm going to be the new COO here," I introduced myself to the lady who strolled into the elevator next to me.

"I'm sorry?" She looked at me in bewilderment. In all honesty her expression, the orangey-red hair that sat too neatly on her head and the thick layer of makeup caked onto her face made her look crazy.

"I said I'm Greyson. I'm currently on summer vacation from college so I think I'll work here for now. Aren't you uncomfortable in that skirt? It looks unnecessarily tight. Anyways, I have an interview with Jonny Meyers on the top floor. I'm excited and seeing that there aren't many girls here I think we should get to know each other. That would probably make this job a lot more fun. Have you seen the men that work here? Most are a bit old, but those who aren't have some serious sex appeal." The lady looked at me very steadily, listening to every word I said.

"Did you say you were being hired as COO?" She asked, smirking slightly. I didn't really like how she looked at me, but seeing how much attention she was paying to me, I figured she was someone to keep around.

"Yeah, something like that." The elevator opened up to floor fifteen, her floor, and I watched her walk out, not saying much else to me.

I rode up two more floors before the elevator opened again to show a big group of professional looking people speaking in hushed tones, "We'll get the next one." A dignified, fatherly looking man said, smiling politely at me.

"No need, I'm stepping out." I smiled kindly back, looking at his eyes through his thick-rimmed glasses. Everyone was so nice and that was awesome. I walked a few paces before pausing to take a look around.

The floor I was on was very clean, quiet, professional, colorless, bland, stupid, depressing, deathly. Okay, so the office space was nice at first glance, but after being here for some time it was apparent that it definitely needed more liveliness, color, conversation or something! One note to self was to get on the interior design committee.

"Are you okay?" A voice called from behind me, causing me to turn around. A handsome blond smiled tentatively at me, as he waited for the elevator.

"Isn't this place kind of boring?" I said frankly, walking towards him, which revealed that he was even more attractive up close.

He chuckled sexily as the elevator dinged open. I quickly followed him inside it, "Sadly, a lot of floors here are strictly business, including mine. Wow your eyes are gorgeous." He looked at me so deeply, with a smile so soft on his lips I could seriously melt.

"Thanks," I smiled brightly, considering in my mind the countless times I've gotten that exact compliment, "I guess your eyes aren't too bad either." I said with the roll of my eyes as he clicked the button for the fifteenth floor on the elevator. I guess he worked on the same floor as that other lady, "Well then I hope I don't work on your floor."

He laughed, like the actual laugh that makes a person throw their head back. This was good, it told me that this one wasn't too stuck-up and business-y. This was a good person to keep around. "Yeah you definitely don't want to work here, but it would be nice to work with someone like you. So you're new?" He said as the elevator came to a stop.

I decided to follow him, considering the fact that he was certainly flirting with me and it would be nice to have a person to visit from time to time, "Yeah, I actually have an interview today. I'm confident though because Jonny loves me. Oh hey girly!" I saw that same red-head from the elevator, her face was a lot more pale though. I didn't think that was possible with an inch-thick layer of makeup.

"Please tell me you weren't lying about being hired for COO." She came over to me, sweating slightly. Ew, not a nice combination with that whole, I-have-a-pole-stuck-way-up-my-ass, look.

"That's what big boss Meyers said to me." I shrugged, "Are you okay?"

"You're being hired for COO?" Blond boy now looked bewildered. What the hell was so special about COO? I should probably figure out the meaning of the title, but it didn't sound too bad. I knew it wasn't janitorial so what was the issue? "That's, um, strange?" He stated, well more like questioned, looking to Miss. Red-Head for answers to his obviously confused concerns.

I figured this was my time to exit, since they were being kind of rude, so I sighed and left for the elevators for what felt like the hundredth time already.

"Hey, where are you going?" Blond boy came after me, aw he was sweet, I liked him.

"Sorry, I just have to get to my interview." I smiled at him, "Don't worry, I'll come around from time to time."

"Yeah, good luck! And please do." He smoothly slid his hands into his pockets. I really liked him and his laid back character. I was certain that he was going to be fun to keep around.

I finally got to the top of the building, where Jonny's office apparently was, and quickly scoped out the receptionist, "I'm here for an interview with Mr. Meyers. Oh, your necklace is really beautiful!" I looked at the super thin silver chain with a small heart hanging down it.

"Thank you," She said politely, "He's in that room at the end, I'll call him now." She smiled, and picked up the phone.

"Wait, no need. I want to surprise him." I winked and she smiled in agreement. Nice lady, very reserved, but nice nonetheless.

I actually really liked Jonny's floor. Everyone seemed to be less stressed and more relaxed. Although the color palate of the floor was still very monotone, it was a tad brighter than the other floors I've been to and that filled me with good vibes about my boss.

I walked up to the double doors, took a deep breath and swung them open, "Good afternoon Mr. Meyers!" I strolled in to witness a scene I didn't really understand. However, I quickly ignored it when Jonny smiled super brightly at me, and the really unpleasant man simmered in silence for whatever reason.

While Mr. Boss Man was telling me the description of my job, which was starting to sound a lot more difficult than I had wanted, I could feel the other guy staring at me. For the entire interview, I was considering the idea that I was possibly taking his job, but that wasn't possible because I was being partnered with Jonathan's son, who worked alone prior to this.

"So after the training and after you get comfortable I simply want you to be present at the meeting in Tokyo and use some of that charm of yours on the men there. I'm sure whatever you end up saying at the meeting will be this company's ticket." Mr. Meyers spoke and a smile was growing on my lips from the flattery.

"That sounds like fun."

The interview ended in a weird place. I didn't entirely enjoy the fact that the childish man beside me was my partner, although he helped make it the most interesting interview I've ever been in. I also didn't like how he had the nerve, through his immature tantrum, to call me the childish one. Not to mention my distaste for seeing Mr. Meyers in a very unhappy place.

However, it dawned on me that this might make my time here a lot more worthwhile. I was sure I read somewhere about the health benefits of a little office drama. Besides that, everyone I've ever met seemed to warm up to me eventually. Well, kind of. So I decided right then and there to understand where he was coming from and become his friend.

"I'll see you in our office later," I contemplated for a short moment how to address him in the nicest way possible, to show him that our little mishap shouldn't stop us from being friends, "Partner." I smiled when he looked back, very wide to show my apologies for being a hot-head.

He nicely returned the smile, and with a wave walked out. I guess he wanted to be friends as well. How nice.

"I apologize for my son, but he'll come around." Mr. Boss Man smiled reassuringly at me, and called in someone to give me the tour.

"Nah it's fine. I'm sorry for being rude. Don't worry though, I'm good at making friends so I'll play nice." I laughed for a moment, then followed my tour guide out after a final good-bye.

"So are you excited about working here? I here you have a very important position." Old Man Tour-Guide asked me. He walked kind of slow, very dignified and I was already bored with the tour.

"Yeah, yeah. Hey listen, I'm the play-as-you-go gamer, not the whole, read-the-instruction-booklet-before-playing gamer. So if you could just show me to my floor and office, I can handle the rest." We walked onto the elevator and he raised an eyebrow at me.

"Are you sure you belong here?" He said so steadily you'd think he was a gentle soul. Well he wasn't kidding me. What a rude old man.

"Well, it's hard to get hired at a place you don't belong." I tried to be as polite as possible. The biggest relief was when the elevator opened up to the same floor Blond Boy worked at. "Well thanks for, um, nothing?" I shook his mean hand vigorously and walked on out. I didn't even let him show me where my office was, due to how peeved his pretending to be kind made me. It wouldn't look nice on my resume to be fired on the same day I was hired.

To my surprise it wasn't all that hard, seeing how men with desk pieces were walking in and out of it. I walked on in and Connor, I believe that was his name, was angrily typing on his desktop keyboard. "Here you go." One of the men working on my desk gave me my chair and a laptop, "The computer is courtesy of Mr. Meyers." He smiled nicely and went back to work.

"Aww that's so sweet. I love Mr. Meyers, he's great. Thanks!" I sat down and opened my new Apple MacBook.

The red haired lady walked in now and gave me a stern look before walking up to Connor. So much for all the hospitality. She spoke to him in a hushed tone signaling it was time for me to do my own business.

I opened up my laptop with a stupid grin on my face for the lavish gift and finally decided to search up COO. The word apparently had a lot of buzz and I wanted to know why.

"Holy shit!" I whisper-screamed to myself as I read up on the definition. Mr. Meyers was cool and all, but actually kind of nuts. I was about to enter my senior year of college, for my Bachelor's degree, and he was basically giving me CEO status. Was he out of his mind? I was sure this wasn't a very smart business move, not to mention really nonsensical. No wonder people were surprised, like damn, even I was surprised! I had absolutely no credentials for this job. What idiot boss gives a college student this much power. "I'm COO of Meyers Motor Company." I let it roll off the tongue, trying to get a feel for it.

I chuckled a bit, shaking my head in the process, as I pulled out an apple from my purse. I set down my laptop and watched the men quickly assemble the expensive looking desk. It was the same beautiful brown color of my partner's, but slightly smaller.

Holy shit. The current COO is my partner. I'm also a COO. The second highest ranking man in the office space was sharing a title with a college student.

Ha, no wonder he was pissed. I took a bite out of my apple.

"Sam, I fucking get it. Do you think I don't get it? Can you seriously just shut up and go do your damn job." Everyone, even the men working on my desk got awkwardly quiet. The red-head, Sam I was guessing, scurried out of the office in no more than two seconds.

Um, oh hell no. I wish someone would talk to me like that, they'd get smacked in a moment.

This Connor guy would need to learn how to control that tongue of his or end up having it torn out. I stared at him in disbelief for a moment until he finally looked up at me and I scoffed, getting back to work on my apple.

"All done." The same man who gave me the laptop nicely told me and they all left moments after.

"Thanks hun!" I waved and slid myself over to my desk. The hardwood floors made it especially fun in the spinny-chair. "This job is great. Hey partner? What should I be doing today? You're supposed to teach me how to do this job right? Like, I can't even believe your dad gave me the COO position, I bet this must suck for you, right? It's cool though, I'm not here to steal your job away from you." I laughed at my statement, considering a college student taking the job away from someone a bit more experienced. I turned on the desktop computer the desk came with and looked at all the lacking materials on my desk.

I couldn't wait to use the money Meyers told me I'd have for renovating my desk space, "I brought a notepad and pen, for the small notes." I rummaged through my purse for my stuff and brought it out, "I don't have too many materials today, but I'll work on it this weekend." I finally finished my apple, and started searching around for a trashcan, "Hey do you have a trashcan?" My spinny-chair swiftly made its way over to my grumpy partner's desk.

"Do you always talk this much? Listen, I didn't sign up for babysitting, that's a decision Jonathan made on his own without consulting me. I have my own job to do, so figure out what you're supposed to do on your own time." Meyers Jr. scolded, not even giving me his full attention. What an asshole. I guess he truly was pissed.

I studied him for a moment instead of opening my mouth, which mind you was really difficult since I really wanted to curse him out. He was obviously older than me with a look-at-me-I'm-sophisticated-and-can-wear-a-suit kind of arrogance. I mean, yeah, okay, so he did indeed look like a poster-boy model for some magazine like GQ, but he was mostly basic. Clean shaven with short meticulously neat light brown hair on top of his head, boringly dull brown eyes (his eyes were only dull because his whole personality was lackluster and they in general could potentially look nice on anyone else), and that whole "I was in the sun for exactly two hours and twenty-three minutes to get this specifically even tan." Beyond that his facial features were nothing to be impressed about.

To be fair, his thick eyebrows kind of allowed him that cool sunken in eye thing, not to mention how his eyes were heavily hooded that aided in the mysterious factor. And if we were talking about jawline, then holy frickin' shit, my friend had that going on. His lips were kind of thin, but with his constant scowl, they kind of had a slightly pout-y effect which wasn't too bad. Plus his lips looked soft which was always a bonus wherever kissing was concerned, but I swear everything about his looks weren't that great at all.

If he took off that jacket though, I bet he'd have those beach-boy muscles that weren't too bulky, but not too lacking either. Again though, beyond that, he was mostly just some ugly guy. No one would ever look at him if it wasn't for his job title, I swear.

"Are you honestly just going to sit there and stare at me?" He finally turned towards me, looking ready to bite my head off.

"Just returning the favor since you stared at me for the entire duration of my interview, jackass. Actually, right now I think I'm going to find better company," I finally swiveled back towards my desk and gathered my belongings, "Maybe then you will have gotten your head out of your ass and can grasp the idea that you ain't working alone anymore baby-boy."

I angrily stormed out, slightly embarrassed that I was literally staring at him so absentmindedly. His constant negative mood was honestly just a bit too much for my usually cool demeanor. I found a trashcan finally, and launched my apple core into the bin. I took a deep breath and finally found my composure. It was time to scope out blond-boy, especially since I didn't have his name.

I found the receptionist, a very old woman with really short white hair, and an overall petite and fragile look, "Can you tell me where the office to a blond-haired man is?" I smiled nicely at her behind the huge desk-space I hadn't seen before near the elevators.

"So you must be Greyson. Congratulations on getting a job here, how's your first day going?" She smiled brightly, and I instantly fell in love with the woman. She was the nicest person in the entire building, I was certain of it.

"Thank you so much! It's been kind of weird honestly. Not to mention how my partner really doesn't want me around. Despite him, I've met some amazing people today, like you and my blond friend. Oh and Big Boss Meyers, of course. I'm not too certain on some people though. Some have acted nice, but I'm not too sure they like having me around. So what's your name? I've been forgetting to ask people for their names, which isn't cool, but I'll work on it. So that's been my day mostly, without all of the grueling details," I laughed for a moment, thinking through all of the events of the day, "Do you talk to Connor Meyers a lot? Is he always such a negative person? I really hope he isn't, I'm hoping that we'll become friends with time, but I've also been wrong before so who knows. I really like how you have your desk organized, so pretty and classy-" I stopped talking when she began to chuckle.

"Greyson, slow down a moment. I'm not sure anymore if you want any of your questions answered or if they are all just rhetorical." She laughed again and grabbed my hand which had found it's way on her sticky notes, giving it a gentle squeeze. I laughed back at her good nature. I knew my conversational habits were slightly overbearing, but hopefully she'd get use to it and like me nonetheless.

"Well, for starters, I'm Amanda." She began, looking ready to answer all of my questions, "About Connor, I hate to say this to you, but Connor is usually at his best when left alone. He can be very negative and scolding if you talk to him for too long. He definitely prefers to keep to himself with business, only talking to his advisers when necessary. So you may be out of luck with him becoming friendlier. Either way, don't take any of his rude remarks personal." She tried to sound reassuring, but it only made me feel worse.

"That's really upsetting to hear," I pulled off my hat to fluff my hair, "Well he hasn't met me before, so I'm confident I can change this bad reputation he has here. Don't worry Amanda, you'll see. Just give me till the Japan meeting, and we'll be the best partners the world has ever seen! Anyways, I'll talk to you later, I have to raise a white flag." I smiled confidently and retreated back to my new shared office space.

I swung the door open and looked at my target straight in the face, "Before you say anything, I just want to apologize. I know this is probably a very uncool situation you've been tossed in straight out of the blue and I think I can try and understand where you're coming from. Maybe you just need some time to warm up to the situation we're in, I don't know. So how about I go home for the day, and maybe we can get some work done tomorrow?"

I went to retrieve my awesome new laptop, and made sure to smile often to the profile of the man who was obviously ignoring me. "So what time should I come in tomorrow?" I made one last attempt to speak to him before leaving.

He finally looked at me with a slight smirk on his face, "six-thirty." I was sure that smirk grew significantly when I frowned so dramatically back.

"You're joking... A.M?" I asked in complete shock and his response was one smooth nod. I made a huge and childish grunting noise and contemplated asking him to show me mercy. No matter how I tried, no words came out of my mouth, so instead I just stomped my heels out. This was the exact moment the office became the total opposite of my dream job. I didn't even get up before nine for college, and now I would have to wake up at like five just to make it in time! That's four hours of sleep, gone.

Whatever, I wasn't prepared to give up on this job anytime soon. It would simply be like that time my roommate challenged me to play and beat some super scary video game without chickening out straight through one night. I ended up beating the entire game, though at the cost of nearly a heart-attack, and was able to have my laundry cleaned for that week.

This was basically the same situation. I was up for any challenge, even if that required getting up at such an unholy hour.

Game on.

Chapter Three

Chapter 3- She's Moronic (Connor's Perspective)

It was six-forty-two when my supposed "partner" walked through my office. I had been sipping on some coffee, wondering if she would even show up today. It appeared that sadly, she would.

She didn't even make an attempt to look in my direction as she tiredly made her way to her desk. After loudly dropping her things to the floor, she plopped her head onto the wooden surface of the desk and with eyes closed she grumbled, nearly unintelligibly, "Mornin'."

I spent nearly three hours in the gym the day before, ranting to Adam about the situation I was thrust in. He was usually just my closest adviser along with my best friend, but last night he also made a great personal therapist to rant to. Adam wasted no time in agreeing with me fully and also getting angry with Jonathan for his awful business decision.

I went home after that and took an extremely long shower, cursing to the heavens about the aggravation my father was exceptionally good at making me feel. Sleep did not come so easy, but I had to admit that the few hours of sleep I did manage to have did seem to calm me down a bit. Only a bit.

I was still extremely angry with this ultimatum, but my mind was finally clear enough to deal with the situation appropriately. She would soon see that this job was too much for her to handle and quit. My only issue would be dealing with her while she was still here.

"Good morning," I finally said, still watching her lifeless form. To be completely honest, I felt kind of bad for the girl. Mornings were never my strong suit, and it took me years to become accustomed to working early. So I could definitely empathize with her.

"This is hell!" She shot upright, throwing her hands in the air. This Greyson girl was probably the most animated person I had ever met, "Just kill me now and take me out of my misery!" Did I mention that she was also very dramatic?

"I'd be happy to if it were legal." I finished my coffee and set the mug down. The corners of my mouth pulled up a bit in amusement at her pain.

"It's too morning to deal with you right now." She hunched over her desk using her hands to prop up her head.

I surprised myself when I chuckled at the combination of her bad grammar and completely different persona from the day before. I instantly coughed away the laughter, trying to understand why this childishness was even remotely amusing.

"Someone's in a better mood today," She peered over to me, smiling, "So what's on the agenda for today?"

"Well, it's still early but I need to look over some papers before my schedule gets busy," I pulled out the files that were sent to me from people on every floor, "Maybe you can go get yourself some coffee and figure something out for the time being."

"Coffee only messes with the nervous system and stains your teeth. And I don't brush my teeth twice a day, keeping them whiter than snow, just to mess 'em up with that nasty drink. I'll wake up in no time and I'll be back to my usual self, you'll see. However, today I'd like to do some actual work, instead of a whole lot of nothing like yesterday. Maybe I can look over some of those papers of yours. How about that?" She rambled on and on. If I were guessing, I'd say she was already fully awake.

I think I liked her best when she was too tired to function, "You don't have any idea what you'd be looking at. Besides, these are files I personally check in order to ease my own mind. You doing that wouldn't help at all," I looked at my watch, shocked to see it was already five past seven, "Listen if you go off to do something now, I'll give you an actual task later on."

"Fine." She said and actually left. Even though she was obviously reluctant to do so, the fact that she was gone remained and I was able to breathe easy.

Four hours went by, and I was back to my usual work routine. Papers were getting looked over and edited peacefully and efficiently. Samantha sat across from me, signing documents and reminding me of what I still had to look over.

Over the many years of hiring and firing many assistants who couldn't keep up with my pace, Samantha was truly amazing. She even worked faster than me from time to time which made the decision to keep her around fairly easy.

It always boggled my mind, however, that someone whose brain I used to literally pack information in like a filing cabinet could even find the time to gossip. Either way, I couldn't deny that she did her job and she did it well.

"Adam wants you and the others involved in the merger to have an informal meeting about certain things he feels the need to discuss. Your down time today is around three, so we can attend that for about half an hour. If it runs over I can always come back and finish up on signing these papers." Samantha smoothly let out, never missing a beat.

"Okay." I easily let out as I continued writing up the letter I was working on.

"Hey, Connor?" My focus was rudely broken when an already too familiar, and nonetheless annoying, voice called out to me, "Hey girl," Greyson acknowledged Sam's presence before returning to me. I hadn't even heard her come in, let alone notice her presence over my desk, "When is lunchtime?"

"Whenever," I angrily let out, trying to regain my focus on the letter, but failing. Did she really need to ask me about that?

"Yeah, but like when do you go to lunch?" She asked again. This girl didn't allow for simple conversation, which was a real pet peeve of mine.

"Does it matter?" I hated opening myself up to conversation, but since I obviously wasn't going to be able to write my letter with her around, I guess it couldn't be helped.

"Well, yeah. We're partners and it's my first official day, so I thought we would eat together." Her neutral expression turned grim after a moment of silence, and I wondered if she realized how ridiculous she sounded, "Never mind. Just let me know when you have my task for me. Oh, so you will never believe what Amanda said to me! She's so funny, you'd never guess it from just looking at her. Well actually, you probably don't care. Hey, what's your name again?" She quickly regained her usual smiley form, and the form that talks nonstop.

"Samantha Snyder." Sam looked at her like she was an idiot, which wasn't too far from the truth.

"Alright." Greyson frowned again and walked out without another word.

"I cannot believe you are letting this girl be your partner." Samantha looked at me in disbelief. I guess we weren't going to just get back to work.

"I'm not, Jonathan is. Don't worry, I'll get rid of her. Just consider her a challenge to deal with for the time being." I tried looking over the letter to see what I was typing to hopefully continue with it. I would have been done with it by now if it wasn't for the distraction.

"Oh are you scheming some kind of plan? What is this plan and can I be involved with it?" I could feel the snake-like smile that formed on Sam's face without having to look at her.

"It's basically to make her realize that this job is way too advanced for her and have her quit. If she quits, Jonathan can't do a thing about it or stop me from my business. It's a win-win situation."

"Ah I see. Well then I can't wait to put it to full effect," Sam stood up and gathered her belongings, "Will you survive here alone with that infant for two hours? I can reschedule my doctor's appointment if you'd like." Samantha was scary when she wanted to do something bad to someone. Part of me contemplated if it was a good idea to tell her that I had plans to make Greyson quit. Especially considering how willing Samantha would be to create a war in my office.

"I'll manage." I shooed her off, already not enjoying the great possibility of having to break up a cat-fight due to being a loud mouth, "Samantha. I'm going to deal with this Greyson situation on my own."

She paused for a moment, "Well alright," I could feel her reluctance, but I knew she'd drop it, "Just remember that today as a whole is supposed to be very laid back. In other words, please don't go overboard with the workload." She winked at me and with a wave left my office.

The peace of being alone felt amazing and I took advantage of the situation to finish up my letter and read over the rest of the papers.

Adam had called me about an hour later to make sure I was going to be able to make it to his business meeting and also to give me updates on what he had been up to, "Yeah Connor, I have all of that taken care of. So tell me, am I going to have to bail you out of jail for seriously harming this new partner of yours?" I could feel him smirking through my cell, which instantly pissed me off.

His joke wasn't exactly what set me off, it was everyone, including him, talking to me about her like she was my main focus. Everyone in the office was becoming more informal with me, only asking how I was feeling about my new partner situation. It was almost as if a family member died and everyone was trying to sympathize with me with questions like, "Are you okay? Will you be able to handle this? This situation must be rough considering the merger coming up, right? How about we ignore all the paperwork we're supposed to be doing and just talk about how this girl is affecting you?" So that last one wasn't exactly something I'd been asked, but it might have well been.

"I'm not in the mood," I simply said, pacing around, looking through the glass window-wall at the people and cars passing down below.

Adam simply laughed through the receiver, "I'm just messing with you. Just be happy there isn't media coverage on this. Press would only take up more of your time."

"Don't remind me," I sighed heavily. The thought of the reputation the company would receive from this was too much to swallow. I found it easier to ignore all of the details and work on getting her out of the office as soon as possible.

"Well anyways, Brian finally called me back. Everything is looking good on that end also, but I'll discuss the details of that at the meeting," Adam spoke on, giving me the run down for later on.

"Hey," My concentration that was on the valet at the entrance of the building was diverted when I felt a finger poking me in the back.

"Adam, I'll call you back," I hung up and turned around to find a smiling Greyson and her piercing green eyes staring directly into mine. She had such a surprisingly confident aura that always seemed to surround her. It was almost unnerving coming from a college student.

It was the first time I was standing directly in front of her and in her heels she was exactly my height, and being over six foot, this was new for me.

"Do you have my task?" She cut straight to the point, pushing her mane-like curls out of her face. I finally noticed the leather jacket and skirt combo she wore today, again, not at all proper in any business setting.

I broke the eye contact by moving over to my desk, trying to quickly think up something, "Yes, and I made it really simple for you," I mentally rejoiced at my task for her, "I haven't had lunch yet and I have a meeting at three. I just need you to go down to the café and order me whatever pasta they have for today." Since my assistant wouldn't be back till the meeting, this would actually be beneficial for me.

"Mhmm," She mumbled from her place behind me and walked out, surprisingly without another word.

——

It was four-thirty when Samantha left my office to go back to hers and finalize what my schedule was supposed to look like for the next day.

It was four-thirty when I realized I had not seen or heard from Greyson in awhile.

It was four-thirty when I realized I hadn't had my lunch.

I was ready to call Greyson and ask what the hell happened, but it was also at this time that I realized I didn't have her phone number.

The amount of anger that I felt was almost immeasurable when I stood up to go find her. I was going to call Sam and have her figure it out, but it was more important that she fixed up my schedule. There was also the fact that Sam dealing with this would probably only further my anger, if that was even possible.

"Connor?" Amanda, the receptionist, softly called as I repeatedly pressed the button for the elevator. She looked at me for a moment, and I got the message she was trying to send very clearly.

"Do you know where the-" I cut myself off, trying not to lash out at Amanda, "Have you seen Greyson recently?" I tried again, noticing my right foot tapping impatiently on the floor.

"Not since she headed down to the cafeteria," She slowly informed me and the elevator dinged open. Without another word I walked onto the elevator, clicking the button for the lobby, "Breathe first..." Amanda's voice trailed off as the doors closed.

I understood that she was just watching out for my temper. I've said some cruel things to people, especially inadequate assistants, in the past that was probably a bit overboard. However, in all honesty

I didn't care to have her trying to give me a pep-talk right now. If I managed to emotionally scar this girl for managing to waste so much of my time in only two days, then so be it. I welcomed the idea of seeing her cry if that meant I would never have to leave my office or stop working for her sake again.

Fuck her sake and fuck her too.

People quietly passed me as I nearly stomped my way into the cafeteria. When she was nowhere to be found, I was sure my teeth would break off with how hard I was grinding them.

There were no words to describe the anger felt when there was a specific job you were supposed to be doing, and were doing so well for so many years now, and all of a sudden you were spending your time trying to find someone who wasn't in any way beneficial to your job. Yet that person shared your job title and only seemed to want to destroy all of your progress!

As I was ready to head upstairs and forget looking for her altogether, loud and annoying laughter erupted from the kitchen. I weaved my way straight through the small tables, avoiding the few people who actually ate in the building, and through the double doors of the kitchen.

Greyson had on an apron and was chopping up some vegetables with a huge smile on her face as she spoke to the head chef. All the cooks' heads darted in my direction when the doors slammed against the wall and Greyson's smile only grew when she saw me, "Hey Connor! Guess what? Miguel here is teaching me how to make his famous stew."

All the words I wanted to say to her, including a few very colorful ones, completely vanished from my mind. I was sure I looked slightly insane with my mouth slightly opened, but the moment was just too surreal. Was she just pretending to be oblivious to piss me off or did she honestly not understand how unbelievably terrible she was?

"You were supposed to bring me my lunch hours ago," I finally said, the anger bubbling over my limit.

"No I wasn't," Her smile faded and she put down the knife, "That's your own job, or your assistant's job, but not my job."

In that moment all of the cooks retreated near the back of the kitchen silently.

"Playing chef isn't your job either, but here you fucking are."

With a long pause, neither of us breaking eye contact, she slipped off her apron, gathered her bag and jacket, and walked in my direction, "Thanks for everything Miguel, I'll make sure to stop by from time to time," She walked past me, nearly bumping her shoulder into mine as she exited. I followed her to the elevator, using all of my willpower to not cause a scene.

"Why the hell are you even working here? It's obvious you have no credentials to be here, let alone the fact that this is all just a joke to you," I spoke up after the elevator doors closed, "You're just making my life difficult at such a crucial time. If you want I can just give you money if you quit and never show up here again. I'll even pay you more than you would've made working the entire summer. I'm just asking that you go." My voice remained incredibly calm as I attempted to solve this situation once and for all.

The elevator came to a stop on my floor and Greyson walked out without saying a single word to me. I followed her to my office, ignoring everyone else, especially Amanda.

"Um, Connor?" Sam questioned as we got to the doors of my office. She was waiting outside, probably wondering where I was. Despite the obvious concern in her eyes I quickly dismissed her with a wave of my hand.

"I'll call you in later," I simply said, keeping my focus on Greyson.

When I finally closed the office door behind me, she dropped her belongings on her desk and faced me. Her expression was a strange mixture of anger and indifference as she opened her mouth, "I am trying my hardest to understand how this situation must feel for you. I really am, but I need to make a few things clear about this situation we're in," She took a long pause, almost tempting me to speak up, but I didn't play into her game.

"First of all, I thought that if I stayed in the cafeteria and out of your way for the rest of the day, you'd be grateful. It was obvious to me that you weren't ready to give me an actual task, so I decided to give you more time. I don't appreciate you lashing out at me like some kid who did wrong. I tried doin' one thing and you didn't like that, so I did the opposite and I'm still wrong in your eyes! You can't just get angry at me for not doing my job, but when I try doin' my job, not even help me out like you're supposed to! That's not fair-"

"Yes, because-" I started and was quickly interrupted.

"Can I please say exactly what I'm thinkin' for once? Or are you gonna just talk down to me again? We can do this where we both keep cutting each other off, but I think we are old enough to do this maturely." My jaw clenched tightly as everything she was insisting with that statement registered in my brain.

I strongly wanted to give this disrespectful brat a piece of my mind, and it would have been so easy to do so. I've cut off multiple people in my life, but something held me back. Instead of lashing out I bit my tongue, went over to my desk and sat down, allowing her exactly what she wanted. Besides, I didn't work in an office for as long as I did to allow my stubborn nature to just get the best of me.

She followed me and stood in front of my desk, across from me, not bothering with sitting down, "Secondly, and probably most importantly, I want you to finally understand where I'm comin' from. Whether you like this situation or not, I am your partner. I am the COO of this company right now just as much as you are. Just because I'm younger, or as you put it, lacking credentials, I am done with you talking down to me. You disrespected me in the cafeteria, scolding me like a child, and I don't appreciate that! I don't give a shit what you or Samantha want to believe about me! I ain't no goddamn child!" Her voice rose drastically and a strong urban-like accent came through.

She paused a moment, looking towards the floor before beginning again, "I don't care if you hate me for working here until I die, but I won't sit back silently as you try talking down to me. No matter what, I am not lesser than you. Now, thirdly and finally, let me make something really clear to you. I am not a fuckin' hooker. You can buy a hooker with your money, but I'm not sellin' nothin'. Yes, I'm working here 'cause I'm getting paid, but I have a job to do and that's what Mr. Meyers is expecting of me. Oh and believe me, I fully plan on doin' my damn job." She was hunched over my desk now, stabbing her finger into it as she spoke.

She finally broke eye contact and went to her desk, picking up her belongings. I said nothing the entire time.

"I'm gonna head home a bit early today. It's obvious I won't be doing any work here anyways. Maybe this will give you some more time to actually figure out a task for me to complete and maybe I can finally start proving you wrong about me. No matter what, I'm hoping that we can actually start getting down to business tomorrow and put this childishness behind us. Goodnight," She sternly nodded at me and strode out.

Not too long after her disappearance, Sam walked in. "I said I'd call you in." I sighed as I placed my laptop in my briefcase, ready to go home myself. Although I usually worked late nights, I had a great need for a shower and some solitude.

"Are you going home already?" Sam looked down at her watch, confusion evident on her face. I hardly left the office before eight anymore, and she usually stayed back with me, no matter how long I stayed. Even on the many occasions I stayed overnight in the connecting room to my office that had long been converted into a bedroom, she would always stay the night with me.

"Yes," I stood up now, ignoring the fact that it wasn't even six yet.

"Shouldn't we go look over a few things?" I could hear her heels clicking directly behind me as I made my way out. I said absolutely nothing, simply waiting for the elevator to get to floor fifteen.

"Email me whatever you need me to know." I finally said when my elevator opened. I watched the look of confusion on her face as the doors closed. I couldn't deal with the idea of her nagging me for any details regarding Greyson. In fact, just hearing her voice for any longer than I had already heard it was surely going to give me a headache.

I easily ignored the greetings those on the lobby gave me and went around to the back where my car was always parked. The hot Florida sun made it absolutely necessary to slide my suit jacket off, and once the car was turned on and my seat belt buckled nicely, I placed a hand on the steering wheel and paused.

My mind finally went over the interesting lecture I had received basically moments ago. I thought about everything, from my decision to let her speak without reserve to how hard she tried to create and keep a professional mannerism.

I was really shocked with my decision to let her disrespect me so openly. Before this moment, anyone who would even dare to raise their voice at me received an ear-full and was promptly fired or our company never did business with theirs again. I wasn't sure if it was how bold she was or what, but something in me just couldn't bring myself to yell back. Maybe it was the fact that I personally couldn't fire her. Whatever the case, the most surprising thing was how I wasn't feeling angry in the slightest.

And boy was that surprising.

Then out of nowhere I started laughing. I was uncontrollably laughing and I considered the idea that I was actually losing my mind.

Then, just the idea of me thinking there was a possibility I was going insane made me laugh even more.

I desperately wanted to ship Greyson off to China for the rest of my life, along with my father and Jackson. They were seriously plotting to kill me. I had no doubt about that. The visual of packing them all into boxes and sending them out over the ocean seemed to bring me back to myself and the laughter subsided.

With a shake of my head, I put the gear of my car in reverse, and backed out of the parking lot to the company that would hopefully be mine one day, if it didn't burn down first. For the entire drive home that day, despite myself, the sides of my mouth stayed curved upwards in what was almost a smile.

And in a way, I was happy about that...

And in another way, it made me consider how long my jail sentence would be for homicide...

Chapter Four

Chapter 4- He's Always Angry (Greyson's Perspective)

"I absolutely hate him!" I practically yelled to Jayden as I rummaged through the refrigerator.

"Grey, don't say that," Jayden, or Jay as I called him, said trying to be the voice of reason, "He just never met someone as amazing as you and it's hard for him to come to terms with the fact that his entire life has been empty 'til now."

I couldn't help the smile on my face as he said this. Jay always knew how to make me smile and I loved him for it. Jayden and I met during our freshman year of college and we instantly clicked. He was probably the only reason I had so many crazy stories from college to share.

We decided to become roommates in an apartment our sophomore year, despite me wanting to take care of my mother, and it was the best living arrangements I could ask for. No one else was able to deal with being around me for too long, since I tend to be very high-energy, and he was the perfect mixture of excitement with an easy-going persona to put up with me.

"I guess you might be right, but he's still an asshole," I finally found my protein shake, behind a cluster of Tupperware, and was all set to go. I recently learned that there was a free-of-charge gym at my job thanks to Miguel, the head chef, and was excited to finally start back up with my workouts.

I was way too broke to afford a gym, and the gym back at the university wasn't available due to summer break.

"I'm not saying he ain't an asshole. He probably is. But you've dealt with enough in your life for me to know that you can find a way to be cool with him." Jay slid on his shoes to finish up getting ready for work.

"I don't know how you can go to work so early in the morning, I'm surprised I'm even up right now," It was four-thirty in the morning and the only reason I was so awake was due to falling asleep unusually early the night before. Everything about my first official day exhausted me beyond comprehension, and I was out cold.

It worked out in my favor, though, because I wanted to begin an exercise routine and stay toned during the summer. Morning would be the best time for that. Although, knowing me, I wouldn't be able to get up early on enough days to keep myself on such a schedule.

The other positive point of waking up so early was being able to rant to Jay. My job and his job schedule were already proving to keep us away from each other until the weekend. My job was twelve hours a day for five days a week. His was eight hours a day for four days a week. Why I decided to take on a full-time job over the summer as a party-loving twenty-one year old college student was beyond me.

"You'll get used to the early mornings," He said and I gave him a look of disbelief, "Alright, I'm lyin'. You just have to remind yourself that it's only for the summer and that makes it a bit easier." He smiled and grabbed his bag. The reassuring look in his beautiful honey-brown eyes made me decide to trust his wisdom.

I think our eye colors were another reason we became so close. His skin complexion was slightly lighter than my own, but dark enough that the bright and contrasting lighter color of his eyes stood out prominently and beautifully. We met by an exchange of liking the other person's eyes. I think he was a lot more surprised though that my eyes could even possibly be green.

I followed him out of our apartment and to our cars, "Bye Jay! Have a great day and remember that my day is already worse than yours." I laughed, acting like my job was really horrible when it honestly wasn't that bad. Connor was seriously the only downside. Well, that and the early mornings.

"Deuces, nugga!" He threw me a peace sign, acting like a true thug straight from the hood.

"What it do though?" I threw him a peace sign back, having no idea what any of our brief conversation meant, but loving it anyways. I slipped into my car, putting all my bags and junk down on the passenger seat. As Jay drove off, he honked a few times, obnoxiously. The corners of my mouth rose in amusement though as I watched Jay's sexy-self speed down the street.

Now don't get me wrong, a person with so much sex-appeal definitely caught my eye. We actually dated for a while and it was fun, but we both realized we weren't exactly compatible in a romantic sense at all, but luckily our friendship only became stronger. Which is also kind of weird, I know.

I think it was for the best that we decided on staying friends. He was basically my older brother and I couldn't imagine life without him. We were family and even our individual families considered it so. His parents loved having me around and he was always welcome to all of my family reunions. We'd even refer to each other as brother or sister from time to time. It was the perfect set up.

I breathed deeply a few times, throwing my hair into a sloppy bun to get it out of my face for my workout and silently prayed I wasn't forgetting anything. I had a tendency to do that.

——

It was strange walking into the spacious gym at almost five in the morning. The space was incredibly empty and it was obvious by its neatness and amazingly clean smell that not many people came to work out at all. That, or the cleaning crew was absolutely amazing.

Ignoring how lonely I was, I pulled out my headphones and plopped them in my ears allowing my collection of high-energy workout songs to fill my ears. I placed my water bottle in the cup holder of the treadmill and started a quick warm-up before beginning my work out.

———

By the time I showered and was properly dressed, I was completely late to work. Which, considering how early I was to even get to the place, was unbelievably unfair.

So yeah, I was never a very timely person, but I had high hopes for myself. Especially after trying to prove my maturity the day before, since apparently he sees me as a child, or so says the red-headed lady.

I breathed deeply a few times again, trying not to bring back the memories from yesterday when she rudely told me that I was basically a child. I was prepared to let all hell break loose on her right there. I breathed deeply again, remembering what my old therapist had said.

Oh, but then she had the nerve to be like, "I've got an appointment to get to. Please allow the man to work in peace and continue the grown-up business he has to attend to." Boy, I was not even two seconds away from getting arrested for assault. She thinks she can just smile at me and use her thesaurus words to act all kind and understanding. I see straight through that.

I had hoped she had counted her blessings and really considered if it was a smart idea to get smart with me again. I inhaled deeply once more on the elevator, "I wish she would fuck with me today." I cursed out loud to myself in the elevator and on my exhale I dropped the situation entirely.

I decided to focus on the fact that I was already late by over an hour. I tried to make it seem not so bad in my mind, but the reality was that I was incredibly frickin' late! I couldn't really deny it.

In my defense, it would usually take me just thirty minutes to get ready with my outfit already chosen. So, I obviously only gave myself thirty minutes before I was supposed to clock in to get ready. However, after showering off the sweat, I realized that tight business clothes didn't just slip on slightly damp skin. It took me some time to put on the clothes. Then I put on my make-up which was no big deal, but then my hair came into play. My hair was not trying to play.

I wouldn't have washed it, but it was too dirty not to, and I usually washed my hair after working out anyways. However, I couldn't just have my hair dripping wet while resting on my clothes while working. I usually don't mind it doing that, but that wasn't appropriate in a business setting, which wasn't something I'd accounted for before washing it.

My last option was blow-drying my hair. Which, blow-drying was an effective option, but with my hair's density, no blow-dryer could dry it enough in a short amount of time. So I blow-dried it for a while, getting it somewhat less-drippy and brushed it into a bun. I wasn't especially fond of buns since it was hard to do with thicker hair, but I didn't mind them when I had time to make them look neat. I didn't have the time, so my hair came out looking extremely unkempt.

I was effectively a mess.

I hoped my partner, the younger of the Meyers, was laughing in his smug way at my lack of punctuality. I'll give him this win, because okay, so maybe I wasn't the most "grown up" when it came to time management. I'd still prove him otherwise with every other aspect.

I said a quick hello to the amazing receptionist, Amanda, and busted through the door of my shared office room. I definitely startled the man-child with my abrupt entry. I would've felt awesome about startling him, if it wasn't for the fact that I was even more surprised to see him standing a few feet from the door, instead of sitting at his desk like usual.

I also took note of how if he was one step closer, I would've slammed the door straight into his face. Not expecting to see him so close-up kind of threw me off my game plan, but I quickly regained my composure.

"Yes, I'm late. Incredibly late for that matter. However, I want you to know that it wasn't because I was sleeping or something like that, I was actually in the office since a little before five. If you want to yell at me for that, okay, but what's done is done. Today I'm fully prepared to get down to business." I said and mentally rejoiced. Exercising always put my mind in order, well temporarily, but I managed to stay focused and that's all that mattered.

"Don't worry, I have an actual task for you, but right now I'm actually running late for a meeting, so we'll talk when I get back. So do whatever for now, but be here when I get back. If you're not, I'm going to assume you aren't prepared to take this job seriously and you can forget my help." Meyers Jr. spoke quickly, rushing to get to his meeting. Without another word, or smile, he was gone.

That went better than I had thought, and I was completely stunned with his non-scolding tone of voice. I stood for a moment, trying to figure out if that encounter was real or if I had just imagined him being so good-natured, or well, as good-natured as a grumpy person can be.

Then, when the moment registered as real in my brain, another issue became present. I didn't know when his damn meeting ended! What if I left and he came back in only half an hour and I wasn't around?

I sat at my desk, preparing to just sit and wait, but I had no idea how long his meeting would be. What if he was gone for two whole hours? I would probably die of boredom at that point.

Trying to stay positive I set up my supplies and tried to do some busywork. The problem was that I lacked any tasks to do. I started tapping my foot on the floor impatiently, while also clicking my pen. I bit my bottom lip a few times, trying to figure out what to do.

Taking out a piece of paper I decided to test out my drawing abilities. It didn't take long to find out I had none. I stood up and decided to browse the room. I looked at some bland pictures on the wall and stopped at a door. Despite my better judgement, curiosity got the better of me and I opened the door to reveal an entire bedroom! It was so boring and modern looking, but interesting nonetheless.

Did Mr. Grumpy Partner sleep in here? That was so weird, there was even a bathroom attached. The monotone color scheme and lacking flavor was really upsetting though and that too became boring.

I finally decided to check my phone for the time and found that only about five minutes went by. I loudly groaned, and decided to stop lying to myself. I couldn't just be in the office without any work all alone for an unknown amount of time.

I wished myself all the luck in the world to get back in time and left. And to be completely honest, it wasn't much fun where the people were. Everyone was all about business and being so serious all the time. I could not handle that.

I decided I'd go on the elevator and play a game of random elevator number. This was the game where I'd randomly select a floor button and explore wherever I ended up. However, before I got to the elevator I ran into a very attractive person who also had a familiar face.

"Hey stranger," The blond-boy greeted me with that notorious smirk/half smile, "How has your first week been going so far?" I'm not sure what it was about him, but he just had the ability to lift my mood with only his presence. And I still didn't know his name.

"Eh, it had its ups and downs so far, but I can't give you an exact answer until this week is over and done with." I laughed, wondering if this week would get worse or better. With my partner being in charge of that, it seemed he would determine my fate, "So what's your name again? I'm horrible with names."

"Peter Thorne," He proudly greeted, "Is Connor giving you trouble? He has a tendency to do that to most people. Don't take it personally, he likes targeting specific people to give hell to every now and then. However, he might actually have a personal vendetta against you due to having to share his job title with you. In that case, I'm so sorry for you."

I frowned a bit, thinking about this until Peter Parker started laughing. I then remembered why I liked him specifically. He wasn't so stuck up and uptight. "If I die in the coming week, make sure you let the cops know that he's been out to get me since the beginning," I whispered, going along with the joke.

He just laughed some more, "So I finally did my research on you," Peter said, and I instantly went into defense mode.

"What?" I let out flatly, not trying to overreact.

"Well, we hardly get newcomers, and they're hardly ever interesting. You, however, have been the latest buzz around here and I like interesting people," He said, but I was still unsure of what he was talking about.

"Wait, so do you mean you like snooped through my personal files or something?" I tried laughing it off, wondering if there even were personal files on me.

He just laughed some more, "I'm not a stalker now. No, I just finally learned how you ended up in our wonderful car company oasis. Is it true you're only staying for the summer though?"

Yep, I truly enjoyed this person. He was a funny person, "Oh ha ha, well Mr. Meyers would like me to stay longer, but with college and such I can't say right now. So have you heard about the fancy-pants dinner this weekend? Well, I'm sure you have, you've worked here longer than me. Anyways, I'm really excited for it, but I kind of want a date. And I know just the Spiderman for it." I smiled widely, not ashamed of my directness.

He laughed, I guess recognizing how his name was Peter, and Spiderman's was also Peter. "You are absolutely hilarious, I love that. Well, I usually go to company dinners alone, but I could always use a Mary Jane."

Oh, he was smooth. "Then it's a date," I said simply, "So, aren't I keeping you from your work right now?" I eyed my office, making sure my partner was still in no way in the vicinity. And to think I was going to just sit there. Due to leaving, I now had a date to my very first high-class company dinner.

"Well, if I needed to go I would. I always have work to do, but since I'm still waiting on Connor's approval for my main assignment right now, I have some down time."

"Okay, I get that. Well, I actually have to go and talk to Mr. Meyers actually, so just grab my number from Amanda, she has it, and text me. Talk to you later, Spiderman." I waved him off and went to the elevator.

I pressed the upmost button, glad to have remembered that I needed to ask my boss how flexible my work hours were. I knew he said he'd be lenient on me for being so new and young, and although I was more than willing to use my ability to show up and leave whenever, I didn't want to take advantage of it either.

"Jonny! It feels like it's been years since I last saw you," I said happily, when Meyers Sr. invited me in.

"I've been meaning to call you in to check in actually," He smiled that same warm smile that made crinkles form in the corners of his eyes, "How has Connor been treating you?" He was so welcoming and understanding, it was hard to believe that he worked in such a busy environment.

He would make a much better Ice-cream Man for sure. "Well, he's still not too happy with our partnership, and he's a bit hard on me, but don't get worried just yet Jonny. I'm sure he's only being difficult because he's testing to see if I'm a worthy partner. I'll just prove to him that I can work as hard as he can." I said confidently, trying to believe what I was saying myself.

"That's the fighting spirit I like about you. If he ever gives you too much grief, you just come to me, okay?" Meyers Sr. gave me a very stern look and I nodded in approval.

However, there was no way I was going to be a snitch, even if my partner put me straight through hell. I didn't need to run and tattle on anybody, I could handle everything on my own.

"So, is there any specific reason you're here today though?" Mr. Boss Man said, getting to the point. I kept forgetting that everyone was actually working here, and not just able to have random conversation.

In my defense, I still had no job of my own to tend to, so it was hard to keep busy. "Oh yeah, there was something I was going to ask. Hmm, what was it?" I racked my brain, completely forgetting the primary reason I even came to his office, "I honestly can't remember." I sat there for a moment, still dumbstruck, while trying to unlock the storage part of my memory.

"Well I'm sure it'll come to you eventually. On another note, I wanted to call up Connor and talk to the both of you together, so stay here a moment." Meyers Sr. picked up his cell-phone and I felt instantly uncomfortable.

Why was he calling up Connor? Why did he want to talk to both of us at the same time? I still wasn't on great terms with the guy, so there would probably be some tension in the air. What if Jonathan asked me about what job I was working on? I wasn't working on anything!

"Alright, see you here." Meyers hung up his phone, and I felt even more uneasy.

"Um, are you sure I have to be here?" I asked, awkwardly.

"Is there an issue?" Jonny shot back easily. Touché, I'll give you that one.

"No, just wondering." I replied, and in not too long at all there was a knock at the door before Connor came strolling in.

I think my issue was the fact that we hadn't truly spoken to each other since my little outburst the day before. The only time he spoke to me was when he was rushing to a meeting, and I had no idea if he was pissed at me or not.

He gave me a very deadpan look which didn't help my case at all. I couldn't read any expression on his face to tell if he was surprised to see me in his dad's office, or just mad at me in a general sense. Did Jonny tell him on the phone that I was here? I hadn't paid any attention to his phone call to know.

Connor sat down in the chair directly next to mine and I kind of just looked at him. Well, more like stared to be honest. I didn't have much shame at all to feel weird about staring at people.

I looked at his suit and took note that the charcoal color looked especially nice on him.

But that was beside the point. He glanced at me for a moment with a raised eyebrow, probably questioning why I was just staring at him. I'd never seen him so reserved. We weirdly looked into each other's eyes for what felt like an hour, until I got bored and looked over to Jonathan. I couldn't read any emotion in his eyes, so I just prepared myself for this little meeting to go as bad as possible.

"So, you asked me to be here?" Connor broke the silence, addressing his dad. Jonathan was kind of just looking between the both of us, probably wondering if a fight was going to break out. I was wondering the exact same thing.

"Yes, I wanted to see how the partnership is going so far, of course. I was thinking of waiting till the end of the week, but knowing how headstrong you both are, it seemed appropriate to meet with the both of you before that time." Jonny spoke slowly, keeping his eyes directly on his son, probably trying to see if he'd finally change his expression to something that could be interpreted.

If the car industry ever failed for Connor, he would make a great statue. Like those people who get painted in silver or gold and are forced to just stand still without moving their face or anything. Yeah, he'd be good at that for sure.

"Well, it's forced me to change around my schedule drastically to make room for the new tenant in my office, but I'm sure it'll all work out in the end. I've already gotten this far in my life, and I'm sure you've given me bigger obstacles to deal with in the past."

Ouch. Talk about low-key shade being thrown. How he managed to sound so sophisticated while also calling me an obstacle in his way was straight up amazing. If I hadn't listened in so steadily I would've never caught the obvious disapproval of our partnership. Not that I was surprised, I knew he didn't like having me around. That didn't make his honesty hurt any less, though.

They ended up talking amongst each other and I just spaced out. At first I was trying to decide if I was as distracting as my partner liked to believe. I came to terms with the idea that I had always been a lot to handle, but I tried staying out of his face for the most part since I understood how I tended to be.

I was also really hungry. I looked at Jonathan, trying to figure out what he was saying, but nothing was registering in my brain. I didn't eat enough after my workout and I never had a proper breakfast since I woke up so early. I looked at my phone for the time, but even that wasn't really registering in my brain.

"Can I go eat?" I interrupted whichever man was talking. I stood up feeling really on edge. "Wait, I think I have a granola bar in my purse actually," I rummaged through my bag, and to my surprise actually found one, "Never mind." I sat back down and started to peel away at the wrapper.

My ability to pay attention was always completely shot when I was hungry. It was as if hunger made my entire brain shut down, only being able to think about the emptiness in my stomach. Something about blood sugar was what doctors told me in the past.

"Okay, is there anything you need from me specifically? I really should grab some actual breakfast soon." I announced after I finished my granola bar.

"Oh, um, yeah," Jonny said, seeming a bit dumbstruck. It was at that moment that I realized they had watched me eat my entire granola bar without talking. That wasn't awkward at all. I slowly turned to Connor to see the expression on his face.

Still nothing. Good. Eating a granola bar wasn't weird anyways. These people were weird for always acting like they've never seen actual humans.

"Yes, can we hurry this up? I have to get back to work." Connor said to his dad, and I was starting to get annoyed with him not talking to me. It was good in the sense that he never spoke to me kindly anyways, but I didn't want to be ignored either.

"I just wanted to inform and formally invite you, Greyson, to a dinner we're hosting this weekend. We tend to have these every once in a while, but this one is specifically for all business partners of Meyers Motor Company. There will be a lot of people there that I'd like you to meet." Jonny smiled, and I was glad for the formal invite.

"I love dinners! I would love to go, thank you." I returned his excitement with my own smile, showing him just how honored I felt.

"Fantastic. So, since you are both currently partners, maybe Connor, you and Greyson could go together...?" Jonny timidly suggested.

There it was! Classic Connor finally came back! Instead of the emotionless face he tried to sport this entire time, his face finally contorted into what looked like annoyance, disgust, and my personal favorite, bewilderment.

"Jon-" Connor started to interject, but I decided it was my time to shine.

"No need for such a proposal, I already have a date to the event. Thanks though." I easily let out, and received two confused glances.

"I'm sorry?" Jonathan asked.

"Miguel already told me about the dinner yesterday, so I already have a date. He works here too." I said proudly, thinking of Peter's nice smile.

"Who?" Connor finally addressed me and I smiled so wide at him, you'd think I was crazy.

"His name is Peter. He works on our floor. He has blond hair and is really nice." I described, turning my entire body towards Connor, "I'm not sure what he does though, and I forgot his last name, but I'm sure you'd know him if you saw him." I continued on, just excited to be questioned by the man-child partner of mine.

"Peter Thorne? Peter is actually going with you?" And that's how the excitement crumbles. I'm sure he recognized how rudely he said that, but when did he care about how mean he was to me?

"Yes," I said firmly, "Is there an issue with that?"

His face finally softened from its shocked expression, "No, just wondering," He didn't miss a beat when he turned towards Jonathan, "Well if that's all, I have to go." Connor stood up and I quickly followed.

"Yeah me too." I said and left before Connor could. I remembered that I needed to get to our room before he did so that he would give me an actual assignment.

I hurried out without a proper goodbye and got to the office in about two seconds. Or, at least, that's what it felt like. I sat down behind my desk and folded my hands while I waited patiently for Connor's slow moving self.

He took slightly longer to get to the office than I would've preferred, but he did come eventually. "I'm here before you are so this means I get an assignment." I giggled teasingly, feeling proud of my abilities at being cunning.

Meyers Jr. was obviously not as impressed with my awesome talents. Whatever. He placed his briefcase onto his desk, opened up the straps, and pulled out the first paper sitting inside it, "Here."

I slid my chair over to his outstretched arm to receive the paper. The only thing on it was a picture of one of the company's cars, and the name of it. "Um, this is a nice picture?" I ended up saying as if questioning him, not able to understand what this paper meant to me or my task.

"It's a car model from a few years back." He said, as if that wasn't obvious.

"Oh really? Wow, and here I thought I was looking at a salad."

Connor gave me the most pissed face I'd ever seen him portray yet. He was obviously through with acting like stone, apparently. His facial expression seemed to be questioning if I really responded to him sarcastically.

Well, yes I did! So I looked him straight in the eye, challenging him. He could intimidate anyone he wanted, but that attitude wouldn't fly with me.

"Ms. Lewis, you're working in an office. If you want me to take you seriously, act it." He shot back and I was half prepared for the worse. He finally hinted at the conversation we had the day before. Well, more like the one-sided arguing that happened the day before, but he quickly dropped it. "Take this car model of ours, do research on it, and present it to me at the end of the week. Make sure you set it up to portray how you'd present the information in an actual meeting, keep your presentation professional, and be prepared to answer any questions I may have."

"Wait, what kind of research do you want me to do on it?" I stopped him as I rolled myself back to my desk, trying to find a pen to write out everything he wanted from me.

"That's what you get to figure out."

"Okay, so what did you want me to remember for when I present this to you?" I finally found my fuzzy pink pen and matching notepad.

"I already told you." Connor waved me off, turning to his computer, and the papers in his briefcase and on his desk.

"Wait, just repeat it one more time, please." I rolled my spinny chair back to his desk, stopping directly beside him on the same side of his desk and not across from it. I needed to get straight up into his face if he would ever give me the time of day.

"Present it in the style you would for a group meeting, keep it professional and answer my questions." He quickly spoke, tapping his fingers on his desk impatiently.

I scribbled the notes into my notepad as quickly as I could, "Okay, last thing. What kind of research did you want me to do on it, exactly?" I stared intently at my notepad, ready to jot down whatever came out of his mouth.

"Are you serious? I just answered that question." He nearly yelled at me, fed up with my questioning.

"I just want to make sure I have it all written out is all." I remained calm, but was internally upset with how impatient he always was.

"Research whatever you think is important to know. Now, can you please go back over to your desk?" His voice visibly softened as he tried to match the tone I used.

I wrote that out too, just to make sure I wouldn't forget. "Okay, and when exactly do you want me to have this done by?"

"The dinner is Friday night, so have it to me by Friday morning. That gives you about three days if you count today."

"Wait, can't this wait till after the dinner?" I didn't like the idea of having to worry about this and getting ready for a fancy party all in the same day.

"No."

Go figure. "Okay..." I trailed off, writing the date down in my notepad as well. I finally slid back to my desk, when all was said and done, and gathered my things, "I'm going to go get some food, but I'll get to work on this right after that." I grabbed my wallet and phone, leaving everything else put. I was borderline starving.

I was at the door to exit when I heard my name being called from behind me. "Yeah?" I turned around to look at Connor.

"Is Peter Thorne really going with you to this dinner?" He didn't make eye contact with me, he just continued typing on his computer like he hadn't asked me a question at all.

"Is there a problem with that, Mr. Meyers?"

Connor didn't say anything for a long while, so I turned back around. I didn't have time to deal with him acting so self-righteous. My hand was on the handle of the door when he finally spoke up, "You just seem too young for his taste."

I easily let go of the handle and turned back around to face him. He still didn't lift his head to look at me. "We're all adults here, Connor. I understand that I'm the youngest employee in this building and that you only view me as an ignorant and immature child, but I don't care. I'm not stupid and I can carry myself maturely. Just because you can't see that doesn't mean it ain't true," I went off, finally letting it all out. I was tired of beating around the bush when we all knew what the problem at hand was. "I was told office relationships aren't exactly shunned upon here, so don't concern yourself with my dating habits. If you're worried a relationship will get in the way of my work ethic, I'll tell you right now that I don't intend on letting that happen. I can be professional."

Connor finally looked at me. He didn't say anything at first, and I really wished he would. It would be so much better if he just said what he was feeling so we could move on. You'd think he would say something, after seeing how quick he was to argue on my first day at the office. However, it appeared to me that he was trying to pick up a habit of just letting me talk, and it made me feel really awkward. I'd rather just argue.

"I'll see you later," I said and with a roll of my eyes I finally opened the damn door.

"Enjoy your breakfast..." Connors voice trailed off as I shut the door behind me.

Now what was that supposed to mean?

Chapter Five

Chapter 5- She's Still Unskilled (Connor's Perspective)

I had no idea why it took me so long to give that girl an assignment. With work to do, she was literally out of the office and out of my way.

I easily shut her out of my consciousness and reverted straight into my old busy-bee self. The amount of work that got completed was astronomical. Which, considering how behind my schedule I was, this was a relief.

All the tasks I set for myself were completed, so I just sat back for a moment, waiting for the phone call I was supposed to make in about ten minutes. I could actually hear myself breathe, and the solitude was helping me release some stress.

If I really had to deal with Greyson for the entire summer, I would surely grow gray hairs and burn-out. I wondered if the simple task I assigned her was causing her any problems. Knowing her idiotic nature I could easily picture her confused face as she researched pointless information on the car.

Connor, stop. My face contorted in frustration. She was finally out of my hair and I had finished all of my work, so there was no need to be spending what was supposed to be a relaxing time for me thinking about her. In the short span of less than a week she was actually managing to slowly eat away at my sanity, and I needed to be the stronger person to properly deal with her and Tokyo.

Yet I still couldn't wrap my mind around why learning about a car you could easily Google about was keeping her away from the office for so long.

And that's how quickly the beauty of solitude crumbled. I decided I needed to call in Samantha since being alone was, for the first time in my life, not total bliss. I still had about six minutes before I needed to make the call, and dealing with Sam now would at least be beneficial to other matters.

"Yes?" She easily said when she walked in, ready for anything I needed her for. I watched her approach, staring at the neat and tidy red bun that sat high and tightly on top of her head. I could admire how much time she must've put into getting it to look so perfect. She wore her hair up most days, but I never really took much notice of it.

Greyson had worn her hair in a bun for the first time since she got here today. It wasn't nearly as kempt as Sam's, and lacked in every department. Yet, with Greyson's hair out of her face, you could actually see more of her facial features and how prominently her eyes really stood out.

"You're going with me to the dinner Friday." I calmly blurted. I then rolled my eyes at the flash of excitement that became evident on her face.

"Are you actually taking me out on an official date?" Her eyes sparkled mischievously. The day I made our relationship a bit more than a boss and an assistant, I made it clear to her that sex did not mean we were anything more than a boss and an assistant. I didn't want to date, I didn't want a girlfriend, and I didn't even want her to label us as lovers.

She managed to stay around for the past year or so because she respected that and never tried to make us anything more. "Jonathan never liked me going to these things alone, and maybe this will persuade him even more that I'm ready for his job."

And just like that the glint of hope for anything more left her eyes. "I understand," she professionally stated, "Should we get lunch at two in the cafeteria?"

"Sure." I shooed her off and with a sly smirk, she was on her way. I knew she was still excited about us going to the dinner together, no matter the circumstance, and I could only hope she wasn't going to think this was my way of actually wanting more from her. Why did I ask her to the dinner again?

Oh wait, I still had a phone call to make.

Finally at about half past one, Greyson finally made her way back into the office. I was still ahead of schedule with everything I could possibly do, so I had resorted to idly reading a few emails. She had a huge smile on her face and greeted me by waving.

Yes, waving, like she actually raised her right arm in the air, while the left was holding onto papers and her laptop messily, and wildly shook her hand side to side at me.

"Hey Connor!" She said, and went over to drop her things haphazardly onto her desk. "How's your work coming along?" She walked to stand across from my desk, hands on her hips, while panting slightly as if she ran here.

I could never get used to her random outbursts, "Fine." I said, flatly.

"Awesome, my work is coming along fine as well, and I just thought you'd want to know that. It's nearly eighty degrees outside right now, and there's a beautiful breeze going on too. It feels absolutely heavenly."

She strut back to her desk and grabbed her purse. What was the point of that conversation? I could already feel the mild anger rising in me at how unconventionally she spoke.

"I'm gonna walk around the block today and see if I can find some place to grab lunch. It's too nice right now to spend my lunch confined indoors. I'll see ya."

"You're going out alone?" I was mildly curious to know if Peter Thorne was taking her out. Mr. Thorne was a great employee, and usually kept to himself for the most part. The idea that he'd taken interest in this train-wreck was utterly surprising.

"Well apparently partners don't eat lunch together so obviously." She pulled the hair-tie from her head, allowing her thick curls to fall from the sloppy up-do she was sporting today.

"So you're going to walk around the building alone?"

"I'm not five Connor, I think I can handle being outside alone." Her tone quickly became defensive, and her smile was gone. She repeatedly grabbed at her hair, fluffing out the curls, keeping her gaze on a photo hanging on the wall.

I knew she thought I was just seeing her as a child, but in a way it wasn't too far from the truth. I was babysitting her against my will, and with how all over the place she was, she really could get lost outside. At the same time, if she never came back, there wouldn't really be an issue there.

"Okay, bye." She finally finished fixing up her hair and left. I wasn't getting paid nearly enough to continue dealing with that girl.

Not too long later I was in the cafeteria with Sam, enjoying a soup and sandwich while she spoke endlessly about the dinner coming up and picked at her salad.

"Is there any particular color you'd like my dress to be? I'm not sure if you want our outfits to match at all or..." She trailed off, waiting for me to input something to the conversation. Her way of questioning was a mixture of business and casual, and I was already regretting my proposition.

It was possible that I had been too spontaneous in my inviting her to be my date, and being a person who enjoys fully planning my moves, I was frustrated with myself. My mind was blank as to why I had opened my mouth without a second thought.

"Well, maybe it'll be easier if I choose a few that would look nice and then have you decide from there." She stabbed at the salad she ordered with her fork and picked up her phone, possibly to respond to whoever made it vibrate the moment before.

I was facing the entrance of the cafeteria and had been looking out at the lobby where the entrance to the building was. Greyson hadn't returned from her lunch yet.

Typical. Taking extremely long lunches was pitiful, and I noted it in my mind as just another reason why she wasn't mature enough to work in our specific car company. Not that this mental note was all that useful since my father didn't seem to mind hiring children to run a car company.

"Will Ms. Lewis be attending the dinner?" Samantha's voice snapped me out of my thoughts.

"Hmm?" I questioned, still half focused on the people walking in and out of Meyers Co.

"The girl you're currently forced to work with. Is she going to be at the dinner Friday?" She spoke again, louder.

I finally allowed my eyes to land on Sam's. That famous smirk of hers landed its way on her face when she knew she had my full attention.

"I believe so." I kept my tone nonchalant. I didn't really enjoy how Samantha tried using topics to get under my skin just for the satisfaction of getting my attention.

"Wow, Jonathan must really be serious about this if he's going to let that hoodlum wreak havoc at an event where all of his business partners will be present." Samantha scoffed, taking another bite out of her salad.

"I'm sorry?" I questioned. Something about her statement rubbed me the wrong way and I wasn't entirely sure if I had only heard her wrong. There seemed to be some underlying assertions Sam was making with that statement and I'd be damned if she was saying things like that in general, let alone to me, her boss.

"This girl, Greyson. She is a mess and as serious as a clown. Not to mention her upbringings... She'll probably lessen our credibility, and at such an important event like this dinner, it won't be surprising if she runs our good name straight to the ground."

"What about her upbringings?" I tightened my grip on my soup spoon, and my jaw clenched as I sat in disbelief at the woman who had worked for me for so long already.

She took notice of the change in atmosphere and her composure quickly diminished. "I um- Well, I- I didn't mean anything specifically. Just how out of this world of business she is. I'm just upset that you, you who has done so much work to build this company and put in so much effort to show your abilities as a leader now has to deal with this unexpected change of plans. Especially since we are so close to the Tokyo merger. I'm just hoping that you can get her out of our hair before anything detrimental happens." Her face had turned a scarlet shade that almost matched the color of her hair as she rambled on.

With much effort I bit my tongue and just focused on the spoon I was holding. After a moment, I nodded my head a few times, seeming to agree with Sam, and stood up. I tossed the spoon on the table, slipped my phone from the table to my pocket, and walked away.

For about the next hour and a half I was in multiple phone call meetings with multiple people getting information on what was going well and where there were setbacks. I had been pacing back and forth in front of my full wall-window, paying attention to the cars driving up and down the block, and the people who were also passing by.

After my last phone call, I noticed that Greyson's stuff was still messily lying on her desk, and that reminded me that I hadn't seen her come back in at all.

I smirked to myself at the idea that she really got lost. With how frivolous she pranced around, maybe she found a van full of hippies and decided to travel with them to some mountains in another continent.

I ended up over at her desk, rummaging my hand through the mess she left. I opened up her laptop and in it were some pieces of paper. The one on top had the name and model of the car on top so I decided to look through them.

:: The car comes in more than one color, like black, silver, shiny gray, white... Boring things like that, but there's also red, this interesting blue color, and this tan color that I really like for some reason. More things like that, but this is probably not important to Mr. Grumpy partner anyways. ::

I couldn't help but smile at not only her already horrible notes for this presentation, but the way she was addressing me. I set that page down and looked at the one underneath it.

:: WHY IS THIS ASSIGNMENT SO BORING!?! HOLY SHIT! ::

I laughed now, not expecting her to be so dramatic even while writing. I felt satisfied that this was causing her so much grief. I set that page aside also and looked at the last page she had stuffed into her laptop.

:: Pretend you are writing down something worthwhile about this car that Peter has so kindly decided to tell you about, but since he is talking so fast and this information is boring you still have no idea how the hell you are going to pull off this stupid presentation. I wonder what color dress I'm going to wear Friday. Oh, he said the car was a top seller the year it came out. I did get that info. I'm awesome. I think I'm hungry again. Note to self- get Peter to email you all the things he just said. ::

There was a dead stick figure drawing at the bottom of the paper, and I was surprised by how much I enjoyed reading her notes. It was comforting to know she really couldn't handle such a simple task.

Especially since a few hours before she had told me everything was going well with the assignment.

The amount of time it took her to get what little information she did have was also interesting to think about. This girl was never meant for a company like this, and it only solidified my hypothesis that Jonathan was going out of his mind.

I walked back over to the window, looking down once again for a sign of bushy hair, but found none. I hated to admit that I was getting slightly concerned about the whereabouts of Greyson, but she was gone for nearly three hours now on lunch, and it was unlike her to not make her presence known if she had returned.

I made my way out of the office and over to Amanda who was typing away on her computer. "Good afternoon, Mr. Meyers." She smiled as I approached the desk.

"Have you seen Greyson within the past hour or so?"

Amanda raised an eyebrow at me, as if I just asked a really stupid question. "Weren't you just in your office?"

"Yes?" I questioned back, now looking at her like she was the one losing her mind.

"She came back from lunch a while ago and had been in your office ever since." The confused face didn't leave Amanda, nor me for that matter.

"She's not in my office." I stated the obvious, peering down at the receptionist who had worked here before I had even started college. Fed up with the circles this conversation was going in I decided to finally do what I should've done a while back, "Give me her cellphone number." I pulled my phone out of my pocket. It honestly didn't make sense that I didn't have her cellphone number yet, especially since we were technically partners. I guess I had still been hoping that this was a joke and that she would have been gone by now.

After I had her number, I went back to my office, and looked around it, not understanding why Amanda thought she was in here.

My eyes landed on the door to my connecting office bedroom, and I stared at it for a moment.

There was no way she'd be in there for hours without notice.

Despite my better judgement I headed over to the room and opened the door. And guess who was sitting on the edge of the bed, in the flesh.

She was facing away from the door and was hunched over, speaking in a hushed tone. She peered her head over at me, quickly turning back around. "I know. I know. I have to see her though. I'll be fine. Listen, I gotta go. I promise I'll call you after, but I really need to see her and I can't wait till the weekend. Okay. I promise. Alright, bye."

Greyson finally stood up, and kept her eyes to the floor as she walked back into the main office space.

"Were you in there this entire time?" I asked in disbelief. She usually didn't stay in one place so quietly. "That's not your room to use whenever you want." I added, not liking how she sat in my private room for hours as if we shared that too.

"It won't happen again. Sorry." She packed up all the junk on her desk, her expression fully grim.

She was never so agreeable, and that's when I started to feel the gravity of her new demeanor. This wasn't just some random bad mood, but she was actually really upset.

"I'm going home to do some more research peacefully. I'll see you tomorrow." She picked up the rest of her stuff and without a single glance in my direction she walked out of the room. I was left standing in my place, completely dumbstruck.

And, for whatever stupid force that was working inside me, I was also completely concerned.

Chapter Six

Chapter 6- He's a Party Pooper (Greyson's Perspective)

Meyers had a closed driving course. A closed freaking driving course and no one bothered to tell me about it! Luckily for me, I was fully capable of doing research and could find out about it on my own. So, on the very morning of the presentation and company dinner, I was at the driving course.

I had been home most of the week, taking care of matters, while Connor and everyone else in the office believed I was just working on the presentation I was supposed to do. To be fair, I tried to do research and come up with information for my assignment, how else would I have found out about the driving course, but it wasn't easy staying focused at home. There was television, Netflix, constant snack breaks, random old things I kept finding in my room, walks around the block, and not to mention how many times I found myself switching tabs on my laptop to watch Youtube videos or play weird online games.

And to be quite honest, sometimes I just found myself laying on the floor in a pile of papers and food wrappers while my feet rested above me on the bed or couch. I'm not quite sure how that happened, but it happened often, and I'd usually be texting multiple people for a while before I even realized I was upside down.

I refused to believe that I was procrastinating since I had actually been trying. It was just a boring assignment that didn't really have much information that made sense to present. Give me some credit here.

Therefore, going to driving course was probably my best option. Well that, and the information Peter emailed to me about the car. I figured, if I drove the car, maybe my presentation would sound more like it came from me after getting a feel for it firsthand. It all made perfect sense. And due to being COO, I had the right to test out company cars and drive them for however long I wanted to for free.

My buddy John was even nice enough to find the pretty tan colored model for me, and was going to drive me around as fast as it could go. John was the man in charge of the driving course. He and some of the others that worked the driving range usually tested out the cars for speed, brake power, steering wheel reliability, and all that other fun stuff. John used to drive NASCAR, and since he could probably make the driving experience more fun, I decided to let him be the one behind the wheel.

I even got to wear a helmet, that's how cool this whole thing was.

"John, you are awesome!" I said once we finished. I was dizzy, my hair was sticking out at weird angles, and the adrenaline rush was absolutely amazing. "We definitely have to do this again with a faster car!"

"Agreed! You are welcome here any time, Grey. It's been a pleasure." John pulled me in for a hug and I squeezed him extra tight as a final goodbye.

As I walked out of the course, waving goodbye to all the guys working there, I pulled out my phone to check any missed messages I might have received. Which, to my displeasure was actually quite a few. Connor had called me twice and sent me more than a few text messages asking where the hell I was since, again, the presentation was today.

I said a silent prayer under my breath as I dialed his number. "Hey Connor," I quickly said, trying to ignore how unhappy his 'hello' sounded. "So anyways, I'm on my way to the office right now, I'm just down the block at the driving course getting in some final research before I present to you what I have. It's still morning right?" I pulled my phone away to check the time on the screen. I'm pretty sure half-past-eleven counted as morning. "So I'll be there in like three minutes, okay?"

I waited a moment for him to reply, but received silence. "Is that okay, Connor?" I tried again.

"Three minutes." Came his response before the line went dead. Talk about pressure.

I took a pill to help me stay focused during our meeting. I was unhappy about that decision, but I was determined to not screw up.

I quickly did a small prayer to make it in on time and headed to my car.

Maybe it was the look in his eyes, or the frown on his lips. Or maybe it was even the way he rested his hand on his hip, tapping his fingers impatiently, or quite possibly, the steam that was blowing out of his ears. Whatever it was that had clued me in on his specific mood, I was certain that having appeared in the conference room over ten minutes late wasn't something he was fond of.

"You should be fucking fired." He spoke through gritted teeth. Yeah he totally wasn't happy with me.

Well, he was never happy with me anyways, even when I did try. Like how I was trying now. "For someone who works in the professional world, you curse way too often." I walked past him, setting up the information I pretended to have on the one side of the long table.

The room was actually really cool. It was the smallest room for holding meetings on our floor. Yes I gave myself a tour on all of them, and this room was the most adorable.

"You tend to bring it out in me." The strong annoyance was hard to miss in his ever so cold tone of voice. Either way, he took a seat a few chairs down from where I was sorting my papers, obviously ready to hear my presentation anyways. I kind of wished he would just cancel it until another day.

"Aw, I'm flattered. I've been told I bring out strong emotion in guys. But flirting won't get you off the hook with me. You really should watch your language around ladies such as myself." I smiled while continuing to sort through my mess of papers for the notes on the car Peter had emailed me.

"What?"

"Listen, you also need to lighten up. I can't give my presentation when you're obviously unhappy. It's bad atmosphere, and I'm all about good atmosphere. Plus, bad moods make me nervous, and if you're already mad before I even begin then I'm obviously only gonna fail from here!"

"Can you just begin already?" He loudly, and not to mention unhappily, insisted.

"Alright! Damn." I finally stopped searching for the paper, remembering that I had left it with Jay to hold a few days ago so that I wouldn't lose it. I guess that was bad karma for not having done the work myself. "Um." I just stood there, looking down at the papers that didn't hold anything about the car. Wow, the irony was just amazing. It was messed up, but still amazing.

"Ms. Lewis..." Connor trailed off, implying that I should really start speaking.

"Yeah so, you see, the car, it's called a Meyers Conqueror. It has four doors and a sunroof. It comes in a lot of colors like red, black, white, and even a shiny tan color, plus more. Apparently, it was a top seller the year it came out. It's also pretty fast, when you drive it fast, and can do some pretty sharp turns. It's cool for doing racecar things like doughnuts in the road, burning rubber, and the brakes work really well too."

Connor had the most expressionless face I've ever seen him pull off to date. It reminded me of the time we were both in Big Boss Meyers office, and he looked like he had turned to stone. I couldn't tell a single thing from his face, and that was a bad thing. This whole deal was a bad thing since I didn't have anything on the car at all. I knew I semi-looked over the notes Peter sent me, but my mind was turning up blank to whatever information I did read.

"Yeah I think it would be good for families, maybe not exactly NASCAR quality, but pretty good. Oh, um, and the seats are leather. The gas thing is on the driver's side. Um, yeah. I think that's all. Thank you for your time." I smiled brightly, ending on a strong note.

Thinking over everything I just said, I started to feel confident that I did an alright job. It wasn't as awesome as I had intended it to be, but it wasn't too bad either. I remembered some points of the car which was nice. I gave him information like he asked, and I did it on my own. Yeah, this presentation went awesomely, especially for my first time.

My smile faded slightly as I waited for Connor to give me his feedback on my presentation. It's not like he knew I was missing any information, so he shouldn't have anything negative to say. I continued the staring contest we were apparently having, quickly becoming annoyed with his lack of response.

"That's the only information you could come up with in this time?" He said simply, and I nodded in agreement. He silently got up, and walked over to the door of the conference room. He was leaving? Without saying anything?

When his hand reached for the knob, that's when I snapped myself out of the daze I was in to speak up, "Wait. How did I do?" I asked, and quickly regretted opening my mouth. Truth be told, I think I always knew it didn't go so well, but sometimes lying to myself was much easier than facing facts.

"I'm already so sick and tired of dealing with you and it's only been about a week," He let go of the doorknob to turn and look at me. "Do you honestly think I enjoy this? Do you think I wanted this partnership? I think I made it more than clear that I never asked for any of this!" He raised his voice, and I just kind of stood there, not really sure what to say.

"I don't want this and I don't want you. I honestly do not," He brought his voice back down, but not bringing down the harshness of his words. "I sat down the other day and let you go on and on about being mature and capable of working here. You wanted to be taken seriously, and. I. Did. That. I gave you something to do, and I said to myself that if you took this seriously I would at least take the time out of my busy fucking schedule to teach you about what it means to be the Chief Operating Officer, as if you deserved such a title! Which, let me tell you, you don't and you never did!" The volume of his voice rose again, and I still just stood there, allowing him to say whatever it was he wanted to say.

"And this little shit-show was proof of that. You gave me basic information anyone just looking at the car could say! This was a total joke to you and I feel like the ass here since I was the one who thought you'd actually take this seriously!"

What he was saying was really starting to hurt and I felt the need to defend myself, "You never told me exactly what you wanted! You just vaguely told me you wanted information. You never gave me a setup or helped me at all along the way. This was my first presentation and-" Connor intervened.

"You never asked me for help! The only time you came to me was when you told me everything was going well and then you went home for the next couple of days to do research. In the real world you can't just expect people to come help you when they have their own work to do."

"It's not like you would've helped me anyways! You would've just been all pissed and told me to figure it out. You've never wanted to help me, and I didn't want you to know I was strugglin'. I wanted to show you that I could do this, so maybe, just maybe you wouldn't always be so mad at me all the time." I loudly spoke back. I didn't like that he was yelling at me and making me feel like I was just some giant fuck-up.

"Well look how well that turned out," He paused for a moment, staring dangerously at me. His brown eyes had turned black and unforgiving. "You wanted to show me that you could do this, but this presentation did all to prove the opposite. And don't act like you have me all figured out, because if you would've come to me with a specific question involving this assignment, I was completely ready to help out. I fucking wanted you to prove me wrong! At least that would have made my job just slightly fucking easier, and yes, I'm fucking cursing at you! But no I'm not cursing in front of a lady, I'm currently cursing at a fucking child, and that's what makes me the fucked up person here!"

That didn't feel too nice. "Connor..." I spoke calmly, trying to bring the volume of the conversation back down.

"Don't you fucking dare. Shut up! Just shut up!" He shook his head at me a few times, his eyes never wavering from mine, not even for a second. "I'm so done with this! This is a waste of my time. I don't care what Jonathan says, I'm not doing this." He finally turned back to the door, opening it, "If you want to continue working here go right ahead, but you're going to have to find someone else to do this because I'm done." He took half a step out the door, "You're less than pitiful" He walked out, slamming the door shut behind him.

"...Well that went well." I said to myself and stuffed all the papers back into my bag.

I avoided the office for the next couple of hours, thinking that was probably a good idea. During this time Connor stayed in the office, even having Samantha bring him food to the room instead of leaving to get his lunch himself.

I figured that was probably for the better since I didn't want to be yelled at again. However, that made me realize how much it sucked to share an office. I felt exiled from my own space that I had full rights to, and now I was basically a nomad, sent to wander the floor looking for a place to temporarily be at.

Which wasn't fun since I, once again, didn't have any real work to do. This whole situation sucked. It sucked major ass actually.

Amanda was nice enough to let me pull up a chair behind the front desk, but I was dying inside to do something. Anything!

"Do you still not want to talk about it?" Amanda asked for about the fourth time, after hanging up the phone for about the twentieth time.

It's not that I didn't want to talk to her about it. I didn't like not talking about things that bothered me. What held me back was the fact that she was always picking up the phone, or needing to write something down. I didn't like the idea that I'd have to pause my story frequently while she did her actual job.

"I'll tell you about it some other time. I think I've wasted enough time here anyways. I'm not doing anything so I might as well go home and get ready for the dinner tonight." I got up reluctantly, feeling like absolute crap. "You're coming tonight right?"

"No, honey. I'm sorry, but my husband and I already have plans." She gave me a half-hearted smile, and I frowned forcefully back.

I sighed heavily, "Alright. I guess I'll have to fend for myself tonight." I grabbed my stuff and with a sad goodbye, I left.

Back at my apartment, I wasn't feeling any better. I sat at the edge of my bed, looking at the long black dress Jayden had graciously given me for this event. Before I left in the morning to the driving course, I had set it out on my bed, excited for the night. Boy how things could change from one moment to the next.

The dark storm cloud that was seeming to be permanently over my head was really starting to piss me off. I was not a person of bad moods, and Connor just had to be the mean person I was partnered with who hated me so much. Although I wanted to blame him fully for being upset, it was more aggravating to know deep down that this was slightly kind of my fault.

"Can't it be dinner time yet?" I said to no one in particular, and flopped backwards onto the bed. With some grunts and sighs, I finally forced my body up and into the shower.

When I finally finished drying my hair and slipping the dress on, I had to admit, I was looking mighty fine. The gown style dress came all the way down to the floor, just barely scraping it in my tallest black pumps. There was a long slit down the side that came all the way up my left leg. Its elegance was prominent in the way the top of the dress came all the way up to my neck and down my arms, hiding even the idea of cleavage.

My favorite part however, was the back. From my shoulders down my entire back was bare. The fabric of the dress only being seen again at the very base of my spine. Who said elegance couldn't be sexy? Since I was having a moment with myself, it only seemed appropriate to grab my hair brush, blast Whitney Houston from my phone, and lip sync to I Will Always Love You in my mirror, acting like a true diva.

It was fitting. Definitely a bit overboard, maybe in the right person slightly shameful, but I was feeling myself, and I was the COO of Meyers Motors. I was about to be the most fly person at this dinner, and the fact that this dress was personally tailored by one of Jay's closer friends made me smug knowing I'd also probably have the cheapest dress.

"The queen has arrived," I said to myself in the mirror, turning around to check out my butt. I was totally shameless. The storm cloud over my head had officially dissipated, leaving a rainbow in its place. All I had to do now was apply some makeup, and wait for my date to pick me up.

The look on Peter's face when he got me was super reassuring. I was sure the smile on my face stretched from ear to ear when we walked into the fancy dining hall. He looked mostly the same in his suit, seeing how he also wore a suit to work. Guys were always more boring with their formal-wear. If they were working, at an important event, or even getting married the whole suit or tux appearance was the same in my eyes.

Either way, a man in a suit was always a turn-on, and I wasn't totally bothered by it. The place we were having dinner at, on the other hand, was totally amazing! I had met Mr. Meyers and his brother while waitressing for my school at an alumni event he attended, and I had thought that place was fancy. This place however, put that other place to shame easily. It was like going to a huge expensive wedding!

There were big round table everywhere, waiters and waitresses walking around with drinks and finger-foods, a stage on the far side with a band playing softly, and a crisp off-white color-scheme going on making the place very classy. I was expecting something nice, but this made me feel like I was about to meet royalty. I was sure the Queen would pop out of nowhere at some point with a British accent to ask me how I felt about scones.

Definitely not a dinner party I was used to, but I was loving the culture shock anyways. People were standing around talking, or already settling into tables, looking at menus.

"Who knew a car company could be so classy?" I said under my breath, still smiling like a maniac.

"Do you want to meet the rich old people who sponsor us? I can definitely help you grow your network with some of our partners." Peter placed a cold hand on my back, trying to bring me closer so I could hear him over the voices of everyone around us. With my heels on, he was slightly shorter than me and I thought it was absolutely adorable.

"Do they bite?" I joked, and he led me through the crowd of fancy-pants to meet a man who worked in the commercial aspect of the car company. Apparently he worked in our building, and I hadn't even seen him till now.

"I know a thing or two about visual media! Graphic design and creating short commercial type videos is my specialty. I can't draw, but I can definitely do some cool designs through the computer." I was telling the guy, really excited to be able to talk about something I actually understood. "Actually one time, a group of friends and I entered a video creating contest on the quote, 'Out of this World' and we started off with the video sounding very educational with planets and everything." I paused to grab some weird mini egg-pie looking thing from a waiter.

I've never seen eggs in a pie crust, but it was adorably small and actually tasted amazing, "Anyways, it was my idea to add a huge alien clip art and we changed the music for a dramatic effect and thanks to my artsy friend we had the alien eat all of the planets! It was like Godzilla attacking! Anyways, the video ended and after all the chaos, Earth was the last planet that remained and we had the alien with a quote bubble saying, 'Stay in your World,' it was totally awesome." I chuckled at myself, remembering creating that beautiful video with my friends, "It was such an awesome play on words in my opinion. We were actually disqualified for that video because the background music had profanity and I guess even at the college level, people still get scared of a few curse words in music. That was depressing, I'm sure if it wasn't for that we would've won the gold." I ended the story, glancing around to find Mr. Meyers with his brother.

"Well that was... Interesting?" The commercial guy was saying.

"Hey, no problem. Actually I have to go say hi to a friend, Peter I'll meet up with you a bit later." I hugged Peter quickly and shook the guy's hand, "It was nice meeting you! I'll be sure to visit you in the office later to talk more." I waved before I walked off and made my way to the man I hadn't seen since waitressing.

There wasn't so many people that walking was a hassle and I was happy for that. It could easily become claustrophobic in this dining hall if there were any more people, but I guess Mr. Meyers was smart enough to understand that as well.

"Jackson!" I yelled when I finally got to the brothers, "It's been a while, I've missed you." Jackson Meyers turned towards me, ready to scoop me into a huge bear hug.

"Greyson! I was wondering where you were just now actually. How have you been?" He smiled that same old smile of his that made the skin around his eyes crinkle in the way that only a truly happy person who's lived many happy years could pull off.

It was weird, I only met him once before now, and he had a way of making me feel like we knew each other for an entire lifetime. "I'm great, this job is awesome. Thank you again for this amazing opportunity." Both of the Meyers brothers really made me feel like I was in their family and I was grateful for them helping me out like this.

"Well of course! But there's no need to say thank you for this. You deserve to be here because of who you are, not because of us." Jackson was saying, making me feel like a priceless gem. I felt kind of bad being talked about so highly. I still hadn't done anything specifically to deserve such a compliment.

"You look very pretty tonight Greyson. I'm glad you made it." Jonathan Meyers said to me, giving me a warm smile. Oh yeah, my ego was definitely through the roof at this point. "Have you found a table yet? I'd like for you to sit with us so I can finally introduce you to some people." He said before him and his brother walked me to the only rectangular shaped table in the entire place. It could fit way more people than all the circular tables, and that was the moment I truly felt like royalty.

I wasn't just a peasant at this formal event, I was a princess who was allowed to sit at the all-exclusive VIP section. That was incredibly humbling. I didn't necessarily sit so close to them at the end of the table, but instead I sat somewhere down the side. I placed my purse on the seat next to me for Peter, and watched as seats quickly filled with people who seemed to be already acquainted with one another.

A woman with a navy blue colored dress sat next to me, and spoke to some other lady across the table. They were both older and judging by the rocks on their finger, I assumed they were both married to the men that sat directly next to them.

Starting to feel bored and out of place, I took out my phone and texted Peter to save me from my despair. Once he came, I was finally in a right enough mind to ask him a question I should've asked since the beginning. "Isn't this all just a bit too much for just a dinner party for a car company?"

Peter had his arm around my shoulders, always seeming more laid back than everyone else. A quality I always liked about him. "Yeah, it would be for just any dinner. However, this specific dinner is something Jonathan does only once a year. And this specific year is probably the biggest since this is right before the meeting in Tokyo, and everyone has been working to make a compelling argument for our friends in Japan. If that meeting doesn't go well, it will be hard to finally expand this business into Asia and everyone will lose money instead of gaining. So I guess this is kind of his way to say thanks for everything and to get everyone motivated for the little time we have left before that meeting." Peter explained, and I tried so hard to keep everything he told me permanently in my mind.

This dinner was only once a year. This was the biggest thanks to Japan. Japan is important because we want cars there. No cars there means no money. The world runs on money. And for some odd reason, Jonny Meyers thinks I'm a key factor into making himself more money. Yup, definitely no pressure there. It's not like I didn't know how to do my job or anything. It's also not like I didn't even know what the hell my job was for Japan.

Well shit.

At this time, Connor and Samantha finally appeared and sat down at the two seats left vacant at the table. I was starting to wonder why those seats weren't filled too. The awkward irony was the fact that those seats were directly across from Peter and I. Samantha sat in the seat across from me and it was nice to see someone I actually knew at this event, despite how she disliked me.

Ignoring Connor, who I was sure still probably wanted me dead, I focused my attention on Samantha. She was wearing a really pretty red dress that seemed to work with her orangey-red hair. "Hi Samantha! How are you doing?" I smiled at her. She was saying hello to the lady beside her, but took a moment to look at me with a cold expression. Talk about bitch-face.

"Good." She rudely replied, quickly turning back to the lady beside her. I knew I didn't like her, yet I was always trying to make peace with such a person. She was lucky I was a kinder person or by now she'd be in a hospital on life-support.

"Uhh, excuse you, but that attitude of yours really needs to be taken care of because I don't appreciate that kind of bullshit." I took a sip of my water, ignoring how a few people at the table were looking at me and the situation that was being created.

I could tell Samantha was shocked herself at how blatantly I came at her. I didn't care where I was, if someone wanted to be disrespectful I would easily call them out on it right then and there. She opted to look at Connor who was sipping on some alcoholic beverage. She seemed to suggest to him to do something about the situation. Samantha had no backbone. Go figure.

I locked eyes with Connor, his face blank as he finished off his glass.

"She isn't worth it," Peter ended up saying, breaking the tension that was slowly growing. "Have you looked at the menu yet? I'm thinking I want the steak." He easily diffused the entire situation, and everyone slowly went back to their business. I did, however, take notice of the side-eye the ladies next to me had given me before picking up where they left off in conversation.

"Yeah that looks good, I'm hungry." I decided to drop it, not trying to make Jonny-boy reconsider his high opinion of me. I looked around to find a waiter, trying to get some actual dinner. What kind of dinner party was this? "So when are they gonna play some good music? I'm tryin' to dance. I love dancing." I eagerly looked at Peter, since he was so smart and always had answers for me.

"This isn't really a dancing kind of party." He laughed lightly, and my entire face dropped.

"What kind of party with a live band doesn't have dancing?" I whined, but just then a swarm of waiters arrived to take our dinner orders.

Peter and I were having a blast during our entire meal, laughing and telling embarrassing stories. It was nice of him to just talk to me since

I didn't know people, even though he knew a lot of the people that were present.

"I think you might have me beat." He finally calmed down from laughing at my latest story. I had embarrassing stories for days. "If I'm ever playing truth or dare, I know who to call."

"Daredevil is my middle name, what can I say." I shrugged, trying to act cool, but couldn't help the smile on my face. "Let's dance! Please?" I nearly begged Peter, already standing up. Some of the older couples had been swaying back and forth to the crap music that was playing and I was ready to bust a move.

"Mr. Meyers is about to speak right now actually." Peter gently pulled on my arm, causing me to plop back down onto my seat.

I watched as Jonathan and his brother made their way to the stage. Ugh, someone should just kill me now. I hate speeches.

While Jonathan and Jackson were speaking, I was browsing Instagram on my phone under the table. It was all I could do to keep myself from going to sleep.

"...Greyson Lewis!" I heard my name echo through the speakers, and looked up to find Jonathan pointing in my direction and people staring at me. Shit, I missed something.

"Stand up." Peter whispered to me, causing me to awkwardly rush to stand up. The chair squeaked loudly behind me, and I quickly gave my phone to Peter so no one would know I was distracted.

"Hi!" I waved weirdly, not sure what I was supposed to do.

Jonathan said more words that I didn't catch since I was trying to make eye-contact with everyone all at once. Peter tapped me twice on the leg, and I took that as a sign to sit back down. He passed me my phone, and I looked around a bit longer, not sure what just happened. Everyone went back to looking at the Meyers brothers, and that's when I decided to ignore it and continue browsing through my phone.

When he finished talking everyone clapped, and I sighed in relief. Speeches should be illegal in my opinion. They make parties super boring.

"So I've been thinking that there's something different about you today, and I think I finally realized what it is," Peter said to me once everyone began to start talking amongst themselves. The same slow boring songs were being played, and I was just about ready to go home and hang out with Jay.

"Oh yeah?"

"Yeah, it's like you're calmer today. You're usually very high energy and bouncing all over the place, but now you seem more relaxed."

"And to think it only took one pill to make me all boring for the whole day. Crazy, right? It didn't even help me on my presentation. But don't worry, it's slowly wearing off. Actually, I have to pee." I got up, looking around for the bathrooms. "I'll be right back."

After weaving through all the different tables I finally found the ladies room. It was much more dimly lit than the main hall, which didn't make sense to me. I could hardly see myself in the mirror, so retouching my makeup was super difficult.

The door to the bathroom opened and guess who walked in. If you guessed Samantha then you deserve all the cookies.

"You must've really pissed off Connor if he doesn't even want to look at you anymore." She strode over to the sink beside me, pulling out some powder from her clutch, caking it on. Her already pale face looked nearly chalklike under all that powder and I couldn't help but think that the fake effect it gave her matched her personality perfectly.

"Why do you hate me so much? What the fuck have I ever done to you?" I set down my lipstick and placed my hand on the edge of her sink, getting all up in her business, as I towered above her.

The strong front she kept trying to put on faded, and she actually looked scared of me. I did not grow up in the hood for nearly all my life to not know how to be intimidating. I already had her type all figured out. She was sneaky, someone who liked to twist words and be manipulative. Given the right conditions and she could probably really terrify someone.

However, she had no power over me. And since her job description was below my own, it would be silly of me to give her that kind of control.

"I dislike you, because all you're doing is jeopardizing Connor's chances of successfully carrying out his plans for Tokyo. All you've done here was create unnecessary stress for Connor and as his assistant I care about what's affecting his ability to do his job." She said, trying to regain control of the situation she put herself in as soon as she walked into the bathroom. To be completely honest, her argument was kind of strong. Those were some valid reasons to dislike someone.

"Well I guess you're just gonna have to hate me then. Because honey, I'm staying here for the entire summer, I will be present at the meeting in Japan and if you think you can honestly keep being a disrespectful bitch, I will see to it that your ass gets fired. You here tryna tell me I'm childish when you're the one comin' at me with the scare tactics of a middle school girl. If you wanna play these games, I have no issue with being the tattle-tale." I snatched all my shit from the counter and walked out with my head held high.

So maybe I lied a bit, but she didn't need to know that. I wasn't one to run to someone to take care of my issues, but if it scared her enough to leave me alone then there was really no problem.

Something about the means being justified by the end results, right?

On my way back to the table, I saw Connor duck out the front door. I was sure he came with Samantha, so it didn't make sense for him to be leaving without her. Maybe he was getting some air?

I looked over towards the table I was sitting at, realizing maybe I needed some air myself. Oh and maybe, just maybe, I also owed someone an actual apology for the mistakes I made. Yeah, I needed to do that too.

Once outside I found Connor pacing along the side of the building with his phone to his ear and his face pointed to the floor. He didn't look up to notice me, and I just watched him for a moment. I wasn't sure if I should make my appearance known so he'd hurry his conversation along or if I should just wait for him to finish and not piss him off at me any more so. Yeah, I opted to wait.

He stopped pacing for a moment to pull out a small box from his pocket. From the box he pulled out a cigarette, placed it in his mouth and returned the box to his pocket. He still managed to speak to whomever was on the phone, while also pulling out a lighter and lighting the cigarette. My face cringed as he sucked in a long breath, bringing in all the chemicals from that cancer stick with it.

This totally dropped his attractiveness levels. Not that I thought he was attractive in the first place, I mean he was, but that was beside the point. He wasn't my type.

But what was it with wealthy men and celebrities having a particular set of genes that was so blessed anyways? Either way, now with his little smoking deal, he became super unappealing.

"Fuck you Adam. Enjoy this now when you can. I'm only giving you till Tuesday," Connor said and hung up, not bothering with saying goodbye.

Great, he wasn't in a good mood. Just my luck as always, "Hey." I waved when he finally turned my way and looked up. I decided to just ignore the look on his face altogether instead of allowing myself to understand the degree of dislike towards me it held. The option I chose was much kinder.

"I know you hate me, I know it's my fault, but I just really need to apologize." I kept my distance, allowing my hands to fiddle with my dress as I questioned in my mind what the hell I was trying to accomplish. The last time we spoke was only a few hours ago, and that was when he was telling me how much he was done with me. Maybe I should've given him the weekend before talking to him. It also didn't help that I didn't plan anything to say, but leaving things as it was for a few days probably wasn't a good idea either.

"Do you really think I want to hear anything you have to say right now?" He placed the cigarette back into his mouth, inhaling more of the nicotine.

"No, but I don't really think there's going to be any other time where you're gonna want to hear what I have to say. So I just picked the soonest time I could. Connor, look, I'm sorry." I swallowed all of my pride to humble myself to such a jackass.

He turned his head away from me, exhaling a thick white cloud of smoke, and taking in another breath from the cigarette.

"I know I messed up. I didn't take the assignment seriously, and I know I don't deserve to have you take me seriously. I don't deserve any more chances, but please just gimme one more. Just another assignment, and if I mess up, I..." I trailed off, not exactly sure where I was going with this, "Look if I mess up, I'll move to a different office on a different floor and figure out everything on my own. I'll stay out of your hair for good." What the hell was I proposing?

Connor snapped his head towards me, his eyes slightly widened as they stared straight into mine, probably considering the stupid friggin' proposal I just made up.

"But," I said, trying to not completely screw myself over, "I want us to work as the team we should be on this. I get that it'll be my assignment, but I don't want you to hate me the entire time either to the point where I feel like I can't come to you. I really want us to be friends, even though you're not the nicest. So before we start work next week, on Sunday I want us to go to lunch like actual business partners and start over on the right foot." Yeah, I think that was much better than the deal I almost made where I would be sealing my fate to him so easily.

"You will actually leave me alone for good?" He finally said, only looking at the aspects of the deal I was making that benefitted him. I guess he really didn't want to be friends.

I nodded once, still not exactly happy with how excited he was to the idea of never seeing me again.

"Alright fine." He said after contemplating the details of the proposition I literally pulled out of my butt.

"Cool, then we are partners!" I tried my hardest to look towards the bright side of the whole ordeal, "And as your friend, I should let you know that smoking is not a nice look for you. See ya Sunday." I smiled and turned to go back inside. My smile faded as soon as I turned from him.

I knew he could say a lot of cruel things, but was having me around really all that bad? I could understand that he disliked me, but did he hate me so much that he was okay with never even seeing me again?

Maybe I should get out of his hair. I mean, apparently, I was making his life so terrible by being around. He only knew me for a week, and was so quick to jump at any opportunity to have me go. It kind of hurt to think I had caused a person to hate me so much. Especially since I was trying to do the opposite this entire time.

Connor never even apologized for how he constantly treated me. Did he truly think he was never wrong? He verbally abused me constantly for the past week, and yet it was like he thought he was never wrong for that.

"Hey, you've been gone a while, are you alright?" Peter said when I finally got back to the table. Waiters were finally coming by to serve desert, and my appetite was completely gone.

Connor came to the table then too, and took his seat. We made eye contact for a moment, and I looked away. I stared down at my hands, not sure what to do.

"Yeah I'm fine." I lied, not even bothering to look at Peter. No, I wasn't fine at all. Everything was not alright. I felt absolutely terrible. "I want to go home, I'm tired." I started feeling very claustrophobic, and stood up, ready to bolt.

"Okay, we can go now." Peter started to slide his chair backwards to get out.

"No, you stay." I finally got around my chair, trying to gather everything into my purse.

"Greyson, everything okay?" Jackson called from down the table. Everyone got quiet to stare at me.

No everything wasn't alright! I was the most worthless piece of shit in the entire company, yet my job description had a yearly salary that was so above me that being here was a complete joke. "Mhmm." I responded, not trusting my voice to stay level.

Why was I hired? Was this just a prank, something for Jonathan and Jackson to laugh about? Who would ever hire me for any job ever? I was barely a C-student, with a GPA so low you'd wonder how I ever even got into college. I was a joke.

Who wouldn't hate me?

"Are you sure you don't want me to take you home? I don't want you out on the street at night alone." Peter rested his hand on my arm and I yanked it back.

"Because a kid like me can't handle it, right?" I accidentally snapped at him. I felt bad just as quickly after.

Finally closing up my purse I made one last glance at Connor and left. I wished that when I looked at him he wouldn't have been looking back, but he was looking back. I wished he wasn't my partner, but he was my partner. I wished I tried harder, but I didn't try harder. I even wished his facial expression was neutral or hateful, but it wasn't.

I guess that was the thing about wishing. It didn't really change the reality of the situation. It only made a person fantasize about what wasn't.

Why did he look concerned?

Chapter Seven

Chapter 7- She's Impulsive (Connor's Perspective)

It was an amazing deal. Instead of working towards making her quit, Greyson was basically giving me a simpler alternative that worked just as well. It would be so easy to give her an assignment she couldn't do and then she'd leave my office, my floor, and most importantly she'd leave me alone for good.

How could I not like such a deal?

"And as your friend, I should let you know that smoking is not a nice look for you. See ya Sunday." She was saying as I was thinking of the beautiful situation I was about to be faced with.

She flashed me her signature smile, but this time it was different. It didn't reach her eyes, and before she completely turned away from me I noticed the corners of her mouth drop.

That didn't matter though, because in about a week, I was going to be stress free and would have my office to myself again. It would be completely quiet and I would finally be alone.

I would be alone.

I looked down at the cigarette I had been smoking, letting the words Greyson said register in my mind for a moment. I tossed it on the ground, crushing it under my foot before walking back into the dining hall.

As I was making my way over, I briefly made eye contact with Jonathan. His eyes, that I was told reflected my own, locked on to mine, and in that moment I came back to reality. Even if Greyson wanted to leave my office on her own accord, he had all the power in the world to simply deny such a proposal.

When I got to the table, Greyson quickly glanced at me before looking down at her lap. I could feel Samantha eyes on me, wanting me to turn towards her and actually converse with her. I elected to ignore her altogether. She had been down my throat the past couple of days that Greyson was gone, throwing snide comments about her every chance she got. I was fed up with hearing about matters that didn't pertain to my job.

I continued to watch Greyson, quickly becoming aware of how fidgety she was acting. Despite her constant animated behavior, this time her shifting seemed uncomfortable. She always seemed to hold an aura of confidence, but now it was like she was completely unsure of herself.

She shot up out of her seat, something she had done way too many times this evening, but this time it was as if she was overwhelmed or scared even? I didn't understand what happened from seeing her outside to now that caused such a dramatic shift in her demeanor.

Everyone was staring at her now as she haphazardly gathered her belongings. What the hell was she doing now?

"Because a kid like me can't handle it, right?" I eventually zoned in to hear Greyson snap at Peter, yanking her arm away from him. She looked at me for a moment with eyes full of betrayal as she turned around and started heading for the exit.

Whoa, what did I miss?

I looked to Peter to see if he was going to follow her out. When he didn't I slid my chair back, ready to make sure Greyson wasn't about to find a way home in the middle of the night alone, but Samantha grabbed onto my arm, stopping me. I was halfway out of my chair when I was forced to stop. I snapped my head over at Samantha, silently demanding that she let go of me.

"Connor, sit down and look around yourself." She calmly said to me in the tone of voice she used when I was overworking myself. I sat back down, not bothering to look around. "You don't want to cause a scene in front of all these people and Jonathan at such a crucial time. Don't subject yourself to her childish ways."

At this time the servers arrived with deserts for our table. The hall had become quiet, thanks to the dramatic exit Greyson had made. I looked over to Jonathan once again before my eyes shifted over towards the entrance to see if she'd come back or if she was really about to go home by herself.

"Connor, look at me," Samantha said and this time I did, "She is trying to make a joke out of the position you so proudly hold. Don't give her that power." She gave me a stern look, before turning from me to talk to Richard's wife.

She was absolutely right. It was unlike me to make a scene, and yet I was about to do just that in front of the entire board, sponsors, and other people who viewed me on basically the same level as Jonathan.

Yet, despite knowing that, I still couldn't take my mind off the idea that a person as erratic and childish as Greyson was out alone at night, in a dress even. And not just that, but the question still remained in my mind as to what the fuck just happened?

By the time the dinner was over, I was effectively a mess internally. Just because I didn't like Greyson meant I wanted her to end up being raped because not one single person was decent enough to take her home.

"Sam, have the valet bring the car to the front for me." I nearly tossed my keys into her hand as I rushed to go find Peter before he left. To my luck, I found him just as he was finishing saying his goodbyes to his colleagues. "Peter, come here." I said as soon as he locked eyes with me. I walked him away from the cluster of people waiting to be brought their cars.

"What's up?" He said, leaning up against the wall behind him. He crossed his arms over his chest, trying to be the most nonchalant person in the world as always.

"Why did you let Greyson leave alone?" I cut straight to the point, consciously restraining myself from becoming disrespectful to Peter. I always had high regards for him, but right now I couldn't understand why the fuck he didn't take his so called date, home.

"Because she wanted to leave alone," He responded simply. I could tell he quickly grasped the severity of my tone by the way he took his back off the wall, trying to stand tall in front of me.

"Yeah, but you brought her here, so she was your responsibility."

"She's a big girl, not a dog. She can handle herself." He shot back, and I could feel myself clenching my fists in my pockets.

"You know that's not what I meant."

"Connor, you and I go way back. From the moment you hired me because you knew I'd be good at my job, I've been loyal to you. We've hung out in both professional and unprofessional settings, but despite that, right now I'm not quite sure what the tone of this conversation is. So excuse me if I come across as disrespectful, but why the hell do you care how Greyson gets home?" He paused as if taunting me, "From the way she talks to me, it's as if you wouldn't even care if she dropped dead." He finalized, that damned smug look plastered on his face.

Of course I cared, I'd care for anyone's safety! It was just the normal way to react. Then I thought about Samantha in the same scenario. Would I care then?

"I care for the safety of all my employees, Peter. You're right, I don't like having her in my building. You want me to be honest, there you go. But no matter what you think of me, as long as she's working for our company, with me directly, then yes, I want her safe. I'm not a fucking monster," I took half a step forward, wanting to make sure he not only heard me, but knew just how serious I was. "I guess I should apologize though. I thought, since you brought her here as your date, that you actually gave a damn about her, but that was my mistake." I spoke firmly, then turned to walk away. I could feel my blood really starting to boil, and I really didn't want to do something I'd regret at such a delicate time before Japan.

"Oh please! Don't act so self-righteous. This entire week, you and your assistant ostracized the poor girl, making it more than clear that you can't stand her and want her gone." I stopped myself mid-stride, turning back around to make sure this didn't become a screaming match right beside the few people who were still waiting for their cars. "I'm the only person who's tried to accept her as a serious employee. What, you don't think I at least messaged her to make sure she got home safe? No, you wouldn't think that, would you? Because, again, you'd never even care enough to do that yourself. Tell me again how you're not a monster, boss."

When I stomped my way back to where Peter was standing, all I could see was red. I had to deal with Greyson talking back to me because I had no control over her employment, but him? He was fucking nothing! "I don't know who you think you are, but you don't fucking talk to me like that."

"Or what? You're going to fire me right? You're going to fire me like I'm one of those assistants of yours who doesn't mean a damn thing to you? All because what I'm saying is true and the truth pisses you off? I get it! I do. She's not one of those assistants you can use for a week and then get rid of. No, you can't fuck her and fire her like the others so you're pissed! You're stuck with her because Jonathan said so, so now all you can do is hope to emotionally scar her so badly that she quits. How fucked up is that? But you know what, this girl is resilient. I've seen so many girls leave your office crying because of this or that, even Samantha cried after her first hour because you yelled at her for messing up a stupid coffee order. Yet no matter how much you are trying to put Greyson through, she hasn't backed down yet and only becomes more determined to prove you wrong. And now you're giving me this bullshit that you care if she got home safe? This bull that I, after this entire week of being the only one to help her out, am some bad person? Is all this caring about her safety shit, just to clear your conscious of having been a complete dick to her this week? What, you're using this to call me a horrible employee and you, the best boss ever? Go on and fire me then. Fire me because you have that power."

"You son of a bitch, you know I can't fire you right now. It's really cute of you to grow some balls at a time like this and speak to me like you have any idea what it's like to be in my shoes. I don't give a shit what you think about me or what I've done, but don't act like you have me all figured out. You want to think you're a great guy? Go right the fuck ahead, you're a saint Peter. Do you really think I care about that? This has nothing to do with my conscious, or being the most loved piece of shit here. My main concern is this company and working towards expanding it. My methods have always worked for doing just that and because of this, everyone gets paid more. And it's because of the pay-raise that you've stayed here. If you ever disliked my vision, you could've easily given me your two weeks' notice. In fact, you can quit right now, but you're not. Why? Because your main concern isn't ethics, and it never has been. You only care about you. Go ahead and talk about my affairs when, as far as I'm concerned, you've only ever lied and cheated your way into the position you hold now. Yeah Peter, you're a saint." I ended the conversation, and left.

To say I was pissed was an understatement. I hated to take any negativity to heart, but I couldn't stop myself from reflecting over the opinions Peter had of me. If he was anyone else I could've easily disregarded whatever bullshit that person decided to say and go about my business.

However, Peter was someone I knew for a few years now with ideas and plans that were borderline genius. He was unstoppable with computers, coding, engineering and anything else I needed basically. He also had a chilling ability to go from talking to people in plain English to elaborate textbook terminology from one moment to the next like a light switch. He was able to spot mistakes or strong suits for possible automobiles before anyone ever even drew the first draft of it. Peter Thorne was one of the best decisions I'd ever made, and a person I considered a friend.

Due to all of that, I spent my entire Saturday and the next morning going over the words he so disrespectfully said to me. It made me consider if there was a negative consensus amongst my employees about me as a leader. If Peter could generally be on my side, but still think I was a horrible person, then what did that mean for those employees I hardly even spoke to?

I didn't care if people feared and respected me, but for them to actually think I was incapable of being a proper successor was kind of concerning.

I ran my fingers through my hair, finally getting up from my bed. Fuck Peter for making me think about this.

It was about eleven-thirty in the morning, and Greyson hadn't contacted me at all about the whole lunch thing. I walked over to the huge window-wall in my condo. Looking down nearly fifty stories I watched the waves hitting the tide at the beach. Out of all the things that were now currently bothering me, the one thing that shouldn't have been, but was nonetheless, was still not knowing what had made Greyson leave the dinner early in the first place.

Despite myself, I decided to text her. When's lunch? I kept it short, not exactly sure why I was contacting her in the first place.

Forget it, we dont have to do that anymore. She responded not too long after.

What the hell? I went over to sit down on my couch, staring off at the small green plant on my sleek and modern coffee table. The entire interior of my condo matched the sleek and modern style. Everything was a crisp white with gray tones and not much else. I didn't spend much time at home, therefore I kept it relatively plain. If it wasn't for the hot Miami sun that flooded the space due to the multitudes of windows, my place could almost seem depressing. Either way, I liked it for how peaceful it was. No matter how stressful my day got, I could always come back home to relax and escape.

Now, however, having nothing but my thoughts, this place was like a prison. Are you skipping out on the deal you made? I shot her another text, Peter's words on my being a monster towards her resurfacing in my mind.

Yep, imma get out of your hair though, dont worry.

That text hit me like a ton of bricks. She was the one who made the proposition in the first place. So now all of a sudden she was the one backing down? My mind quickly went back to the look she gave me before she left the dinner Friday, for about the hundredth time now, and the idea of actually being so terrible that I personally emotionally scarred her.

Thanks Peter.

It dawned on me then, even though I couldn't really process why, that she might have just left the dinner early because of me.

But why was any of this my fault? She had only wasted my time, and gave me that crap presentation on such a simple assignment. I told her I wanted nothing to do with her because she couldn't grow up and take anything seriously! How did any of this mean I was wrong or the bad guy here? After all the crap she was putting my company through, I even decided to give her another chance to fuck up my merger. Even though I technically had no control over that.

And what exactly happened from me agreeing to go through with this and her excitedly wanting to become my friend, to her leaving all angrily at the dinner meant I did something wrong?

Despite knowing I had been unnecessarily forgiving towards her, I was still feeling like the jackass here! If the merger went horribly, I promised myself that I would personally make Peter Thorne's life a living hell.

I grudgingly exited out of my messages and scrolled through my contacts to find Jonathan's number. "Dad, I need Greyson's address." I nearly demanded once he picked up.

Greyson didn't live in the most put-together neighborhood. I guess, considering she was a college student of probably not such a wealthy background, this made sense. Apparently she lived in one of the clusters of apartment buildings that took up an entire block or so. Her specific apartment was on the first floor of a building that looked slightly old and unkempt.

People on floors above were sat out on the balcony on plastic chairs, talking amongst each other from a few houses away. Children were out playing in yards, screaming loudly. Despite the apparently monstrous reputation I had in my own office, I actually liked kids. Before the countdown to the Tokyo merger got increasingly smaller, I liked personally holding fieldtrips for the local elementary school children to our building.

However, I only liked dealing with children on my time. Having one constantly in my office, now that was an entirely different aspect altogether. And not one I was too fond of.

"What the fuck am I doing here," I said to myself as I looked down at my phone for her apartment number that I had typed down. I walked over to what was apparently her door, and with all the regret that I was sure I would feel from this, I rang the doorbell.

"Coming!" I heard a voice, quite like Greyson's, yell from the other side of the door. I could hear a loud and quick constant thud, before the door was being swung open unnecessarily fast. Her face went from happy to complete shock the moment she locked eyes with me. "Connor? What are you doing here?"

It was interesting to see her go from over-the-top, what she called proper office attire, to oversized sweatpants, a black tank-top and the mess that was her hair sloppily tied back in a loose ponytail. I went to speak, but she cut me off before I could get a single word out.

"Oh my goodness, is that your casual wear? Khakis and a white button-up? It's like a slightly toned down office suit, but if the office needs you, you're still totally ready to go back to the building without anyone ever even thinking that you were dressed casually! That's so weird. You have the brown dress shoes on and everything, oh man." She ranted on. Here came the regret I knew I'd feel. If she thought I was a horrible person to her, she definitely had a weird way of showing it.

I don't think I've ever questioned what the hell to myself as much in my lifetime as I was this weekend.

"Come in, come in!" She moved to the side, gesturing me in the house. "I was just cleaning since I had nothing better to do, so ignore how out of place everything is right now. I found a yo-yo and had been messing with that for the past half hour." She laughed, walking me over to her sofa.

The place was definitely not something I was used to. It was abnormally small and cluttered with non-matching furniture and there were paintings along the wall that made the space feel even smaller. She sat me down on a couch that was covered in plastic. The couch was actually wrapped in plastic, as in, there was a couch, made of actual material, underneath an entire wrapping of plastic. Was this not supposed to be cut off once bought or something?

I continued looking around, noting the dishes that littered what I believed was supposed to be a coffee table. The television was blasting crap music and there was an air conditioner making a loud whirling noise. Despite the yellow light coming from her outdated incandescent lightbulbs, the space was pretty bright thanks to the curtains being pulled open widely. She also owned a lot of odd plants that were placed everywhere.

"So," She came over from whatever place she fled to and sat down across from me on a brown loveseat. She brought her legs up to cross them underneath her and looked at me like she was so amazed at me actually being in her house. Watching her was literally like seeing a five year old prance around, "Why are you here again?" She grabbed the remote from the mess of things on the coffee table, turning down the volume on the TV.

"You said we were getting lunch today." I stated simply, and her famous smile faded a bit.

"Yeah, but then I said forget about it. You win Connor, I'm giving you your office back and gettin' out of your hair for good." She shifted in her seat and pulled her hair out of the ponytail it was in.

There it was again. After hearing this in the flesh, I wanted to be able to rejoice at just the idea of her deciding to give me what I want, even if it probably wouldn't have been a reality. Yet for some stupid fucking reason, I wasn't overjoyed.

I stared at her for a moment, allowing a silence to settle between the both of us.

She wasn't looking at me anymore, she had resorted to twirling a strand of hair in between her fingers while her eyes rested on the remote she had placed back onto the coffee table. "Greyson," I said flatly, making sure she was looking at me, "I came all the way over here, we're going to get lunch." I finalized, and her eyes lit up like that same five year old, but now in a candy store.

"Okay! Let me change my pants first," She sprung out of her seat, becoming instantly electric, "Give me two seconds! You can change the TV if you want to!" She yelled over to me.

The sides of my mouth rose at the sight of her always dramatic reactions, and I shook my head at how wild she was. I didn't bother with the TV, I decided to check my phone for messages instead. In no more than a minute or so, she returned in very short jean shorts made shorter by her extremely long legs and bright neon orange sneakers. In my opinion, her clothing ensemble was always odd so I guess it shouldn't have come to a surprise that this was the case with her outside of the office.

"Okay, I know a great diner that isn't too far from here. Do you wanna drive or should I?" She asked as she scurried around, turning off the TV and grabbing her purse and keys.

"I'll drive." I said, following her out of the house, "You want to have lunch at a diner?" I asked, confusion evident in my voice. There was so many decent places to eat and diners were usually associated with families and the elderly of a middle to low socioeconomic class.

"Yeah, the food is good and cheap. You can't really beat that." Greyson nearly skipped beside me, as I lead her to my car.

"Expense isn't really a concern." I countered, unsure if she knew the financial benefits of working in a very wealthy company.

"Greyson! Where ya off to?" An older woman knitting on the balcony of the second floor called to us. She was sitting on a rocking chair, with orange and yellow yarn all over the place.

"Gettin' some food." Greyson stopped walking to respond to the woman, though still bouncing excitedly in place, her smile never wavering. "This is my business partner I was tellin' y'all about! His name is Connor." Greyson spun on her heels to face me, "Connor, that's Mrs. M. If you're ever sad, she will get you laughing in a second! She also has this apple pie recipe that is the bomb! There's nothing like it, but she's selfish and won't share her secrets with me."

Mrs. M laughed at that, "I'm makin' some more tomorrow honey! Make sure you stop on by before they all gone." She waved once at Greyson, still laughing softly to herself.

"I work tomorrow, but please save me a slice! If you give Jay two slices and I get none, we're no longer friends. Bye M!" Greyson waved frantically, and grabbed my arm to start walking off.

I waved politely to the laughing woman, not entirely sure what happened. I guess it shouldn't have been too surprising to know that someone as talkative as Greyson was really close with her neighbors. However, seeing how multiple people outside were talking to others around the building, I wondered if that was just a normal occurrence in these kind of apartment complexes. I only ever saw my neighbors during house parties growing up.

Maybe this was normal with most people and I was just the odd one out.

"Okay, it's called Sunshine Diner, it's only about three blocks down. So all you gotta do first is drive down this street." Greyson had started her usual fast paced rambling the moment I sat in the seat of my car.

"I'm not eating at a diner. I'll choose where we go." I stated, driving in the exact opposite direction of where Greyson had pointed me.

"Even demanding on your day off, huh?" I could feel her eyes directly on the side of my face, "Alright, I guess I can trust that you only ever eat at places with good food. Only the best for his majesty, I'm sure."

"You done?" My tone was cold, already overly annoyed with her childishness.

"Do you realize," She ignored me, "how surprising it is that you came to my door today? It's like, you showing up wasn't the most surprising part about you showing up," She giggled at herself. "Nah, it's surprising because this literally means that you actually want to work with me. See, I knew you didn't hate me."

Having stopped at a red light, I allowed my eyes to glance over at her briefly. My face was expressionless whereas hers was full of joy and mischief. Her signature wide pearly white smile was plastered onto her face as if she had just figured out the greatest piece of blackmail on me to ruin my entire life.

"I have absolutely no desire to work with you. If you quit tomorrow, I would probably be the happiest person alive." I retorted simply. I didn't have to look over at her to know that her exaggerated smile became an, as exaggerated, frown.

"Well, I gave you an option to never see me again. That' almost like me quitting. But again, here you are, so that obviously means you want to be partners."

I had finally pulled into the parking lot of my regular lunch spot. The Lounge was a nice modern looking place with good food, great employees and the best part was that it also delivered.

After parking my car, I pulled my key out of the ignition before turning to face Greyson. "You can't just choose to get a new office on another floor. Although Jonathan could do that, he won't and knowing him, he'd give me hell for going along with this whole thing. He wants to screw me over, and since he owns this company, he can do whatever the fuck he wants with it." My voice became angry as I thought about my father and this whole mess he got me in.

I turned away, throwing the door open and getting out of the car. I had spent my weekend considering the idea of being the worst head of a company to ever be born, and just a horrible person in general for making employees hate me. Yet instead of being thanked for trying to alter that notion, the person who I had apparently scarred so badly, thought this situation was funny and petty.

Greyson obviously didn't think I was that bad if she had enough time to joke about everything. What a fucking kid. Peter really had me going for a moment too about this 'bad boss' business. They could all go to hell for all I cared.

I had nearly stomped my way into the building as Greyson followed, mostly silently, behind me.

"Mr. Meyers, it's been a while." Matthew, the manager of the place, greeted me with a smile and firm handshake. I frequented The Lounge regularly for small business meetings and casually as well.

"I know, work has been hectic recently." I smiled back at him, returning the familiarities.

"I can imagine. You're starting to grow more gray hairs than me," He joked, laughing heartily.

I laughed back, "Not quite yet Matt," he patted me on the shoulder, loving his joke, "I need a table for two." I said, and he finally noticed Greyson slightly behind me.

"Ah, new friend of yours?" He asked me before gesturing to her, "I'm Matthew. I am the owner and founder of this fine establishment." He took her hand and kissed it, like he's done to countless girls. I rolled my eyes. No matter how old he got, he would probably always hit on whatever girl walked in the place. "I hope you find it to your liking." He held her hand for a moment longer than he needed to.

"Well hello Matt! I'm Greyson, but you can call me Grey. And it's really pretty in here, I love it already." She giggled, shamelessly flirting back. I guess she liked his flirting ways.

"Rooftop table." I interjected, hoping to move things along.

"Sure thing," Matthew turned his head, signaling to one of the waiters, "Find our guests a table on the top."

"We're going to be eating on the roof? Wow, that's so cool. I feel so fancy." Greyson started her weird bouncing-in-place thing. "I should've worn something nicer."

"Enjoy," Matt had said before moving over to talk, and probably flirt, with more customers.

Greyson couldn't stop talking from the moment we entered the elevator, "Wow, I've been to many interesting places, but I've never eaten on a rooftop before. Isn't this for just the super wealthy people? Like those men who can actually afford the all exclusive golf clubs? I want to join one. Hey what's your name?"

"Kevin." The waiter responded simply.

"Hey Kev, I'm Greyson. You look young, how old are you?"

"Seventeen."

"Wow, that's awesome. Seventeen working in this beautiful place, man you've got a great situation going on. When I was seventeen, hmm, how long ago was that? About four years?" The elevator dinged open, and she was the first to step out, staring around, slack-jawed. "Oh wow, this is so pretty! Plants everywhere and a fountain! Oh wow, and look at the view! I can see all of Miami from here." She walked around, ignoring how rude it was to those trying to eat.

"Your table is right this way," The waiter told me, and I followed him to the far side of the roof. He handed me the menu and left, assuring that he'd be back soon to get our drink orders.

During this time, I watched in horror as Greyson walked to all corners of the space, inspecting everything with a goofy grin on her face. I was partially tempted to just get up and leave with how pissed I was already with her behavior. However, I, admittedly had gotten myself into the situation I was in, so I didn't.

"Greyson," I said through gritted teeth the moment she decided to start conversing with a table of people.

She looked around, confused for a moment, trying to find me, "Oh, there you are," She smiled once she saw me, and finally came over.

I wasn't smiling.

She sat down across from me, grabbed her menu and started flipping through it. If there was anything that annoyed me more than her random outbursts, it was her acting as if those outbursts weren't completely deranged.

"Wow, everything is pretty expensive here. I mean, I guess it makes sense, considering how fancy it is in here and all, but still..." She trailed off, never lifting her face from the menu.

The waiter came by not too long after that.

"I'll have a cup of coffee; two sugar, one cream, and a shot of espresso." I easily let out. After the waiter wrote down my order, he and I looked towards Greyson, who was still hidden behind the menu. "What are you going to drink?" I said kind of harshly, my patience already running super thin.

"Um," She looked up at me for a moment before looking back down at the menu, "Uh, can I just have a water?" She said, slightly timidly to the waiter.

"Sure." He responded, writing it down, "I'll be back with those in a second." He told us before leaving.

"You just want water?" I asked her, slightly curious as to why her option was so odd. This place had a plethora of drink options, and it seemed kind of out of place considering the person sitting across from me.

"Yeah, I'm fine with water." Her tone remained very detached, and she wasn't really making eye contact with me.

Never needing to look at the menu, I sat and watched Greyson do just that. Not bothering with words anymore. She kept flipping through it again and again, her face very serious, as she, or as I believed, considered the options.

Nothing had changed by the time the waiter came back. "What can I get for you two?"

"Um, maybe just some fries? A small size." Greyson responded.

"What?" I basically spat in confusion.

She just looked at me.

"No, just give us two of the steak entrees, mine medium, hers well done. The mixed vegetables are fine, and yeah bring fries if that's what she wants. And would you please bring this girl something to drink. I don't know, how about you get her the strawberry lemonade, that's probably fine." I grabbed Greyson's menu and handed hers and mine to the waiter, trying my best not to snap.

She really had a knack for getting under my skin.

"I'll have that right out for you." The waiter turned and left.

"That is really expensive." Greyson trailed off.

"It's not like you're paying, and considering what I make, this isn't all that costly at all."

"I am paying for my food! I just didn't get paid yet. We can't all be living the lavish lifestyle."

"Yes, this probably is a bit more lavish for some people, but it isn't for me. I understand that you are just a college student who just started this job recently, therefore I, who once again can buy a few nice things, never expected you to pay."

"I can pay for myself though."

"It's not about what you can or cannot do. You probably can pay for yourself if you really want to, but I want to pay, so I am and that's the end of that. Do you know how many women don't even bring a wallet, expecting to be paid for? And you, of all fucking people, are trying to fight me to pay for your own food."

We really couldn't get along for even a moment.

She didn't say anything after that. I decided to use that time to look at my phone and see what emails had been sent to me. One of the advisers had sent me updates to where everything was standing with the company since I had been busier with the merger.

I sighed a breath of relief seeing that everything was going well and those who had taken my place for the time being to make sure the company runs smoothly were really keeping everything together. We were also doing really well in the sales department and this would be a really great quarter with the stocks. At least there were still some order with the company despite the chaos I was currently dealing with.

I looked up to see what Greyson had been up to. She was rocking side to side, humming to some song while she messed with the silverware. She met my eyes and smiled that wide genuine smile of hers.

"You wanna hear a story?" She said to me, her eyes glowing with excitement. I could never get used to her random outbursts and mood changes.

"Not necessarily."

"Okay, so it was my first year in college," She started, the excitement never leaving her face as she completely ignored my response.

I watched her tell me her story, almost in disbelief. She was so loud, being completely inconsiderate of those sitting around us. She used her whole body to talk, and she looked directly into my eyes the entire time, laughing loudly when she felt appropriate.

It was almost hard not to laugh along with her, especially when her story itself was so unbelievable.

"I was covered from head to toe in mud, and the pig was so freakin' pissed!" She laughed again, scooting in closer to the table, "Whatever though. I caught him, so I made over two-hundred bucks that day. To this day some people still call me Miss Piggy. I'm not so proud of that one actually." Her story ended just in time as the food arrived.

I was surprised at myself by the time we finished eating. It was actually a decent time, and considering how much I couldn't stand this person, I could not believe I left the restaurant without the urge to murder her, let alone leaving the restaurant having enjoyed myself.

"That steak was so good! When I get paid, we'll come here again. My treat." Greyson said when we got into my car. I just shook my head as I started the car. She laughed at that. "This is serious!"

Her phone started to ring and she looked at it for a moment before picking it up, "Hello?" She answered, her mood shifting, "Oh hey Susan, what's up?" I kind of eavesdropped, not necessarily meaning to, but there was only so many options in a car. "Oh man, that doesn't sound too great. I'll stop by later today, okay?" She listened to the lady for another moment before hanging up.

It was quiet for a moment, and being a person who generally stayed out of people's business, I considered not saying anything. However, the silence that followed the phone call wasn't pleasant either, "Did you need a ride somewhere?"

I looked over at her for a moment, catching her eye before turning my attention back to the road.

She sighed deeply, "No, I don't want to head over there right now." She started playing with her hair and leaned against the window. The rest of the ride was silent.

When I pulled up to her apartment complex, she didn't move at all. She was biting on her lip, looking off in the general direction of her building, but her mind was obviously elsewhere.

"Hey," I finally said, getting her attention, "You alright?"

"Sorry," she started gathering her things, "Yeah, I'm fine. Hey, thank you for lunch. It was a good time, that place was truly amazing. I'll see you tomorrow." She smiled, getting right back to her bubbly self. "Thanks again!" She leaned in, reaching an arm out toward me. I moved back, confused as to why she was getting so close to me all of a sudden.

She paused then, matching my confused glance, before pulling back, "Oh haha, sorry. I'm still working on my professionalism. Bye." She waved at me as she opened the door and left.

It dawned on me then that she was reaching in for a hug.

I watched her walk over to her building, making sure she got in okay. When her door finally closed behind her, I pulled away from the curb. I couldn't help thinking about what that phone call was about. I also couldn't get my mind off of how rudely I rejected her hug.

And yes, I also thought about how I shouldn't be thinking about these things at all.

What the fuck was I doing?

Chapter Eight

Chapter 8- He Complains (Greyson's Perspective)

It was a beautiful day! The morning sun wasn't quite yet fully beaming, but the birds were chirping and Bob Marley was playing on the radio. Everything was already great.

"Today is my day!" I said to Jay, who was barely waking up. I woke up super early, finally happy to be at peace with my partner. I had a feeling this was going to be a great week and that was all that mattered.

"I really don't care." Was Jay's groggy response from his room.

"Whateva. Don't hate just because you ain't working for a huge ass car company." I danced to the tune of Bob Marley, turning up the radio before going over to Jay's room, "Could you be loved! And be loved!" I sang at the top of my lungs, a wide smile on my lips. Jay looked at me a moment, before getting up from his bed, half dressed, and danced slowly to the beat while getting his clothes. "Aye!" I cheered him on, happy to see him in a good mood, "Today is our day, boo!"

I twirled out of his room, gathering the rest of my belongings before finally leaving our apartment.

"Good morning," I said softly, trying to contain my excitement as I entered the office.

Look at me saying, "the office," like I was all official and what not.

"Morning," Was Meyers Jr's response. He looked up at me for a quick second, before easily going back to typing on his computer. He did not look as excited as I imagined he'd be.

"How are we doing today?" I strode over to his desk, coming right up beside him.

He quietly sighed under his breath, "I'm fine, you?" He finally stopped his typing to give me his full attention.

"I'm doing absolutely amazing!" I went over to my desk, finally satisfied, "What are we doing today?" I dropped into my spinny-chair, smiling over at stone-face Connor.

"Okay, I think I'll go over some of the basics, since you obviously don't know anything. Maybe assign you a task to those things we go over so you can look more into them in your spare time." His demeanor was very serious, and it made me miss his slightly more lax self from the day before.

I guess this was what professionalism meant. But boy was it boring. "Sounds good," I said, already forgetting what he was going on about. This didn't seem all that awesome anymore. "Can I just go grab a drink real quick?" I rummaged through my wallet, already deciding I was going with or without his permission.

"Sure." He said, already going back to clicking on his computer. How could anyone do that every single day?

While I was out and about, I decided to look at the bright side. Connor wasn't completely pissed at me, and ready to actually work with me and help me out. Beyond that, I was still working at this amazing place, and I had already made a few friends. Not to mention, payday was coming up.

I guess it wasn't all bad after all.

With my newfound hopes, it felt like the perfect time to visit Mr. Spiderman.

"Peter! How are you doing on this fine Monday?" I pushed open his door after he gave me the okay. He was here super early which was nice.

"Fine," He said simply, completely against his usual nature. He was speedily typing on his laptop, seeming absolutely pissed. I hadn't heard from him since he asked me if I got home okay after the dinner. Maybe he was mad at me for leaving? I actually never really thought about how he'd feel about my abrupt exit.

Then I also remembered the attitude I gave him before storming off. Wow, I was a terrible person.

"Hey," I went over to him, grabbing his arm. He stopped typing to look at me, "I'm sorry about how rude I was at the dinner. I shouldn't have left you like that." I sincerely apologized, and his face softened.

"Oh, don't worry about that. No, you didn't do anything wrong. Actually, how are you doing?" He gestured for me to sit down. His words were extremely relieving.

"I'm great actually! I think Connor is actually okay with me now, he's being so much nicer. He's even finally going to help me with this whole thing." I eagerly told Peter, and his face became hard again.

"Oh, is he?" He said, sounding peeved.

"That's good, right?" I was really confused now. Not sure why Peter wasn't sharing my excitement. "Are you okay?"

"Yeah I'm fine. I just have a lot of fucking shit to do. Can we talk some other time?" He looked away from me, going back to his stuff.

Wow, okay. What the hell was that? That did not look fine. Whatever.

I got up and left without another word. Dad always said, sometimes you have to give people in a mood, some time to be in their mood.

Headed back to the office, I noticed Amanda at her desk. "Amanda! Please tell me you're in a good mood today." I pleaded with her and walked over with a sad smile.

"Grey, I'm doing great. How was the dinner?" She asked, enthusiastically. I knew I could count on her.

"Eh, it was interesting. Enough about that though, I've got great news!" She looked expectantly at me, "Connor ain't mad at me anymore! He's finally gonna help me with all this business stuff. We got lunch together yesterday and I think he may just finally be warming up to me! I'm so excited and it's taking a lot of the load off. I feel so relieved, I thought he might hate me forever. Oh man, the place he took me to though had some really great food! We ate on the roof! It was so fancy and great."

Amanda laughed, cutting me off from my rant. "He really did all of that? That's good. I'm happy you both are finally starting to get along."

"Thanks. Yeah pray for the best for me," I laughed, "I gotta go find me some snacks downstairs before we start, so I'll see you a bit later." I waved and headed to the elevator, my excitement finally starting to soar.

When I left the cafeteria, I had two of everything. I decided that it wouldn't be nice to not get Connor anything. He probably got hungry for some snacks too, but just couldn't do much because he was stuck in meetings or whatever. I had water-bottles, fruit, some granola bars, and even some chocolate. I was mostly into healthier snacks, but since I wasn't sure about him, I also brought chips. It took me some time to figure out which chips he'd prefer, but I didn't bring my phone to ask him, so I just kind of had to guess.

I wasn't the best at guessing people's favorites.

Doritos was something everyone enjoyed though, right? Either way, I got both the red and blue flavors, so he could choose from there.

Walking back through the lobby, I looked outside for a moment. It hit me then that I would probably be stuck upstairs for some time, with no hopes of feeling the warmth of the outdoors. The building was unnecessarily cold. It made sense to go outside for a bit, take a quick walk before actually getting down to business. Considering how I wasn't gone for too long yet, that is exactly what I did.

I came back inside feeling wonderful. The early morning sun wasn't as hot as it surely would get later on in the day. The sight of all these successful people around me was such an inspiring thing. Everyone, though too serious, really strived for greatness. I envied that. I wanted to be that determined one day for my job, too.

"Good morning Greyson," I heard from behind, and spun on my heels to see Jackson Meyers in the flesh.

"Jack! What are you doing here?" I ran over to him to give him a hug. I knew Jonathan was the one who worked here specifically. Jackson, I think I was told, was only around when Jonathan wanted a second opinion. I could've been wrong though.

"Jon has some business for me, so I decided to stop by and see how everyone's doing. What are you working on this week?" He gave me a similar smile his brother was good at giving and I felt instantly comfortable.

"Oh, I'm working with Connor this week! I think he's warming up to me. We had lunch yesterday actually! It was a really great time. Anyways, I think he is going to start teaching me about this and that, and maybe I can finally start helping him with more of the big boy stuff. I'm excited."

"That's good," He smiled brightly. Jackson looked super interested in everything I had to say and that made me want to talk to him forever. "Connor is very into his work, so he always comes across as a bit mean to those who first start to work around him. Usually, those who get to see him elsewhere can really see a great side of him, but since he's almost always working, even when he's off, it's hard. Jon told me you both were having some issues, but I'm glad you're saying that you're both starting to get along."

"Oh yeah, don't worry about that. Wish me luck in learning though. I really want to be more useful to you all. Am I keeping you from anything? I know about the importance of punctuality here." I laughed, realizing the irony since I personally wasn't all that great at being punctual.

"Oh no, of course not. I'm here kind of early. I was just going to say hi to a few people before seeing Jon. Am I keeping you? You have a lot of food there, did you miss breakfast?" He gestured to the bags in my hands. I kind of forgot I was even holding them. The water was probably warm now. What a shame.

"I had some yogurt for breakfast, I probably should've had something else, but that's why I have all this. I think I'll just have a second breakfast. There's fruit and stuff in here, so it'll be pretty good. But this is mostly just for snacking throughout the day. I get hungry when I'm learning. Well, actually, I'm always hungry. Plus, I think I'll share some of this with Connor. I'm not sure what he likes to eat. Maybe this will be my way of saying thank you, actually."

"Are you going to be fine with just that for food?" He asked, looking skeptical. He was adorable, like another dad.

"Yep, I'm perfectly fine with this. Believe me." I waved him off, shifting the bags into one hand.

"Okay, well, I guess I'll go now to say my hellos. Have a great day Greyson, I wish you luck while you're here. When we've merged with our friends in Japan thanks to you, I'll personally throw you the best party you've ever seen." He made me laugh, but he seemed really serious about that.

"You're hilarious. Have a great day!" I waved him off and watched him retreat to the elevators. Now I was feeling slightly stressed. He and his brother had this really inflated idea of my ability to do some crazy big stuff.

No pressure though, right?

I looked away from the elevators when they finally closed, and just watched the people walk in and out. All of them were going to a specific place, falling into their extremely boring looking routines.

My eyes landed on one man who locked eyes with me and seemed to be heading my way. The dude even had this smirk going on, with one hand in his suit jacket. His gaze was mischievous, and it rubbed me the wrong way.

"If the rumors are true, you have to be the infamous Greyson Lewis." He came right up to me, extending his hand for me to take. I just kind of looked at it before looking him up and down.

Mr. High and Mighty over here, had almost a full buzz cut, with slightly more hair directly on top of his head. He was freshly shaved, acting so clean with what was probably an unnecessarily expensive suit. He had blue eyes and a super thin pointed nose. He had the same slightly tanned look that Connor sported, but he wasn't as strong looking and wasn't all that special overall.

"Excuse you, and who would you so happen to be?" I quickly pointed at him, my guard quickly coming up.

"Feisty too, Connor does not lie." He put down his extended arm and was now full on smiling, looking entertained.

"Do not give me that bullshit honey. Believe me, I am not the girl you want to be fuckin' with. But try me, I'm in a good mood today and I would love to put someone in their place." I crossed my arms in front of my chest, ready to hurt someone's feelings.

"Wow, I'm impressed. Can't say anyone ever spoke to me like that. Jon hired you, huh? Super interesting. Anyways, I'm not here to cause waves. I'm Adam, Connor's closest adviser. I'm just excited to be meeting the new co-COO of our auto shop." His smile felt like he was mocking me and I could not get over it.

"Why haven't I seen you before?" I asked and he gestured me towards the sitting area of the lobby.

He sat down on one of the cushioned chairs and I did the same to the one opposite his. He sat like a typical guy but with way more authority. His legs were super spread out, his arms rested on either side of the armrest, and he had set his briefcase on the floor beside him. It felt like a power tactic. Make yourself seem super big and relaxed to instill fear and maybe this sense of importance.

I actually liked that, it was like showing this confidence and it really worked. He really did seem super into himself.

"So you asked why you haven't seen me yet. That's because I'm not in this building every week. I usually end up doing Connor's dirty work, and I'm in another state or country. So that's where I've been.

I'm back home now and you'll probably see a lot more of me because of the merger. Speaking of which, I hear you are the golden ticket for the merger? That's fun." He sat forward now, crossing his hands over his lap, keeping his elbows on either armrest.

"Well apparently you already know everything there is to know about me. I have nothing new to say." I mirrored his body language, keeping my legs a good space away from each other, without becoming indecent due to wearing a skirt. I scrunched my hair quickly before crossing my hands on my lap, leaning forward to get closer to him.

I could tell he was really paying attention to my every move. Ready to judge everything I did and come up with his opinions about me.

Well go the hell ahead, Adam.

"You really don't like me," He chuckled, "I'm sorry if I came across too heavy. Anyways, despite how Connor feels, I'm actually excited to be working with you, Greyson. If you need anything, you let me know." He winked, grabbed his briefcase, and got up now.

He outstretched his hand to me again, and I took it this time, making sure my grip was firm and my eyes stayed locked on his. He chuckled softly looking fiercely into my eyes before loosening his grip and finally walking away. "I'll see you upstairs." He called over his shoulder.

Wow, I did not like him. He made me feel inferior, and that was not okay. He was like a snake and snakes ain't ever been known for good.

I got up from my seat, straightening out my skirt and grabbing my bags. If he was going up, so was I. I wouldn't let him faze me. Nobody was about to faze me.

And today was still my day.

Chapter Nine

Chapter 9- She's Unbelievable (Connor's Perspective)

I was going over sales reports for our company from the time our business started till last month when Amanda called the office phone.

"Yeah?" I asked, still skimming through numbers and adding them onto my documents for the merger.

"Adam's here to see you." She said simply.

"Send him in-" I was saying when Adam came bursting through my doors. I really hated the lack of respect there was for my office space nowadays. I had no privacy whatsoever.

"Buddy, how are you?" Adam walked through, hands wide in the air. "You owe me drinks."

"Weren't you supposed to get back tomorrow?" I clenched my jaw a few times, trying not to get annoyed with, once again, being interrupted from my work. I closed out of the documents, trying to let my frustrations go.

"Don't seem so excited to see me sooner. You must be stressed, huh?" He smiled, taking pleasure at my expense. He had dropped his stuff, sitting down at the edge of my desk. He completely ignored the comfortable leather seats I had specifically for the sake of sitting.

He got nice and comfortable, messing with my name plate, smiling even wider knowing how much he was pissing me off.

"Adam." I warned, glaring dangerously at him.

He just laughed, "Relax, you're always getting so angry at everything." He finally got up and walked over to Greyson's desk. He turned around with eyebrows raised, pointing at the small space she occupied in my office. "Wow, this is actually real. There's a desk and everything." Adam was obviously entertained as he snooped through the things she had scattered all over her desk.

"Can you just tell me how it went?"

"Do you think I'd come over here to mess with you if it went bad? Everything is exactly the way you wanted it, Connor."

I sighed in relief. He was at least capable of always doing the tasks I assigned him, "Thank you so much for not being a complete pain in the ass." That was going to be one less thing to worry about, meaning I was even closer to making this meeting in Japan go absolutely perfectly. Well, if my dad's stupid addition doesn't fuck it up.

"So I met her," He finally walked back over to sit in one of the seats across from me, instead of my desk. I looked straight at him, not enjoying his dramatic pause. "Boy does she have an attitude. I've never seen anything like that. It's kind of hot though and Connor," He looked at me with a mischievous glint in his eyes, "she's very pretty. For a black girl at least."

"What?" I snapped at him in confusion. I wasn't sure if I had heard him correctly and I was really hoping that I hadn't.

Before I had time to process what was going on, the door to my office was being swung open once again. Greyson strolled in with grocery bags in her hands, looking directly at Adam with a scowl.

I regained my composure, her abrupt entry bringing me back to reality. I looked back at Adam who was watching her with a smirk on his face. "Adam, can you give me two minutes." I stood up finally and headed to the door to get him out.

What the hell did he just say to me?

"Sure," He said, while still looking at Greyson. He got up then and casually strolled over to where I was. I easily shut the door behind him the second he was out.

Greyson set her bags down at her desk and smiled at me. I walked over to her desk, trying to think up something she could do. There was no way I was going to deal with her here while also dealing with Adam. Goodness, why did I have to be dealing with anyone in general.

"Listen, I know I said I'd help you out today, but I wasn't expecting Adam, who's one of my advisers, to come now. I'll be going over things with him, so I need you to just get a head start with things on your own," She looked blankly at me, her big green eyes staring almost uncomfortably into my own. "I'll make it easy for you. Find out about exactly what a merger is, and the importance of this one.

Write me about one page of what you find out and email it to me whenever. You can go home to do this."

"So you want me out of the office?" She continued looking straight at me.

"Yes, what we're going over might distract you and you'll only get in the way anyways." She pursed her lips together and turned her head towards the bags on her desk, which caused me to look at them.

Oh great, I hurt her feelings.

"If that's okay with you," I added.

"Just one page on mergers is what you said?" She finally looked back at me, and I shook my head in agreement. "Okay," She shrugged her shoulders and started gathering her belongings.

"Thank you," I felt relieved as I walked back over to my side.

"What choice did I have?" She mumbled under her breath, finally grabbing her purse, the laptop and the grocery bags. She didn't even look in my direction as she headed to the door.

"Hey, did Adam say anything out of line to you?" I asked, before she could grab the handle of the door. I didn't necessarily mean to ask, but my mouth had other ideas.

"Nope." She still wouldn't look my way as she walked out without another word. Not even seconds later, Adam made a reappearance.

However, this time, Sam had come too.

Fuck me.

"Does no one, but me, have an actual job here?" I went straight back onto my computer, trying to give the two a hint.

"Connor, we've got some catching up to do. You have to tell me how you are handling this whole thing. I have to say, I'm impressed you haven't given yourself a heart attack yet." Adam chimed in, sitting in Greyson's seat and rolling himself up to where I was sitting.

"Is it true you went to lunch with her yesterday?" Samantha finally spoke up, giving me a death glare from across my desk.

"Oh, so you are trying to get a piece of that young colleague of yours?" Adam placed his hand on my shoulder, "I see. That's how you're going to handle this, huh? Where's Peter? I bet he'd get a kick out of this."

That was when I remembered my current situation with Peter.

Ugh.

I dropped my face into my hands and pushed them forward into my hair, probably messing it up in the process. I could feel myself getting angry again, so I got up. There was no way in hell I was going to deal with this now.

"Do neither of you realize how serious the shit I have to deal with is? I don't come to work to talk about whatever bullshit is going on. Talk to me about that when I'm not working. I swear you're all fucking children here. I'm going home to finish what I was doing and tomorrow, I don't want to hear from either of you." I shut down my computer and quickly grabbed my belongings.

"Connor," Adam started when I got to the door.

"Find your job, do that, and talk to me when I'm not working." I cut him off, opening my door, "And both of you can get out of my office now." I stayed as calm as I could, not trying to have a repeat of the situation with Peter.

Which once again reminded me that I still had to deal with that.

I knocked on Peter's office door, only entering when he said so.

A thing everyone should learn how to do.

He looked up at me and instantly stopped doing whatever he was doing. He stood up calmly, making sure to keep eye contact. He leaned on his desk behind him, crossing his arms over his chest.

"I'm here to apologize for my actions on Friday. I was out of line and I don't want to put an awkward wedge between us. I value you as a part of this company and as a friend. I let my emotions get the best of me and that was wrong." I smoothly let out, my professionalism back in full swing and all the anger I felt from before being pushed to the very back of my mind.

"So you got lunch with her yesterday?" He shot and my jaw clenched.

When did Meyers Motors become a high school? I could deal with Samantha's occasional gossip, but now everyone had their nose in my business and felt so bold to tell me about it. This was not going to happen and I once again was not going to entertain this unprofessionalism when I had a company to run.

"I'll let you get back to work." The tension was thick when I walked out, closing his door gently behind me.

That was the straw that broke the camel's back. I didn't even want to think about work anymore. I needed to go to the gym.

After spending an intense two hours lifting weights, the cold water from my shower felt heavenly. I stood there for a while, letting the water run down my body, the cold contrast on my overheated skin helping subside any anger that had remained.

I elected to ignore the events of the day. I would deal with them some other time. Food was already on the way and that was all that mattered.

I left the shower, wrapped a towel around my waist and grabbed a cup of coffee that I had set to brew beforehand. After the food arrived, I sat at my desk and continued looking through emails. My mood was finally better and I could calmly get back to work.

While I was in the process of looking through sales reports, something I was trying to do at work, a notification popped up signaling I had a new email. I opened it up, quickly learning it was from Greyson.

I've attached the thing on mergers here. First of all, you never gave me your email! Since you were super busy I ended up having to ask your dad. Which, to be fair, wasn't all that big of a deal, but I feel like you should know how sloppy that was on your part. Anyways, you better actually stick to your word about helping me out tomorrow. I'm trying to get serious, so if you try to complain I don't do enough, that shit's on you right now! Alright, I'm getting off track (I never send emails so this is interesting for me lol). Have a great night Connor! You can look over this if you want, but just know I already did all that and I think I deserve an A on this! Lol.

I smiled a bit after reading this. I never met someone so unorganized and all over the place. She didn't only talk out of focus, but she even typed that way.

I ended up opening the attachment and reading the page she wrote on mergers. There were a few grammatical errors and there were some places where the focus drifted, but overall it surprisingly wasn't all that bad. In fact it was a lot more than I had ever expected from her.

My phone buzzed and I looked over at it to find a text from Greyson.

Connor! I sent you the assignment. I emailed it to you, so look at it when you get a chance :)

She was truly something else.

AN: Another short one. It just didn't make sense to make this one too long.

Chapter Ten

Chapter 10- He's Boring (Greyson's Perspective)

She was still sleeping. Which, considering how incredibly early it was, made a lot of sense. I wish I could also be sleeping. Mornings were evil.

She looked at peace when she slept. It was like nothing ever changed. I could almost imagine her opening her eyes and calmly telling me to go find my father and bug him with all my "hyperactivity" as she always used to say.

"So work seems to be getting better," I whispered. I enjoyed talking to her most when she was sleeping. It was a lot easier for me. "I mean, I don't know for sure. Connor seems to be in charge of whether or not I'm havin' a good or bad time and that depends on his mood which switches like crazy. I kind of question if it's worth it since I'm only staying during the summer anyways. Jon and Jack really believe in me though, and you didn't raise any quitter."

She inhaled deeply and shifted gently in her bed. That made me smile. It was like she was agreeing with me. "Jay says hi. Also, Mrs. M sent me with some pie for you. I don't think she's doing too well. I think that's why she's been makin' a lot more pies than usual. Maybe I'll visit her soon and see what's been going on. It's some lemon pie this time around. Part of me wants her to stay upset to keep making the pies because they're so good." I laughed to myself, "Nah, I'm not that messed up."

I watched her for a bit, then focused my attention to the window. I kept the blinds closed so she wouldn't end up waking up. It was still pretty dark, the sun was just starting to rise.

"This job pays well at least. I'm really surviving the grown-up world. It's weird to think that I'm a grown-up, but I am. I survived long enough to be able to say that. I did it without you, too," I stared hard at her sleeping features, "It's really messed up that you left me alone like this. Have I ever told you that? Maybe that's messed up for me to say. I sometimes think I'm a selfish and terrible person for thinking that way. Either way, I do think that sometimes. Even if I don't tell anyone out loud. Keepin' it a secret doesn't make me any better."

I took my phone out of my pocket to check the time. I was already about an hour late for work. I still wasn't entirely sure how bad it was to be late. My job title seemed lax in that sense, but since I was so new, maybe I'd walk in one day being super late and get fired on the spot.

That would suck.

"Okay, I guess I have to go now. I'll come by some other day when you're up."

I made my way to the door, thinking about what I just said to her. I was never that honest with her out loud. I felt a lot more relieved though. I stopped walking then, thinking about what else I wanted to say since I was already on a roll.

"Before I go, I want you to know something else. I always like to think that I've forgiven you for leaving me like this, but then there are times where I still think you were selfish for what you did. When I think that, I say to myself, have I truly forgiven you? If anyone asks I don't hesitate to say that I have, that I am perfectly understanding with what happened, but mom," my gaze was unflinching as I spoke to her, "I really don't know if I have. Life is hard mom."

I left without another word. I didn't really feel sad or angry. I was mostly indifferent.

In the car, I blasted the volume on the radio, singing loudly to whatever song came on, easily brushing the chat with my mother out of my mind. I had working with Connor as partners to look forward to! That should be exciting. I hoped he liked my paper. I worked so hard on it! That was not fun in the slightest.

As soon as I walked into the building of Meyers Motors, my phone rang. It was Connor. Wow, his timing was amazing.

"Hello?" I answered, smiling to myself, as I made my way to the elevators.

"Why do you insist on wasting my time?" He scolded easily. It didn't even sound like he cared, just repeating some line he had said a billion times. Damn, why'd he have to be so hard to read? It really made responding difficult. I wasn't sure how pissed he was on his pissed scale.

"Walking in the elevators right now. I'll be up in a second, okay?" I clicked on the fifteenth floor button about a thousand times while the elevator doors closed painfully slow.

The line went dead. I pulled my phone back looking at the screen in disbelief. He really hung up on me! Oh hell nah, this boy was actin' super disrespectful and I was not okay with that.

And if there was anything between us that was similar, when I was pissed, I'd sure as hell be quick to show it.

As soon as the elevator dinged open, I stormed over to the office, ignoring Amanda altogether.

"Greyson?" I heard her ask from behind me, but I was not having that right now. What professional just hangs up on people? It made me more mad remembering it wasn't the first time he did it.

I busted through the office doors, ready to get an apology, one way or another. Connor was standing in front of his desk, sipping on some coffee, looking expectant.

"You do not just hang up on me." I walked right up to him, pointing a well-manicured fingernail at him. Word to my girl Lynn on Eighth Street too for getting my nails so on point.

"Are you sincerely trying to fight me on that right now when you're walking in late?" He, not so kindly, smacked my hand out of his face, stepping forward so that our noses were about an inch from touching, "You do not run this place, so cut the high and mighty bullshit out. I'm doing you a fucking favor, so you're on my time."

He slammed his coffee mug on his desk behind him, not breaking eye contact. I stayed glued to my spot, not allowing him to get the upper hand in this situation. "So while you're on my time, you don't show up whenever you want, you don't talk to me however you want, and you better be ready to put in some fucking work. Do I make myself clear?" His voice rang throughout the office with power and his eyes pierced straight through every crevasse of my soul.

I might have appeared unintimidated with my unmoving stance, but to be completely honest, his tone made me nervous. Considering how much angrier his tone got whenever we got into these arguments, I was beginning to think that he'd soon cut me off completely. Which surprisingly hadn't happened yet.

And that nervousness of him finally giving up on me really pissed me off.

Why did I have to watch what I did so that I could please his ever so particular self? Why was he always picking fights with me? Why did any of this make it okay for him to just hang up on me!?

"I had shit to do this morning. I understand that you're helping me, but that does not mean you can waste my time either by changing up plans last minute. Just because you think that everything you do is more important than what I do, doesn't mean my time ain't valuable. Yesterday, you had no issue with just pushing me to the back of your 'to-deal-with' list." I made air quotes with my fingers for emphasis.

I started shaking ever so slightly with the rush of emotion. I knew I was messing up our partnership once again, and that was bothering me much more than I wanted it to. But at the same time, he could really just go fuck himself.

"Besides, stop actin' like I messed up your entire morning. You, being the busy bee you are, just got more time to work on whatever else you're always working on." I paused, then laughed lightly at a revelation I had, "This isn't even about how late I am! You're just looking for any reason to get out of helping me! Oh my goodness, why do you hate me so much?" My voice cracked just the slightest bit, and that was enough to make me snap, "You're such a stupid fucking dick! You know what, fuck you!" I stabbed my finger into his chest, wishing it was my fist, and stomped my way over to my desk. "Sorry for actually thinking we were making progress." I turned on my laptop, trying as hard as I could to ignore how bothered this conversation made me.

Connor sighed loudly, causing me to look up at him. He pulled on his hair with both of his hands before quickly jerking himself around to face his desk. He grabbed his name plate and angrily threw it across the room at the wall, "Fuck this." He growled and stomped out of the office, slamming the door very loudly on his way out. I jumped slightly at the noise it made.

I dropped my face onto my desk, groaning into the wood.

I guess that was the end of that.

Not even five seconds later, the door was being swung open once again, causing my head to fly up from my desk. Connor reappeared, slamming the door shut behind him. He looked straight at me, which was slightly terrifying, but not as scary as him also rushing toward me.

I remembered being told at one point in my life that when a predator, such as a bear, comes towards you, your best bet would be to make yourself as big as possible to hopefully get them to leave you alone.

That advice was obviously given by a person who's never had a bear come up to them because that shit ain't easy.

I didn't even bother with getting up, I just made myself as small as possible in my seat like a trapped bunny.

"I don't fucking hate you!" He literally screamed at me, causing me to flinch. "I know your time is important, I'm not trying to say it isn't. I'm just..." His hands clenched into fists on my desk and his jaw tightened, "I don't..." He trailed off again, "Forget it!" Connor shook his head, breaking eye contact.

He went over to his desk and immediately went back to work, tension heavy in the air.

I think he was trying to apologize?

Okay, maybe, just maybe, I was personally being a bit overdramatic. I sighed to myself. I wasn't even mad anymore. I got up and walked over to his name plate that was laying on the floor near the wall. It said his name, Connor Meyers, in a big golden font that screamed power, but was still very simplistic in nature. It was really pretty honestly.

I picked it up, feeling the lettering for a moment. Man, I could use one of these. I turned to look at him. He didn't spare me a glance as he angrily typed away on his keyboard. I made my way over to him, a soft smile on my face. He didn't hate me, which meant we could still work past this.

I smoothly set down his name plate where it had been, and walked right up beside him. Thinking about what I particularly enjoyed doing when I was apologizing to someone, I instinctively threw my arms around him.

My grip tightened around his wide upper back as I awkwardly bent down to be hugging him sort of at eye level. He froze instantly. That's when the realization dawned on me that maybe he wasn't so into hugs as I was. Correction, I was pretty damn sure now that Connor was not a hugger.

Fuck it. I was already hugging him so I had to follow through.

"Hey," I nearly whispered, moving my face back, but as painfully awkward as one can imagine, still keeping my arms loosely around him. He didn't even look at me to make matters worse. "I know. Your time is really important. Definitely more important than mine, that's for sure. I don't mean to keep wasting it." I looked firmly at the profile of his face, taking in his features, "We just need to work on our communication skills with each other a bit more." I squeezed him tightly one more time, before finally letting go and straightening out my legs.

He finally looked at me, and to my great surprise, didn't look like he wanted me dead.

"So, awesome! Let's start learning about doing the thangs!" I skipped over to my desk, getting my stuff ready.

There was silence as I shuffled through my mess of things. I was thinking about what Connor's next move would be and also what I would be eating for lunch later. This whole situation was taking a lot of my energy.

"Alright," Connor finally said, straightening his posture.

Fuck yeah.

As I was looking for a pencil, there was a knock at the door.

"Come in," Connor said without missing a beat, and in walked Samantha. She looked at me for a long moment as she approached him, kind of curiously. She finally shifted her focus, ignoring me altogether. How typical.

"Hey, everything alright with you?" She questioned and I wondered if that had anything to do with the door slamming that happened not too long ago.

I bet she thought it was my fault too. Typical.

But it actually was my fault...

Well... She'd have a point there, I'll give her that.

"What do you have for me?" He ignored her completely. Boy, he could really be cold.

I decided this was my time to not be around.

"Hey, I'm going to grab a fruit or something real quick." I gathered some of my belongings, trying to leave before I had to ignore whatever it was they would surely be going on about. Super boring.

"Greyson," Connor called me as I was almost at the door.

"Yeah?" I turned my head, still opening the door.

"Come right back." He raised his eyebrows and tilted his head down while he spoke. He really wasn't joking.

"I promise," I assured, smiling to show him he had nothing to worry about. His stern look didn't fade in the slightest. "See you in like, two minutes."

After grabbing a banana in our floor's breakroom, I obediently made my way back to the office. I made eye contact with Amanda and smiled.

"Everything okay in there?" She whisper-yelled across to me. Of course it slipped my mind that angry Connor had thrown doors every which way, probably concerning the entire floor of the possibility of him going Hulk and taking the entire building down with him.

"Yeah, I handled it," I assured her with a wink. She didn't look very convinced, eyeing me warily as I started opening up the office door.

Well unless my douche of a partner was still mad, I was being honest to the best of my ability. Whatever.

Samantha was no longer in the room, thankfully, and Connor was on the phone, not surprsingly.

"No, I'll do it next week if I have to, but that kind of screws me over. I'm not exactly ready for that yet," Connor was saying on the phone. I wasn't one for eavesdropping, in fact, I sucked at it, but something about his conversation sparked my interest. "I know, these guys are all about self-interest, even to the expense of others. If it all goes well, next time we have shit to do, they go by my convenience. Alright, bye." He hung up, looking up at me.

I peeled my banana, taking a bite, and with a mouth full of fruit, I asked, "So what do we have going on next week?"

"We have nothing, I have to fly out to Europe to take care of some business."

"We're goin' to Europe!? That's awesome! I have a passport and stuff, but I've never actually been out the country! What should I wear? How many days? Oh, that's so cool! This job is lit." I was nearly hopping around in excitement. I was going to Europe! Oh man, Jay was going to be super jealous.

"I'm sorry, are your ears not working? You aren't going. Can we get to work now?"

"Is your brain not working? We have the same exact job in the same exact company. That means, whatever you do as a part of your job is also my job to do. Duh."

"Oh, so do you want to run a meeting? How about organize piles of paperwork, write emails, read emails, make estimates, create business moves that favors the company, lead everybody on this floor and take phone calls day in and day out for starters?" He looked at me blankly, "I didn't think so. We don't have the same job. You get paid to sit here."

"Whoa wait. I would love to do all that," I lied so boldly. I forgot half the things on his list, but I was sure it was all super boring and infuriating, "I don't do anything because you won't let me. I'm going to Europe." I took another, way more fierce, bite out of my banana and grabbed my phone.

Jonathan would settle this.

"Great, so I'll get everything ready for Spain next week, thanks!" I knew my face oozed with smugness with the perfectly crafted scowl Connor was giving me. I set my phone down, and crossed my arms across my chest.

"You really want to screw me over, huh?" I could tell Connor was starting to grow really tired with me with the way he easily accepted this instead of fighting me on it. He kind of just sunk into his seat, staying quiet. It almost made me feel bad for being so obnoxious towards him all the time.

Almost.

But who could be mad? I was going to Europe, no, Spain to be exact in just a few days!

"It's going to be way fun-er with me there anyways. You'll thank me later! While we're on this subject, can we talk about how boring this office is?" So I was on cloud nine, and my filter went out the window as my excitement rose with every thought of the next week. "You need some color, fun furniture, a rug or something!"

"Am I going to help you or not?" His voice rose ever so slightly.

"Yes, yeah. We'll get to that, but I think I can help you too. I think we need some music." I went over to my laptop, pulling up YouTube, thinking about a good song to play.

"Greyson..." I heard Connor warn from behind me.

"Oh, I know exactly what to play!" Earth, Wind and Fire came to mind, naturally, and I quickly searched up their song, September.

As soon as the melody started playing, I quickly turned up the volume to the highest it could go, really wishing I had brought some speakers. The office, being the large size it was, was hardly doing the song justice, but it would have to do. My head was already bobbing to the beat and not long after my entire body followed.

I slowly danced my way to Connor, who was looking at me like I was absolutely insane. The chorus was finally coming up and I couldn't help, but sing along, "Ba de ya, say do you remember. Ba de ya! Dancing in September!" I went on with singing and reached for Connor's hands. He pulled back.

"Are you serious right now?" He said. I finally grabbed one of his hands and only got his arm to start making worm-like movements while the rest of his body stayed frozen. No fun whatsoever.

Letting him go, I twirled around the room, stopping at the huge glass wall, looking below as I belted out lyrics. Turning to Connor who was still graciously watching my performance, I hopped and spun to him, keeping stern eye-contact as I sang and danced.

He leaned back in his seat, as I was getting dangerously close, and raised an eyebrow in curiosity at whatever I was plotting. I reached my hands in front of me, snaking them around each other right in his face, trying to remain dead-faced with my eyebrows scrunched together, but once I saw how scared he was starting to look I bursted out laughing.

I laughed so hard I fell to the ground, failing at trying to compose myself. "I can't!" I said through fits of laughing. "Your face." I tried again, remembering the look of terror in his eyes.

"Are you okay?" Connor was clenching his jaw, trying so hard not to laugh and that made everything much funnier. "Greyson, get up." He chuckled once, not allowing himself to really feel his emotions.

The song had long since ended, which was a shame. Finally relaxing from my fit of hysteria, I slowly made my way up, wiping tears from my face. Sighing, I said, "Alright, teach me the ways of the company." I grabbed my laptop and some paper and pens, and went to sit across from him at his desk.

"You are something else." He softly smiled to himself, typing something on his computer.

I looked at the profile of his face, studying it. His eyes were ever so gently crinkled at the corners, which slightly reminded me of his father when he was smiling. Except you could tell Jonny smiled more, with the way his crinkles were etched into his skin permanently. I also noticed how much more Connor's eyes lit up when he seemed happier. He didn't look like his usual stone statue figure, and this was only from the slightest of smiles. I came to the conclusion that he should smile more. And dance more, but that was beside the point.

He still wasn't looking at me, but I smiled back at him.

I liked him smiling.

Chapter Eleven

Chapter 11- She's Wild (Connor's Perspective)

Surprisingly, for the first time in a while, I had finished all the tasks I had set up for myself at work early and had gone home just to relax. Adam, who was a lot more excited for me than I was, came over bringing whisky along with him to celebrate. At the same time, Samantha was texting me constantly about work matters.

You never truly left work.

Adam finally emerged from my kitchen with two glasses. He set them down on the coffee table, pouring the brown liquid into both of them. Passing me one he sat adjacent to me on the white love seat that matched the couch I was on. His feet lifted off the floor and landed on my coffee table as he made himself very comfortable. Too comfortable. I watched his actions, making sure he didn't do any harm to my plants.

Wasting no time in taking a swig of his drink, he downed his glass, and with a slightly pained expression, went right away to pour another. "Don't be modest on the drinks, I have another bottle in the kitchen."

I finally decided to take a sip, wincing at how strong it was. I almost forgot that Adam wasn't one to mess around when it came to his alcohol. He was borderline alcoholic, there was no denying that.

"So tell me," He finally started, taking a smaller sip from his glass, "Have you figured out what you are going to do with this merger considering your current female situation." He raised an eyebrow at me.

That was definitely the question on everyone's mind. Especially after a certain dinner where everyone was informed of the situation in the first place to be able to question it. It was fairly easy to ignore, except when one of those people were sitting directly next to you, asking so bluntly.

Samantha had texted me then. If you hand me a few suits tomorrow, I can get those dry cleaned for you before Spain.

I took another, more eager sip from the glass, Okay. I responded to her, setting my phone on my lap.

"Connor?" Adam asked impatiently, obviously not taking my silence as an answer.

"What do you want me to say exactly? Everyone knows how fragile this situation is. We all know how our relationship with our Japanese counterparts are. Hell, if anything I know exactly how particular this situation is. Yet instead of going to the man who decided to screw our chances, everyone, including our partners, stockholders, and even you are coming up to me about it." Slamming down the rest of my glass, I quickly sat forward to pour myself another one.

"Connor, everyone knows Jon is on his last leg. The only reason our stockholders are still on board is because we all know if anyone can figure it out, it's you. You always do." He smoothly let out, leveling out our conversation. "Have you asked Peter? He's a devious fella."

"No, I haven't asked Peter." I spat in disgust. "He fucking loves her." I could feel my temper rising at the thought of all the disrespect I encountered from him. His interest in Greyson was really putting a wedge between us and I still partially wanted him out of my building for good.

No, I couldn't afford such a thing. If anything Greyson was the real issue here. Why should I even want to sacrifice good workers for someone who did absolutely nothing?

My phone buzzed.

Hey Connor! So, I know we're gonna be in Spain for 3 days. How many outfits do you think I should bring for that? I'm ignoring pajamas, I already have that figured out. OMG are you excited?! It's coming up so soon! I can't wait!! Greyson texted.

Speak of the devil.

Adam spoke, "Peter isn't stupid. He would never let a girl get in the way of a great opportunity. He's probably just being nice to her so that he can sleep with her. I don't blame him. Either way, I bet he already has some ideas on how to get rid of her."

I focused my attention on my phone, trying really hard to ignore the crawling feeling under my skin. Three days. So three outfits and a business suit. I replied to Greyson.

"Connor," Adam sighed, "I am actually here right now. Let's think about this shit. I'm not in the business of plotting against people per se, but as your adviser I have to think about what's best for all of us. And this girl, although cute, really isn't the gimmick we want to use in Japan. So if we actually think together on this, we can probably figure out how to get rid of her."

My phone buzzed again, twice. One message was from Samantha, I ignored that one. Greyson's read, I'm thinkin' 7! No, that's a lie. How about 8? One extra just in case.

This girl was truly something else.

Adam spoke up, "I agree with Sam, this girl is fucking you up." He apparently had one drink too many. The fucking bastard.

"How do you, or Sam for that matter, figure?" I retorted angrily. So they were casually talking behind my back now?

"I didn't ask her. However, from the short time I've been here, I've noticed something. You talk to her differently." He pointed at me, smiling mischievously. "If you want to have sex with her, nobody is going to fight you on the age difference." He paused.

"What?" I replied in confusion way too quickly. I then realized that was the exact reaction he hoped to get from me.

"Or is it that she doesn't want you?" He teased.

"Adam, fuck you. You do realize we're talking about a human right? Not someone who's just there to fuck. Why is this always about sex anyways? You're a perverted piece of shit." I got up then, taking my glass and myself to the kitchen.

"Relax. Why are you always so defensive? I'm just messing with you." He got up then, but didn't follow me to the kitchen. "Hey, you enjoy the rest of your night. Keep the extra bottle on me. But you listen to me Connor and heed my warning. You better figure this shit out before it all comes crashing down right on top of that pretty little head of yours. The merger is coming up and if you keep ignoring the issue, for whatever reason you're choosing to, you're going to regret it. Kiss everything you've worked for goodbye!"

He grabbed the bottle of whisky from the table and then his keys. I bit my tongue, allowing silence to take its place instead.

"Enjoy your night Connor." He finally said before leaving my home.

Was I really taking this situation too lightly? That was simply impossible. I had gotten pissed about a thousand times already about the fact. I'd spoken to Jonathan, I'd spoken to Greyson and I even talked to Jackson for fuck's sake! There was truly no outlet.

I could treat Greyson like absolute garbage, but not only was that bad for my own morale, it did nothing to get her to leave. If anything it just meant having a person who knew absolutely nothing about our company as a key factor in the merger. That wasn't an option. If I could at least prepare her to know enough to be there, she wouldn't make an absolute fool out of us. Or would she?

Was that even the best option? Working with her meant wasting my time. Not to mention how much I hated it. She was just so immature and just plainly stupid. And her boldness to argue with me instead of listening to me, was becoming ridiculous. I never had to take such disrespect ever, and now that's all my life was starting to consist of.

I looked at the bottle of whisky Adam had left me. Seeing how I still wasn't feeling any calming effects of what I had already drank, I poured myself some more. I just needed enough to feel relaxed.

How could I even relax? Why did Jonathan do this to me? Now of all times?

I wasn't sure how many times I had gone over this same endless and unprofitable thought process, but I couldn't help it. I took comfort in finding light in troubling times and this was the only time I really couldn't make any sense of the situation I was living in.

How do I get rid of a person I can't fire in a way that doesn't upset them?

And there goes another issue. Why should I even care if Greyson hates me? Why did my morale depend on her happiness? I'd never see her again anyways. Here I was though, constantly giving her attention and trying to work with her. Me, Connor Meyers, was really trying to work with some kid on the biggest business move of his life.

I made my way back over to the living room, dropping down onto my couch. I checked my phone, quickly skimming through Sam's text and finally landing on the text thread between Greyson and myself.

Although I could never truly accept it, I knew I had to have some admiration for someone so self-assured, no matter how over-the-top.

Considering all of the bad qualities, she did possess a few decent character traits. She was very courageous, confident and, in her own weird way, authentic. Authenticity wasn't something I saw often.

So, how are you? I texted her without any thought whatsoever.

Not too long later came her unnecessarily long reply. I'm super excited, that's how I am! I even missed a party to begin packing. Maria even came over to keep me company since Jay went to the party. She left a little bit ago actually. I'm eating some food right now. Courtesy of M. What are you up to? Are you at home?

There was still no way Adam was right. I could never want to be with someone so... So... Just so her!

Yeah I'm home. I sent and tossed my phone beside me. Having a conversation with her wasn't helping ease my mind.

Another drink.

At this point, my phone started buzzing repeatedly. Sam was calling me. That girl was becoming the biggest pain in my ass. Her con list was starting to outweigh her pro list and that needed to stop sooner rather than later.

I picked up, but my mind was already getting so fuzzy that most of that conversation didn't register properly in my mind.

"Let's talk tomorrow." I said, in the middle of a speech she was giving, and hung up.

I tossed my phone once again, and dropped my head back, closing my eyes. I really needed to clear my head.

After what could have been one minute, or five hours, I was startled awake by a loud banging on my front door. I looked down at my watch in confusion, it was nearing midnight.

"Housekeeping!" I heard coming from the opposite side of the door.

"What the fuck?" I breathed, now in even more confusion. I wasn't at a hotel.

I looked at the door for a while longer, not sure if I was imagining things. Louder banging followed.

I got up then, "I'm coming." Nothing made sense. I mean, I did own a doorbell at the very least.

I went to unlock the door, realizing Adam never locked it in the first place on his way out. I turned the knob, and pulled it towards me, my eyebrows never ceasing to be scrunched together.

"What the fuck?" I said again. Apparently I had a catchphrase now.

"You're not the only person who can stalk someone's place of living," a big smile stretched over her face while my brain was slowly trying to process everything going on.

"Greyson?"

AN: A shorter one, I know! It just so happens that it ended perfectly right here, so this is what I give you.

I hope you're all enjoying this. Thank you everyone for your continued support! I appreciate all of you reading.

Chapter Twelve

Chapter 12- He's Whatever (Greyson's Perspective)

There was nothing but excitement coursing through my veins. Well, there was also blood, but that was beside the point! I had never been out of the country, which meant my passport was actually going to come to some use. This also meant my life was finally cooler than Jay's, so I was surely going to bring back a story that would make him super jealous of my life. Wasn't that what friends were for?

The only flaw in all of this was that I had absolutely nothing to wear! I came up with a few raggedy outfits of mine, but I definitely needed to get to the shopping plaza ASAP to make sure I'd look my Greyson Lewis best. That was on the top of my priority list.

Considering all the energy (and blood) coursing through my veins, I could not possibly stay home. Maria had left and I needed an outlet. That was why, after finding out that Mr. Meyers Jr. was home, I called up Jonny-Bear, who was super nice despite being woken up, and found out my partner's address.

I was driving through the night, my head bobbing from side to side at the Michael Jackson I was blasting on the radio. I was just a sucker for older music since it always brought back so many good memories.

Connor didn't live as close to me as I thought, which wasn't fun in regards to the gas I was wasting. That was whatever though. I'd worry about that another day. Also, I just wanted to take a moment to talk about how he lived in a freaking condominium. And not just your average Joe kind of condo, no, more like the one that's also by the beach and is the super expensive kind.

Well, I guess if you have the money.

I couldn't even hate, it was so massive and pretty! I walked into the huge front doors, and there was a front desk situation. It felt like I was at a five star hotel. Nobody was there though. I stood in front of it, looking around. I wasn't sure if I was allowed to just go on up or not. Oh, this was weird.

There was a name plate too. "Con... Conci... Concert? Concerto... Concord? Consumer...gi?" I tried pronouncing the word, or name, and I really just couldn't. "Fuck it." I walked off in the direction of the elevator, opening up my phone. I had Jon send me the address in a text because there was no way I was going to remember it.

Thinking about it, it made absolutely no sense for Mr. Meyers to send me Connor's address. I could've been an axe murderer for all he knew. He was way too trusting. His son could be dead right now all because he decided to hand out his house address. I mean, I did tell him it was for something Connor asked me to send to his house, but that he forgot to give me the address and I couldn't ask him because he was asleep, but still. That could've been a lie. I mean it was, but the point I was trying to make was that I could've literally committed a murder at this very moment all thanks to Jon.

I finally came up to Connor's suite. It was even fancy looking from in the hallway. Oh man, I could just imagine how shocked he was going to be to see me there! He'd probably hate me again, but I was too optimistic for that trail of thought. If anything, I was just returning the favor.

I raised my fist and banged loudly on the door. He could've been sleeping for all I knew, and there was no way this journey was going to waste. "Housekeeping!" I called out for good measure. I was nearly dancing in my shoes.

After a minute or so, I decided to knock again. I was prepared to do this all night.

"I'm coming." I could barely hear him say from the other side. I was smiling so hard I started giggling. This was great!

The door was finally being opened and the look on his face was everything I hoped for and more! He looked confused, but too tired to be mad.

"You're not the only person who can stalk someone's place of living," I rested both of my hands on my hips, loving this new expression of his.

"Greyson?" He asked, and I took that as my invitation in. I pushed passed him and he didn't really resist. I could hear him closing the door behind me.

After a few long strides, I stopped dead in my tracks, "Oh my gracious!" I was absolutely star-struck by the coolness that was his home. It was like being in the future. Everything looked so smooth. There was a whole lot of white, which made me feel kind of scared to touch anything and get it dirty.

"So you're a pretty clean person? I guess I could've expected that." I thought back to how messy my house would be if Jay wasn't there to constantly help with cleaning it up. Even though there was a lack of color in Connor's house, he had a few plants, which just made the green pop out pretty nicely.

I loved his house.

"Greyson, why are you here?" I made my way to his couch and noticed an opened bottle of alcohol on his coffee table. It looked unnecessarily expensive. I dropped down onto his couch, and kicked off my shoes so I could cross my legs. I already invited myself in, I might as well have gotten comfortable during my stay too.

"You came to my house. It's only fair that I do the same. Besides, I had too much energy to sleep." Connor sat down on a sleek looking recliner across from me. He dropped his head back and closed his eyes. He then started rubbing his temples.

I looked back down at the bottle of alcohol that was more than half way empty. It then dawned on me. His calm demeanor wasn't a result of being tired.

"Connor are you drunk?" That didn't seem like the most responsible thing to be doing on his part on a weekday.

"Adam brought that over." He responded, still with his eyes closed.

"Okay," I paused for a moment, "So are you drunk?"

"I don't know," He said defensively, "Why, did you want some?" He finally brought his head back down to look at me.

"Ew. I don't drink." I scrunched my nose in disgust.

"Oh are you too young yet?"

I looked at him in disbelief. "No, I am still twenty-one." Yeah, he was definitely drunk. "I got drunk only two times in my life and that was the worst. I did some stupid stuff, I had like no control over myself and the next day felt like hell. Me and being drunk is not a good combo."

"Why are you here again?" He spat out. He was really starting to get on my nerves. Nothing new there.

"You should just accept the fact that I am here. Your questioning is gettin' us nowhere. What you should be doing instead is giving me a tour of this place. I've never been in a condo before." I jumped to my feet, going over to help the drunkard up.

We walked throughout the entirety of his bachelor pad, which consisted of me saying, "Oh wow!" to most of it. If I had to choose a favorite thing, it would have been that beyond the kitchen you could walk out onto a balcony and view the beach below. It was incredibly high up, which was kind of scary, but super cool at the same time.

During my tour, I had also taken note of the way Connor was when he was drunk. He didn't really seem all that drunk, which was the interesting thing. He didn't stumble while he walked, nor did he slur his words too badly. If anything he just did things a lot more slowly and his breath smelled disgusting.

"I'm going to go light a cigarette." He started walking in the direction of the balcony.

I scoffed in disgust, "Connor, do you know what day and age we are livin' in? Stop being stupid, cigarettes ain't even good for you! You're too smart for that. It doesn't make any sense." I went back to sit on the couch, annoyed. So I wasn't very fond of smoking.

I started playing with the leaves of the plant on his coffee table, flicking them back and forth. I stopped doing that after a second, that wasn't very fun actually.

Not too long after, Connor came by and sat on the smaller couch next to me. He sighed. "I'm not going to smoke right now." I smiled at that. "I can't stand you." He said, way too seriously.

"Well it's a good thing you're sitting down then!" I laughed. Dad jokes were my specialty. And a good defense mechanism against hurtful words. "So, Mr. Alcoholic. How about you tell me your entire life's story?" I easily blurted out. Actually, after asking out loud, it made me realize I really didn't know much about Connor at all. It was weird because, I argued with this man so many times to learn he was a complete jackass, but I had no proper understanding as to why he was such a Debbie-Downer.

Oh yeah, I really liked this question.

"What kind of request is that?" He asked, unsurprisingly.

"A good one," I quickly replied and stood up, "I'm going to go grab something to drink from your kitchen. While I do that, start gatherin' up your memories."

His refrigerator didn't have much content in general. A few water-bottles, some fruits and vegetables, miscellaneous, more miscellaneous, coffee creamers and a drink whose name I couldn't pronounce. The water-bottles looked pretty fancy, so I went with that.

I snooped in his freezer too, for good measure, and found one pack of frozen meat and some bags of frozen fruit. Connor probably had about zero clue on how to cook. Which wasn't surprising actually. It would be surprising to know that mister works every single moment of every single day was also a decent chef. Lame.

I slammed his freezer door shut and then also realized he didn't have any magnets. That was a shame since his refrigerator was so big it just looked naked without them. I started thinking that I should have brought one of mine to donate to this cause. It was like looking at those neglected pet commercials, the ones that had, In the Arms of an Angel, playing in the background. Nobody should ever own a fridge and leave it so unloved. Who was the ASPCA to call for refrigerator cruelty?

The clanking of glass behind me snapped me out of my thoughts. I saw Connor wiping his mouth, and settling himself back into his seat. With my fancy water-bottle in hand, I made my way back over to the living room.

"Did you just drink more alcohol?" I accused, with very good reason mind you.

"There's no way I'm going to tell you anything about myself if I am even feeling, in any way, sober in the slightest." His words were finally starting to sound more slurred.

With an angry huff, I dropped back into my seat and twisted the bottle cap open. I brought my legs back up to be in full pretzel position. I decided not to argue because the devious side of me was excited that this was even happening at all. Oh, he was surely going to kill me the next day.

"Alright," He finally said. He was back in his relaxed mode, with his head thrown back and his hands loosely clasped together on his lap. His eyes were watching the ceiling, "Where do I start." He was talking super slowly, which was burning my soul.

Connor wasn't going to kill me.

Nope. Not in the slightest because from what I knew of drunk people, at this point that he was, he wouldn't even remember any of this happening. Which reminded me that the only reason I was here was to get him to tell me all the cool things that was going to happen in Spain so that I could have really cool dreams.

Not that I was complaining. I was about to receive some top secret, presidential eyes only, type of information. The type that was stored in a computer with uncrack-able coding in a metal safe, in an indestructible room, guarded twenty-four/seven by only the best spies the US government could afford.

That meant that I should at least try and be patient with how slowly he was starting off his story.

"So I was born."

I groaned internally.

"Right after that my mom left," He continued. I immediately felt bad for mentally groaning.

"Why did she leave?" I interjected.

"I don't know. Jonathan says she wasn't ready to deal with the lifestyle he was living. I guess giving birth to me reinforced that idea in her." He let out very easily. My heart was already breaking.

"Oh."

"Jonathan never remarried. He decided instead to just sleep around with different women every now and then. They are normally employees that he, himself, has hired for the sake of sleeping with."

"That doesn't sound like good workplace ethics," I thought about the time I went through training at this one company. I didn't end up working there because I didn't actually have enough experience, which was bullshit, but they spoke about what wasn't good to do. Dating was frowned upon, but if the boss was to have a relationship with anybody he could potentially be charged for sexual harassment. I never forgot that because there was no way I would allow someone to harass me like that.

"If no one has an issue there isn't an issue. I can't say either way though, I'm no better." He paused and I didn't add anything. "Anyways, growing up, I was homeschooled until high school, that's when I first went to a private school. That was also where Adam and I first met. What time is it?"

That was a really good question. I went in my purse to find my phone and clicked on the home button, "It's nearly one-thirty."

"I have to get up soon." Connor groaned. I nearly laughed.

"Oh you are going to hate yourself in the morning. That's what you get for drinking." I smirked.

"If you leave my house now, it won't be too bad." I stopped smirking.

"Wait, wait. Just finish your story first. How was your childhood?"

"Well, it was okay," He kept going. This was great, he was actually telling me everything! "I didn't have a necessarily normal childhood. I studied really hard for this company. I was alone quite a lot too. Except when Jackson was around. Maybe it would have been nicer to have a mother around. I don't know. My grandparents' house was nice to visit too." He rambled.

I couldn't even imagine Meyers Jr. as a child. Especially as one without a mother. I couldn't believe she would be so selfish and cold. That was horrible. What was it about moms and thinking about themselves first?

"College was a good time for me. I became passionate in taking over Jonathan's business and it turned out I was great at running things. That's when I started working in the company and I proved to everyone that I was capable."

I looked around his space again, "Was your dad able to pay for your entire college tuition?"

"Yes."

"Wow." I was really starting to get a feel for the differences between us. Having the same job title made me forget, but we really came from two different upbringings. "It must be nice being rich." I tried not to feel jealous. I knew he had his struggles too, but at least he had a good amount of money to fall back on and that allowed him to overcome his issues.

"I suppose." He looked at me, "I rarely feel rich, though."

I thought about that one for a moment. I never really even cared to have so much money in my life. As long as I was happy, I always thought I could live as a troll under a bridge and that would be fine. Maybe I was spending too much time around luxurious environments.

"Connor, I hope you find your richness. The one that really counts." I uncrossed my legs and slipped my feet back into my shoes. "I'm gonna let you sleep now because I really should be sleeping myself. I don't care if you hate yourself for staying up and being shitfaced, but I don't want to feel the regret I surely will for my lack of sleep."

He went to get up and I could see him really struggling to control his limbs.

"Don't worry, I'll let myself out." I went over to give him a hug, "Goodnight!" I smiled as he tried so hard to act sober.

"Goodnight." He half-waved back.

I drove home with a new perspective on Connor.

Chapter Thirteen

Chapter 13- She's Childish (Connor's Perspective)

It was the very early hours of the morning of our little excursion to Europe. Despite the unholy hour, Greyson was jumping, yes actually jumping, around the plane and our small group.

I stopped speaking to the group at some point to watch her in the darkness. Her bags were scattered on the ground and she kept going from person to person, trying to properly release her excitement.

Yeah, like she could ever actually release her excitement.

"Does anyone want to switch seats with me?" I said, mostly serious, but everyone laughed it off anyways.

We were going in our small company plane, but there were still enough seats for her to not have to sit next to me. So that brought the question of why exactly was she supposed to sit next to me then?

Well, apparently that all happened a few days ago. I had woken up still kind of drunk and kind of hungover. I was absolutely pissed at myself for being so irresponsible, especially because my reasoning for drinking myself blind was to not have to deal with thinking about everything Adam had been telling me. Not to mention, I didn't even remember drinking all that much. Adam had a way of getting unexpectedly strong alcohol.

I wasn't generally one to try and ignore my issues by drinking them away. However, being angry at myself wasn't helpful to the growing migraine I was dealing with, so I just accepted what the situation was. I got to my office a bit late and made sure Amanda and Sam knew to leave me to deal with my business alone for a few hours.

My migraine was centered in the front of my face straight back into the very core of my brain, so instead of reading emails, I rested my head down on my desk. Too many things were spinning in my mind.

And then, to add icing on my ever so beautiful cake, Greyson threw my door open and at the top of her lungs screeched an unnecessarily peppy, "Good morning!" I don't think I have ever hated her more.

To make matters worse, yeah, because things could've actually gotten worse, she laughed and said, "Oh you are so hungover! This is why you shouldn't drink. Maybe you'll learn a lesson here."

Her voice was way too high and her spot on accusation left whatever brain space I had control over in confusion, "How do you know I was drinking?" I whispered, hoping she'd get the, let's-be-quiet, memo.

In all too many words, which led to me regretting the question, she explained how she was over at my house the night before. I remembered Adam, but I thought the parts of my memory that included her was part of a terrible, horrible nightmare.

If it was any other day, I would've told her off for coming over to my place, I would have even asked her how she knew where I lived, but the pain my brain was in didn't allow me to do that. It was reassuring, however, to know that she only came over, in her words, for a little while to discuss our business trip. She added in there that I had promised her I would sit next to her since she still isn't very close with everyone. My drunk self wasn't the best at decision making. Apparently.

So that was the situation I was currently dealing with.

"Hey, haven't we met before?" Greyson stopped prancing to look keenly at Grant. He was like a veteran in our building, having worked with Jonathan's father before the company was ever actually put together. He was incredibly smart.

"Yes, on your first day I was going to give you a tour. Which never happened because you didn't want it." He replied.

"Oh... I remember now." She frowned a bit and quickly walked off. Grant shook his head in disapproval.

When we finally got settled into the plane, Samantha, who was sitting directly across from me was going over some business we'd have to try to work on during this trip and immediately when we got back. Greyson was sitting by the window, staring out of it.

"How does taking off feel? I heard it's kind of scary. I don't know, I'm thinking about it too much, aren't I? I feel a bit nervous." She was still smiling, tapping her feet repeatedly on the floor.

"You've never been on an airplane?" I asked, slightly amused by how scared she was.

"No." She opened her eyes really wide and went back to looking outside.

The captain's voice rang through the overhead intercom, reminding us to review safety protocols and to fasten our seatbelts because we were about to take off. Greyson grabbed onto the armrests on either side of her seat, and she finally stopped smiling.

Was it bad that I was finding so much enjoyment at her expense?

The plane finally started its takeoff, and Greyson's eyes shut instantaneously. She was definitely overreacting, which wasn't all that surprising. I opened up my phone to turn it on airplane mode. While I was away, Adam was going to be taking care of some of my business back at the building.

Since he was always traveling out of the country, I let him stay back and watch over things for me. We worked more efficiently anyways when we were both working on different aspects of the company. He was definitely a lot more involved than your average adviser and it showed in his salary.

We lifted off of the ground and Greyson took that as her opportunity to say, "Lord have mercy," under her breath. I almost laughed at that.

Once the plane leveled out and was smoothly gliding in the sky, Greyson's usual personality sprung right back. She was glued to the window, making gasping sounds every other second. The moments she wasn't vocally showing her amusement, she was pulling on my arm, trying to get me to look at all the sights down below. It was mostly city lights, seeing how the sun hadn't come up yet.

Everyone else had decided to use this time to catch up on some sleep. Samantha was typing some things up on her laptop. On these kinds of trips, she usually tried to stay up for as long as I did. She was honestly great at her job, all things considered.

Eventually, I drifted off to sleep and woke up to bright light peering in from the window. Everyone was in the process of waking up with laptops out, already on work schedule. Since this trip came a bit out of the blue, no one was completely caught up with things back at the building.

Sam was still asleep and I decided I much rather have it like that for the time being. Looking beside me, there was no sign of Greyson. I turned my head in the opposite direction, scanning the aisles and couldn't find her anywhere. Maybe she was in the bathroom.

I wasted no time in opening my laptop to check on some of the different committees within the company. They always sent me updates, upon my request, but I didn't always actually look at them.

Within an hour or so, everyone was awake, talking amongst each other and going about their business. Sam had taken to reading a book she brought along. I was sipping on some coffee.

Greyson still wasn't back, and I was actually starting to feel a bit nervous. She could've passed out in the bathroom and I never even considered that.

"Samantha, can you check the bathroom and see if Ms. Lewis is alright?" I finally asked and was given a stern look in response. She quietly placed her book down and started to unbuckle her seatbelt.

At the same time, the curtain separating the cockpit from our seats were being swung open. Looking straight ahead, I saw Greyson appear from the other side of it. What was she up to now?

"Alright everybody," She spoke. Of course. "If for whatever reason both the pilot and copilot can't perform their duties, I've now got enough knowledge to land this baby myself," She smiled, "So not to fear because, Greyson Lewis, is here." After a quick bow, she skipped over to her seat beside me. "Connor, I learned so much! Well, actually," She looked up at nothing for a moment, "I don't quite remember everything they taught me, but I have decent instincts, so I'm sure it'll all come to me."

I looked over at Sam who was rolling her eyes. Ignoring that, she stood up, "Okay everyone, as a quick reminder I'm going to go over the plans so we're all on the same page," She had her iPad in hand and everyone stopped what they were doing to pay attention. "We'll get there around noon, so we'll have a quick lunch and head off to the first meeting. That will be mostly an outline for the next day, and making sure everyone knows who they need to be connecting with. Tomorrow, we'll be starting at seven in the morning. We'll all gather together for a discussion, then you will be breaking off to cover your specialized areas. After that, please type up your required assignments. The next morning our team will come together to debrief. The plane leaves that day at eleven in the morning. Thank you."

She sat back down and Greyson scoffed at the information, "Wait, what about sight-seeing?" She asked, mortified.

"This isn't a vacation," Sam shot back, "If that's what you were expecting you should have never come in the first place."

Surprisingly, Greyson chose not to respond, instead she looked at me, her eyes pleading.

"I thought you said I told you what was on the agenda for this trip?" I spoke softly to not add to the waves Sam was trying to create. I really wanted to put her in her place.

Greyson's bright green eyes broke away from me, "You didn't make it seem so bad." She mumbled.

"This is what jobs are like. If you can't handle that then you really shouldn't be working here." Samantha shot. Greyson looked at her, so instead of giving Sam a piece of my mind, I held back to see what would ensue. Greyson then looked up at me with an empty expression for a moment, and turned back to look out the window, propping her head on her hand.

Sam shook her head, smirking in victory. The next second she was focused on her cellphone.

I leaned over towards Greyson, "I'll try to fit something in between meetings." I whispered.

Her head quickly whipped around and she was grinning madly, "Yes, please."

I turned back to my laptop, feeling more relaxed myself.

We had finally landed and were finishing getting settled into our hotel rooms. Greyson, having spent no time getting herself ready decided to come over to mine. She was sitting on the edge of my bed as I fixed my tie while also organizing my belongings into my briefcase.

"We could all be outside exploring Spain right now. What's taking everyone so long?" She huffed.

"Everyone needs to go over their notes," I told her. I really had no clue why I even let her in. She was entirely too distracting.

"They all did that on the plane! You are all more than ready. This is such a waste of time," She groaned, "What am I even supposed to be doing at this meeting?"

"Just observe it. Maybe you'll learn a thing or two." I was trying extremely hard to be reasonable. Sam was texting me. Since she was leading our time management, she was rushing me so that everyone would have enough time to eat.

"I hate this job sometimes," She continued on in her hysterics.

Feeling the aggravation of all the things my mind was trying to keep track of I quickly quipped, "Feel free to quit anytime." I then grabbed my belongings, texting Sam back to get everyone ready in the lobby and left the room.

After lunch, we all headed in cars to get to the where our meeting was going to be held. Upon Sam's request, we took a car for just the both of us so that she could speak with me about something.

I waited for her to speak up.

"You know I'm on your side, right?" She started and I already knew what this speech was going to be about.

"I have no fucking time for this. If we're not talking about what's going on with this meeting right now then you can keep your mouth shut."

To say I was sick and tired of all the bullshit was an understatement. I didn't need the talk of Greyson to take precedence over every aspect of my job.

"Connor..." She tried leveling with me.

"Sam, stop. This whole side thing is childish and unprofessional. You're all so concerned about Greyson messing up everything, which I understand could be a legitimate concern," The car stopped in front of our intended destination, "But think about this for a moment. Where did all this little faith in me come from? Don't I know how to do my job? Haven't I always succeeded despite the circumstances? Now all of a sudden, everyone thinks I'm not capable enough because of one person who doesn't even really care about this job! Focus your energy in not underestimating me and trusting that I know what the hell I'm doing." I threw the car door open, stepping out without another word. I quickly composed myself, walking up to our small group.

I looked at the line of cars on the side of the street, noticing we were missing one. Readjusting my focus to the group, it didn't take me very long at all to realize what was off.

Where, in the honest fuck, was Greyson Lewis?

Chapter Fourteen

Chapter 14- He's Completely Business (Greyson's Perspective)

"Cheese!" I smiled wide as a stranger took a picture of me in front of a Spanish stop sign. I was in Spain for goodness sake! That was incredibly exciting. So of course I needed one or two pictures. "Gracias," I thanked the guy in pretty good Spanish, if I did say so myself. I pulled the photo up to examine it.

Perfect.

So I skipped out of the meeting I was supposed to be in. Did I feel bad about it? Nope. I had absolutely no purpose in being there. There was no way anyone could expect me to just sit there and listen. If anything, I was doing everyone a favor for missing it. Not that they wanted me there in the first place. Whatever.

I was going to enjoy my time here no matter what. I was even going to make it feel as much as a vacation as possible too, just out of spite. I could be selfish. Anyways, Barcelona was alive with tourists, so I didn't feel out of place. And from what Google had been telling me,

Barcelona also had a beach. I just had to know if it was better than Miami's.

While sitting on a bus to the beach, my phone rang. It was Connor, "Hey partner! How's the meetings going?" I received silence in response, "Hello?" I asked, unsure if the connection was bad.

"Greyson, where are you?" He asked simply. I guess it didn't cross my mind that someone would be forced to ask where I was if I just disappeared. I probably should have sent a quick text to him at some point.

"Oh, I'm so sorry I didn't say anything! I ended up stayin' back at the hotel. I thought you'd all do better without me there so I..." He cut me off.

"Greyson. Where are you actually?"

"Aw man. Okay, I'm caught," I had to give him props for seeing right through my lie. Well maybe all the people talking around me weren't entirely helping my case either. "I'm on my way to the beach. Please don't make me go back. I'm no help there. And I know that you know that there is no way I can just sit still and listen. You didn't even want me to come on this trip in the first place. I'm helping you. I know I shouldn't be just having a fun time either, but I've never been out of the country and this was the only way I could have done this."

"You're out alone in a foreign country. Do you realize how dangerous that is?"

"Okay, dad." I sarcastically responded, completely offended. He was always trying to treat me like I was a stupid kid, "I know how to take care of myself."

"When you get to the beach, you stay there. I'll leave this meeting early and come get you," He hung up.

"Why does he always do this!?" I said aloud to no one in particular. Everything always had to be his way. Well if he thought I was just going to go back without having some bit of fun, he was going to be really disappointed.

Since the bus was taking far too many stops and my mood was already not in the happiest of places, I decided to call up Peter, Also known as Spiderman, to check in and cheer myself up.

"Ms. Lewis. What do I owe the pleasure?" I smiled, he was good at cheering me up.

"I'm in Barcelona! Safe, mind you, which might not have been the case if the pilots weren't good at flying planes. Anyways, how are you? I'm headed to the beach right now, which sounds great, right? But it actually isn't because Connor was all like, what are you doing?" I imitated his annoyed, deep voice as well as I could, "And I was like, you don't even want me at the meeting, so you're welcome. And then, he was like, you wait there I'm coming to ruin your day! How messed up right? It's not too bad though. I'm still going to have a good time. Anyways, how are you?"

"Tired. However, I've been looking at trends in Asia and I'm actually pretty shocked because..." He went on and my mind spaced the moment I realized he was talking about car business, "...but I know Connor is too stubborn to pay me any mind," I came back to the conversation thanks to hearing a specific trigger word. Connor was that trigger word, which should be added to my mental notes because that was just horrible, "But, it's all good because you are also the chief operating officer which means we can really do some good for this company."

I smiled. He thought I was important, which seeing how ignored I usually felt, was very reassuring.

"Yes, Peter that's so cool! I'm more than happy to help. I won't let you down, I promise. You keep doin' what you're doing, I'll survive this little trip and then we can start doing some damage once I get back. Nobody will know what hit them! I'm so excited! Thank you. Hey, my bus is stopping, so I will talk to you later, bye!" I hung up before he could say goodbye back.

Bad habit of mine sometimes. I couldn't say why I did it even if I tried.

The lay of the land was beautiful. Small local shops here and there, some gimmicks for tourists and I could smell the salty sea water blowing in the wind from where I was. I could definitely live here.

Walking closer another, more glorious, scent hit my nose. Local cuisine. Even though I just had lunch there was always space in my belly, for just one bite more.

Let's play a good old fashioned game of, who's that calling me?

Before pulling out my phone, I really thought about it for a moment. Could it be Jay? Probably not, he would have still been working. Hmm. Maybe Peter? Nope, he wouldn't be checking in so soon.

Oh I know! Let's say Connor for 600?

Checking the caller ID, I was happy to find that I would have gotten all the points on a real game show.

"What's up?" I answered, trying to sound like I was all about business.

"Where are you?" He spoke fast and unpleasantly.

"I am at the Galeria!" I happily proclaimed. "It's near the beach, I'll stand outside so that you can see me." I snapped my phone shut and strutted outside...

Hah! That was a joke. Nobody had flip phones anymore!

Not too long after, thank goodness, Connor appeared in the all-black batmobile. He stepped out from the backseat, looking at me all intense-like, "Come on," He said through gritted teeth. He grabbed onto the door, opening it wider for me.

"Didn't you say something about ending that meeting early? That means, you have some free time. And that means, we can actually enjoy my time here. So let's go! Vamanos!" Oh yeah, I was really pushing my luck. I didn't care though, Connor didn't scare me. Well, honestly, maybe a little. He would never need to know that though.

Acting tough got me this far, right?

"We'll call for you," I said to the driver and grabbed Connor's wrist, effectively pulling him from the car door and shutting it with my foot. "You have to see the artwork in this gallery." I told him, smiling at the little resistance I was receiving.

I rejoiced too soon. Two feet from the door, I was yanked back.

"Did I not tell you that I'd try and make time for some leisure? Why are you so incapable of following the simplest of directions?" I underestimated him.

"Connor," I said, calmly.

"Stop it. I'm tired of leveling with you. That's all I ever do," His voice was far too calm to make me feel at ease.

"Okay," I sighed in defeat. I was about to swallow all of my pride and my dignity too while I was at it, "You are absolutely right. I am in the wrong here and I'm sorry. I promise for the rest of this trip I will follow whatever you say without any complaints."

It was the exact proposal I gave to my mom sometimes when she got to a point where she was too tired to argue with me. It generally gave her some relief, but I usually felt miserable actually following it. I didn't generally propose this as a result. I was sure I could be stubborn forever. But every now and then I felt kind of bad.

And Connor did promise to have something fun happen. I remembered that clearly just in case he ended up forgetting. Which he didn't have to do, seeing that he also didn't want me here, but he did it anyways.

He ended up sighing himself, "I need a cigarette," He mumbled to himself. I didn't dare say a word, despite how much I couldn't stand the thought of anyone I knew smoking. "Well are you going to show me the gallery or not?"

"But didn't you say..?" I tried to not get excited, "What about the meeting?" My voice got higher in pitch.

"I already left it because of you," He played with his shirt button near his wrist, looking at that rather than me. I tried to read his face, uncertain if this was just a test or not.

"Um, okay," I hesitated, but the excitement was already bubbling over inside my body, "Yeah, okay! I just want to show you two things real quick!" I almost sprinted to the shop.

———

It was the night before the day we would be heading back into the states. Due to Connor's promise, we were all hanging out at this really nice, classic, Spanish-style bar.

Although I wasn't too enthusiastic about having to stick to the promise I made to Connor, it turned out not being all that bad. The meetings were incredibly long and I almost shoved a pen in my eye just to put myself out of my misery, but it wasn't always boring.

When everyone broke off into a different area, I got assigned to the best group ever in my opinion. I quickly became friends with the Spanish guys and that was great. I can't say the same happened with the guy who actually worked back in Florida with us though.

Anyways, Connor also complimented me on being so great and that felt really good. Not that he had a huge effect on me feeling good about myself, but considering how crappy he usually made me feel about being able to do this job, it felt nice to be commended.

At the bar that we were at, everyone was sort of talking about things at tables, getting drunk and enjoying the atmosphere. The bar had a pool table which was my saving grace.

I had invited the one Spanish man, Antonio, from the group I was a part of to join us which was great because, he was willing to play against me in pool. Not to brag, but I was incredibly good at pool, so he had no chance.

"Eight ball, corner pocket," I announced, leaning over the table. With a smooth stroke, my stick propelled the cue ball forward, causing it to smack against the surface of the eight ball pushing it directly into the pocket I called, "Aye!" I yelled in a gruff tone, dropping the pool stick on the table and doing a quick dance.

"You're pretty good," Antonio said to me in a thick accent.

"The best," I smiled and gave him a hug. "Who's next?" I looked around at my boys who were seeming to have a really fun conversation.

In total, eight of us had come on this trip. However, Samantha and the old guy who really hated me didn't show up to the bar. I wasn't complaining though, the air felt lighter without them around and Connor seemed to be having a decent time. It mattered if he was enjoying his time because, when he was having fun, everyone was too.

"Connor!" I called to him above the music and chatter. He looked over. "Come play me in pool. I promise to go easy on you." I stepped forward to the pool table, grabbing my stick and the chalk.

He shook his head and waved me off, "No, I'm alright over here." He took another sip of his beer.

I felt my shoulders drop in disappointment. He could never just say yes to me.

"Hey Mr. Meyers, this girl here, she is really good, but you're the boss. You have to play her and win," Antonio told him. I smiled at that. The guys back at the table were already pushing him up.

"Yeah show her who's boss," They were saying and my smile grew. COO versus COO. That's the battle of a lifetime. I wouldn't let my friends back home down.

"Alright, fine." Meyers Jr. got up willingly now, grabbing his beer to bring it over with him. All the guys followed, ready to watch me as I beat their precious king. Connor grabbed a stick and started chalking it up, "Who's going to break the rack?" He asked. He looked at the table with the same focus he usually had when he did his job.

Seems someone was taking this very seriously. Great.

"You can," I told him and helped Antonio place the rest of the balls in the rack, "Let me tell you all a story," I looked around at the boys, making sure I had their attention, "I have been playing pool for as long as I can remember. My dad was in a bowling league, which his team was really good, but that's beside the point. So after watchin' that, we'd all play some pool in the back. I got so good, I'd make grown men cry. Anyways, in my second year of college, word got around as word does. My English professor found out about this skill of mine."

The pool table was set, but Connor was just hanging onto his stick, listening to my story as everyone else was.

"I had a D in that class and was pretty close to a C, but wasn't close enough that he'd round it up. And, to be honest, I was only at a D because I had some friends write certain things for me, if not

I would've surely failed. Not important. So, I made a bet. I win, I get a C. I lose, not only would I get a D, but I'd dress as a bumble bee for an entire day, going to his classes and stressin' how much I loved English."

Many of the guys started laughing, "What?" Someone asked at the ridiculous nature of the bet I had made. It was crazy, especially back when I had made it.

"So there was no way he could pass that up, right? Long story short, we ended up playin' three games, I won three games and I passed English with a C. Beautiful time for me. It really was." I thought back to the cake I bought for myself to celebrate, "So Connor all I gotta say is, good luck." I winked at him.

He rolled up his sleeves, showing off his veiny forearms, and got into position. In a swift motion, the cue ball struck all the other balls with such a great force, it sent three balls into pockets straight away. Two solids, one stripe. He looked up at me with a smirk on his face. He shrugged his shoulders and grabbed his beer to take another swig.

Well shit.

I was lying in my hotel bed, tossing and turning around in anger. That scumbag actually freaking won. Apparently Connor had skills beyond his knowledge on stupid cars. That seemed so out of character for him to be good at anything cool. He never cared about things. Just his work things.

I sighed.

I should've kept my big mouth shut. I spoke so much shit, I was basically asking to get my ass beat. It always came down to humility.

Screw his friends too. I was certain that they all actually knew he was super good. That was why they encouraged him to go against me in the first place. They all cheered and got more drinks to celebrate. I was too proud a person to give Connor any credit. He even tried to shake my hand, the bastard. Maybe I would have too, if he wasn't flashing me his stupid teeth in his own excitement for himself. I didn't speak to him at all for the rest of the night. I only really talked to Antonio which was more than enough to keep me occupied anyways.

My phone buzzed. It was Samantha. Due to a change in plans, we will not be meeting early in the morning to debrief. Please be in the lobby of the hotel by 10:20am so that we can make it to the plane on time. Thank you.

Thank the Lord for that. I was not about to get up at dumb early o'clock, to talk about things that could've been talked about on the plane, or back in Miami, or never for that matter.

Then my mind went back to losing pool.

I would never get over that unless I had a fair rematch and won. Screw Connor Meyers.

Chapter Fifteen

Chapter 15- She's Completely Crazy (Connor's Perspective)

I was currently feeling stressed internally as I smiled and mingled with men externally. As per usual in more recent years during the summer months, my father hosted quite a few early dinner parties at his place. Jonathan had added on an entertainment space in his backyard that included a bar, a pool, a few cabanas and a grill he was extremely fond of. Although most months were fairly hot in Florida, meaning there was usually good enough weather to host these, the summer months were probably some of the slowest months for us at the office, considering that's when all of our newest models were already completely finalized and the main concern was sales.

Of course, sales indeed were very important, but once we'd crafted a great automobile and gave the stamp of approval to the marketing team, it was then up to the people to buy the product.

This slowdown during the summer was the main reason why this was the time I was focusing on my pitch for Japan. Which was the exact reason I was feeling stressed. With Greyson having set me back, I definitely wasn't paying enough attention to what I needed to do. Although I generally didn't mind coming to Jonathan's dinners, I truly had more important things I wanted to spend my time on.

"Oh yes, of course," I had smiled to the man I was speaking to. Anderson. He was someone I had now known for a long while, yet never completely trusted.

Thinking about how Greyson had set me back, it should be mentioned that after our trip to Spain, I was pleasantly surprised to find that we were finally starting to come to equal grounds. She seemed to be more understanding of my need for space and silence while I worked, and she would do her work elsewhere when she couldn't stay quiet any longer.

Greyson was also actually doing work. It was probably incredibly messed up on my end, but I had given her some files from a few years back to look at and mess around with. So far she had done every single one of them wrong. I could tell that after a few she was starting to give up on them. Even still, she would never ask for help, so I let her be.

With how much less of a pain she was being, I also tried to be more understanding toward her. I started to give her some time to talk about whatever she wanted, something she enjoyed way too much of, and I'd occasionally get lunch with her. I really disliked it, since I usually sat down with Sam and got updates from her and the rundown of my schedule, but I figured I could spare a few times out of my week.

Peter had come now, wearing pink dress shorts paired with a white button up and white loafers. It was very like him to do a pairing like this. "Hello Mr. Anderson," He extended his arm to shake his hand, now standing between us, "Connor," He turned toward me to shake my hand with a firm grip as well.

Although we had never spoken about the incident between us, we were currently on good terms. I assumed that he, like myself, had decided to just drop the matter altogether. This was the best thing that could have happened in my opinion.

It was still early on in the party, so not many people were around. I was still on my first bottle of beer, not in any rush, knowing that Adam would soon show up with some drink that would have an unnecessarily high alcohol content.

About an hour later, the party was in full effect. People were sitting under the cabanas, others were in the pool, and it all seemed laid back and relaxed. My mind was still racing, so I was texting Sam every once in a while to have her see to some of my business.

"I don't even think you realize how much you getting this deal and then becoming the CEO will suck, Connor," Adam was saying, clearly a bit intoxicated already. He was still the same Adam I met in college. Loved to drink and party, yet still so smart that he maintained an almost perfect GPA. Or in this case, out of college, smart enough to do his job well.

"Why does it suck?" I smiled, not actually expecting him to say something like that.

"We'll never see each other anymore." He pouted, and some of the men from my floor started laughing.

"Speaking of that, how many of us are you going to give the boot when you become mister big man?" Charlie, one of my employees, asked.

I laughed at that too. In their mind, there was no debate on whether or not I'd get Japan, only, what would happen when I did.

"All the men I've hired myself are some of the best men in this company. Hopefully we'll all get raises instead." I responded, receiving some cheering and happy faces.

Charlie raised his glass to that and the rest of us followed, "To Connor. The near future, C...E...O..." Charlie exclaimed, and the men around either applauded or howled like dogs.

Clearly many of them were intoxicated.

At some point, Greyson had come around, going up to Peter to give him a hug.

I still didn't particularly enjoy whatever that situation was.

"Sorry I'm late, hi Connor," She smiled at me, and I nodded at her, "My car broke down this morning because that's just my luck. My roommate has been out of town visiting his cousins for the past week already, so I had to figure out how to get an Uber on my own, and then when the Uber came I was still getting ready which made me stress out and-" She stopped herself, "Well, I'm here now!" She laughed it off. Waving at the others who mostly waved back. "And

I can't believe I'm in Star Island right now! Like shit, this place is so big! But I'm sure all of y'all are used to this. I'm going to go get food." She skipped off and Peter followed.

I finished my glass and motioned to Adam to pour me more. He easily got up from the chair he was lounging on to grab the bottle.

"Connor, can I steal you for a minute?" A woman I was far too familiar with grabbed onto my arm. I didn't even look at her as Adam finished pouring my drink.

"Sure." I said nonchalantly and once my drink was poured she pulled me in the direction of the next cabana over that didn't have many people occupying it.

Her name was Daisy Knicks. She was the daughter of a friend of Jonathan's, and for years she had been quite determined to marry me. No, not just date me, but actually marry me.

It didn't help that at some point I had involved myself sexually with her, something I wasn't proud of. However, thankfully I made a bigger mistake by having sexual relations with Samantha. Another regret, but Sam being the vicious girl she was, made sure that Daisy would get lost. So basically I had gotten rid of one problem by adding on another. At least the latter had more use to me in terms of business. However, that problem wasn't around, which meant this problem could run rampant.

I'm guessing the terms and conditions were limited to not include social events where Samantha was elsewhere.

"What?" I finally asked, after a moment of just standing with her staring at me. She was a tall woman, yet still quite a few inches shorter than me, with dark brown hair that was cut in a blunt straight line right at the base of her neck. She was fairly thin and her skin was quite pale with pink undertones. Her small eyes were a pale blue color and she kept them focused on my face.

"I just want to know how you're doing. I haven't seen you in a long time I feel." She spoke softly, finally looking directly at me. She was actually four years older than I was, but did not act it at all. I didn't find her to be unattractive, she was actually fairly pretty. But she was obsessed with me and annoying, and frankly, I just couldn't stand talking to her for very long.

"I'm good," I said shortly. I looked away in the direction of the pool. There were more people swimming than I had expected. Some pop song was playing on the speakers, creating background noise while most people stood or sat around and chatted.

My father was still grilling some food with about ten men he knew standing around smoking cigars. Greyson had walked up to them with a plate in her hand already filled with food. She had her famous goofy smile plastered on her face.

"Connor," Daisy sighed and I refocused my attention to her, "Can I just talk to you?" She looked ready to cry, and that really pissed me off.

"Aren't you doing that right now?" I took a large sip of my drink and set that down on the nearby table and reached into the pocket of my khaki shorts to pull out a pack of cigarettes.

She sighed again. "Maybe this isn't the best time, but I want us to grab coffee together soon."

After placing the cigarette into my mouth, I returned the pack to my pocket and replaced it with my lighter. After inhaling the smoke, I held it in for a moment and blew it out of my nose and once again looked at Daisy. "Now's not a good time for that." I sucked in more of the nicotine and then took the cigarette out of my mouth, holding it between my index and middle finger.

"I'm asking you to give me about an hour or two of your time. You can't give me that?" She asked, obviously getting more frustrated and I could tell she was now consciously trying to hold back tears. I nearly snapped.

Leaning in, I looked her directly in her tear-filled eyes, "That's exactly what I'm fucking saying."

She looked down, "Why are you so mean to me?" Her voice cracked. She was such a spoiled brat. When she didn't get what she wanted, she'd play the victim until she could guilt-trip a person into giving in. I absolutely despised it.

I tried to smoke some more to calm myself down, but the more I thought about how much I couldn't stand this girl, the angrier I became, "Daisy," I said through gritted teeth, "I-..."

"Hey Connor," Greyson walked up, cutting me off. My focus now moved to her and she frowned in confusion, "You don't look so happy." She observed. Then she saw the cigarette in my hand, "Are you smoking again? No wonder you look all mad, you're messin' up your life with this shit. You know that right? I only say this because I care."

Daisy chimed in then, "Excuse me, we're having a conversation." Both Greyson and I turned then to look at Daisy whose eyes were so red you'd think she found out her mother had passed away.

"Um, I think you could have said that nicer honestly," Greyson responded, looking down at Daisy's feet and then back up to her face again, "Are you high?" Greyson asked her, taking note of her eyes. Daisy opened her mouth, but Greyson interrupted, "Wait, no, I don't actually want to know. Connor. You're why I'm here," her face softened as she refocused herself, "Peter said he has absolutely no intentions to go swimming. Which I thought was a joke since this is a pool party, but most of the other guys were like, agreeing with him! Are you going to be swimming at least?"

"This is a dinner party. There just so happens to also be a pool." I responded.

"Are you saying you aren't going to swim?" She looked completely dejected.

"I'm not going to swim," I told her.

"Well what if I say I'm not going to accept that?" She asked and I almost smiled.

"Connor, can I finish talking to you?" Daisy interjected.

Greyson sighed loudly and rolled her eyes, "Okay, fine, I'll go. This isn't over though Meyers. I expect swimming," Greyson gave me a stern look before turning on her heels and walking off. After about two steps she turned her head back, "And stop smoking, I mean that." She added before rejoining the men who worked on my floor.

I watched her for a moment, amused at how unorthodox she spoke to me.

"Daisy," I said much calmer than I was feeling before, "I don't have any romantic feelings for you. Whatever happened between us is in the past and that's that." I tapped the end of the cigarette against the chair nearest to me, extinguishing it, and after grabbing my drink walked over to place the cigarette into a trashcan. Without turning around, I kept on walking over to the next cabana, completely ignoring the girl behind me.

———

It was now dark out and I was decently drunk. There were some lights on around, keeping the place pretty bright and the volume of the music was raised. My father was playing poker with some of his friends and I couldn't tell where half the people I was originally with had went off to.

I was sitting on this chair telling a story to about six girls who were gathered around me. One of them was sitting on my lap, a blonde girl I was sure I had never met before.

"Connor," Jonathan had called to me from his table, "Do you remember that lousy slogan that intern was trying to have us use for our Fortem car model?" I grabbed the girl on my lap by the waist and slid her over so I could get out of the chair.

"That was a few years ago now. I almost forgot about that," I rubbed my chin, trying to think back to that time. That boy was probably one of our worst interns. He always had some idea he felt was absolutely revolutionary and just needed it to be implemented.

He reminded me of Jackson with his ideas, the only difference was my father wouldn't listen to this kid. Thank goodness. "I can't actually remember what it was."

"It was something ridiculous. Anyways, letting that kid go was not so easy. We needed security to escort him out," My father was saying, and the men laughed, their eyes still trained on the game at hand.

I chuckled too, remembering how the kid had just decided not to move, forcing us to call security. My eyes glanced around to catch Adam talking to Greyson by the edge of the pool. She had a towel wrapped around her, still dripping wet, and he was standing very close to her.

I then looked around for Peter, since he had picked up a habit of being by Greyson's side whenever he could. I couldn't see his pink shorts anywhere.

"Hey Charlie," I asked my employee who was also playing cards with my father's friends.

"What's up?" He looked up at me for a moment, before refocusing his attention to his cards and the moves of the other players.

"Have you seen Peter?" I asked, then looked back to Adam who had his arm around Greyson now, walking her to the far side of the patio.

"Yeah, um, I think he went to the bathroom actually." Charlie set his cards face down and started grabbing poker chips to throw into the mix.

"Thanks." I said absentmindedly as I watched the situation between Greyson and Adam with confusion on my face. I went back to where I had been sitting and sat down. The girls got closer to me again and started talking about something. I couldn't even hear them I was so focused on what was happening between Adam and Greyson.

It gave me a bad feeling in my stomach and I did not like it.

After more talking, Greyson stepped back a bit, and Adam grabbed her by the wrist pulling her in. I tensed up and looked at the house, then back to them.

"Hey Connor, what's up?" One of the girls asked.

I looked over to her, trying to relax a bit. I went to open my mouth to respond, but then I heard Greyson's voice.

I couldn't make out what she was saying, but she was speaking much louder now, poking a finger into Adam's chest. As she turned to walk away, Adam kept his hand wrapped around her wrist, and she tugged it fiercely, making him release her.

Angrily she walked in the direction of the house, but then turned around to grab her clothes that were on a table. I finally stood up, and without saying a word to the girls, followed Greyson in the direction of the house. I looked over at Adam who was still standing at the edge of the patio watching Greyson's retreating figure.

A wave of anger flooded over me. I nearly changed course to go over to Adam and ask him what the hell just happened, but I decided against it.

I finally made it into the house and weaved my way around the people that were talking amongst themselves, looking for any glimpse of curly hair. I found Peter on a couch, drinking while two girls were talking to him.

Ignoring that, I made my way out the front of the house to find Greyson sitting on the ground, fiddling with her phone.

"Greyson?" I questioned, making my presence known.

She turned her head in my direction and smiled, "Oh, hey Connor. Sorry, I don't think I actually said goodbye to anyone. I think I'm gonna go home for the night," She returned to looking at her phone, "Just need to find the Uber's number."

I was now standing directly in front of her. I looked down at her for a moment, considering what to say, "What did Adam say to you?"

She looked up into my eyes, "Oh, nothing really. Don't worry about it." She broke eye contact.

"Greyson, tell me." I crouched down, frustration bubbling within me. I was leaning in a bit too much, a habit of being slightly drunk.

"Nothing." She pressed the call button on her phone and brought it to her ear. Without hesitating, I grabbed the phone from her hand and ended the call.

"I'll call my driver to take you home." I handed her phone back and stood up to grab mine from my pocket.

"Connor, I can get myself home. Don't worry about that." She stood up now, grabbing her shirt from the ground and pulled it over her head. While she picked up her pants and started putting those on, I was already dialing up the driver.

"Pull up to the front." I told him before hanging up.

"Connor..." Her voice trailed off, almost warningly.

"Ms. Lewis."

She groaned in frustration and brought the towel to her hair, ruffling it around.

In no time at all, my driver pulled up in front of us and I walked up to open the door for her.

"Thanks," She said quietly before entering. I scooted in beside her. "You're coming too?" She asked, sounding very unenthusiastic.

"Yes," I replied, offering no explanation. She had a history of disappearing on her own, and as much as I hated to say it, that made me incredibly nervous. To let her take the ride alone meant she could have the driver take her anywhere and I was not trying to raise my blood pressure any higher tonight.

"Fine," She huffed and grabbed her phone. The rest of the ride was spent in silence.

When we pulled up to her apartment complex, I stepped out of the car and held the door open for her to exit.

She left out of the other side of the car.

I tried my hardest to ignore the string of anger that shot through me from that.

Shutting my door slightly harder than I had meant to, I followed her up to her door. Once there, she stuffed her hand into her purse, searching for her keys.

"Are you okay?" I asked, and leaned in a bit too close once again.

"Connor, I'm fine," She found her keys and pulled them out and then looked at me. "Hey, thanks for the ride and checking up on me," She wrapped her arms around my neck and I followed by wrapping my arms around her waist, pulling her into me a bit closer than I meant to. "I'll see you at work tomorrow, okay?" She relaxed her arms around my neck and pulled her face back a bit, but her body stayed close to me since I didn't loosen my grip.

"What did Adam say to you?" She stayed silent so I released my one hand from around her to grab her chin, angling her face upwards so that she'd look at me.

"Don't worry about that, it was nothing." She looked down at my mouth and up to my eyes again. I then looked at her full lips. I could feel her body tense up. I leaned in slightly and she froze, her eyes refocused to my mouth. Our lips were about an inch apart. In the next moment, she dropped her head, looking at the floor, "Goodnight." She said, and this time I completely let go of her and took a step back.

"Goodnight," I turned and walked off without looking back.

———

I was sitting at my desk, sipping on coffee, reviewing notes for a meeting I needed to go to that day. I had a bit of a headache from the night before, oh the joys of growing older.

Speaking of the night before, I didn't even want to think about it. I was so baffled at and annoyed at myself for whatever the hell that was.

Greyson walked into the office, that infamous smile of hers plastered on her face, "Good morning!" She said cheerily. She smiled way too often.

Gripping the handle of my mug tightly, I nodded in her direction, returning to my notes. She quickly got the tone and became fairly quiet.

"I'm going to work elsewhere for now," She said after having sat in her chair for not even a minute.

There was a knock at the door, "Come in," I called and in came Samantha, smiling that wicked smile of hers.

"Good morning, how was the party last night?" She came over to my desk, ignoring Greyson's presence as per usual.

"It was good. Daisy was there though," Sam's smile quickly became replaced with a scowl. She lived for this kind of thing.

"What did she want?" She asked, very interested in whatever was about to leave my mouth. Out of my peripheral, I noticed Greyson walking out.

For the next couple of hours I got a great amount of things done. My meeting went well with the information it presented and in terms of what certain task forces were getting done.

I was currently working on a statement piece that I needed to read for one of the boards I sat on when Greyson came back in.

"Connor, I have to show you what Peter and I have been working on. It's actually so good so far! Like Connor," She dumped her notebooks and laptop on her desk and looked at me wide-eyed, "It's lit." She started opening one notebook when her phone started to buzz. She sighed before answering it and placing it on the desk to continue looking through her stuff.

I stopped what I was doing, thanks to how over the top of presence was.

"Hey Jay," She spoke aloud to her phone, flipping through her notebook.

"Grey," The voice on speakerphone replied, "I got home from my cousins early today and guess what I saw when I got here."

"What?" She got to a particular page in her notebook, and folded the rest of it back.

"Someone ain't taking their meds, huh? Grey, we spoke about this shit, man." She rushed to grab her phone, taking it off speakerphone and placed it to her ear.

"Hey, let's talk about this tonight, okay?" She spoke in a hushed voice and not too long after, hung up.

I became fairly curious.

"What are you taking medicine for?" I asked, bluntly.

She paused, staring intently at the page in her notebook, "It's for ADHD." She nearly whispered.

I nearly snorted, "No wonder you're always so off the wall, you actually have issues." I said without a second thought.

Greyson kept her eyes on that page in her notebook. After what felt like an hour she quickly and quietly placed all of her belongings in her oversized purse and zipped it up, throwing it over her shoulder. She pushed her chair into the desk and abruptly turned to face me, her deep green eyes piercing into mine with a certain heat. She stomped up to me and I straightened myself in my chair.

She slammed her hand down on my desk and gripped the edge of it. She then leaned forward until her face was three inches from mine, looking down at me.

I did not like the inferior position I was in.

"Connor," She poked a finger into my chest, hard.

My eyebrows scrunched together as I tried to read this angry emotion in her face that I had never seen before. It was clear to me that I struck a nerve.

"You can go fuck yourself."

Chapter Sixteen

Chapter 16- He's Despicable (Greyson's Perspective)

I was so angry I was almost seeing red.

"Grey..?" I heard Amanda say and I completely ignored her. I didn't even want to face her and see that knowing look of concern on her face. I had no desire to be comforted, I was so mad I had half a mind to turn back and punch Connor in the face.

Instead I kept going. I pressed the elevator button and nearly sighed in relief when it opened up instantaneously. I clicked the ground button furiously, impatiently waiting as the doors took a lifetime to close. I was annoyed when the elevator made more than one stop on the way down, others deciding to join me.

I really didn't want to replay what had happened in my mind, but my thoughts still drifted to how badly that man had treated me my entire time being here. Every single time I let a bit of my guard down because he was being nicer to me, he had to go on and lash out at me.

He hated me and I knew it all along. I was stupid to think we'd ever truly get along permanently.

He was just waiting for the summer to end so that he'd never have to see me again. We would never talk after this. Why was I even trying? I hated him too and this stupid job.

The elevator finally opened on the ground floor and after everyone ahead of me stepped out, I walked off. I took one look around the lobby, the men in suits and people on their phones while everyone looked so busy with all this car bull. This place was no fun, it wasn't even nice to look at. It was like a prison.

I really hated this place.

I spun around and reached my hand out to stop the elevator from closing. Walking back on, I looked at the buttons. Floor twenty, the top floor. The floor Meyers Senior worked on. I pressed that button and felt a new surge of excitement and anger wash over me as the elevator door closed.

Once I stepped out, I walked over to the receptionist I had only seen a few times since working here. "I want to speak with Mister Meyers," I said boldly.

"Did you have an appointment, Miss Lewis?" She asked very politely, just as she always had. I focused on the really pretty necklace that was around her neck.

"Um, no, but actually this is really important. If he isn't busy, could you see if he'd be able to talk for five minutes?" I spoke much more softly, not trying to take out my anger on her.

"No problem," She smiled at me and picked up the phone.

I looked around at the floor, it was by far my favorite floor of the entire building. It was much brighter and had a bit more color. I always wondered why that was. I looked at the room at the far side, Meyers' office. It was really big. Adrenaline was definitely pumping through my veins as flashes of my wretched partner flashed in my mind.

"Jonathan can see you now," the receptionist told me with a smile. I half smiled back and made the walk over to his office. Without a second thought, I opened up the double doors and came face to face with one of the nicest bosses I'd ever had.

He gave me his kind smile, "Greyson, what do I owe the pleasure?" He stood up as I walked up to stand on the other side of his desk.

I looked at the name tag on his desk, steadying myself before making eye-contact with him. I didn't even bother with sitting down, "Mister Meyers, I want to just thank you again so much for this opportunity you have given me. The pay has been so helpful and I don't deny that it is probably so much more than I deserve. You've been really nice to me and I appreciate that," I broke eye-contact for a moment as his smile faded.

"Greyson..." he started and I spared no time cutting him off.

"I'm here to quit. Or I guess it's more appropriate to say resign. I don't know, I'm not actually giving two weeks' notice, but I know that's usually just there so y'all can find someone to replace me, but this was never a job that even needed two people. And Connor already has the job. Either way, I don't want to be here for two more weeks. I'm going to stop working this very moment, actually."

I opened my mouth to say more, but I let silence take its place feeling a little bit choked up.

Jonathan stepped around his massive table and studied me closely with nothing but concern on his face, "Tell me what happened." The power in his voice as he said that to me reminded me of Connor. Specifically, after Jonathan's party when he was interrogating me about what I was talking about with Adam.

That false niceness he gave me, just to be mean to me again.

"Nothing." That phrase rolled off my tongue as easily as it always had whenever someone asked me for details I didn't feel like sharing. "This is just the right thing to do." I grabbed his hand and shook it, before turning to walk away.

"Greyson," He said a bit more sternly. Without another word I walked out.

There was no expression on my face as I made my way back on the elevator, no expression as I walked through the lobby, I walked passed Alfred, the valet who had taken my keys the first day I walked in.

"Good afternoon Grey," he said to me, kindly.

There was still no expression on my face as I nodded to him and walked off to the employee parking lot. I got in my car, put the key in the ignition and listened as the engine hummed alive. As I grabbed the seatbelt, what happened in Connor's office finally played back in my mind. As I clicked it in place, a teardrop landed on the back of my hand.

I was so upset and angry and mad and frustrated. And I was so sad. Why did he think so little of me? Why did everyone think so little of me? Was I really so unfocused and annoying?

I cried harder as memories of all the things people had said to me flooded my mind. The teacher that told me I would never get anywhere, the friends that stopped inviting me places because they just wanted a peaceful time, how even my best friend would rub her temples sometimes and ask me if I was forgetting my medicine that day and then being sent off to my aunt's place for a week because mom just needed a break from me.

Wiping my face on my blouse, I knew I needed to stop. Thinking about everything was doing nothing, but bringing me further down. What I really needed to do was go home, take a hot shower, nap for a bit and then after some food I could vent about it to Jay.

So I did some deep breathing, and consciously refocused my thoughts to what I'd like to eat later that night and drove myself home.

Once I walked in, I found Jay on the couch, watching the television. "Home early?" he asked, grabbing the remote to turn down the volume.

"I had a really bad day, but I only want to talk about it later, okay?" I responded, and he just nodded before going back to what he was watching. Jay was one of the best people in my life. So understanding and nice. I guess I did know some really good people.

I told myself that I was just being dramatic in the car and ignored that small lingering feeling that most of the people in my life were only staying around because they felt bad for me. The hot water in the shower felt really nice on my skin and I let my mind go through random scenarios involving all the different food I could have for dinner.

Once I was out of the shower, I made my way back to my room and noticed the notification light flickering on my phone. I went to grab it to see I had a missed call and text from Jonathan Meyers. I opened up my messages.

Greyson. I would like to have a conversation about your decision to leave the company promptly. I'm inviting you to dinner tonight. I've attached the location of the restaurant to this message. Call me back to confirm time. JM.

The message came across very demanding and serious. There was no doubt he wasn't exactly excited with me. I never realized how much he and his son had in similarities, especially when they both were unhappy.

After calling him back, I had about an hour to get ready to meet up with him. I really didn't want to go out at all, especially considering how in the shower I had decided I'd order Chinese take-out from my favorite place. The eggrolls would now have to wait. It felt like I owed Jonathan at least this. Not to mention the fact that he wasn't really asking me to talk with him, on the contrary he was telling me that we would talk.

Better now than later, I guess.

At this point I wasn't even surprised at how nice the location was. I probably would have spent more time admiring the interior, but I was really nervous as to how this conversation was about to go with Jonathan. I was sure he was disappointed in me.

I walked up to this man in a really fancy suit. Even knowing that this would be an elegant place, I still felt underdressed wearing the nicest skater dress I owned. "Hi, I'm here to meet Jonathan Meyers," I said, assuming this was the kind of place you needed reservations to eat at.

"Hello Miss Lewis, right this way." He led me through the nice columns and beautiful decorations. I spotted Jonathan and he seemed to see me as well, standing up as we approached.

The waiter pulled a chair out for me and Jonathan waited for me to sit down before he sat down himself.

"I hope you don't mind, but I've ordered for us already," Jonathan said.

"Yeah that's fine." I responded flatly as a weird silence fell over us. I didn't really know what to say, so I just fiddled with a clump of curly hair that fell in front of my face.

"I want to tell you about why I want the Japan merger." He told me and a wave of interest washed over me. I mentally rejoiced that I had reluctantly decided to take a pill before coming out to meet with him. I knew it would help me focus and this was actually a really important thing to pay attention to.

"I never even thought to question this, okay." I replied, and quickly shut up to have him go on.

"I've now known Hitomi Matsumoto for over ten years. He's the man we're trying to work with. My father once told me that it would be a wise decision to one day bring our cars to Asia. He gave me a plethora of reasons, but he never got the chance to pursue it. His legacy involved expanding this company into Europe, which he was successful in doing. Picking up where he left off, I had decided that I would see this company make it into Asia before I ever retire."

There had been a glass of water on the table since before I sat down and so I picked it up and took a sip, already creating a movie of Jonathan's story in my mind.

"After years of research and work, I finally landed on the perfect company to merge with. That company belongs to Mister Matsumoto. The first time I ever presented the idea to him, he easily said no. He said it was too much of a liability with the stature of our company. I felt crushed that he wouldn't even look into my plans, but I would not give up so easily. Meyers Motor Company continued to expand and bring in a healthy profit. I played around with the details of my merger and presented it any number of times over the years I've known Matsumoto. For one reason or another, he kept saying no."

At this point servers came out with our dishes. I was presented with a beautiful pasta dish in this white sauce. I couldn't tell what all was in it, but it sure did smell good. Some of the men placed these small bowls of salad and a soup on the table. Jonathan didn't get a pasta plate like I did. I guessed he was just going to eat the soup and salad. The one server presented a white wine to Jonathan and after he nodded, the man poured it into our glasses.

"Enjoy," The man said and walked off with his crew.

I grabbed one of the two forks on the table, almost certain that given the fifty/fifty chance, I'd still grab the wrong one and went right for the pasta. Before tasting it, I decided to add something to what Jonathan had been saying, "Why are you trying so hard for it?" I asked and let the smooth and buttery pasta hit my mouth.

To think I wanted take-out.

"I'm a stubborn man. A really stubborn man and I'm sure that'll be the death of me." He grabbed the same fork I was using and started on his salad. I knew I picked the wrong fork. I definitely appreciated how he never really judged me.

"This is a really cool story, but why are you sharing it with me all of a sudden?" I asked.

"My entire life has been devoted to this job. I love this company. However, as I grow older and get closer to my retirement, I can't help but reflect back on my life. With my stubborn ways, this job has basically been the entirety of my life. I want to tell you some things." He took a bite of salad and sipped on his wine before giving me all of his attention.

I had basically been shoving the pasta down my throat. I decided to drop my fork and take a sip of my water.

"My ex-wife, Connor's mother, was a free spirit. I really cared for her, but put my work ahead of her. She had no intentions to ever become complacent and all I ever was, was complacent. I screwed up my marriage because I wasn't willing to give her the love she deserved."

"That's really heartbreaking." I said, entirely wrapped up in the story of Jonathan's life.

"It's taken me this many years, but I finally realize the error in my ways. I look at my brother who's only ever lived his life how he wanted to. He never cared for this company, he only took the job I gave him after I begged him to do so. But if you ever sit with him, he'll tell you so many stories from his life, it's mind-blowing to me. I never knew he saw so much, did so much."

I quickly took a mental note to meet up with Jackson and have him tell me these stories.

"Anyways, I have a point I'm trying to get to. It's about Connor," He paused, probably noticing my expression turn more solemn. "He is truly his father's son. He is as stubborn and dedicated to this job as I am. But I don't want him to become sixty and then realize that living so seriously is a mistake. I know you think that giving you this job title doesn't make any sense. And in all honesty, it didn't make sense. As a business move, it was a really stupid thing to do."

I think I sank a bit in my seat.

"But Greyson," I looked back into his brown eyes. I hadn't realized I shifted my focus, "I still think it was one of the best moves I'd ever made. In fact, I know it was a great thing to do. I'll admit, my reasons for hiring you were completely selfish. After Jackson gave the idea, I truly felt that you were the secret to my merger. I still believe that. But I also believed that you, with such a beautiful and wild personality, would help my son find more to life than just work. And whether you've noticed it or not, there has been a shift in him. He's loosened up, even if just a little. And believe it or not, he cares about you."

I snorted. Jonathan was literally going crazy.

"You don't have to believe it. Now, I know he can be good at pushing people's buttons. I'm sure he's really hard to work with and I know he can be stubborn and mean. I don't know what he did to you today that pushed you to the point to quit. However, I'm still going to ask, at least for me, that you sleep on this decision and take a day off to truly think about it."

He grabbed the napkin that was on his lap and dabbed his mouth before standing up. He pushed his chair in and rolled his wrist to check the time on his watch. "Maybe I'm wrong, but I think this job has done some good for you, as well," he looked back at me, placing his hand in his pocket, "I have more work I need to attend to, but please, finish your food. If you want anything more, they'll get it for you so don't worry about cost."

He smiled my favorite smile at me, "Greyson, I want you to have a great night," He turned around and took a step forward, "Oh," He turned back around, "And when you come back, we'll start discussing the first business meeting you'll lead." My eyes lit up and he smirked in response.

I felt as though Jonathan had thrown a lot of information at me and I wasn't really sure how to connect it all, to be honest.

The primary thing my mind was on was that business meeting. That sounded incredibly cool, but did I really want to keep working there?

I finally thought about what Connor had said to me. He told me that I actually had issues. In his mind, I was always just some person with problems. I was a problem.

How could Jonathan even think Connor cared about me? Connor must have talked so nicely about working with me when I wasn't around. If Jonathan saw how it really was, he'd never think that.

I was a problem...

Was that enough for me to quit?

Chapter Seventeen

Chapter 17- She's Simple (Connor's Perspective)

I hated how I felt.

I was feeling absolutely horrible for what I said and I hated it. I didn't like to regret the things I did, but there I sat, wishing I could take it back.

My bad feeling was more of a conglomerate of how the entirety of the day had gone in terms of Greyson. I was mad at myself for the entire situation I had created the night before at my father's house and I had taken it out on her. Then I had to go on and say she had issues for taking medicine and I felt bad about that.

The way she looked at me. I didn't even want to think about it.

I remembered back to when Peter basically called me a monster.

"You have work to do," I said to myself, under my breath. It was never good when I got into these thinking spells. It felt like in more recent months, I had been doing that a lot more often. I usually predominated in ignoring things I didn't want to think about.

I grabbed my phone. I scrolled through unread messages, stopping when I got to the name, Daisy Knicks.

I really need to talk to you soon. It's a time sensitive matter.

She had sent that this morning and I remembered how just seeing her name made me ignore it altogether. However, knowing that I would keep beating myself up for the Greyson thing, despite knowing of the work I had to attend to, this seemed like it could be a decent way to occupy my mind.

Although, on the other hand, it could also create for me unnecessary stress.

Let's grab coffee at the shop near my building in 20 minutes. I texted back, despite that other hand.

Okay. Came her response, almost instantaneously.

I was sitting at the coffee shop, slightly early. Which wasn't surprising considering how it only took about two minutes to walk there. I had my coffee like I always did, two sugar, one cream and a shot of espresso. I took a sip, a knot still in my stomach still present as a constant reminder in some part of my mind about Greyson.

In my defense, I didn't think I said anything too horrible. If she had ADHD, didn't that literally mean she had some issues?

Daisy walked in then and softly smiled as she made eye contact with me. She had on a simple blue sundress and sandals. She made her way over, sitting in the chair across from me. Her icy blue eyes looked at me with a sort of maturity about them that I hardly ever saw in her.

Her very meticulous brown hair was clipped behind her ears and she was still as pale as always, despite the Florida sun.

"Would you like me to order you something," I decided to be nice. Just thinking about how mean I was to the women in my life was really starting to get to me. I thought about how cold I was toward Miss Knicks the night before. Then I ignored that thought.

"Actually, no. I just want to say what I have to say and be done with it." She looked timidly at her purse, before opening it and grabbing a few sheets of paper.

I eyed them a bit, but before I could take a good enough look at them, she set them face down on the table. I took a swig of my coffee, before placing it down and looking in her eyes.

"I know that at Jonathan's house, you thought I was there concerning our relations in the past. That's only partially true," She sat very still, very composed. "Connor, I'm moving out to California."

To say I was shocked was an understatement. From the time I had known Daisy, she was not the type to just get up and go.

"I've met a man. I know that might sound a bit surprising, but he's a really good man and we are planning on starting a relationship. He recently got a promotion which means he'll now need to be in San Diego. So I'm going with him," She stated and her eyes got slightly glassy. "I'm really happy, although a little bit nervous about this new chapter in my life."

"Congratulations," I said, one eyebrow raised. This was all still quite surprising to take in.

"Thanks," She smiled, "I wanted to tell you so I can finally close this chapter with you properly. I know I have been interested in pursuing you for some years now. I'll admit, you denying me was really frustrating. But I've finally come to terms with it. I really moved on," She smiled again and wiped away a tear.

I grabbed my porcelain coffee cup, bringing it to my lips, "When are you leaving?" I thought back to Jonathan's party. I completely read that situation wrong. Not that I could ever guess these news. She herself was aware of how obsessed she was with me.

She honestly tried to marry me for goodness sake.

"Next week," She smiled quickly before her face became serious, "But before I go, I wanted to give you this." She grabbed the papers that were on the table and folded them in half. "I'm not sure that they matter to you at all. However, I felt that it was important that I tie up all my unfinished business. And I think it is important that you know that your assistant, Samantha," She paused for a second, "That woman is a bully."

She handed me the papers and stood up.

"Well Connor, I still hope we can keep in touch." Tears streamed down her face and she wiped them aside and gave me a sad smile before turning around and leaving.

I watched her go. She opened the door of the shop and looked at me once more before disappearing. I tried to let it sink in that I probably wouldn't be seeing her again for some years. That was a really crazy concept to wrap my mind around.

I finally looked at the folded papers in my hand. I probably sat there for no longer than a second, considering what she said to me before unfolding them.

———

I had an absolutely horrible night. I had decided to talk to Daisy in hopes that she'd present enough of a distraction from thinking about what I had said to Greyson.

She did just that and then some.

The papers she handed me were emails sent to her from Samantha over the past couple of months. Almost all of them fell under harassment and three others also contained some blackmail. All of which would be seen as criminal in the eyes of a court.

Now, I always knew Samantha wasn't the nicest of people. However, all of the mean things she thought and said were what I considered, mild levels of harassment. Nothing that a person would sue her about.

In the emails, she made some serious threats to Daisy to ensure I wouldn't hear much from her. I didn't know it went so far.

To add icing on this particular cake, all of it was sent in emails. Which meant there was literal evidence that could be used in court. Which meant that if Daisy was giving me the entirety of their conversation without withholding anything terrible she might have said back, this could've quite seriously become a legal issue. If that didn't sound so bad as it was, let me also add that Samantha added my name in most of the emails, making it seem that I was condoning this behavior.

Now, I didn't think that Daisy would ever bring this to court, but this made me skeptical. Were there any other people Samantha had done something like this to? That thought was almost too much for me to handle.

It came to no surprise that I didn't get much sleep that night. Why did all of this have to happen at such a crucial time before the merger? This was going to screw me over so bad and I wasn't entirely sure what the best route to take in dealing with it was.

I felt betrayed. If it wasn't for the shock factor that was in effect, because, all things considered, a girl as smart as Samantha should know that even if she were to make such threats, that was not something to do via the internet, I would've also been absolutely angry.

I wanted to fire her. I did, but at the same time, hiring a new assistant took time and effort. Not to mention, right now Samantha knew my entire schedule, she knew all of the people I worked with, she was completely up to date with the entirety of the company, my business and my merger. Nobody would be able to pick up so much information in time for the meeting.

Why did this shit have to happen now of all times?

Although I knew I would have to confront Sam about all of this when I saw her, I also had the Greyson situation to think about. It quickly became the less stressful thing on my mind and so I decided to think about just that.

I was standing in line at this bakery near the office. They made fresh goods every morning, so I decided I'd grab one for Greyson. Anyways, I thought to myself, knowing her, she was probably already completely over the situation from yesterday. She'd walk in, late, and ramble on about some small detail that she felt was important enough to be noteworthy.

"How may I help you?" The elderly woman at the register asked me. She smiled up at me and I half smiled back. On the few occasions I'd visit the shop before work, she was always working. I was pretty sure she was the main baker at the shop.

"How about we go with a blueberry muffin," I pulled my wallet out of my pocket, searching for my card.

"Anything else?"

All I had to do was tell Greyson that I recognized how insensitive my comment may have come across. Then I'd hand her a muffin as my apology. Most likely, she'd smile really big and try to hug me, saying something about how she was never all that upset.

"No that'll be all," I swiped my card. My phone vibrated as the woman went over to place a muffin into a small box.

It was Samantha. I'm sure I frowned slightly as I opened up the message, I spoke to Anthony yesterday like you wanted. He said he'll talk to Ian and that he'll email you the papers. Accounting also has those files organized for you, finally. We are really getting everything together for your merger! This is exciting.

How ironic. Things were coming together and falling apart at the same time.

"Here you go," The woman handed me the white box, the smile still on her face. I wondered for a moment if all of the stressors her entire life presented her with could even come close to comparing to the stress I dealt with in a single day.

I had been in the office for two hours.

I had the papers Daisy had given me sitting on my desk, thinking about exactly how I wanted to present it to Samantha. After an hour of considering it and wondering where Samantha was, I remembered that this was the day she generally grabbed my suits to get them dry-cleaned and run other small errands for me in the morning.

My mind was completely frazzled. It was unlike me to forget details like that.

Knowing that getting angry at myself for that would only create unnecessary stress, I knew I needed to get my mind focused on work. So I paced back in forth in front of the huge glass wall, looking down at the people walking while talking on the phone with Anthony.

Sam said she took care of it, but I just wanted to hear the information from him myself. In my mind, that seemed like a good way to not only get my mind on work, but also get me more relaxed with the good news.

I was really going to have to visit the gym soon.

While my foot pivoted to spin me around to pace the other way, my eyes landed on the box with the muffin also sitting on my desk. Greyson being late was nothing new nor surprising. Not being able to make it so early in the morning was the few things I could sympathize with her about.

"Yeah that's great," I was responding to something Anthony was saying. Nothing registering properly.

My office phone rang.

"Okay. Hey, I have another call coming through, so I'll talk to you later, but everything's sounding good. Mhmm, bye." I quickly hung up my cell to answer the phone on my desk, "Yeah." I said flatly.

"Good morning Connor, Mister Meyers senior is here to speak with you," Amanda let out evenly.

"Jonathan?" I sounded nearly baffled.

"Yes," She responded.

What in the world did he need to come down to speak to me about? And why now of all times? "Send him in."

Not a moment later, Jonathan was strolling in my office, looking around the place a bit as he walked up to my desk. I studied him quietly, still not able to think of any reason he'd feel the need to stop by for.

Without saying a word himself, he sat down across from me and looked over at Greyson's desk for a long moment before refocusing his attention on me. He had a decently blank expression on his face as he sat there, watching me.

I took note of his cropped salt and pepper hair, gaining more 'salt' with every time I saw him. He was a tall man, getting slightly shorter the older he got and always stayed in shape with this heftier build to him. With his improved outdoor space, he sported a bit of a tan, his nose more on the red side of the spectrum.

He had more wrinkles being etched into his face also, but he didn't exactly look like he was soon entering his later sixties. He looked more like early fifties to me and as I looked into his eyes, it felt as if I was looking into my own.

"So," I shrugged, "What did you want to tell me?"

"Congratulations," He said flatly, "You did it."

I could feel the vein in my neck pulsing. One of my biggest pet peeves were people who spoke to me without saying their meaning right away. I hated having to guess what it was and I hated all the time it wasted in conversation.

I said nothing for a moment, trying so desperately hard not to become disrespectful as the anger rose within me, "For what?" I asked, simply.

"You did it," He emphasized, pointing a finger in my face. He then pointed over at Greyson's desk. He looked over at it again and then looked at me, "She quit." His arm remained outstretched, his finger pointed right at the space Greyson occupied in my office.

"What?" I spat, none of the details coming together quickly enough in my mind to form a cohesive enough thought about what he was telling me.

"You win," his voice was gruff, "I don't know what you did or how you did it, but Greyson quit yesterday," He relaxed a bit in his chair, composing himself. "She wouldn't tell me what happened, but Connor I'll tell you this. Whatever it was really pissed her off. Tell me, are you proud of yourself?" He stood up and stepped behind the chair, pushing it back in place.

"Greyson quit?" I questioned, mostly to myself, not being able to believe such a thing.

"That's what you wanted, right?" He had his hands resting on the chair as he continued watching me.

He asked if that was what I wanted. It is what I wanted, right? That was the plan I had. If I couldn't fire her, I'd make her miserable enough to quit on her own.

My stomach twisted. I didn't really think it would ever happen.

"Connor, I want to speak to you as your father for a moment," He softened his voice drastically, "You are my son and I've always been proud of you. I've always known that you can accomplish great things. I also know some of your strengths and weaknesses as a leader, hell, I have some of them," He looked down at the chair for a moment, "Only you know what has happened in this office with Greyson the short while she's been here. Tell me something, did the way you treat her reflect the way a CEO handles his business?"

I was dumbstruck. I didn't know what to say. So many things were swirling around in my head. There was a pregnant pause in the air as everything he had said to me was sinking in.

"I know you think your judgement is better than mine. And that may honestly be so, but this..." He shook his head a few times, "Connor you better fix this." He stated definitively and without another word, walked out of my office. There was an unsettling quietness that took its place.

"Greyson quit..." I let the words linger in the air.

Why would she do that? I thought to myself as unwanted memories of how hard I'd been on her over the past month and a half resurfaced.

My gaze rested to the white bakery box on my desk.

"...But I was going to apologize."

Honestly, thank you all so much for how patient you are with my updates! I know I have no set updating time and I hate that I can't guarantee a regular upload schedule with this one.

I was actually not going to post this just yet and possibly play around with it a little bit as I write the next one. However, I don't think I want to touch it too much and I just really wanted you all to get this as soon as possible.

See you all in the next one! <3

Chapter Eighteen

Chapter 18- He's "Mature" (Greyson's Perspective)

The doorbell rang.

I groaned loudly, rolling over in my bed so that my face was in the pillow.

The doorbell rang, again.

With another groan I turned my head to the side, "Jay! The door!" I called out, my voice sounding much huskier than usual. I dropped my face back into my pillow, pulling the blankets up. My body easily got comfortable and my thoughts got fuzzy.

The doorbell rang, again.

"What the fuck!?" I threw the blankets off of me and sat up at the edge of my bed. Wiping the sleep from my eyes, I pulled up my phone to check the time. I nearly cried when I saw that it was still way too early in the morning.

My thoughts finally came to me and I remembered that Jay was probably already at work. I also remembered that I had recently become unemployed. Which meant that this was my day to sleep in until noon, at the earliest, and then spend the rest of the day goofing off and considering if I should go back to work like Jonny had asked me to do.

So who in the world could possibly be disrupting my ever so meticulous schedule for the day?

The doorbell rang again and I was sure the person on the other side of the door had a death wish.

"Coming!" I called out and finally stood up, all too quickly. My head spun. I slid on my slippers slowly and walked over to my dresser. I wiped my eyes one more time and examined myself. My shorts were too short and my tank top too revealing to be answering the door.

I scanned my room and found one of Jayden's black hoodies on the ground. I pulled it over my head and rechecked the mirror. The shorts were still too short, I was now nearly sweating, but the bigger mess was my hair. It really looked like a bird attacked me and I lost. Curls and tangles were abundant.

I shrugged. Whoever was at the door was at fault for coming so unannounced and at such an ungodly hour.

My feet shuffled through the house until I finally got to the front. I undid the lock and pulled the door open, probably much wider than was necessary.

My heart nearly stopped as I took in the person standing three feet in front of me. Out of all the people who could've visited me at my house, he was by far the worst person to do so at that moment and had no business doing so. I had half a mind to shut the door in his face.

And I should have done it too.

He stood there, about my height, with this meticulous black suit, looking like he came straight from the office, his eyes peering into mine. He had a brown paper bag in one hand, his other sat in his pant pocket. There was this slight smirk on his face that seemed to mock me.

"What are you doing here?" I nearly spat.

"I just wanted to have a little chat," He looked me up and down, "Can I come in?"

Hell no! I thought to myself. But that seemed weak and I did not like for him to think he intimidated me in the slightest. So instead I said, "Sure thing," I paused for a moment, "Connor's friend."

"It's Adam," He winked at me as I moved aside to let him through. The moment he stepped foot in my house I could feel him judging everything. He walked over to where the couches were and turned to face me, "I brought you a gift." He extended the bag to me.

Hesitantly I took it from him, opening it up. I pulled out the bottle inside, it was a red wine. A fancy looking red wine to be more specific. Probably not the most specific, but I wasn't too knowledgeable on wines and I couldn't really read all the complicated looking words on it.

"I don't drink," I said flatly, still examining the bottle, "But Jay does so maybe he'll like it. Thanks, I guess." I looked up at him, or Adam was his name, not able to read the expression on his face, "You can sit on either couch, I'll just put this in the kitchen."

As I made my way to the kitchen it felt like there were lasers being shot at the back of my head. I really didn't like having him in my house. But, I was the one who invited him in so I guess I was dealing with a 'me' problem. I was still going to blame him though.

I just placed it on the counter, trying to avoid some dirty plates that really should've been in the sink. Then I remembered just how horribly I looked. He was in a suit and I was in pajamas with my hair a mess and no makeup gracing my face. Oh, he was judging me so hard.

As I made my way back, my hands kind of found their way in my hair, trying to finger-rake through it a bit so that it wasn't such a disaster. It probably didn't do me any good, but I was more optimistic than that.

Adam seemed to have made himself comfortable, sitting with his arms resting over the back of the couch. I sat across from him on my other sofa, the cold plastic covering it making me uncomfortable as my bare thighs came in contact with it.

"So I'll ask again, why are you here?" I started, trying to get the upper hand. I didn't like him from the beginning, but my feelings for him got progressively worse, especially after our encounter at Jonathan's house.

"Right to the point, huh?" He smiled that snakelike smile of his, "I knew I could catch you before you went to work today. It worked out since you have a tendency to show up late," I just glared at him, "Okay, I'll waste no more time then."

It was hard to focus on what he was saying when I was so preoccupied with how much I didn't like him.

"Connor and I have been a little bit stressed about the merger coming up in Japan. Now, I know you don't like things to be sugarcoated, so I won't do that."

He had no idea if I liked my information sugarcoated, he didn't know a damn thing about me. Maybe I liked coats of sugar on whatever people wanted to tell me. Did I look like the kind of girl who didn't like sugar? Or coats for that matter! I could not stand hearing him talk like he knew me!

In all fairness, he was right, I didn't like my information sugarcoated. That was beside the point.

"You being at this job has created some more stress, naturally, since you have a position that's a bit above your qualifications." He stated his words so carefully, like I didn't see the full implications. It was definitely rude, but something else came to mind that made that a secondary thought. He didn't know I quit. Granted, I should've figured that out when he said he was trying to catch me before work, but in my defense I was still waking up.

I smiled a bit. I really did have the upper hand here. Or well, if not the upper hand, at least the element of surprise.

"I just want to know what you plan on doing at this meeting, exactly." His steel blue eyes peered into mine.

"Since we are having a frank conversation, just to be clear, what you actually want to know is how I plan on fuckin' shit up? Right?" I brought my knees up to sit crisscross applesauce, making my own self comfortable.

He chuckled a bit, "Sure." He crossed one of his legs so that his left ankle rested just above his right knee. I was studying him incredibly closely.

I twirled one of my curls as I considered the question. Spiderman, or well, Peter and I had been going over some details of the merger for a few weeks now. He confused me most of the time with what he was talking about, but what I did grasp, I was totally on board with. Anyways, Connor, who was my freaking partner for goodness sake, wasn't doing anything to prepare me, so whatever Peter's plan was, it was at least teaching me things.

The most important thing about Peter's plan was it didn't really require me to do much if things went well, which they should've. I had emphasized to Peter that I honestly didn't want to give Connor more of a reason to hate me by stepping in on this since it was apparently so important to him.

Look how nice I was really trying to be for him and he still hated me.

"I know how important this thing is for Connor. I wouldn't sabotage it just for fun," I said to the snake in front of me.

"What do you think are the possibilities of you skipping out on this meeting? Money is no object."

Oh no.

Oh hell no.

He had me fucked up. He really thought he could just sit there and bribe me? Connor did the same shit to me on my second day of working to get me to quit. What did I look like? Honestly!

"I know you're a dense piece of shit, so let me make this clear to you," I snapped. I was not about to try and be the bigger person here, he was in my home for goodness sake! He had some nerve walking into my place and insulting me, "I. Ain't. A. Hooker." I enunciated every word, "I'm going to be at that meeting, so you can shove your money up your ass. I already told you, I'm not going to say a thing that'll screw your boyfriend over, so you can go fuck off and fuck him." I noticed that my hand was balled into a fist, punching into my other hand with every syllable and that I was leaning forward. I had no idea why I did that.

It reminded me of the times I had gotten into a fight. It always started with arguments that got heated, I would do that punching thing or even start clapping out syllables, which was funny because it kind of seemed like I was in second grade, and then I'd stand real close to the other person, tempting them to punch me with my chin in the air. Hands got thrown not too long after.

I knew the situation at hand would never become a fight, but I also knew that I really should watch my temper before I did anything that could have negative consequences.

We both sat there for a moment, I was regaining my composure while he just looked at me, the smirk still evident on his face. That made composing myself extremely hard to do.

I tried to breathe deeply a few times.

"That temper is truly something," He said.

Oh, I hated him. And I was pretty sure I made it clear just how much I disliked him, but he didn't seem to catch that, oh so evident, hint.

He stood up from the couch, so I immediately stood up also, "Do you remember what I said to you the other night?" He walked up to me, keeping this intense eye-contact. It made me uncomfortable, but I didn't look away. "I wasn't kidding." His breath hit my face, smelling like some minty gum before he backed off. "I'll see you soon, Greyson." He walked off, letting himself out of the house.

I just stood in place, almost as if I was frozen as the memories of Jonathan's party resurfaced in my mind. I cringed just thinking about what he said to me.

I had gotten out of the pool and just wrapped a towel around me when he strolled on up. He was asking me about how I enjoyed my swim and such, obviously drunk.

We made small talk for a few minutes until I stepped back, telling him I was going to check on Peter. He grabbed onto my wrist, pulling me into him. I was sure my face showed my disdain, but he didn't seem to care.

And that's when he told me, "Greyson," His blue eyes seemed darker, "I want you," His breath smelled heavily of the alcohol he'd been drinking, "And I will have you."

My phone rang.

I groaned, "No, please no. Stop." I sleepily said. Adam stopped by super early, so naturally I went back to sleep.

My phone continued ringing.

With another groan I rolled over on my bed to be next to my nightstand. I grabbed my phone and looked at the caller ID, "Just my luck." I frowned.

It was Connor and it was only eleven in the morning. So much for sleeping in on my day off.

It wasn't even a day off. I quit. I was supposed to be free from all the madness. I slid the green call icon over, "Hello," I grumbled, pushing myself to sit up.

"Greyson?" He asked. I rolled my eyes.

"That's who you called," I coughed a bit, trying to wake my voice up for the second time that day.

"You quit?" He asked, sounding kind of concerned. I was completely surprised by the worry in his voice. Although, I couldn't tell for sure if I was hearing him properly. It could've just been my sleep deprivation followed by the fact that I was listening to him over the phone.

It was also kind of annoying to know that he knew I quit. The whole Adam situation made me definitely want to continue working. Or well, I was pretty sure the idea Jonny gave me of leading my own meeting made me pretty excited. Even still, I hadn't considered that I'd still have to face him eventually.

"Yeah," I stood up, walking to my dresser to look at myself.

"Greyson," He sighed.

I waited for him to continue on, but received nothing. Another moment passed and I pulled the phone back to see if he was still on the line, "You there?" I asked.

"I'm sorry," He blurted out, "I'm really sorry for what I said to you and how hard I was on you."

I pulled the phone back once again to look at the caller ID, "Is this Connor?" I asked, not being able to connect the kind apology the person was saying to something Connor would say.

"Yes?" He responded, but it sounded more like a question.

I wasn't sure what to say. I still didn't even like to think about what had happened the day before. "Well, I know you'd rather not have me work there, so like..." I trailed off, not sure where to go with that since again, I was still considering not actually leaving.

It got really quiet for another painfully long moment. "I," he hesitated, "I don't want you to quit."

Immediately I scoffed, "You're joking." I really could not believe what I was hearing. Not for a second.

"I don't really know. I just," He paused again. I don't think I had ever heard him sound like such a mess before, "I don't like what I said to you and I don't like knowing I'm the reason you quit."

I was playing with a comb on my dresser as he spoke to me. I looked up at the reflection of my face to see my jaw hanging open. I really couldn't believe it. "Connor," I spoke slowly, "Are you saying that you don't want me to go?" I asked, really not knowing what to expect.

It was feeling like I was talking to an alternate universe Connor. He was literally the Connor I had always wanted my partner to be. It was all too beautiful a thing to be real life.

"Yeah," He spoke as if he was questioning how foreign he sounded himself.

"Yeah, what?" I decided to push the boundaries of this new, nicer Connor.

Another moment of silence. This conversation was killing me in more ways than one.

"I don't want you to go," He finally said and part of me felt really good, but the other part of me didn't know if I should even trust it.

Did this mean he didn't hate me? If he didn't, which I still wasn't sure about, he was still such an asshole to me. My mind was spinning. There was too much going on this morning.

"Pigs must be flying," Was the only thing I could think to say.

"Listen," His voice was still really serious and I stopped my heavy thinking to hear him out, "What I said about you taking medicine, I truly do feel bad about that. It was an ignorant thing for me to say. If I could make it up to you" He paused, "I would."

"I really don't know what to say. If you feel bad or whatever, then why do you always treat me like shit? It's like, some moments you are super nice to me and then the next you seriously hate me! You always say you want me gone, so why would I believe you actually want me around? I guess you're havin' one of your good person moments, but we both know this ain't gonna last," The thoughts of the day before kept repeating in my mind and I knew I was starting to feel on edge,

"I'm literally giving you what you wanted. Why do you keep trying to confuse me?" My hand pushed into my table and I shook my head in disbelief.

"Let me make it up to you," Was what he responded with.

I was really mad and frustrated. What he said to me really hurt, how he always was to me hurt. I really wanted to hate him forever. However, I knew I wanted to keep working at the car shop. Not for him, but for myself. Being able to work there gave my summer meaning. I was able to be more responsible for myself and act more like an adult. Beyond that I really liked Peter, Amanda, Jackson, and of course Jonathan. Plus, I was making money and people were counting on me. People believed in me.

Part of me didn't even care how Connor felt. Wanting to work there didn't have to do with him. But a bigger part of me really hoped he was being sincere and actually wanted to work with me. Call it my stubborn nature, but I wanted us to get along since the beginning. I was determined to show him I was likable. I knew that I really shouldn't trust his apology. I needed to keep my guard up and just ignore him, but I couldn't do that. It was totally against my nature.

Since we were partners, I would want to work with him. I would want us to be a great team. I thought again about how mean he was and about his apology. Was it worth it?

What was the worst that could happen?

...That was a question I didn't actually want to answer.

"How are you going to make it up to me?"

I could hear him sigh in relief, "I will."

"Do you promise?" I asked.

"Yes."

"You have to say it."

"I promise I'll make it up to you."

I smiled a bit, "So what am I missing at work today?" I tried to lighten the seriousness of the conversation.

"Nothing interesting." I could hear how much more relaxed he sounded. I smiled more.

"Hmm, that doesn't sound fun. How about we skip work today?" I started walking around my room, looking at piles of clothes, wondering what to wear.

"You're already skipping," Came his reply.

"Yeah, but you aren't. I have an idea. My uncle is barbequing today. I wasn't going to go because I had work, but even if I called out sick, I wouldn't have gone 'cause Jay's at work. Let's go to that! My aunt makes really good cornbread. It's sometime in the afternoon so you have time to get ready."

I picked up a tank top and sniffed it.

More silence followed and I was really getting fed up with his slow responses, "Is that a yes?" I asked, raising my eyebrows.

"Fine." He couldn't sound more unexcited.

"Yay!" I cheered anyway, "Go home and get ready and I'll pick you up in like two hours, okay? Bye!" I hung up, tossing my phone on my bed.

I was sure all of this could backfire. I was sure I forgave him too easily. What he said hurt, but I didn't like to feel hurt. I liked being happy instead.

So that's what I decided to be.

I was definitely going to need to take a pill.

"Hello?" Connor answered his phone after the fifth ring. The fifth ring. I was sure it was going to go to voicemail.

"Connor, I'm here! Come on down." I said, impatiently. I arrived at his place about two more hours after I said I would.

It didn't actually take me too long to get ready. It was just still too early. I texted him, telling him that I'd stop by a bit later. Which I'm sure didn't piss him off because it gave him more time to do work or whatever.

"Okay." He replied and hung up without a goodbye.

For some reason, whenever he did that my jaw instantly clenched in annoyance.

I was parked out front of the huge building. It looked so much nicer during the day. It was definitely not a place for just anyone.

Surprisingly it didn't take Connor too long to walk out of the place. He wore long tan pants and a blue patterned button up. I didn't think I had ever seen him in shorts. Always work ready.

He walked up to the open passenger side window and peered inside at me with his mocha brown eyes. "I'm driving." He stated.

"Hello to you too." I responded, "Where do I park then?" I didn't even fight it. He had this weird thing with driving.

He walked over to my side of the car, "I'll park your car," He opened my door, giving me space to step out. He wasn't smiling at all, just kept this expressionless face while looking at me. He seemed nicer on the phone. Instead of walking out I climbed over to the other seat. It was the quicker option.

Then his majesty sat down and shut the door. I just sat there and looked at him, waiting. I wasn't sure what I was waiting for, but I guess I just expected something. Maybe a hug, maybe for him to say, 'Oh Greyson! I'm so glad you're staying!' I don't know, something! He shifted the gear to drive and went off to the building's parking lot. Without a word.

So I continued staring. I couldn't read him at all. It was so frustrating.

He finally parked my car, took the key out and stepped out. He didn't even seem to notice my staring. Why was he always so weird? He parked my car right beside his, his was black, shiny, but nothing too fancy. I had seen the car before, but never took too much note of it. I assumed it was a Meyers' car, but it still wasn't as flashy as you'd think someone who had a car company would own.

We got into his car and he handed me my keys before placing his own in the ignition. Once the car started up he placed both of his hands on the staring wheel and just froze. I had a record going on of me staring at him so that's what I continued to do.

"Greyson," He finally said, and the unexpected sound of his voice made me jump a little in the otherwise silent car, "I really am sorry." He looked at me for a long moment then.

Talk about feeling awkward. I looked him back in the eye and then at my lap. It was one thing hearing him apologize over the phone, but it was an entirely different beast to hear him say it out loud. It was like his apology became real. Not that I thought it was fake before, but once it was said in person, him saying it on the phone completely didn't matter.

From the short moment I looked in his eyes, I could tell he was sincere. I guess that was why he was quiet for so long. I imagined it wasn't that easy for someone as stubborn and proud as him to admit he was wrong. The silence became unbearable and so I did the only thing I knew how.

I hugged him.

"Thank you," I said quietly, getting almost choked up as I said it. To my surprise, he hugged me back. Which, I knew he had done before, but he was drunk the last time he did so willingly. I breathed deeply, feeling entirely too comfortable in his embrace.

I let go and looked at him. He was still expressionless, I sported a lopsided smile. "Well, I'm glad now. I thought for sure you were mad I was trying to make you skip work to go to this, but now I know you aren't! So let's hit the road," I smiled and unlocked my phone trying to go to the GPS. My uncle's house was probably about a half hour away, but I never bothered learning the route. That probably made me a terrible niece.

We had taken off and drove in mostly silence for some time. I had been playing with his radio, but nothing good was on. I gave up eventually on a standard pop station, but then a thought I had earlier resurfaced in my mind.

"Hey, Connor?"

"Yeah?" He kept his eyes trained on the road.

"Don't take this offensively, but why is your car so boring?" I asked and I saw the corner of his mouth lift a little in amusement. The brick statue could actually smile, huh? "Like, I know you are super wealthy. Plus, you literally have a car company. I'm not saying your car isn't nice, it's way nicer than mine, but like," I paused, considering my words, "I don't know, I would have like a Lamborghini or maybe something like a Stingray. Something fun. Or multiple cool cars."

"This isn't the only car I own," He replied, still slightly smiling.

"Oh, how many do you have?" I asked.

He considered this for a moment, "A good amount," he finally said. "I drive this one a lot through the city."

"When do you drive the others? Or more importantly, what kind of others do you have? Or even, where do you keep them?" I rattled off a few more questions, not dropping the subject.

"I have some nice ones," Was all he offered, "Maybe I'll show them to you."

My eyes lit up, "Well now you're going to have to show them to me! Maybe we can do that tomorrow," My mind wandered to what kind of cars Connor Meyers could possibly have. I also wondered what he meant by, "A good amount." To me, two cars was a good amount, but even fifteen cars could be considered a good amount.

"Unless you are still planning on leaving the company, you have work tomorrow." He said. Bummer.

I looked out at the road, seeing some familiar landmarks. We were definitely getting close to my uncle's place.

"I'm glad you decided to come with me to this," I looked over at his profile, his eyes were trained on the road and my GPS I had set up for him, "I mentioned this idea to you, almost certain you wouldn't agree to it, but I'm happily surprised you did!" I smiled brightly at him and then looked out of my side window.

"I had some things I wanted to get off my mind anyways." He said without going into it and I decided not to ask about it.

We finally made it to the house. Connor parked by all the other cars that were already there. I recognized most of them. Every get together was like a family reunion on my dad's side. It always made me happy to know I had a big family.

"Okay, here are some things to know before we walk into the lion's den," I spoke up after he pulled his key out of the ignition, "They might offer you a lot of food, don't feel bad for not taking it. They will even insist, you can still say no," I started thinking about my aunt and how if it were up to her the whole world would be incredibly obese, "Also, my family likes to hug. I know that's not your thing, but I would just let it happen. I don't know how to nicely get you out of that." I chuckled a bit.

Connor was just looking at me, seeming somewhat interested in what I was saying.

"So beyond that, I don't know," I tapped my finger on my chin, thinking hard about anything that may have been a culture shock for the king, "Oh, well also, if you want to leave at any moment, just tell me and we can do that. They do this often, so I won't be mad to leave early once, okay?"

He nodded.

"Great let's go!" I threw open the car door and hopped out crossing my fingers for a decent time. It all seemed like a great idea when it was just an idea. I was having my doubts now being in the situation.

Instead of ringing the doorbell, I just walked in. My uncle never locked his door. He would always insist that he wish someone would try and walk in. He'd then flash us the gun on his waistband, going on about that person having a death wish.

My uncle, like my dad, had gone into military service, wanting to follow in his older brother's footsteps. However, he didn't stay for long, but continued on being a police officer.

"Grey, is that you?" My aunt poked her head out from the kitchen and instantly rushed over, "Hey baby," She smiled widely before pulling me into a death grip of a hug. She gave the best hugs, "How you doin'?" She asked when she pulled back, flashing a gold tooth.

My aunt DeeDee was a short and stocky woman. Or big-boned, as she would say. She was sporting a black bob weave and this bright yellow dress that I considered to be tacky, but that was her entire style. She had this deep and raspy voice, partly due to smoking habits and wore thick gold chains around her neck and arms. I loved this woman.

"Hey auntie, I'm doing well. Um," She looked over at Connor, and that's when I realized that maybe I should have at least told the family I'd be bringing him beforehand, "This is Connor. He's the one I told Uncle Tim I've been working with."

DeeDee wasted no time in smiling and pulling him into a hug. Surprisingly, Connor smiled nicely back and hugged her like he really wanted to. "It's nice to meet you, Connor." DeeDee said, and released him from her constraint.

"It's nice to meet you too," Connor paused and looked at me. I looked confusingly back at him.

"Oh my name is Dejah, but everyone calls me DeeDee or Auntie. Whatever you like, honey." My aunt brushed it off and started walking toward the kitchen.

I was the greatest at introducing people, apparently.

"Grey, everyone's out back, the food's still bein' made." She said and tended to her baking.

"Alright, we'll go say hello." I grabbed Connor's wrist and ignored the people on the couch, going straight to the back. There were too many people to introduce him to and I really didn't want to do it at all.

I walked through the screen door and saw so many faces all at once. There were kids running around the yard and playing in the small inflatable pool. My uncle and a good amount of men were surrounding the grill. Some ladies had formed a circle of white plastic chairs, all talking together. You had somebody's grandmother already drunk dancing to the music that was playing out of the two speakers on either side of the yard. The neighbors on the other side of the metal chain fence were also outside enjoying the weather, the one guy was hovering over the fence, talking to someone on our side. There was a table set up with more guys playing some card game shouting about one thing or another. You even had these awkward preteens hanging around their mothers in the circle. It was mayhem.

It made me instantly happy.

"Alright, let's meet the mothers," I told Connor and walked over to the plastic chair ring, "Hello, hello." I said when we got closer. They all looked up at us.

"Greyson, they said you wasn't comin' today." My aunt Aliyah stood up to give me a hug. Everyone was saying hello and I was trying to hug all those I could from their chairs.

"Yeah, I was able to get out work," I laughed a bit, "And I dragged this one along," I motioned to Connor, "This is Connor, my work partner." Aliyah leaned over someone to give him a hug and everyone else who wasn't trying to get up simply waved from their place. Thank goodness.

"Thanks for having me," Connor said.

"Grey, you workin' with a white boy? What job you got now?" My smile faded, as an old family friend spoke up. These women had no filter ever.

"She got a job at a dealership. She sellin' cars now," Someone else spoke up. I sighed internally. It's like you tell someone a story, they hear one part of it, then make up the rest in their minds. That's what made them so good at gossip.

Mostly everyone else nodded in understanding.

"I thought you was workin' for a mechanic?" A different person said now, and I was already rolling my eyes.

"No, you're all wrong. I'm working for Meyers Cars. Like the actual car brand. This is the owner's son. His last name is literally Meyers. I do a really important job and I'm makin' big money right now." I tried to explain as simply as I could while also making myself seem really important.

"You said what now?" Aliyah had asked and looked directly at Connor, "You're Meyers?" She asked in disbelief, "Grey you brought a celebrity." All the women laughed now and the ones closest to him strained their necks to get a good look at him, "Honey, I don't know if you seen my car out front, but she has some years on her. If you want to hook me up with a new car, I'm not picky." My aunt had said to him and I groaned.

"Listen baby, your newest model is absolutely beautiful. If y'all can spare to lose one, I have no problem taking it off your hands."

"I want a red one!"

Connor was smiling like he was actually enjoying the madness. I was drowning in regret from telling them who he was, "We're gonna go say hi to the men!" I cut them all off and dragged Connor away. "I'm so sorry about that," I whispered to him as we got closer to the grill.

"They were fine," He simply said, still smiling a bit.

"Hey Uncle Tim," I snuck up behind him and laughed when he jumped slightly.

"There she is," He chuckled this deep, hearty laugh and pulled me into an embrace that matched his wife's. At six foot five, he always reminded me of a giant. He had this very sturdy build and worked out daily. He was truly a man to fear. Especially when he was angry. However, seeing him in his kiss-the-cook apron made him look like nothing more than a cuddly bear.

He and my aunt looked like a very odd couple, considering his extreme height and her extreme shortness, but somehow they made it work. His hair was always cropped and he always sported a light goatee. In a way he reminded me of Idris Elba. Very handsome too.

"How's your momma doing?" He asked me, while I went off to hug all the other men around the grill.

"She's alright," I finally answered when I finished the introductions, "Not much has changed." I gave a kind of sad, lopsided grin.

He matched my expression.

"Oh, also," I quickly changed the topic not liking that look since it made him look just like my dad, "This is Connor. He's the one I was telling you I work with."

He smiled at Connor and gave him a handshake. Then Connor proceeded to shake hands with everyone else in the circle.

"He's got a firm grip," My uncle's friend said and laughed.

Then Connor shook the next man's hand and he said, "Yeah, that's a man's grip right there."

I just looked at Connor, still not understanding how he was taking this so well. I was even more surprised at how awkward I was feeling.

I usually didn't care about anything my family said at any moment, but now with Connor around, I wanted them to all just stop talking.

"So the job's going well then?" My uncle went back to messing with burgers on the grill with his tongs. I called my uncle often to talk to him about things going on, but after getting the job, I hadn't updated him much on it.

That was a relief, because if I had told him how much I was struggling with Connor, it would have made bringing him around even worse. At least for me anyways.

"Yeah it is," I responded, "A lot of work, but I'm getting by."

"That's good. How's Jay doing? Why ain't he here?" My uncle started moving some burgers onto a plate off the grill.

"He's working, like always. He says hello though!" I looked eagerly at the burgers being put on the plate. "Please tell me since we're up here we can get food first." I already started to grab a Styrofoam plate from the table near the grill.

My uncle simply winked at me and I took that as a yes. I handed Connor a plate and got to work grabbing a bun.

"Grey!" I could hear my cousin's loud, screechy voice calling from behind me, "How you not gonna say hi to me?" I turned around with a huge smile on my face, watching her approach from the house, "I feel like I haven't seen you in forever."

I placed my plate down to give her a huge hug, "Hey Liz," We let go of each other to take in how we both looked. She was admittedly one of my favorite cousins. She was about my height and just as skinny as

I was. Which meant she understood how it felt to always be told to that we were too skinny and needed to eat more.

She always wore some long wig, this one was wavy and had purple ends that came down to her waist. Her eyes were nearly black, and though she used to own glasses, nowadays she only wore contacts. Her cheekbones were probably one of her most prominent features, she could've easily gotten into modeling. Instead, however, she followed in my footsteps and went to college. She was doing something with photography and movies.

With how smart she was, I was sure she'd get a great career.

She looked beside me at Connor, then back at me and I instantly knew what she was asking. I grabbed my plate and started filling it up, "This is Connor. I work with him." Connor had already grabbed food for himself and was just standing around, being super polite and what not.

"Hi," Liz smiled at him, and grabbed a plate of her own instead of trying to hug him, thank goodness.

Connor just nodded back.

Liz was standing super close to me as she grabbed things off the table, "Girl..." She said, trailing off. My cousin and I had grown up spending a lot of time together. I was an only child and she just had older brothers to deal with so we grew a bond. This meant that we had also mastered the art of being able to understand what the other one was saying, without us having to say a lot.

"I just work with him," I whispered a response. Connor was way too close for her to be talking about him.

"Girl..." She said again. As a translation, I was certain that Liz found him to be decently attractive. Considering I had brought him to a family event, she was certain that this meant I was introducing him as my boyfriend. And if that wasn't the case, then in her mind I should have definitely been trying to make him my boyfriend.

"We're not talking about this," I looked her in the eye.

She sighed, "Fine," She looked up at him and then back at me again, "Please tell me you're coming to Shay's thing. She has a hot tub." We finally had our food and were making our way over to a table near the circle of women.

"Of course I'm going! We all haven't hung out in so long, so you can bet I'll be there."

Liz shifted her plate to one hand to throw her other arm around me and squeeze me quickly, "Good! We'll do more catching up there." Translation, we'd be talking about Connor.

The three of us sat down at the small circular wooden table. I looked at Connor as he sat down, still really surprised at how he was being. I couldn't quite explain what it was though. I was also hoping that Liz wouldn't say anything that was too Liz. She was great at leaving her filter behind.

And I thought I was bad.

"Where are the boys?" I had asked her, realizing I hadn't seen any of my guy cousins in our age group.

"Playing ball," She said and we both rolled our eyes. The guys could play basketball for hours on end without ever being heard from again. "My daddy's with them," She rolled her eyes once again. "Oh, let me show you some pictures I've taken recently." She quickly got up to head into the house.

I grabbed my burger and brought it to my mouth, refocusing my attention to Connor. He had his phone pulled out and was scowling at whatever it was he was looking at.

That's the Connor I knew.

"What's wrong?" I asked, my mouth still full.

"Nothing," He didn't even bother looking up. A moment later he slid his phone into his pocket and finally looked at me. He was still scowling and I had no idea what was going on. "Just, something with work I have to deal with eventually." He picked up the burger and took a bite, looking off at the yard and the kids playing.

"Oh," I decided to drop it, knowing he wouldn't tell me more anyways. "Are you enjoying your time here? We can leave soon if you want." I said, still feeling awkward. He was acting super different, in a good way, but I couldn't tell if it was just him being polite and I really didn't want him to not like my family or something. I wasn't too sure what my deal was, but whatever it was, it was really frustrating me. My head was starting to spin.

"I don't think I want to go back to work today, so we can stay." He responded. I nodded in agreement.

Out of the corner of my eye I saw my uncle walking over, holding three drinks, "Here," He handed Connor a beer that he already opened for him.

"Thank you," Connor clanked it against his beer before taking a sip. He placed it on the table right after.

"Since you don't like alcohol," Uncle Tim handed me a bottle of water. I smiled at him.

"You know me so well."

"So you know some things about cars, huh?" Tim took another sip from his bottle of Heineken.

Connor chuckled, "Yeah, I know a thing or two." He responded modestly. It reminded me of how he tricked me into thinking he wasn't all that good at pool when he really was.

"The boys got a question for you. We tryna settle an argument."

Connor stood up from his chair, grabbing the beer, "Let's see how I can help." He kept a smirk on his face, looking at me for a moment and with a slight nod went with my uncle.

I took two more big bites from my burger when Liz came back with her camera, "Girl he's cute." She said, without missing a beat. "Girl, I don't think of him like that and I don't want him like that. Drop it." I quickly retorted, "Let's see these pictures though."

She paused, looking at me, obviously not satisfied, "Fine," She sighed and did as I said. We went through some of her work, I was completely fascinated with how good they all were.

The opening beat of the song Poison played over the speakers and some of the ladies instantly hollered in excitement. The ones who were completely drunk got up first and easily started dancing. Others joined them and that's how I knew the party officially started.

A few of the guys decided to join the ladies in dancing. My uncle's shoulders were already rocking to the rhythm, and Connor looked so out of place.

"I bet he doesn't dance," Liz said to me. I thought back to when I tried so hard to get him to dance in his office. "Gotta be a white boy." She shook her head, watching him.

That made me frown, "Don't stereotype my friends." I looked her straight in the eye. Race was always a factor for everything and I couldn't stand it. "Let's dance."

A few hours had passed and everyone was going about their business. My male cousins had finally come by and I was catching up with some of them. Connor was still with the guys. They had pulled up a table and were playing dominoes. People were still talking, laughing, and dancing. My auntie finished with her cornbread and Connor let me have his share.

Well, I made him try some of it, but I couldn't resist not taking the rest. There were too many people who wanted some.

I started thinking that I might have left Connor alone for far too long. I looked over at the men, to catch them all looking at me. My uncle laughed and they said more things. Oh, that instantly rubbed me the wrong way. They were obviously talking about me!

I went over suddenly, ready to break it up. "Are the old men behaving?" I asked, directing my question to Connor.

"Old?" Tim's friend, probably the oldest of the group responded, "Babygirl, I'm offended you'd say that. I'm aged to perfection," His eyes closed almost all the way as he said that. Obviously he was drunk, "I'm like a ripe fruit," He laughed and coughed.

"Ripe? More like rotten!" I responded and the other men laughed now, "Come on Connor, before their crazy rubs off on you."

"You're just jealous," Liz's dad said, a cigar nearly falling out of his mouth, "You ain't never gonna know style like ours."

"Amen," Some of the men responded agreeing with him.

"And the young girls still love us," They all laughed some more. I rolled my eyes, dragging Connor away.

When we finally got away from them, I couldn't help, but ask, "What were they saying to you?" I looked slightly upwards at him, and he just held my stare, smirking slightly.

"Nothing," He tried to hide a smile. I knew he was lying and that made me furious.

"Just tell me! Okay?" I didn't like knowing my uncles were talking to him about me and I didn't even know what it was about.

"It really wasn't anything," His face got serious, probably noting how unhappy I was.

"Why can't you just tell me?" I knew I had gotten pissed off. Somewhere deep inside of me, I knew I was overreacting and should have calmed down, but the anger was a more prominent feeling.

In what world does someone find people looking at them, and then going off and laughing, makes a person feel comfortable with ignoring?

"It was nothing, Greyson." That shit was so annoying. Why did he even feel the need to lie?

"I'm ready to go home," I said tightly. I then turned around to walk back to the men playing dominoes to start my goodbyes. "We're leaving," I said, and right away my uncle got up to give me a hug.

"Why you leaving so soon?" He asked as he pulled me into him.

"I've got stuff to do at home," I partially lied. There was always something to be doing. So that was kind of true.

"There's some cookies inside. Make sure you take some. And call me soon." My uncle finalized and I nodded back at him before hugging the rest.

"It's been a pleasure," Connor shook my uncle's hand and did the same to the rest of them.

"Look, you're welcome anytime. Don't forget what I said." Uncle Tim pointed at him and Connor nodded in agreement. My jaw clenched. Without anything more I walked off to say goodbye to the others.

When we got in the car, I hadn't said a word to him. I just stewed in my anger as I brought up my GPS. I handed him my phone and looked out the side window, still ignoring him.

After a few minutes, we were still in the same place and the car wasn't even started. Were we going to just stay there all night? I looked over at Connor in confusion despite myself.

He was looking directly at me, obviously waiting. "They only asked how working with you was going," He said, "I told them it was good, but that you were good at getting yourself into random things. They were laughing in agreement." He broke the eye contact to start the car, "You're pissed for no reason. I told you it was nothing." He shifted the car in reverse and slowly backed out of the space to avoid hitting the cars that were parked so closely all around.

"Since it was nothing, you should've just told me." I was still absolutely pissed. He thought I was overreacting to be mad, but he was being unnecessarily stubborn by not just telling me the bullshit.

"Fair enough," He said calmly instead of arguing back.

He was the most frustrating person in the world! I could never figure him out!

I let silence take over for some time. Then I couldn't take that anymore. "They all seemed to love you." I finally said.

"Your family is nice. Plus, I'm good with people."

I scoffed, "If only you were that good with me."

He turned his head to look at me, but I didn't look back. I just kept my eyes forward on the road.

I shouldn't have said that. But of course, I always had a habit of talking before I thought.

He didn't say anything in response to that, which was probably for the best.

We drove in silence most of the way. I was humming along to songs on the radio.

I looked at the GPS to find we were about ten minutes out when Connor's hand went to the volume knob. He turned it almost all the way down.

I stopped humming and looked at him. I wondered if my humming was bothering him.

He looked at me for a moment before returning his gaze to the road, "Where are your parents, Greyson?" He asked.

Chapter Nineteen

Chapter 19- She's Something (Connor's Perspective)

I was listening to Greyson hum as I drove back to my condo. It didn't seem to matter what song came on the radio, she'd either hum or rock her shoulders to the beat. It made me think about how big her presence was. If a space was silent, she'd find a way to make sure it was known that she was around. She couldn't just blend in, she would rather stand out.

Considering how we hadn't been talking most of the ride, my mind sort of wandered. Something kept rising to the forefront of my consciousness and I could not shake it. While she had introduced me to her uncle, he asked her how her mom was doing.

Greyson did not look too pleased about him bringing her up, and she quickly changed the topic. I took note of that, and it made me think about how I really didn't know much about her or her life. I had only just recently figured out that she had an attention disorder.

My curiosity got the better of me and I reached my hand out to turn the volume down. That quickly got her attention. I looked at her for a moment and she was looking at me inquisitively. I turned to face the road again, "Where are your parents, Greyson?" I asked without a second thought.

There was a long moment of silence that followed.

"Why do you want to know?" She finally asked.

"We were at your family's get together and your parents weren't there." I glanced at her, she was looking at her lap.

"Does it even matter?"

My jaw clenched. She always chose the worst times to be difficult? "If you don't want to tell me, you don't have to." We were finally pulling into the parking space of my house.

She sighed, "Okay well, my dad's dead and my mom lost her mind." Her tone was very stoic and distant.

I really had no words. I never would've imagined that would be her response. I parked the car without saying anything. I wasn't sure what to do. Part of me wanted to pry further, the other part of me wasn't sure if that would be too insensitive.

I turned off the engine, "I'm sorry Greyson..." My voice trailed off.

"Well it's not your fault," She was looking out the window. I watched her without saying anything. She finally turned her head and looked at me with a face vacant of emotion, "Did you want to know what happened?"

Quickly I responded, "I don't want to bring up bad memories for you."

She laughed once, "I've been over it for years now. It doesn't bother me," She tried to dismiss it, but I wasn't buying her attempt to shrug it off as nothing. "So here's what happened. I was ten years old at the time, about to turn eleven in a month. My dad had been a Colonel in the army," Greyson spoke with a weird detachment that made her sound almost monotone.

"He was involved in the military my entire life. I really admired him for it. I was definitely a daddy's girl," She smiled, "So yeah. Then one day when I was ten, a few guys in their uniforms came to the house to deliver the news. They handed my mom his dog tags and a picture he had of us. I eventually stole the tag from her. Well, she had kept it, along with some other of his stuff, in a box and wouldn't kindly give me anything. So one day I just went in and took it. She hadn't even noticed it was missing for months."

I sat there thinking about how inconsiderate I had always been toward her since we've met. I never once made it a note to figure out anything about her. Not even the basics. And now I was learning that she lost a parent at such a young age.

"If I'm to be completely honest, losing him hurt. He was the only one who never saw a problem with me, despite ADHD. To him I was just normal and I liked that. I didn't see him as often as other kids saw their dad, but when I did get to see him, we'd have so much fun. Yeah, that hurt." She just shook her head for a while, agreeing with herself.

She then snorted and smiled at me again, "Enough about that, now I'll tell you about what happened to my mom," Her eyes kind of lit up, confusing me deeply. "To start, I think I should mention somethin'. My mom never really wanted kids. My dad kind of persuaded her to have me, but for her, having me was just something to make my dad happy. She would've also preferred a boy, so I was just nothin' good for her."

"That can't be true." I couldn't help from interjecting. There was no way she could believe her mom was so cold.

"She told me," Greyson looked me in the eye, "Multiple times." She adjusted the air conditioner vent of the car. I hadn't turned it off, considering how hot it was outside. It was blowing in her hair and she moved it to blow down at her lap. "When I think back, I guess she kind of died the same day we found out my dad did. Back then I didn't know what was going on. She just went into a heavy depression. The news destroyed her. In a way she kind of ignored me, and just went into her own spiral of despair," She paused and licked her lips, "Well, I wouldn't say she was horrible to me. Like, I know she kind of tried. She was really great before his death. I think it was how much she changed that really caught me off guard. For about a year, she tried to keep it together, but I guess trying just got too hard. If you ask me, she just lost the will to live without him."

I continued listening, taking in all that she was telling me like a sponge.

"For her sake, it would've been better if she did die. Well she did try. Twice. I caught her overdosing on some of the pills she was taking for depression and stuff. Then when she tried to hang herself is when she was admitted in the hospital." She returned to looking at me, "I wanted to take care of her myself. I don't hate her at all for anything, despite it all. And dad always told me to watch out for her. But she got worse. Ended up with Alzheimer's. I have no idea how she managed that, but she really just let go. And since she wanted me to go to college, I had to let her go. When she was a little better I put her in a home. A lot nicer than a mental hospital. I visit her often though. Hmm," She rubbed a finger back and forth across her bottom lip, "I'm not sure if I'm missing anything. I think that's about it." She gave me another smile.

"Greyon..." I started to say.

"Well, that's my situation, how about you tell me where your mom is?" She quickly interjected. I could tell she wanted to change the subject and since she told me so much, I decided it would only be fair if I complied.

"Okay, well," I tried gathering my thoughts, even though Greyson's story was more prominent in my mind, "Jon and my mother were going through relationship struggles that dated back to before I was born. She wanted him to stop working so much and that was obviously not something he could simply just do. The problems persisted for a few months after I was born and she was finally fed up. She fell in love with a man from her job and moved with him to London, where he was originally from."

Greyson was staring at me intently, her eyebrows were currently furrowed, as if she was appalled by what I was telling her. Although I knew that nothing I had gone through held a flame to what she had.

"My mother and her lover wanted to start a new family of their own and Jonathan wanted someone to take over the legacy of the building. It all worked out that I stayed with him. He was also wealthier, so he was able to afford a nanny and cover my education."

"Wow, how could she be so selfish? That's just terrible," She added and I nearly scoffed. She was looking at me as if my story was the most unfortunate thing she heard could happen to someone.

"Well, eventually when I was in my early teens we spoke on the phone. We also met up once when I was about eighteen so it's not too bad."

"Yeah, but you were still a baby when she left. That's so upsetting."

I could not believe her. "That means I didn't really remember her. It was never too bad. I'm completely fine," I searched her eyes. The green was as radiant as it always was, "But are you?"

"Of course," She blinked a few times, "I always am." She said quietly, more to herself than me. "Thanks again for coming to this with me. I'll see you tomorrow," She smiled and opened the door, pushing it out all the way. She was moving so fast and was already almost out when I grabbed onto her wrist. I tugged slightly causing her to settle back into the seat and look at me.

"Are you really okay?" I knew I was prying too much, but I still had questions about how her life went following her father's death.

"Yes," She smiled in reassurance, "I have to be..." She added on, her eyes fixated on the seat. "If I let myself not be okay, I might end up like her." Her smile faded. She stepped out of the car and I didn't stop her. "Hey, can we not talk about this again? Let's leave it at, what happened in this car, stays here." She hung onto the door, waiting for a reply.

"Okay," I tried to give her a smile.

It seemed to be enough because she matched my expression and went on her way.

Having avoided Sam for an entire day, I knew I would finally have to face her and deal with that situation. There was no easy way out and I had no idea how to go about it. Best case scenario would be if Samantha could give me some really good reason as to why this wasn't true. However, even I knew how irrational that hope was.

"Good morning," Greyson's voice snapped me out of my thoughts. I looked at the time. It was six-thirty-five. This was by far the earliest she had ever walked into the office. I gave her a quizzical look and she smiled, "Yeah, I know. But don't get used to it yet. I'm trying to turn a new leaf."

"Oh yeah?" I asked, still stunned she was basically on time. Especially by her standards. She could've showed up at seven and I would've thought that was on time.

"Plus I have important matters to deal with today. Please, try not to be as interrupting as you usually are." She tried to keep a serious expression, but the corners of her mouth lifted in amusement anyways.

I smiled at that. At least she recognized how bothersome she was. She was wearing jeans and a light blue button up top with the sleeves rolled up to her elbows. Her hair was pulled up into a tight bun.

It wasn't a look she usually sported, but it was probably her most appropriate attire to work. She did look like she was up to some business.

"What do you have going on today?" I questioned, thinking about how she just came back from having quit.

"Jonny didn't tell ya, eh? When he spoke to me the night I quit, he said that if I'd consider staying, he'd let me run my own business meeting. So I've gotta work on that! Can't disappoint the boss." She was pulling out papers and pens from her bag, getting her stuff situated on her desk.

What she told me was news to me. Jon decided to leave that information out when he had spoken with me. I didn't even know he went to talk with her after she completely decided to leave, without giving notice to anyone.

So he was going to try and get her to stay, with or without me talking with her.

"Hmm, you know what. I'm gonna go check out the room I'm going to be leading this meeting in. I'll be back later," She gathered everything she just took out, back into her bag, grabbed the laptop and walked out.

I just shook my head, I couldn't think about that now. I wasn't sure how long she'd be gone, most likely for hours, but now that she was away, it was the best time to deal with the Samantha situation.

I walked over to my attached bedroom. I had a filing cabinet that I had kept in there that I put some documents I wanted to keep locked away overnight. When I gathered the files Daisy had given me I took a quick look at the room. It had felt like ages since I had been there. When I closed the door, I pulled out my phone and texted Samantha to come to the office as soon as she could.

It took her no more than three minutes.

She smiled her devilish smirk, "How are you today? And where were you yesterday? There's so much we have going on!" She sat in a chair across from me and handed me a few papers. I looked over them quickly, it was more of my shit I had her dealing with that she was handling so well. I was stuck between a rock and a hard place.

Without a word I slid Daisy's papers across my desk toward her. She wasted no time in looking over them. It didn't take very long for her expression to turn grim.

She grabbed the papers now and flipped through them. Her face was extremely red. Well, if I wasn't completely certain she had actually sent the emails before, there was now not a doubt in my mind.

"Samantha," I broke her out of her frantic reading, "What the fuck is this shit?" I kept my voice calm and steady, but on the inside I was losing my composure. I had no idea what the fuck to do. I was pissed, I felt betrayed, but firing her wasn't the simple solution. In fact, that would've brought much more problems for me.

She looked at me as though she had never seen the emails before in her life, "Connor..." She shook her head. "I..." She was dumbstruck. How would she know what to say?

"Do you understand how bad this is? You not only threatened her, but you have my name in there as if I condoned this. What if she sues?" I asked, still not sure where to go with this.

I knew Daisy would probably not sue. I knew Daisy didn't think I had anything to do with this. However, there was no denying that this was something I now had to take seriously.

"Connor, she was literally stalking you! I had to do something. I know what this looks like. But if I hadn't gone this far, she wouldn't have left you alone. And she did leave you alone. Isn't that what you wanted?" She pleaded, trying to add reason to a situation that you couldn't reason your way out of.

"Are you fucking with me? Sam, you can't use that as an excuse. I should fire you for this shit!" I threw my chair back and stood up. I paced over to the window, with my hands on my hips. "Fuck!" I yelled loudly, banging my hand on the glass.

A silence filled the space. Samantha didn't say a thing. Good. I paced back over to my desk and saw her face. It was still red and she looked close to tears. Her eyes were fixated on the papers. How could someone so smart do something so fucking stupid?

"Are you firing me?" She spoke so quietly, I barely heard her.

"I don't know Samantha, what should I do?" My voice was loud and harsh, "What would you honestly do in my shoes?" I placed both of my palms on the desk, hovering over it to be looking down at her. She seemed to cower under me.

She didn't offer any answers.

I sighed, moving back and pinching the bridge of my nose. Dealing with terrible situations had to be by far, the best part of my job. It was only better when I had a lot to deal with all at once. Cue the sarcasm.

"Just," I wracked my brain, trying to find the most useful solution, but coming up with nothing, "Get out of my office. Just leave." I walked back over to the window, "I'll figure something out. Go home today." I didn't even turn to face her. I just waited and listened for her to open and close my door.

I then walked over to my desk and plopped down. I held my face in my hands and sighed. Mentally shaking myself out of it, I straightened myself and grabbed the papers, shoving them into my desk and out of sight. I then grabbed my cup of coffee, taking a long gulp. I really needed to figure this situation out.

As I had guessed, Greyson didn't return until about three hours later. She came in with a huge smile on her face. I didn't understand how she always managed to be so cheery. It was like the world didn't affect her.

Before, I would've assumed that she just didn't understand real struggles. But now...

"You have no idea how excited I am about this presentation! I didn't get much done yet, but I did work on my opening slide and I think it's lit." She came over to my desk and placed her laptop down, opening it up.

"It's what?" I asked as she placed her bag on top of my desk, or more exactly, on top of my papers.

"Shush!" She placed a finger up to her lips and started scrolling through her laptop files. She clicked on one that was called, 'The Best Presentation Ever'.

She loaded it up and I could not describe what I witnessed in words. There was a loud sound of, what I was guessing was, an angry bull. On the screen a bull's head popped up and rocked side to side with steam leaving its ears and fire crackling in its eyes. After that finished the title appeared, showing up with a transition effect of the words coming up in a circular old-time news fashion. Her presentation was called, The Running of the Bulls. Not too long after that, her name slid in from the right-hand side.

"Don't you love it?" She looked at me now, smiling viciously. I looked at her blankly.

"What is this?"

"That's my presentation!" Her smile faded.

"Why was it so animated?" I asked, "And we're in a car company. What do bulls have to do with it?"

"Well first of all, why not animation? Second, my presentation can be about anything! I think," She looked off to the side, obviously unsure of herself now.

"Where did you even learn how to make something like that?"

She regained her smile, "I do have some skills Connor! That's what my college major is all about. Graphic design and marketing crap. I can create videos and things. Ain't it cool?" She placed her hands on her hips, lifting her chin in the air.

"Sure, it's interesting. However, it isn't appropriate for this kind of meeting." She went back to frowning.

"This took me so long to do," Now she was full on pouting. "Fine. I can take criticism." She grabbed her laptop and things and went over to her desk. She set her things back up loudly and popped in some earphones. Not too long after that, she was humming along to some song and her focus was completely on her computer.

Even when she was in her own zone she was distracting. I got up then. This was definitely my cue to leave. I had in mind that I needed someone to figure out the Sam situation with. Rather sooner than later anyways.

Once out of my office, I made eye contact with Amanda. "Good morning Mister Meyers," She smiled at me. I smiled and nodded back. I made my way over to Peter's office. He was still one of the wisest people I knew and Adam wasn't going to be around for the day, so it was my smartest option.

"Come in," I heard him say after I knocked. I let myself in to find him furiously typing something up on his computer. His office was slightly disheveled with papers everywhere and a few folders and mail. "Oh, hey Connor. Give me a second." He finally looked up at me for a moment before easily going back to his typing.

I took a seat in the chair across from his desk, still looking at the mess he had going on. In the next moment he finished typing and stood up. I watched as he tried to get himself slightly more organized by creating one pile of all the papers on his desk, he then came to sit in the chair beside the one I had been sitting in, instead of his own chair.

He usually tried to sit beside me when I had stopped by instead of across from me. I supposed out of respect.

"What's up?" He asked, spreading out his legs and getting comfy. He turned his chair to be mostly facing me.

"I have a situation I don't know how to deal with." I started, grabbing his full attention. He scrunched his brows together, ready to listen to whatever I had to say.

I went on and told him the important footnotes of the story. About Daisy giving me the papers, what the emails said, how good Samantha had been doing her work, how I felt like I needed her for the merger. He listened to the whole thing, shaking his head in understanding and without interruption.

"It seems like you're in deep shit boss," He finally said when I was done with my spiel. I couldn't help but laugh. All the stress was taking its toll and I felt like I was going to snap. He laughed along with me.

"Is there a way to go about this that doesn't completely screw me over?"

Peter rubbed his chin. I could tell he was really dedicated in trying to help me out on this. "Well, you said you're pretty sure Daisy doesn't plan on taking this to court, so should you even do anything?"

"Doing nothing will ruin my reputation. And if Sam just so happens to pull this kind of stunt again, there's no denying I'd look like I condone this." I stared down at my black shoes, shaking my head back and forth.

"Samantha has been here the longest out of all your assistants. She does some pretty good work and to be honest, I consider her a pretty decent coworker," Peter started listing, telling me all the things I had already known. "She's also a bit sneaky, manipulative and loves a good rumor."

"What would you do in my shoes Peter?" I finally asked. He had a very sympathetic look on his face.

"Well, luckily I'm not paid enough to make the hard decisions, so you're on your own there." He placed a hand on my shoulder in compassion and I shrugged it off. Of course he'd say something like that. "Connor, you and I both know, that you know, what you should do. What you will do is up to you at the end of the day. I'll support whatever you decide."

I just shook my head in agreement with him. As per usual, he was right. I did know what I was supposed to do. It was all just bad timing.

"On another note," Peter spoke up and I snapped out of my thoughts, "Greyson told me what happened."

This fucking girl.

"I commend you for how you handled it." He said and I smiled lightly at him, although internally I was completely annoyed he brought it up.

He smiled back and I stood up. Following my lead he did the same thing and walked over to be back behind his desk. I placed my hands in my pants pocket and looked at him. "She really likes you, huh?" I said.

"Yeah, we get along." He responded and there seemed to be a slightly awkward silence that fell between us before he started speaking again, "So I have to ask. If you don't plan on getting rid of her, are you going to have her involved in the merger?"

More things I had to deal with. "I haven't given that too much thought just yet." I offered and he shook his head.

"Makes sense. This Samantha thing seems like the thing to deal with first. Alright, well, at some point in time there are some things I want to talk to you about concerning the merger. I've been talking to Greyson about some of it."

I just shook my head, not paying much attention, "Well, I have to get back. Peter," I extended my hand from my pocket, giving him a firm handshake, "As always, thank you." We had completely gotten to a point where our disagreement in the past was just a distant memory.

He smirked, seeming like a giddy child, "My pleasure."

I walked myself to the door of his office, opening it. I paused for a moment. Deep in my mind I knew I shouldn't ask the question that was circling around in my head, but it was really starting to bug me that I did not know.

So despite myself, I turned around. Peter was sitting now, but just looked at me expectantly. "Are you actually dating Greyson?" The words flowed out of my mouth without reserve.

Peter's jaw clenched and I could tell he absolutely hated that I asked. "No." His tone was cold, but fierce.

I didn't say anything or do anything. I just walked out and closed his door gently.

The walk back to my office was fairly short. I took another look at Amanda. She was on the phone and didn't look over to me. Once I opened my door, I frowned at what I saw. In the time I was gone, Greyson had managed to make a mess on her side of the room. There were crumpled pieces of paper all over the floor. She had music playing loudly out of her phone instead of through the earphones. And where was she in all of this? Sitting at the desk.

Oh. But wait.

Not at her desk. No, of course not. She was sitting at mine.

She looked up at me after a moment of not realizing I had walked into the room. Her eyes went wide and she grabbed her laptop and notebook and stood up in surprise.

Which made a vein in my neck pulsate. Did she not expect that I'd walk in at some point? How did that make sense?

I finally walked over and she took a few steps away from my space.

"Connor, I am so sorry. Just let me explain," She spoke and before I could add in my commentary she went on, "You see. I was trying to get in the mindset of working, but there were papers all over my space and my creative juices were just not flowing. I kept hittin' a brick wall so I looked over and saw your chair. I'm not sure you know this, but like, your chair looks super comfy. So I said to myself, maybe if I feel more cushioned that'll relax me enough. So I went over to grab your chair, but then I had another thought."

I really wanted her to just stop talking, but I wanted to try super hard and give her the benefit of the doubt.

"You are always super great at getting work done. No matter what goes down, it's really easy for you to just sit down at your desk and continue on workin'. It made sense that it had something to do with how neat and tidy you keep your desk. So I brought my stuff over and sat down and it really worked! I felt so professional. It was like the energy from your side is just so serious and put together. It's also a little bit grumpy, but that was okay. I just got to work right away and now I am so much further! I guess I lost track of the amount of time I was over here. Sorry." She finalized and scurried back over to her side.

"Instead of sitting at my desk, how about you make your desk more professional and stay there?" I went to my side and sat down. Things weren't as neat as I left them and I rolled my eyes. Ignoring it, I powered on my computer.

Greyson quietly made her way back over to my side. She sat in the chair across from me and slid herself closer to my desk. She then crossed her arms on the table and rested her head in her arms, looking up at my like a sad puppy. "What's wrong?" She asked.

"I just don't see the logic in you invading my space." I said, tightly.

She closed her eyes and shook her head, "No, no. You're not that mad at me. If you were, you'd probably have yelled or cursed or whatever," She looked back up at me, still keeping her head down. "Something is bothering you though."

Since when was she so aware of how others were feeling? "I'm trying to be more patient with you." My jaw clenched. This was not a conversation I wanted to be having and she was easily working her way up on my annoyance scale.

She sighed and picked her head up. "Say whatever you want, but I know the difference between a person who is mad at me or taking other things their pissed about out on me. If you decide you want to talk about it, let me know." She retreated back to her side.

I pondered what she said for a moment. It made me think to our conversation the day before and her situation with her mother. I wondered what kind of things she went through growing up.

I didn't realize I was staring at her until she smiled over at me. "Connor, this is coming out so great!" She laughed and looked back at her laptop. She was always way too excited about little things.

"How does it look?" I asked, thinking about the horrifying bulls head she showed me earlier.

"That, my dear Watson, shall remain a mystery. Are you coming to the meeting? Daddy Meyers said I can do it today." She was still looking at her laptop, clicking constantly.

"But you've just started working on it today. How are you ready to present?"

"Well, it's not a super formal meeting. Plus, I once volunteered at this veterans club. Most of the guys were homeless, it was such a shame," There she went, rambling on about some story. "Anyways, there was this one guy. He had a name like Jimmy, or James. I don't remember. Not important. Every time someone would talk to him, he'd answer them shortly. Like only yes or no. He'd never say a lot." She looked over at me for a moment and turned back, "So one day

I asked him about it. Mind you, the answer was probably the most words I had heard from him, but I liked what he said. He said," she cleared her throat and changed her voice to sound more masculine, "People don't want to spend too much time listenin' to ya. A person asks ya, 'how you doin' today?' But they only wanna hear you say, 'good'. Then you gotta keep on walkin'. So I get my meaning across and say nothing more." She then looked at me once again, "That's some inspiring shit."

I just shook my head at her.

"So I kept my presentation short."

"You're only following that advice to be lazy. You never keep things short." I rebutted, thinking about her story that was as dragged out as a story could be.

She started laughing, "Shush, nobody needs to know that! Let's pretend I'm just following good advice." She shut her laptop close and got up, "Well," She took a breath, "I'm going to go set things up in the meeting room. I think we'll get things started in half an hour if Jonny is available then. You can bring Samantha. I want her to see this."

It was like the universe was forcing me to keep thinking about what I had to do with Samantha.

Greyson made her way to the door and then stopped, "Oh!" She spoke out loudly. "I was going to ask you something and completely forgot. It was about Adam." It felt like my ears perked up at the mention of his name.

I knew something happened at Jonathan's party, but Greyson just wouldn't tell me. It was really bothering me to not know.

Her eyes were fixated on the ground as if she was searching for words. Part of me wanted to ask Adam what was going on, but I knew him long enough to know that he wouldn't say anything. "Actually, never mind. I'll see ya in thirty minutes! It's the smaller meeting room on Jonny's floor. I don't remember the room number, so I might text it to you." And without another word, she walked out.

Of-fucking-course.

After working for some time, I had received the text from Greyson telling me she was about to begin her presentation. I made my way to the room she was in and found her standing at the front of the table, smiling as I walked in. Looking around, Jon gave me a smile and Jackson was sat reading over something on his phone.

The small room was filled with a decent amount of people who Jon worked closely with. They all seemed slightly bored as they fiddled with their laptops or wrote things down on papers. This did not surprise me in the slightest especially considering how unsubstantial I knew this meeting would be to the greater good of the company.

After shaking hands with a few people and giving my hellos to Jon and Jack, I took a seat in one of the few open swivel chairs that was on the opposite side of Jon and made myself comfortable. My attention finally landed on Greyson who took that as a sign to get into action.

"Okay, so thank you all for coming here today," She spoke up and I could tell she was both excited and nervous about the presentation. Her hands were fidgeting with each other, but she smiled brightly and tried to sound as professional as she could. "For those of you who don't know, I am Greyson Lewis, currently working with Connor as CEO, no wait, COO. My bad."

She laughed, the room stayed silent.

"Well, today I'm giving a presentation to show my ability to present. Even though I had no specific guidelines for this, I hope you all learn something anyways." She nodded and went over to shut off the lights. She then went over to her laptop which was sitting on a podium connected to the projector. I looked at the light of the projector, fearing the worse for what would pop up.

She hit a button and the screen went black for a moment before a slow Spanish guitar riff played on the speakers in the room. The screen finally brightened up to a bull walking along a grassy trail. The music picked up as the bull started running slowly and picking up speed really fast until it was out of the shot. The music paused from its crescendo for a moment as the title appeared. It read, "Running with the Bulls –Greyson Lewis."

The music then picked up again and the scene changed to a bullfighter and changed again to an intense scene of the bull versus the fighter. I dropped my head in disbelief. She was showing a video of bullfighting, yet she had called it running with the bulls.

Not to mention the fact that this was unrelated to cars.

Not even to mention the fact that she was showing a video! Usually only those working with the commercials showed videos.

After the intense standoff, the video faded to black and a new slide appeared that only read, "El Toro."

"From our time in Spain," Greyson said, flicking on the lights, "I started thinkin' a lot about bulls. I was in this art gallery and stared at a picture of one for some time. In its eyes I saw power, I saw confidence and I saw elegance." She stared in the eyes of one of Jon's workers, without blinking. "It made me feel a sense of fear that was exhilarating!" She continued speaking as if reading from a book, "I was scared for what it could do, but I felt a sense of respect for the animal. It's a beautiful creature."

She turned to face the screen and hit the button to the next slide. It was a very detailed painting of a bull, head on.

"The running of the bulls in Spain is a tradition that has to do with fear and respect. The same goes for bullfighting. The feeling is mutual for the person and the bull and it is just so intense, but cool!" Greyson threw her hands in the air in excitement.

Classic Greyson Lewis thing to do.

She turned back around to face us, "Anyways, I don't have too much to say that makes a lot of sense, but I do believe that the next car you guys make should be inspired by bulls and this thing about power and respect. That's the kind of car that would sell itself. And it should be called Toro. Thank you for your time." She did a small bow and smiled brightly.

I looked around the room. Jonathan looked like a proud father, Jackson looked like an even prouder uncle.

"That actually sounds like a decent pitch for a car commercial," Some man with glasses said, as he typed away on his computer.

"Right?" Greyson responded.

"My father stood up, signaling for everyone else to stand up. He walked over to Greyson, "Good job." He said sweetly and gave me a curt look that seemed to say, 'didn't I tell you she could do it?'

He walked out and his minions followed. Jackson stayed back a while longer to commend her even more for the presentation.

It really wasn't all that groundbreaking.

We ended up being the only ones left in the room as she packed her things and I waited for everyone to leave so that I could also exit and return to my office.

"Hey," She called at me before I could go, "So, how'd I do?" She stuffed her laptop under her arm and walked up to me.

"The room seemed to enjoy it." I answered back.

"Yeah, yeah, but I want to know what my partner thinks. I know, I didn't give any good facts and it was kind of short. I was nervous and didn't spend a lot of time on it. But it seemed like a good first try. Like, I wasn't even entirely sure about what to do because I've never done a professional meeting. And as you know, the video was a work in progress that I had just done today." She rambled.

I watched her silently as she tried to prove to me that she did as good of a job as she could. I wondered why it mattered so much to her what I thought about it. Then I thought about how negatively I felt as she gave her spiel, while the room was able to see some good in the presentation. Was I unable to give her the benefit of the doubt? Or was everyone being way too nice?

She was still rambling on as my mind refocused to our current conversation.

"It was good for your first meeting." I finally said, slightly surprising myself.

Her eyes lit up. "Okay, cool! Thanks Connor."

"Sure." I responded, raising an eyebrow.

Well, I guess she didn't do too terribly.

I was finally relaxing in bed after what felt like an incredibly long day. I wanted nothing more, but to drift off into sleep, but something I had pushed to the back of my mind was finally resurfacing.

Without me asking it to, the memory flashed in my mind so vividly. I recalled being back at Greyson's family cookout, sitting with her uncles. They were talking about dominoes, and had asked me if I was any good. Once I told them I never played the game, it didn't take them too long to grab a table.

They were all very excited to give me tips and teach me how to play. However, I was sitting next to Tim, the first uncle Greyson introduced me to, so he made sure to stress that he was giving the best advice.

I was actually really enjoying my time. They were all so comfortable with each other, making jokes about one another and just as dramatic as Greyson was. They would slam the dominoes on the table, argue with each other, but laugh all the same. I only played one round and lost horribly according to all of them, so decided to just sit back and watch.

As the game went on, I looked over to Greyson who was standing with a group, smiling as one of them spoke.

"Tim," I finally said, turning my head back around to face them.

"Hmm?" He responded.

"Where are Greyson's parents?" I asked. Considering how much family was in attendance, this question was on my mind for a while. I assumed they'd just come later, but Greyson made no mention of it.

The men became nearly silent at my question.

Tim pursed his lips together and just stared down at his dominoes for a moment. Without looking at me he responded, "When you get the chance, ask Grey about it." The men slowly just got back into the game and that was the end of that.

I wasn't necessarily satisfied with that reply, but I could respect it.

A few more rounds of the game took place and the men were now talking about their wives. Some of the things they said were so bad, but they all laughed anyways.

"Listen, this woman was in the tub," Everyone was trying to stop laughing from the previous story to listen to Eddie's next story. "Her big ass was laying in that goddam tub, like a whale, eating a slice of pizza!" Laughter erupted from the group.

One of them had to stand up and pace in a circle as he laughed. Another guy was banging his fist into the table.

"He said, 'like a whale'." Mikey spoke and coughed up a hearty laugh.

"Man, I couldn't believe it. I said to her, I said, what is your grown ass doing, eatin' pizza in the tub? Guess what the fuck she said to me." Eddie went on and the guys just kept on laughing. "She goes, this is me time. Boy! I just had to walk away! Have you ever heard somethin' so stupid? Who the fuck eats pizza in tub and calls it me time?" I laughed at his story and the way the men were reacting to hearing it.

I looked back over to Greyson and the group of wives who were nearby. If any one of them heard the stories being told, I was sure everyone would get hell for it.

"You can't stop thinkin' about her, huh?" Tim quietly said to me. I raised an eyebrow at him. "You've been looking at her nonstop."

"Greyson?" I asked, confusion evident in my tone by what he was implying.

He smiled at me, "You don't have to tell me."

"I do not like your niece." I said, definitively.

He continued smiling, playing a domino piece down. The guys had finished their fits of laughter and were mostly attuned to our conversation now.

"When I first met my wife, believe it or not, I hated her. She would always act like she was too good for everybody. No matter how much I hated her, I couldn't stop thinking about her. I'm just sayin', whether you are aware or not, you like her."

Mikey whistled at that and the others laughed about it. I just stayed quiet.

"Let me just say," One of the guys whose name I could not remember spoke up, "I don't care whether you're Black, White, Asian, or nothin'. Just don't hurt her. She's been through too much." He gave me a stern look that translated to, I'll kill you if I have to.

"I don't like Greyson romantically. She's also too young." I restated my point while also trying to give them a kind enough reason that would also knock some sense into them, seeing how everyone had now jumped to this conclusion.

"Boy, don't you know that a girl will decide she wants a man, years before a boy will even have the chance to become one! You fine."

"Preach," Mikey laughed. I could tell he was enjoying this the most.

"With how off the walls she is, she's gonna need a man to handle all that!" Laughter erupted after Eddie spoke.

Tim placed his heavy hand on my shoulder, causing me to look at him, "You've got my blessing. Her crazy, is now your crazy." He patted my shoulder a few times and everyone happily nodded in approval.

"Hopefully she won't drive you insane."

Everyone looked over at her for a moment and she looked back. They immediately turned their heads around and laughed about it, trying to get back to the game. I watched as Greyson marched her way over, not looking too pleased about that.

In my room, I was staring at the ceiling in the darkness, the story seeming to repeat itself in my head.

My mind lingered on one place in particular. Whether you are aware or not, you like her.

I had never even dared to think about Greyson in a romantic way. How could I?

Tim had just met me, yet was so sure I liked her.

Most of my thoughts about her were so negative. How could I like her?

Then again, I knew I did care about her. If at least just a little to apologize for the things I said to her. I also cared, more than I liked to admit, about the story of her growing up.

I even cared enough to not want her to leave.

I had thought about hugging her in my car after apologizing to her.

In fact, I thought about every single time we had hugged.

And in the silence of the night, with no one around but myself, I came to a thought I could hardly bare to accept.

Unknowingly, I somehow came to a certain admiration for the person who was causing me the most grief. To put it in words that I swore I'd never say aloud, I liked Greyson.

Chapter Twenty

Chapter 20- He's In For It (Greyson's Perspective)

"Holy shit!" I gasped, flipping through the booklet. "There must be at least over fifty shades of-"

"Grey!" Jay entered my room, cutting me off from my color searching.

"What?" My face scrunched up and I looked at him with attitude written all over my features. It was nothing personal, I just didn't understand why he was barging into my room like he was the police.

"I've been calling you," He walked in and sat on my bed. As he looked down at me I noticed that I was actually laying on the floor on my back, "Whatchu doin'?" He looked at my color catalogue, inquisitively.

"Looking at shades of pink. I have an idea about how to piss off Connor that will be hilarious." I smiled and lifted the magazine toward him so he could see the page of pinks.

"So you good with him now?" He asked. I didn't fully update him on what was going on since we hadn't had a time to hang out in awhile, but I did give him a hint of my anger toward Connor from the past couple of days.

"Yeah, I guess. He apologized for what he said and seemed sincere. I took him to Tim's. That went well. I don't know, I'm just not trying to leave this job right now," I told him and he nodded. "I gave my first, kind of official, presentation this week! Everyone loved it. I spoke about cars and bulls." I laughed.

"Is this job even real?" He asked, shaking his head.

I laughed harder. "Don't be jealous my job is cooler than yours! Yeah, it was good though. I'm proud of myself. What's new with you?"

"Nothing interesting. I'm texting this girl though..." He tried to hide a smile and I flipped over onto my stomach, propping myself onto my elbows so I could look at him right side up.

"Do tell." I smirked, raising an eyebrow. Jay hated sharing a lot about his personal business, unless he was drunk, and the only way I could find out about him was to pry.

"She's cute," He looked up at the ceiling and licked his lips, rubbing his very muscular arm as he thought about her. I could tell he was trying not to smile because he never liked to look vulnerable. But he couldn't hide his true persona with me. He was just a cuddly teddy bear deep down.

"Aw, you really like her!" I smiled. It felt like forever since I was able to just chat with my best friend, and I was enjoying this short moment to the fullest. I didn't realize how much I missed being around him.

"She's alright." He rubbed his chin now, still not making eye contact with me.

"You need to tell me all about this girl! I want to meet her. Plan a dinner for us. I know some good places to grab food from, thanks to this job, but you're going to have to pay," I was already planning his wedding in my mind. My phone lit up with a text message. It was Liz asking if I was ready yet. I bolted upwards, tossing the catalogue to one corner of my room, "I have a hot tub party to go to! Jay, leave! I need to get dressed." It completely slipped my mind.

He stood up slowly, while I was already hopping over to my closet. I was running late. Not that I was surprised, but it didn't make me feel any better about not being on schedule.

"Fine." He easily laughed it off and left.

The people who were going to this were my childhood friends who I didn't get to see often because everyone was so busy. I met Shay many years ago because her dad was in the army with my dad. Both of her parents had a good amount of money, which meant she had a really nice apartment in Miami with a hot tub on a balcony that overlooked the city. By good amount of money, I meant great.

She threw some of the best parties, but every once in a while she'd have a small get together with her different friend groups. My cousin and I highly looked forward to these because we never grew up with hot tubs and nice apartments.

I threw on this simple white bikini I owned and a long, black, slightly see-through maxi dress over it. I grabbed my purse from the side of my bed and ran out of my room.

"Bye Jay, love you!" I called to him, who was sitting on the couch, flipping through the channels. He just waved me off. I rolled my eyes and left.

We had all said our hellos and were finally getting into the hot tub. It was Shay, her boyfriend, Liz, myself and our two other army brat friends, Kyle and Amy.

"Grey, every time we get together you have some crazy story about what's going on in your life. You can never just be like, oh hey, there's nothing new with me." Kyle was saying and everyone was laughing.

I smiled at that, "I'm sorry that I'm such an interesting person and you're boring." I stuck my tongue out at him.

"Me? Boring? I'm in the process of making a successful business in natural juices. I would say I'm doing quite well."

Liz splashed water in his direction, "Yeah, and the last time we got together you was, in the process, of starting up a restaurant." She said, and everyone else laughed.

"You'll see," Kyle said with a smug face. I admired how much he believed in himself. Even if he didn't always accomplish his goals.

"Yeah, but Kyle's right. Greyson. How the hell did you manage to get a job in such a successful car company?" Shay looked at me, honestly intrigued. She had one arm over her boyfriend's shoulder and the other holding a martini.

She was a Caucasian, Cuban mix with such long, light brown hair that curled slightly at the ends. It looked like the type of hair in the conditioner commercials. So healthy. She was shorter than Liz and me, and had more of an athletic build, like those girls who played softball. She also had huge boobs and only wore shirts that showed it off.

Shayla, or Shay as we called her, was a very spoiled girl who cared more about herself than anyone else. Although that sounded like an annoying friend to have, she wasn't so bad to the people she was close with. It was like, she believed that she was at the top and no matter what, none of her friends could match her. With that, she loved giving advice and trying to help her friends because it made her feel like a better person for it. The downside was that she'd expect you to be available to listen to her issues when she wanted to rant. Considering how much of a talker I was, she hardly ever came to me to anyways, so that wasn't even that much of an issue for me. That didn't mean, however, that she didn't expect to be paid back for her service. One way or another she'd guilt trip a person into paying her back.

She wasn't a perfect person, but she was family. And I truly loved her. She was such a great time and never tried to start any issues with me.

"Y'all are going to jinx this for me with your negativity. Talking about my job though," I decided to direct the conversation in a slightly different direction, "I'm super nervous about Japan," Shay nodded her head in understanding, even though tonight was the first she even heard about this potential merger. "I really want to be helpful, but I don't want to piss off Connor. Any advice?"

"Who's Connor?" Amy asked.

I opened my mouth to speak, but was quickly cut off by Liz, "Grey's workin' with the company's most eligible bachelor right now! She brought him as a date to the barbeque." Liz winked mischievously at me and I just rolled my eyes.

I knew she was going to say something about him. Even though it was completely my fault for bringing him up, it still pissed me off.

"Wait, wait, whoa," Shay looked at me closely, "What exactly is your job title?"

I looked around at all the eyes on me. Liz was grinning from ear to ear. I couldn't help, but smile at how cool I was about to sound (I did have my vain moments, I wasn't perfect). "Oh honey, didn't I tell you? I am COO of the company. I work directly with the owners." I was pathetic, true. I tried to play it off as no big deal when everyone's eyes went wide. To think, I didn't even know what those letters meant not too long ago.

"Shut the fuck up," Shay said.

"I truly hate you, Greyson." Kyle spoke up and I laughed.

"She works with the Connor Meyers." Liz unnecessarily added in. It didn't help that she was just about completely drunk. Liz was a lot more excited about my working situation than I was, that was for sure.

"You brought one of the wealthiest men in Miami to your barbeque and didn't think to mention it?" I watched as Shay was actively losing her mind. "Why didn't you bring him here?" She asked and her boyfriend nudged her in the arm.

"Thank God you didn't," Her boyfriend, whose name I honestly just didn't know, said.

"Babe," Shay laughed and kissed him. "I didn't mean it like that! Grey practically knows a celebrity. Wouldn't you want to meet him too?"

"If he has money to spare, I wouldn't mind him helping out my juice business," Kyle, being as shameless as he was, spoke up.

"Yeah, thank goodness I didn't bring him. You're all roaches." I said, playing with the jet below the water. I really didn't want to talk about him. Couldn't we talk about how cool the position I held was? Or anything else honestly.

"Grey could be sleeping with him right now if she wanted to. I can't understand why you ain't." Liz's filter was definitely turned off. Not that she had much of a filter to begin with.

"It really ain't like that." I clenched my jaw, trying to calm myself down.

"Listen, even if you don't like him," Amy started talking, "Sleep with him and tell me how he is in bed." She raised her eyebrows suggestively at me. She was also mostly drunk. "Do it for me." She smiled.

"You're all terrible. Anyways, he basically hates me. So, sorry, couldn't help ya if I wanted to."

Liz scoffed loudly beside me. "Hates you? Girl, that boy loves you." Her screechy voice rang in my ear.

"So Shay, tell me more about what you're currently up to." I ignored Liz, trying desperately to change the subject.

"Wait. Liz. Why do you say that?" Shay spoke, ignoring me. She was my only hope to move past this.

"Let me show y'all this picture I took." Liz stood up and hurriedly stepped out of the tub to retrieve her camera.

I prayed silently to myself that a bolt of lightning would strike me and take me out of this entire situation.

In no more than two seconds, Liz was back with her camera. "Look at this picture I took." She turned the camera to face everyone, and there it was. It was a picture of me, way too excitedly eating cornbread and Connor, standing just a few inches away from me, looking very intently at me, with a smile on his face.

"When the fuck did you take that?" I had no reason to be embarrassed or pissed, but that didn't stop the fact that I was both of those things.

Liz smiled, triumphantly.

"Rich boys don't deserve to be cute." Amy whined.

"Let me look at this," Shay set her glass down outside of the tub and grabbed the camera. "Grey!" She squealed after a moment, "Look at the way he looks at you!" She handed me the camera.

I really didn't want to look at the photo for any longer than I already had. In fact, I wanted the picture to be deleted. Liz was the type to take a joke too far. Especially when it came to boys. We could be walking down the street and someone could say hello to me and she would do whatever she could to make me get his number. She wanted to be a matchmaker so badly, but it was annoying.

I looked at the photo anyways, which was now zoomed in thanks to Shay. My mouth was obviously full in the picture, but I still had a huge smile on my face with my eyes closed. Connor was just watching me, looking amused by it all. I could remember that exact moment too. It was when Connor said I could have the rest of his cornbread.

Amy snatched the camera out of my hands, pulling me out of my thoughts. "All I'm saying is, when it happens..." She looked at me for a moment before returning to the camera, "I'm just a phone call away."

She eagerly handed the camera to Kyle.

I had enough.

"I think I'm ready to go home." I stood up and walked over to the steps of the hot tub.

"Grey, relax." Liz said, rolling her eyes.

Ignoring her, I grabbed a towel and went through the sliding doors, back into the house.

"I was just joking!" I could hear Amy say from the hot tub.

I was entirely aware that I was overreacting, but they pissed me off and I wasn't going to just sit there and take it.

I threw my dress over my head and slid on my sandals when Shay came up behind me. I could tell she was cold, by how she kept her arms crossed under her boobs. She gave me a knowing look. "Shay, thanks for having me. I'm not mad, I just want to go home. We'll get together again soon though." I opened my arms to give her a hug, but she didn't do the same.

"I know we all joke too much, but you usually don't let it get to you. What's up?" She asked, seeming extremely concerned. See? She did have her good moments.

"It's nothing." I responded, automatically.

She put her hands on her hips now, "Lie to me again and I'm never inviting you back here." Her tone was dead serious, and it honestly made nervous. I really liked her hot tub and city view.

I sighed in defeat. Well, they say honesty is the best policy, right? "You guys just don't understand," It just took that statement alone to know that I was going to go into some sort of rant, "Working with this guy has been so stressful. We fight a lot for starters and he treats me like a child."

Shay walked me over to the front of the apartment to be out of earshot of the others. "Go on."

"So, it's like," I blinked my eyes a few time, searching my brain for the right words, "I don't know. He has this annoying ability to get under my skin like no one else can and I hate it. But at the same time, when he's good, it's all great. And I need to work with him, so I want us to actually be partners that work well together." I took a breath.

Shay had her eyebrows scrunched together, really listening to the words I was saying.

"I know y'all are joking, but I can't joke about this guy like that. I can't even see him like that. This job is the first time I'm expected to be professional, so I don't want to get to a point where we are working well together and then Liz is fucking calling me like, So did y'all fuck?" My voice was raising, but at that point, my only concern was getting all of my thoughts out.

"I know I'm hardly ever serious about shit, and I live my life like a fucking joke, but am I not allowed to ever be looked at seriously? I know I'm not good enough for this job, but I'm fucking trying! Why do we even have to talk about him? No one even cares about how serious I'm trying to be!" I stopped myself.

"Honey, you're right," Shay put her hand on my arm. "You deserve to be treated like a capable person and they need to respect when you don't want to joke about something." She finally pulled me into a hug. "I'll talk to them, okay?" She loosened up the hug to look me in the eye, squeezing my arms.

"Sure." I shrugged, focusing on the floor.

"So will you stay?" She asked, and I met her eyes to see her giving me a smile.

I gave her a half smile back, "No, at this point I won't be fun company anyways. I'm even more heated from talking about it!" I laughed it off, "Which is your fault." She laughed too and gave me another hug.

"Drive safe." She finally let go of me and opened the door to let me out.

As I walked to the elevator, I reflected on what I said to her.

I pressed the button to the bottom floor, watching as the doors closed in front of me.

Even though I was nearly shaking from all I said, I was definitely feeling better for letting things out.

I actively avoided my feelings about many things, but as I spoke to Shay, the words seemed to come out of my mouth despite myself.

I truly wanted people to respect me as the adult I was.

The elevator dinged open on the bottom floor.

Oh and one more thing was prominent on my mind. I was tired of King Connor and how important he was to everyone.

For that, I would have to find some way to piss him off.

"Could you send them at-" I stopped speaking to check the time on my phone, "How about noon today?" I brought the phone back to my ear. "Alright, great! I'll see them in the lobby then... Okay, bye!" I hung up the phone with a wicked smile forming on my face.

I could hardly believe I was up and active at nine in the morning on a Sunday. This job was bringing out a side of me I had not known before. Plus, ranting to Shay about Connor brought this newfound motivation to annoy him. I just wanted to piss him off because I knew it would be funny and he deserved it nonetheless.

Now, I knew what I was plotting completely contradicted my other point of wanting to be treated like a capable adult. Even worse, I couldn't find a good enough justification for it, so it would just have to be one of those things that I shrugged off.

Sometimes for the sake of good humor you had to be willing to bend the rules.

I took myself to Home Depot and bought a bunch of cans of my favorite pink paint from the catalogues I looked at. As I placed the cans of paint in my trunk, a mischievous smile formed on my lips. I felt like the Grinch when he had a wonderful, awful idea.

When I got to the building, I was amazed by how little people were there. I knew not as many people worked on the weekend, but I had no idea just how few.

"Here you go." The weekend valet guy came in carrying the rest of my paint. I bought six cans, silently praying that it would be enough.

"Thanks Alfred," I smiled at the man, tossing him my keys.

"My name isn't Alfred," He gave me a confused look. I just shooed him off. I missed the weekday guys. They understood.

As soon as the painters walked into the building, they immediately saw my cans of paint and walked toward me. There were about five guys, without burgers and fries, and I knew this was going to be the best thing I've done since working for Meyers.

They were all dressed in these old, painted up, white overalls, which kind of matched my old, denim overalls and had a bunch of paint-brushes and other painting equipment, "Greyson?" The one in front asked as the group approached me.

"Yep! Hello!" I shook everyone's hands and guided them to the elevator. They all grabbed my paint for me, which was super nice. "Alright," I said, once the elevators closed us in, "So here's the game plan. My partner is a bit of a grump who has the blandest and most boring office ever. Our mission is to spice it up a little bit. Now, I don't want to die early, so I'm not about to go overboard with this little idea of mine. Oh man, I can just imagine his face if I decided to paint his whole office. He would kill me for sure." I stopped my rant as soon as the elevator opened up to the floor.

It was super empty, considering most of Connor's guys also took off for the weekend. It felt like walking into an abandoned space, post-apocalypse. Amanda not being around to greet us made everything feel eerie.

I took the men over to the office and used my special key, that I was entitled to, to open it up. They all flooded into the room, looking around it.

"Okay, so this is not the space we are painting. Follow me." I took them over to the door of Connor's office bedroom. Once inside, I took in the interior of the room. There wasn't much in it, beside the bed and some filing cabinets. There was also a dresser and this portable closet thing that had a few of his suits hanging, with some shoes underneath.

The space was as boring as ever.

"Everything can be moved into the main office space, the bed can just be pushed away from the wall," I spoke with my hands, envisioning how things should be moved. "Any questions?"

One of the men looked at the paint can he was holding and then looked at me, "Yeah, I have a question," I smiled over at him, "Hot pink, huh? How much do you hate this guy?" Everyone chuckled at that and I laughed super obnoxiously. I was very excited about this plan.

"Believe me, he deserves to be as pissed about this as he's gonna be."

It was a few hours later that I decided to buy some coffee and doughnuts for the guys. This project was costing me a bit of money, but luckily the company paid me much more than what I would ever need anyways.

Stepping into the room filled me with both excitement and fear. It looked just as annoying as I had imagined. The pink was so bright that it hurt to look at with the sunlight flooding through the place. The once boring room now looked like a princess's castle, and not in a good way. Connor was going to love it for sure.

"I should've bought matching pink sheets for the bed," I placed the box of coffee I got from Dunkin Donuts on top of the filing cabinet and put the box of doughnuts on the bed.

"Tell us how it goes." One of the guys said, dropping his paintbrush on the tarp they laid out and walked over to grab a doughnut. His fingers, along with his overalls had pink splattered on it.

"Oh I will!" I grabbed a pink frosted one, taking a triumphant bite out of it.

I knew somewhere out in the world, pigs were flying. It was Monday morning and for the first time ever, I was at the office before Connor. I knew it was a bit excessive of me, but I could not predict when he'd see the room. I only knew that I wanted to be around when that happened.

The downside was that all the excitement of the prank had passed and I could only focus on how sleepy I was. The sleepiness was also mixed with crankiness and I wasn't sure if I was in the right mind space to deal with a pissed off Connor. I bought some silly string to spray at him if he decided to be extremely angry. Adding insult to injury was supposed to lighten the mood, right?

I was dozing off, but snapped to attention when I heard the door open. Connor appeared, looking as if he saw a ghost. He lifted his wrist to check the time on his watch and looked at me again. I think he was just as startled as I was.

"Should I even ask?" He said calmly as he made his way to his desk.

"The early bird catches the worm," I responded, still regretting this stupid decision.

"Sure," Came his reply. He definitely wasn't falling for it. He powered on his computer and took some papers out of his briefcase.

"So what do you even do this early?" I finally asked, mostly trying not to fall back asleep.

"Check on some emails. Over the weekend I have a good deal to catch up on. Also, there's always something to do with this merger deal." He actually answered, which really surprised me. I was hoping he'd answer, but I was expecting some type of disinterested response instead.

"Oh, okay." I replied, kind of dumbstruck. I was fully prepared to have to answer sassily.

"What are you up to today?" He asked me, turning his chair to face me. Connor never ceased to catch me off guard. Whenever I thought I had him figured, he'd go off and switch it up on me. He was really giving me his full, undivided attention at work.

The only way I could make sense of it in my mind was by thinking it had to do with how early it was and him not having gotten into full work-mode yet.

"I think I'm going to work with Peter. He's had me working on some things, but with how last week went, I think I'm probably behind on a lot of stuff." Although working with Peter wasn't on the top of my priority list, it had been on my mind that I needed to see him soon and get back on track with him. He was always a much better help at teaching me about the company and believing in my ability to do some assignments.

"Do you like working with him?" Connor was seeming to be really interested in what was going on with me. Wow, was he honestly going to live up to his declaration to be nicer toward me? That was hard for me to wrap my mind around. It just didn't seem possible. His bedroom situation would be the true test to that.

"Peter's a total sweetheart. Working with him has been a lot of help. He's also super funny. He once tripped on nothing while we were walking and, without missing a beat says, I just can't help falling for you. It was so funny I actually choked laughing at it. So yeah, he's been real great." I ranted a bit, remembering the moment and how it was one of the best lines I've ever heard.

Connor just sat there, still facing me.

Before I could think up something else to say there was a small knock at the door and in the next moment, a familiar redhead was walking through, caring a coffee mug.

Every time I had been in the office, Connor already had coffee at his desk. I guess this was one of those things I missed by not being here super early.

Without a word, she placed the mug down on his desk, looking at the floor rather than at him. Odd. "Anything I should be working on?" She nearly whispered.

I blinked a few times, not sure if it was the lack of sleep getting to me or if Samantha was really acting strangely.

"Not right now. I'll let you know." Connor replied. I hadn't noticed, but he was no longer facing me. He was now typing up something on his computer, seeming distracted. Samantha simply nodded and turned around to leave.

The weirdness got to me and I couldn't help, but speak up about it. "Hey!" I called out to Sam, who was already half way to the door. She simply turned around and looked expectantly at me.

No bitchy comment? Something was definitely up.

"Are you alright?" I glanced quickly at Connor now, wanting to see if he'd give some kind of clue. But of course, he ignored us altogether, still typing furiously at his keyboard.

"I am," She gave me a fake smile, and took a step backward, getting ready to turn around and leave.

I knew it was probably a good idea to just drop it and let her go. Something was making her feel uncomfortable. However, who would I be if I didn't pry? "You don't seem okay." I stated matter-of-factly. None of this was my business. But Connor was still acting like he wasn't even in the room and I could not care less if I made Sam uncomfortable. Plus, I was hardly awake so my filter didn't have time to fully activate.

She hesitated for a moment, "Just tired." She said through her very white teeth and walked out before I could say anything else.

There was something quite suspicious about the way she was acting and this easily sparked my interest. I rolled my chair over to Connor, looking at the side of his face as he continued trying to be invisible in his own little typing world. I squinted my eyes, hoping they'd become lasers and burn a hole through his face.

Finally, he sighed and stopped typing altogether, "What?" He asked, pausing for a moment before actually looking at me.

"You can play dumb all you want, but I know somethin' is up with her." I crossed my arms over my chest, looking at him with a raised eyebrow. At that exact moment I decided I was now an investigator and I was determined to figure out what was going on.

He seemed to consider this for a moment, looking at me with the same amount of scrutiny I was giving him. "There is something going on," I perked up in my seat, "But it doesn't concern you." I slumped down again.

"Aw, come on! You can't tell me there's some drama and then not tell me what it is." I whined. I never said I was a professional investigator.

"Drop it, Greyson." He grabbed a paper on his desk and started reading it.

That got under my skin more than it should have. His tone was patronizing, and I absolutely hated being talked to like that.

"Whatever," I rolled my eyes and stood up, pushing my chair back behind my desk and sitting down with a huff.

I looked at my laptop, my email was open, but as per usual, there were no new messages. I had blank pieces of paper around my desk in a messy fashion, some crumpled, some with poorly drawn bulls on them and a few company car booklets I never opened up. I grabbed a pen and spun it around in my fingers. I placed my elbow on my wooden desk and rested my head in my hand.

Coming in early was a mistake.

I let go of the pen to press the home button on my phone. It was still far too early to do anything. It really didn't make sense for me to ever come in as early as Connor. It wasn't like I'd ever have emails or papers to look over.

I crossed my arms together on top of the table and rested my head, facing away from the owner of the office I was occupying. If I could nap for a few hours, I would be able to do something more worthwhile later.

"The situation with Sam is something I honestly can't tell you about." Connor spoke up out of nowhere. I had already nearly forgotten about that situation. I simply turned my head, keeping it resting in my arms. "It's not fully resolved yet." He added on.

"Okay." That was the only response I could think to say.

My phone rang then. I turned my head to look at the caller ID. It was one of the nurses who took care of my mom regularly. I looked at my phone, unmoving as it continued to ring. I spaced out, my mind full of thoughts about the call, but empty at the same time.

I was positive I knew what the nurse was going to say. I didn't want it to linger in the back of my head the entire day, so she would just have to wait until I was ready to call back.

"Any reason you're not picking up your phone?" Connor asked, snapping me out of whatever thoughts I was having.

"It's too early for it."

He looked ready to push the conversation further until his phone rang. Saved by the ringtone.

"Hello?" He picked up, his professional persona springing forward. "Thank goodness." He perked up in his seat, becoming very intent on whomever he was on the phone with.

All I could hear was the muffled voice of the guy he was on the phone with, going on and on about whatever he was talking about.

"That's fucking awesome!" Connor was smiling now, which sparked my interest. Whatever mystery man was saying had such a positive effect on Connor. Not an easy task to accomplish. He was opening the drawers of his desk, quickly shuffling through them, obviously searching for something. "I know I have them somewhere. This is so fucking good though!"

I raised my eyebrow at him. Not that he was looking at me, but I was entirely curious.

"Hold on, I want to find it right now because we need to move forward with this as soon as possible." Connor went back into all of his drawers, flipping through papers even faster now. "Where the fuck..." He said quietly before slamming the last one shut. "You know what, it's been a few months, so I probably put them in my other cabinets. Give me a second." He stood up and started in the direction of his office bedroom.

Shit!

I perked up in my seat, both excited and nervous. Was this really about to happen now? What were the odds he'd go in his room so soon after painting it? My heart was beating so fast. I thought I'd be prepared for his reaction, but I was far from ready.

My mind was racing, I wasn't sure if I should try and stop him from going into it or not. Either way, it was definitely too late because in the next moment the door was being pushed opened and Connor stopped dead in his tracks.

This would have been a good moment to try and run for it, but I was glued to my seat like a deer caught in headlights.

"Let me call you back," Connor slipped his phone into his pocket and turned to look at me. I couldn't tell if his face was red with anger or if it was all of the hot pink reflecting off it. Either way, it appeared that he gathered, from no information at all, I was the person behind the pinkness. He was right, but I didn't like the accusation. Innocent until proven guilty.

"Surprise!" I threw my hands out, smiling meekly. I mentally cringed at my choice of response. The night before I prepped so many better things to say.

"Greyson..." He cut himself off, taking a deep breath and running both of his hands down his face in frustration.

I finally got up. It seemed like just the perfect moment to make everything worse. I couldn't chicken out now, the moment the first dab of paint hit the wall, I told myself to accept how mad this would make him. This was my payback and I was going to enjoy it, even if he killed me.

"I told you forever ago that this office is boring. So I spiced it up for you. At least I didn't touch the main room. Come check it out." I lightly pushed him into the room. He was clenching his jaw, being a pretty decent sport about it, honestly.

Not that he was laughing, but silence was a step forward from yelling.

It was my first time stepping into the pink room since it was painted and it was a lot brighter than I remembered. My eyes were starting to burn.

"You better not complain about this either. It cost me so much money and this is a gift." I stopped pushing him when he was mostly in the room and I stepped around him to hop onto the bed and looked around, admiring my work. I looked at him, who was just staring at me. As a matter of fact, he was staring at me incredulously, but that bit of information was redundant.

I pat the mattress beside me, signaling him to sit down.

He was reluctant, but he finally made his way over and sat down next to me. I watched him as he looked around and then finally laid back to stare at the ceiling. That was the only thing we didn't paint. "You really don't give a shit if you piss me off." He said, but it didn't faze me. I was ready for an argument.

"Payback's a bitch." I retorted, confidently.

"All my life..." His tone was very even, "And you're the only person who's brave enough to constantly challenge me."

My voice got caught in my throat. Whatever that was, I wasn't expecting it.

"You don't even shy away from conflicts," His bright brown eyes pierced into mine with an intensity that caused me to freeze up defensively. "You fight back just as passionately."

I continued staring silently at him. I was completely taken off guard.

He sighed and sat up. With one more look around the room he said, "Tomorrow, this is going to be painted back to normal." He didn't even look at me, he just got up and went over to the filing cabinet. He pulled his keys out of his pocket and unlocked it. He shuffled through it before finding a manila folder that he pulled out and closed the cabinet back up, locking it.

On his way out he paused at the doorway, with his eyes trained to whatever papers were in the folder. "Leave my things alone Greyson." He continued on out without looking back.

What the hell was all that?

Chapter Twenty-One

Chapter 21- She's Troubled (Connor's Perspective)

Having to call up some painters to change the hideous color in my office room was such an unnecessary extra job for me to do.

Saying I was pissed was an understatement.

She could've just bought a stupid pink rug if she wanted to play a prank. That would've required no hassle for me to get rid of.

Having the painters work in the room also sucked because the door needed to be open so they wouldn't be inhaling paint fumes. This was especially annoying because they didn't do their job in silence. Needless to say I didn't get much work done that day. I spent most of it in the gym because at least that meant I was doing something.

Of course, I could've waited until the weekend to get it repainted, but when Greyson specifically asked me to keep it for just a little while longer, I wanted it gone even sooner.

On top of that, I had Sam silently judging the whole situation. She knew better than to speak up, considering her own mess of a situation. Which, don't even get me started on that business. She was only keeping her job because I needed her and that was the only discussion I'd allow on that topic. Still, having her give me very particular glances as the room was being painted was another vein of frustration popping out of my skull.

The cherry on top of this ever so elegant cake was how upset Greyson actually was to have it painted back. I couldn't fathom how in her mind she'd ever think I'd keep it pink. And because she was so mad about it being painted back to a normal color, she protested by spending the rest of the week working with Peter.

Which this news, as you probably guessed, was pushing me even closer over the edge.

It was finally Friday which meant an entire week went by. An entire week of receiving the silent treatment. An entire week of Greyson working elsewhere. An entire week when I finally decided I was going to lose this stubbornness battle.

The office was darker than usual, caused by the rainstorm that had been going on for the last couple of days. It seemed to match the thicker tension between Greyson and I.

Greyson walked into the office, as she did every once in awhile to grab some things from her desk or drop off other things. Every time she did this, she wouldn't even look in my direction, just quickly strut over to her side and shuffle around for a few moments before leaving in the next moment.

A few weeks ago she read a Pinterest article about casual Friday office wardrobe and since then she decided she didn't need to look even remotely professional on Fridays. Today, she sported a frizzy ponytail, white Nike sneakers, black leggings, and an oversized black t-shirt that said 'DIVA' across the chest.

Greyson was the definition of a person with no shame. I had tried arguing that by casual it was supposed to be business casual, but that argument was in vain.

She was shuffling around in her desk for longer than usual. This didn't surprise me as she misplaced things often.

"Greyson," I officially broke the seal of silence.

"No," She responded immediately.

The harshness in her tone got under my skin. It was so hard to be nice to her!

"Are you honestly still mad about me painting back the room you fucked with in the first place?" I retorted just as quickly.

"Yes! I am," She finally turned to face me. This was the first time I was looking into her bright green eyes in days and they were just as intense as they always were, "I paid money for that Connor. I guess I knew somewhere deep down that you wouldn't just keep it pink, but you could've at least apologized for havin' to paint over it! You didn't even let it stay pink for a few days and Amanda never even got to see it." She had her hands on her hips as she scolded me.

How in the world was she trying to guilt trip me for something I was supposed to be angry about? Was I the crazy one for thinking I had more rights to be the one who was upset?

Yet despite the logic, here I was, feeling like an asshole for doing what made sense to do.

I took a deep breath, trying to evaluate what was logic anymore.

"Okay, fine." Greyson spoke up before I could. "I know you're right about this. It just hurt that you painted it back. Not that it should've, but it did. I forgot that because you make so much money, you could repaint it so quickly." She was looking at the floor before lifting her eyes back up to meet mine, "I guess I'm sorry."

That took a turn I did not expect.

Silence filled the space and Greyson took that as her cue to go back to hunting whatever she had been looking for. I looked at an opened file on my monitor I was in the process of filling out. Then I shifted my gaze to the time at the bottom of the screen. It was nearing three in the afternoon.

"Do you still want to see my car collection?" I finally spoke up. Greyson's entire face lit up with excitement.

"Yes!" She nearly squealed closing the drawer she was searching in.

"Alright." I saved and closed out of my document, turning off my computer and gathering my stuff.

"You mean like right now?" She asked, already putting her stuff in her purse.

"Yeah."

"Like, we're going to ditch work?" She asked again, in denial.

"I didn't have much to do today anyways," I grabbed my briefcase and keys.

"Connor, I am shook. This feels unlike you, but I'm absolutely about it!" She gathered the rest of her stuff in a messy pile, shoving it in a drawer and skipped over to me. "I'll accept this as your apology for painting my pink room boring again."

I just rolled my eyes and walked out, Greyson in tow.

"Amanda! If you see Peter, can you tell him I left for the day? Thanks!" Greyson nearly shouted at my receptionist, not stopping for a moment until we reached the elevators.

Amanda nodded, raising an eyebrow in confusion at Greyson, before shifting her focus to me. I could tell she was looking for some answers, but I ignored her, turning back around to face the elevator doors. She was always way too concerned about my business.

It felt like I was riding the elevator with a very tall child. She was quite literally hopping from one foot to the other, bobbing her head side to side as if she was listening to music. It was amazing how easily she could change her mood. Just like giving a crying child some candy. Her moods were contagious, and I couldn't help nearly smiling as I watched her dance around.

"Hey Connor, can we stop at my place really quick? I want to change." She asked as we walked out into the lobby. I exchanged nods with a few people walking around who worked in the building.

"What for?" I asked. If she didn't care how she looked to work, why would she care how to dress to see some cars?

"Well," She stated in a, if-you-must-ask, kind of way, "I'm not sure what kind of cool cars you have, but I definitely want a picture in one to post to Instagram."

I could have chuckled at that. She was shameless. "Fine."

The rain had become a very light drizzle as we left the office. There was still a lot of overcast and I knew it wouldn't be too long before the next wave of rain hit.

I drove behind her to her place and decided to wait outside for a smoke break. I was leaning against the passenger side door, watching as water on the side of the road trickled down into a drain. I looked up at the apartment complex, seeing all the small homes in one building. My eyes landed on a rocking chair, and I remembered that was where, I believe her name was Mrs. B, had been sitting.

I took another puff from the cigarette when my phone buzzed in my pocket.

Are you getting lunch? Samantha was asking. It didn't make sense for me to leave without letting anyone know where I was going, but at this point I didn't care. The only one it truly made sense to tell was Samantha, due to her job directly requiring that she knew what my schedule was, but I really didn't want to have anything to do with her. It probably wasn't the right thing to keep her around, but it was the smart thing to do.

So it didn't actually make sense that I was keeping her around, yet didn't want to talk to her. And I knew I needed to suck it up and follow through with it in an intelligent way. It was just an entirely frustrating situation.

Gone for the day, set up this coming Monday with the meetings we discussed having and check on my email. Thanks. I hit send and slid the phone back into my pocket. I knew when to not let emotions take over my business.

"Connor!" Greyson appeared out of her apartment. Her eyes were opened wide and she looked pissed as she approached my car. I raised an eyebrow inquisitively at her. "Always with this smoking bullshit. How will you feel knowing that if you die, I will be the person completely taking over your job? Isn't that a scary thought? And I don't want to have to do what you do, so please spare us both." She jerked open the passenger door I was leaning on, causing me to stumble forward.

"It's more likely the frustration you make me feel pops a blood vessel in my brain, killing me, than smoking doing that." I slammed the door shut behind her, causing her to jump in her seat.

She was un-fucking-believable.

I took another long drag of the cigarette before dropping it to the ground, crushing it under my foot.

Once I got into my side, I started the car and looked at her outfit. My hand kept still on the gearshift as I looked at her in disbelief.

"What?" She asked, tilting her head to the side with an attitude.

"You're wearing the same damn thing." I replied, clenching my jaw in annoyance.

"Not-uh. I swapped my shoes for these bright red ones and I put on a red baseball cap to match. I decided I can't look too fancy, especially if your cars are super nice. Then it'd be too obvious that I am just pretending to be fancy in the photos we're going to take. I need to look like this doesn't faze me!"

That was the inner mechanisms of Greyson's mind at work.

I just shook my head, "Whatever," I shifted the car to drive and we went on our way.

Greyson was bobbing her head, humming along to whatever pop songs came on the radio. I could tell she was excited by the soft smile on her lips and how her eyes would dart from window to window, looking as the scenery passed us by. "How far is it?" She broke the silence, still looking out the window.

"Well, the garage is already about fifteen to twenty minutes from my place, and from your house to my place is another twenty minutes, so we're looking at about forty."

"I'm so impatient!" She exclaimed loudly. I thought about her ADHD and wondered how she went throughout life when having to wait. The DMV must've been a nightmare.

After about five more minutes of driving Greyson became such a bundle of excitement that she had to talk to keep herself from imploding. "Do you want to work at this place for your entire life?"

"When Jonathan retires, I'll be the owner. I don't think I'm just going to change careers at that point." I looked at her with a face that read, that-was-a-stupid-question.

"Wow, I don't think about how important you are to the company enough. Maybe because you've never actually explained our job title thoroughly," She was looking out the windshield, but the passive aggressive tone in her voice was unmistakable. "I don't think I'd ever be the owner of anything. Maybe that's why stayin' in one job forever sounds like the most depressing situation to me. I'd probably think differently if I was an owner. Yeah, I guess I can respect where you're coming from." She rambled on slightly.

"What do you want to do after you graduate?" After asking the question, I was hit with the realization that Greyson was only ever meant to be here temporarily. With the headaches and stress she caused me, it felt like her employment was never-ending.

In reality, at then end of summer, which was right when the merger was taking place, she'd be going back to school. With how quickly the end of summer was approaching, Greyson would be gone sooner than I could ever imagine.

Oh...

"Um," She hesitated, "Well, I have an idea in mind for right after graduation. Not sure it'll come together just yet. Either way, after that I guess I'll work as a graphic designer or in marketing at some place. I'll probably do that for about five years and then see where the wind takes me."

I don't think I've ever truly considered how different someone's life goals and plans were that grew up in a lower economic class. The careers Greyson was considering were not all that profitable, especially if she wasn't even striving to be a manager.

"What is your dream career?" I heard myself ask.

"Hah!" She laughed, "When you grow up getting really bad grades and having teachers look down on you out of frustration, you kind of just think you aren't good enough for a dream job to be honest. Not that they ever got to me like that, but I don't know," She got quiet for a moment, "Well, actually, when I was in about third or fourth grade we went on this awesome field trip to a planetarium. Looking at the stars and planets made me feel so at peace. I thought about being an astronaut that day. I still really enjoy looking at space, so I guess that would be my dream."

I listened to her words very closely as my eyes stayed fixed on the road. My thoughts couldn't move past her first point. How could she allow herself to not think she was capable of whatever she wanted to work on? She wasn't as stupid as she appeared at first glance. Although she rambled a lot and her focus was a mess, she was actually decently well-spoken.

Then I thought about how often I had considered her to be the most incompetent person on the planet.

"What about yours? Or are cars your whole being?" She smiled at me.

I smiled back, "Being a business owner was always the dream. And I do like cars so I am actually working on my dream job."

"Now all you have to do is become the owner, get an older English butler and you sir will be on the road to becoming the Batman."

And just like that I doubted she ever actually listened to herself when she spoke.

"Greyson, you can have a very profitable career. Don't limit yourself." I spoke and silence soon followed.

After another moment Greyson finally spoke, "Yeah, maybe. This job pays the most out of all the jobs I've had. Luckily it's not all about the money for me. No matter what, I'll be okay."

I didn't say anything in response. I just contemplated her words and the implications. Not too long after, we pulled into the lot where I kept my collection.

"Oh my goodness! This is it, isn't it?" Greyson perked up in her seat, staring out of the windows scanning the entire scene.

It was like the entire previous conversation never took place and her mind could only focus what was going on right this second.

I parked my car beside the garage and Greyson sprang out of her seat, running over to the entrance.

"Open it!" She kept trying to turn the handle, although it was clearly locked.

"Calm down," I walked up slowly, her chaotic energy shot red flags in my mind. "Let's set some ground rules," She hardly looked at me and I could tell her mind was elsewhere. Was it a mistake to bring her here just so she would be happy with me again?

I recognized how even asking that question was proof that I wasn't being myself anymore. Why did she have such a strong fucking effect on me?

"You can only touch the door handles. I don't want fingerprints on everything. Also, wipe your shoes off once we get inside," I looked down, knowing her shoes had to be muddy from all the rain. She shook her head as if she understood, but considering her lacking eye-contact, I doubted she was actually paying attention. "Please just don't break anything." I imagined her getting too handsy with a rearview mirror and snapping it right off.

Yep, this was a mistake.

I put my key in the padlocked door and she bolted in, without wiping off her feet. I pinched the bridge of my nose, trying not to get agitated.

"Wow!" She looked around in amazement. I had a very good collection going and even I was happy to see all of them in one place. Upon tackling the merger, I had decided to stop coming by in order to remain focused. I couldn't wait for it to be over and I could take a few out for a drive. "I love this!" She pulled out her phone and began snapping pictures.

As she pranced around, I strolled through slowly, appreciating the vehicles parked very meticulously by year. I stopped at my all black 2014 Corvette Stingray. It was one of my most recent purchases and one of my favorites. I had considered making it my day to day car, considering it's sleek design wouldn't draw too much attention. However, considering our brand didn't make the vehicle, it wasn't a wise move to do that. I was constantly thinking up different car designs and features we would one day incorporate in a Meyers Motors vehicle that would be my all-time favorite.

I scanned the garage, quickly glancing at each vehicle, remembering exactly when I bought it. My eyes finally landed on Greyson. I smiled slightly at the car she was spending some time ogling. "2000 Lamborghini Diablo." I spoke up, approaching the hot-red vehicle.

"Conn, you have a freakin' Lambo!" Greyson didn't even look at me. She just bent over, trying to see through the tinted window. Surprisingly, she kept her hands at her side.

"Want to check out the inside?" I grabbed the key off the back wall and Greyson's eyes went wide.

"Yes!" She literally screamed and crashed her hand into the door. I flinched at that. "Where's the handle?" I smirked at that and walked over to her side.

"Put your hand in here," I grabbed her wrist, guiding her hand to the top of the door, "And push this button." She pressed it and her jaw dropped as the scissor door opened vertically.

"So cool," She said as she sat inside. I went over to the driver's side and took a seat. "Remember when I said I don't care about money? I lied." She inspected the entire interior, feeling the light tan leather upholstery. "Let's go for a ride!" She looked at me for the first time since entering the garage.

"No." I said flat out and watched her whole demeanor drop. "It's too muddy outside and it can start raining at any moment." I added on.

"True," She considered this for a second, "Another time?" She asked.

"Sure." I didn't really consider it, I just knew saying no would start an argument that I didn't want to get into.

"Awesome!" She threw herself onto me in a crushing bearhug. I wondered if in these moments of hers filled with extreme excitement, she'd possibly get a heart attack. There was no way a person could constantly sustain that level of energy.

She let go of me and just sat there with a small smile on her lips. I leaned my head back into my seat, enjoying the moment of being in my car instead of at work. Before I could get too carried away, Greyson's phone started ringing. It was already in her hand from all the pictures she was taking.

She looked at the caller ID and quitely groaned before picking it up. "Hey, what's up?" She paused and listened for a moment. I couldn't figure out what the other person was saying, but it sounded like a woman. "What? Did you get his name? Really? Hmm. Yeah, I know. I know. What?" Greyson scrunched her brows. I had no idea what was going on. "Whoa, okay. Yeah, I'll come by. Okay. Yep, Bye." She hung up the phone.

I raised an eyebrow at her.

"I gotta go." She avoided eye contact with me.

"Greyson." I called her attention to me without saying anything else.

She sighed, "I have to go see my mom at the home. She got a visitor today, and whoever it was, now she's asking for me. Which doesn't happen often. You know. Because she's losin' her mind."

"Where's the home?" I asked, stepping out of the car.

She followed out, but looked at the Lambo for a moment longer. "Nah, just take me home, I'll go by myself."

"That'll take a lot longer." I retorted. I couldn't describe what compelled me to want to take her. My guess was I had some pity for her ever since she told me her situation with her mother.

"Yeah, I know." She still wouldn't make eye contact with me and I could tell she was in deep thought. That simply intrigued me more.

We walked out of the garage silently and after I locked it up we made our way to my car. I sat in the seat and looked at her as she put on her seatbelt. When she finally met my gaze, I spoke up. "What's the name of the home."

She looked at me for a moment without saying anything, I gave her the same empty expression. "Okay. It's called Vi. It's in Aventura." I grabbed my phone and looked it up.

"It definitely would've taken longer to take you home first."

———

The home was actually really nice. I was surprised at how friendly and attentive the nurses were. My mind imagined dark and gloomy when Greyson mentioned a nursing home. I was looking through a brochure that went over all the services they offered as we walked over to the Alzheimer's unit.

"Hey sweetie! How are you doing?" The receptionist for the unit spoke up and there were quite a few people smiling at Greyson.

"I'm fine, how are you?" Greyson spoke a little quieter than she usually was when greeting someone, but I could've just been imagining that. She already had a huge smile on her face.

"I'm great dear." The woman smiled back.

"Grey!" We all turned our head to the side at the woman who spoke up. She quickly made her way over. "She's still asking for you."

Greyson frowned.

I looked between the woman and Greyson, trying to figure out what I could from the interaction. I gathered that the woman who spoke was a nurse and she didn't look too happy about whatever was going on either.

I knew things were tense with her mother, but I would imagine her asking for Greyson would be a somewhat positive thing. The nurse seemed to fully understand that this wasn't a great thing either.

"Well, let's rip the bandaid right off." Greyson smiled and her and the nurse headed to, what I presumed was her mother's room. I followed a few paces behind, not wanting to be completely nosey.

Greyson walked in the room with the nurse and I stayed behind in the hallway. I walked over to a window and looked out. It was still really cloudy. It made the whole atmosphere seem a lot gloomier. I could hear some muffled voices coming from the room. I tried to focus a little on what was going on, but nothing was truly standing out.

"You are not doing that! Do you hear me?" I heard an unfamiliar woman's voice shout.

"I won't!" Greyson became just as loud. A few nurses, hearing the shouting turned their gaze to the commotion going on." I probably shouldn't have been here.

"Say what you want, but I do care about you." The voice got quieter, but was still loud enough that I could hear it.

Right after that Greyson stormed out, looking extremely upset. "Come on Connor." She grabbed my wrist and shoved a piece of paper into her purse, crumpling it.

"Greyson!" The woman started yelling and Greyson completely ignored it. We were walking really quickly, but I could still hear her mom screaming her name from the room.

I ignored the looks we were getting from the nurses. As we walked, one of them also tried calling Greyson's name. I just followed her out silently. I knew if I tried to calm her down she would only cause a bigger scene in the home. She let go of my wrist once we stepped out, but didn't slow her pace to my car. She got in and slammed the door. I paused a moment before entering my side, trying to think about what was a good approach with her. That felt like a trick question.

I was still thinking about what to say as we drove off in the direction of her house. I wasn't sure if I should've spoken up or not. It was honestly hard to tell with her.

"Thanks," She finally spoke up, looking out the window.

"Are you okay?" I asked automatically.

"No," She looked at me and I could see tears threatening to leave her eyes. "My ex fucking visited her."

Chapter Twenty-One Continued

Cont... (Connor's perspective)

When we pulled up to her house it was nearly black out. It was still the middle of the day, but the rain clouds had accumulated and in the distance we could see some lightning. With all the humidity and light showers throughout the day, it was only a matter of time before we got hit with a tropical rainstorm.

Greyson was looking out at where her apartment complex was, but didn't actually make a move to leave the car. I spent most of the car ride thinking through this whole situation with her and I came to the realization that I was being entirely too stupid and unlike myself for caring so much about her life. It was also ridiculous that I had grown to enjoy having such a dramatic and immature person around.

Taking her out was a mistake and I needed to create some distance.

"You should get in before it rains," I finally said as she just continued to stare absentmindedly out the window. I just waited, not really sure what else to do.

Finally she spoke up, "Can you come in with me? I don't want to be alone." Her voice trailed off. She was a lot more distressed than I imagined. This was unlike her.

"Is your roommate not home?" I was fighting with myself. Her new demeanor made me want to understand more, but this would only drag me in further.

"No. Nevermind." At no point did she look at me as she opened the door and stomped out, slamming the door behind her.

I was completely shocked. I could never predict her next move. Despite all of the logical thinking I had done during the entire car ride, I couldn't help feeling bad. As she was already three-quarters of the way to her door my body automatically reacted and I left the car and headed her way.

When I got to her door, she was still fumbling in her purse to get her keys. The paper she had shoved inside it was getting in the way. She finally found them and unlocked her door. She didn't say anything about me being there, she didn't even look at me. She just opened the door and waited for me to walk in before closing it behind us.

It was dark in the place, again thanks to the impending storm, but Greyson didn't bother turning on the lights. She just made her way to what I recalled was her room. I looked at her tacky couches again, just kind of pacing around, not sure what to do.

"Do you want some water or juice or something?" She called out to me. I came across a picture frame of her when she was in high school. She was struggling to hold up a huge tortoise and laughing about it. The excitement on her face made it hard to not smile along.

"I'll take water, thanks." I called back, setting the picture back down.

When she left her room, her hair was tied in a bun and her bright shoes and hat were gone. I followed her to her kitchen. She just ignored the lights again so this time I turned them on. She stopped once the light flooded the place, "Oh wow, it was dark in here huh?" She laughed lightly, "I didn't even notice." She grabbed a water bottle from the fridge and handed it to me. I looked at her eyes, but she still wasn't meeting my gaze.

"Greyson," I spoke up and she finally looked at me. She kept a slight smile on her lips, but there was no denying she was sad. "Tell me what happened." She looked away just as quickly and started scratching the corner of her one eye.

"Let's go to my room. I wanna be laying down." She stepped around me and made her way to her room. I followed her quietly. There was a voice in the back of my head asking if this was a good idea. I was becoming friends with the worst thing that happened to me this summer, and now asking her to tell me more about her life. No matter how many times I was reminding myself about that, I didn't get any closer to walking away.

Once in her room, she laid down, spread eagle on her bed, facing the ceiling. There was a mess of clothes and other things everywhere, but I managed to step over it and sit on a nearby chair. It was at this point that I realized I probably should've taken off my shoes at the door. The lights were still off, but she had a small lamp that was helping to illuminate the place. I could hear the rain start to pick up outside her window. It was fitting for the mood.

"I'm just gonna say everything, so just cut me off if I say too much," She looked at me for confirmation before taking a breath, "So this particular ex is Dan. He was the first person I ever fell in love with and the first person I gave myself too." She shook her head as if trying to shake that thought from her memory. "Obviously there were probably warning signs early on, but I didn't care. He really helped me ignore things at home and some other bullshit I was going through at the time."

I set down the unopened water bottle she had given me. I was completely focused on her words.

"Anyways, over time things got worse. He only ever wanted to hang out one-on-one when he was in the mood. It's hard for people to deal with my ADHD, so he'd say he could only take me in smaller doses. That sounds mean, but I understood where he was coming from. I have a few more mental shit than just the ADHD, so I could understand that. He always did some drugs, but then he start doing some heavier shit. And he was also dealing, which I didn't always have a problem with. It started to get to me when he started dealin' in some really bad neighborhoods. I was scared he'd get killed and I'd lose him."

She turned to her side to look directly at me. This was the first time she was willingly looking at me and she didn't seem as distraught as she had been earlier.

"So I told him that if he kept dealing in those neighborhoods I would make sure he got arrested," She said and I raised an eyebrow at her. "Then he hit me really hard a few times, bruised a rib and gave me a black eye," She continued on casually, "And I was so angry! I never felt that mad before. I blacked the fuck out and went straight to the police station and ratted on him." Her eyes were wide as she spoke and as she finished her sentence there was a loud crack of thunder.

She went back to laying down and I took the opportunity to take a sip of water. I looked out the window at the heavy rain. It appeared I wouldn't be in any rush to leave.

"He really went through it too. Not only was he strapped," She paused and looked at me, "Sorry. I meant he had a gun on him," She turned her head again, "The cops also found crack in his car and he resisted arrest." She scoffed, "They were pissed. Anyways, I visited him once in jail and he said a lot of nasty things to me. I broke up with him right there and went on my way. I was so upset, I ended up crying that night. But after that I wasn't going to cry over him ever again. And I haven't." She ended her story there. I was surprised she managed to stay so focused on it to begin with.

There was a lot to take in. Everytime Greyson told me more about her life, the more it seemed I was listening to a made up story rather than true events. It was all so surreal to me. Her life was straight out of a movie.

"So what's going on now?" I asked after a couple of minutes.

"Well, he's been outta jail for some time now. I guess he decided he wants to come back into my life or get revenge or something. She turned to the other side of her bed and grabbed her purse from the floor. She sat up and grabbed the crumpled paper from it. "Read the letter he left for me."

I took the paper, trying to straighten it. It was a handwritten letter on lined paper. His handwriting was also messier than a fifth grader's. It read:

Hey babygirl,

U missed me? I been talking around and found out u trying to go to the military. I'm gone fuck that up for u since u tried to fuck with me. Ima let dem u messed up in the head. Shit I should let u go and get urself killed. But nah, cuz that's what u want. U lucky too, cuz that ain't even as bad as what u did to me. But I ain't even mad anymore. Don't worry tho, u will hear from me again.

-Love Dan

Wow. I wasn't quite sure where to start. I just looked up at Greyson who had an unreadable face. She leaned over her bed to take the paper back and crumpled it completely in her hands and threw it on the floor.

"He even had the balls to tell my mom. He knows how she feels about service and how hard I try to keep her happy with me." She took her hair out of her bun and started to fluff at it with her hand.

"Greyson," My voice trailed off, still trying to piece everything together, "You're enlisting?" I finally asked. I knew that wasn't the pressing matter, but that detail stuck out to me.

"Well," She contemplated this, "I don't know. I don't talk much about it. I want to. I think it would make my dad proud of me if I follow his legacy. The only thing is, you can't enlist when you're on medications for mental disorders. I've been trying not to take it, I think you have to be a year without. I'm not even doing well with that because my roommate keeps making me take it. But if my dad never saw anything wrong with me then I don't want to see anything wrong with me either. But I know it can sometimes get out of hand with all the other stuff I'm dealing with." She started to ramble. I imagined she went through this circular reasoning often.

"When are you planning to enlist?" I asked, trying to break her from her rant.

"After graduation in May." She looked at me and then down at her hands. That was not that far off. I couldn't imagine her going to bootcamp, let alone war.

A person like her, being all over the place. She wouldn't last very long.

"Yeah yeah. I know I probably couldn't. I'd have to lie about my use of medication, but I'm totally prepared to do that and suffer the consequences if I get caught."

I didn't like what she was saying. At all. "Greyson, I understand you want to honor your father, but I'm sure he'd want to protect you, not find out you were enlisting just to do what he did."

"I can protect myself," She cut me off, "I don't care. It's what I want to do. And you don't know my dad. He believed I could do anything I wanted." She immediately got defensive.

"Have you ever even went at least a month without your medication? I don't think you've thought this all the way through." I pushed right back.

"Oh whatever Connor. Your life was handed to you on a silver platter with opportunities galore. I'm not denying you struggled, but you just don't get it. You never could." She was speaking louder, I could tell she was heated. Something about this topic struck a nerve.

"Don't say that. I'm sitting here listening to you and trying to understand, so don't give me that." I was definitely starting to get angry myself. How could she be so obtuse to say a thing like that?

"You..." A crack of thunder hit loudly, startling Greyson. The weather was being incredibly ironic. It seemed to have stopped us from getting into a yelling match. I took the opportunity to get up.

"I'm going to the bathroom." I left her room and searched around. It wasn't difficult to find at all in the tiny apartment. I tried to soak in everything we were talking about. I still couldn't believe her in the slightest.

I knew I shouldn't have cared and that it didn't really matter what she wanted to do. She'd be out of my hair long before she even tried to enlist. That's not even mentioning the fact that there's a good chance she wouldn't be able to.

Even still, the thought of her getting caught lying to the government was concerning to me. More concerning was the thought that she'd be in the thick of it, without her medication when she realized she truly needed it. If that didn't happen then there was the fear of her getting deployed and not making it back home. There were many more cons than pros and it was frustrating to me that she was idiotic enough not to think about that.

I needed to leave.

I hardly got one step into the room when Greyson opened her mouth. "I'm sorry. I didn't mean what I said. It feels like there's this constant buzzin' in my head and it just gets louder and louder and it's overwhelming me and that's why I'm getting so on-edge," She pressed her fingers into her temples, focusing on the bed for a moment and then looking back at me, "Let's talk about other things now." She relaxed her posture and gave me a small, reassuring smile.

I looked at her for a moment, considering this, "Okay." I made my way back to the chair I had been sitting on. I grabbed the water she gave me and drank about half of it. She was watching me expectantly. I raised an eyebrow at her.

"So what do you wanna talk about?" She asked, as if I was supposed to be thinking about that. "Oh, you know what! Tell me about something crazy you did. I only ever know about you being all mister work and mister boring." And just like that, the Greyson I was familiar with was back.

"Define crazy. I've allowed Jackson to make some wildly stupid business moves for our company that have almost always been terrible." I replied, thinking about my father's less than competent brother.

Greyson let out a groan and rolled her eyes, "No Connor. That's still super boring and related to work. You're tellin' me you've never gone through some rebellious teenage years? Gotten someone pregnant? Nearly died hiking a mountain? Anything!?" She probed.

Her mind was truly something else. "Gotten someone pregnant?" I asked back. What kind of suggestion was that. She just shrugged it off. I looked out the window at the rain that seemed to be never-ending. "I guess I've done some things in my lifetime."

"That's what I'm talking about! Tell me." She readjusted herself so that she was lying on her stomach, her hands propping her head up to look at me.

"I guess I have gone through some rebellious years, but it was when I started college," I spoke and Greyson gave me her full attention. "I never had many friends growing up. During my freshman year I attempted to make friends. The first group I successfully became a part of was an interesting bunch. They were very unlike myself. Carefree and low-stress. They didn't have many morals or aspirations and at the time I figured this would be a good case study. It would help me learn how to interact with people I wasn't use to, which would of course be a good skill for networking and getting partners and donors for the company."

I could see Greyson restrain herself from rolling her eyes again.

"Anyways, one night they wanted to go to this river that was a couple towns over. Although I needed to study, I realized that didn't help my networking skills, so I went along. We ended up sitting together at a ledge of a small cliff that hung a couple stories over the river. We smoked some weed, although I think I only took it twice and then they started to play truth or dare," I took a pause to drink more water, "To make the story a lot shorter, I got dared to dive into the lake which I ended up doing. I can't tell you what compelled me to do so. The water was freezing cold and a lot more shallow than I thought. I ended up banging the back of my head on a rock."

"Oh my goodness!" Greyson gasped. When she wasn't spacing out, she was great at being an active listener.

"I didn't pass out, but my brain definitely rattled. I completely lost all ability to think clearly and I nearly drowned. They saw me struggling to resurface, but because weed was illegal, they panicked. They did call the police to inform them, but they left right after that. I ended up floating to a dry patch and managed to pull myself onto it enough so that the current wouldn't pull me further down the river. At that point I was shivering and I had a terrible headache and I couldn't see a thing. I blacked out and woke up in the emergency room. I ended up with a pretty bad concussion and hypothermia."

"Connor, you could have seriously died." Greyson interjected. I just shook my head to agree with her.

"I did realize that. So I decided not to hang out with those people and not make crazy decisions like that anymore." I concluded, running my hand through my hair, feeling the spot on the back of my head that needed stitches. I didn't want to give Greyson the full details. It was already a decently bad story, she didn't need to know the extent of it.

"Wow, well points because that definitely doesn't sound like something you'd do. Not exactly the story I expected though." She was still looking at me wide-eyed.

"Your turn." I finally said and felt my phone buzz in my pocket. I was sure I was getting a lot of messages, but at this point checking my phone didn't change the fact that I'd have to deal with it all later on.

"Well, I have a bunch of crazy stories. Obviously." Greyson shrugged like this was no big deal. "I think the mood is too negative right now so I want something funny..." She began rubbing her chin and her eyes were shifting from side to side, as if she was searching for files in her brain. "Not that one," She said to herself and laughed, "But that is a good one."

Her personality was truly amusing. It was the most unnatural thing I've ever witnessed in a person. She was all over the place, which was definitely annoying, but I couldn't get over it.

"Okay, I have one that's not too great, but it may be funny for you." She swung her legs over the bed so that she was sitting up straight and leaned in slightly closer to me. "So this story is about the second and last time I got drunk. The first time was when I was a teenager, that was just a bad night, but when I turned twenty-one not too long ago I tried it again." She took a deep breath, indicating she was ready to ramble through it. "So, first you need to know that people with ADHD are more likely to become alcoholics. That's why I've always tried to steer clear. Being so willing to try anything, this can be hard. I never meant to drink it on my twenty-first birthday, but man all my friends were super convincing."

"I didn't know that." I thought about her generally being more health conscious, especially with her distaste of cigarettes. I also thought back to her family's cookout where she didn't have an alcoholic beverage. I would've never connected those dots.

"Yep! I think it affects us more. Or maybe it's because we don't pay attention enough to stop doing it until we're completely screwed. Like damn drinking is nice, makes you feel real relaxed, but that's the trap I guess. Anyways, I didn't realize I was super drunk until I was already too far gone. My friends were also real drunk too and so we decided to get tatted. This is a good time to say, I don't actually like tattoos. I think it's because my ex had so many. He comes to mind when I think of them. Anyways, I kept talkin' about how sour pineapples are the whole night for some reason and that's what I ended up getting on my body forever," She put her face in her hands in embarrassment. "I swear Connor, I'm not generally that stupid. That's why I'll never drink again. Look how corny this is."

She stood up immediately and started lifting her shirt. I was still trying to process her story when she also hooked her thumb through the belt loop of her pants and started pulling them down. I was pretty sure my face got slightly red, thank goodness the room was too dim to notice it.

Before I could protest she stopped pulling her pants down. Low on the front of her hip sat the outline of a pineapple in red ink.

"Don't ask me why it's red either. Most of this story is just what my friends told me happened. I have no idea where my mind was at." She was saying more words, but my mind had gone a little fuzzy. The tattoo was a little close to her crotch which was now also close to my face from when she stood up. Her brown skin looked incredibly smooth and the pineapple tattoo oddly fit her well.

In the next moment my mind had gone blank and my body reacted on its own. I reached my hand up and grazed the red ink with my thumb, causing her to inhale sharply and stop speaking. I traced the outline a few times and looked up at her eyes that were already looking into mine.

I stood up and she took a step back. Instead of pulling back I pushed forward. Her green eyes were watching me carefully. My thumb didn't leave her hip as my other hand came up to cup the side of her face. My eyes shifted down toward her full lips.

There was a moment of clarity. My conscious was telling me to pull back and not make a huge mistake.

Because this was most certainly a huge mistake.

As I hesitated, Greyson closed what little space was left between us and pressed her lips to mine. The voice quickly disappeared as I deepened the kiss. There was something extremely magnetic about kissing her and my hands naturally slid around her back, lifting her shirt slightly as I pulled her further into me.

Greyson took that as a cue to completely take off her shirt. I took a moment to take in the sight of her in just her leggings and a plain black bra.

She was stunning.

She tugged my shirt up and I immediately obliged and pulled it off. She brought her face back to mine, running her nails along my back. She was acting as desperate as I felt and it was dragging my mind further into oblivion.

I hooked my hands under her knees, lifting her. Our mouths stayed connected until I dropped her onto her bed. Her eyes looked more vibrant and bright with a hunger that I've never seen in them before. It drew out something animalistic within me.

I could see her chest rise and fall with how heavily she was breathing. "Connor..." She said on an exhale and reached her arms up to grab mine and pull me down.

My tongue immediately found her mouth and she responded just as quickly. I couldn't help myself when she was so eagerly accepting me. My hands found her breasts and I squeezed them through the fabric of her bra.

She moaned as I did that and started grabbing at my hair. I couldn't stop. I wanted it. I wanted her so badly.

I grabbed her hips and pulled her into me. I groand.

Her hands made their way to my belt and she easily undid it and started to tug off the button on my pants. Once her fingers slid my zipper down my conscious hit me like a wave.

Another moment of clarity.

Chapter Twenty-Two

Chapter 22 - He's the Worst (Greyson's Perspective)

I nearly jumped when Connor touched me. It was super unexpected and I wasn't sure what to do about it. I just shut my mouth and looked at him. I wanted him to stop, but he was looking at my skin so intently. Did he think it was stupid? That didn't really give him the right to touch it though.

He looked up at me and I froze like a deer in headlights. He was giving me such an empty expression. I hated how I couldn't always read him. It made me feel more lost and confused. He stood up, never breaking eye contact and I finally had some sense to step back. He stepped forward. He was still touching my lower hip and as unbelievable as it was, it had an effect on me. I felt stuck.

His eyes looked black in the darkness of my room. Crap, I only had my lamp on. It seemed like it was midnight. It was also raining really heavily outside.

He grabbed the side of my face, bringing my thoughts back to what was happening.

Wait, what the hell was actually happening?

I didn't know why I couldn't talk, but I just kept watching him. I watched as his eyes wandered downward to my lips. Oh my fuck, was he trying to kiss me?!

And damn his thumb on my pelvic bone was getting a lot harder to ignore.

He leaned in slightly, but just stopped, still looking at my mouth.

I became impatient. If he was going to do it, he should've just done it. This moment would only be weirder if he stopped now. It was obvious he wanted to kiss me. So I decided to kiss him.

It was a weird sensation. Kissing a rich man, who you were only familiar with as your constantly butthurt partner, wasn't something I could describe. I pulled back a little bit and his hand on my face wrapped around to the back of my neck and pulled me in deeper. He didn't want to stop kissing. The guy I was sure hated my guts was really trying to make out with me.

That thought alone got me going.

When he lifted me up so easily and dropped me on my bed, I saw something in his eyes that I wanted to see more of. I never saw Connor look at me so... So personally. The effect it had on me was indescribable.

I knew I was acting impulsively, but I wanted more. I wanted him to keep looking at me in that way. So I tried to pull off his pants. Once I got the zipper down, he came to a dead stop. He looked at my hands for a little and then looked at my face. I stopped moving as well, trying to read him.

His expression shifted to one I knew very well. It was the one that didn't really like me. He looked at me like he was finally realizing who I was and was making the biggest mistake of his life. That look shot through me like a bullet.

I felt stupid. Why did I take my shirt off? Why did I even allow this to happen? I didn't even like Connor like that and now it would look like I was all over him.

"Greyson," He said, already pulling away.

"Yeah, you don't even have to say it," I quickly cut him off, composing myself. "We almost made a huge mistake." I pushed him further back and got up from the bed, grabbing my shirt from the floor and slipping it on. He buttoned his pants and started putting his shirt on. I couldn't help the pang of sadness I felt.

Woah girl, get it together. He's literally nothing to you.

I was able to bring myself back together. There was no need to start acting illogical. "You should go." My voice was cold as I made my way out of the room. He was still gathering his stuff, but I didn't care. I needed him away and to forget this night ever happened.

I already had the door opened when he finally left my room. The rain was hitting the ground hard as he made his way over and I could feel his eyes on me, but I didn't look back. I didn't want to see him at all. He stopped once he was out the door, just under the overhang and I could tell he was about to say something. I spoke first.

"I'll see ya Monday." I closed the door before he could interject anything. I locked it too for good measure. "Cold shower." I said aloud to myself, making my way back to my room.

My alarm woke me up early Monday morning. Instead of spending the weekend thinking about the events on Friday, I was able to completely ignore it and hang out with friends. However, the cruel reality was that ignoring a problem didn't make it go away. The dread of now having to go in and face him was a reminder of that.

Not that it was my fault. It was totally his fault for initiating the whole thing. That didn't make this any less awkward. Which was probably why I was wide awake so early in the morning. I just needed to diffuse the situation and call it a day.

I hated that things were never just normal with us. The worst partnership of my life.

Although I woke up super early and managed to get ready within half an hour, I still didn't get to work until a little before nine. A somewhat more reasonable human hour. It was definitely because I was stalling, but also because I knew Peter usually got in around eight. Peter understood normal human hours. He was only at work extremely early when he had specific business, which he usually did not. And considering I also did not, I felt like nine, although still generally a struggle for me, made the most sense.

Today, however, nine made sense so that I could easily escape the assured awkwardness with Connor and go to Peter. Genius plan.

I also decided not to take my medication. I was starting to take it a lot more regularly and I didn't like it. Having Jay on my back and all the events going on made it real easy to slip into the comfort it was giving me. But that wasn't who I was and I was getting sick of it. On top of that, I was tired to paying close attention to everything.

I slowly peered my head around the office door and Connor looked straight at me. It was times like these that made me super glad to be black. My face got super hot, but he'd never be able to tell. It was unlike him to look at me when I walked in. He was usually busy furiously typing away on his laptop or on the phone. And even when he wasn't doing either of those things, he never really acknowledged me.

Still, it didn't make sense for me to be so embarrassed. None of this was my fault. Thank goodness he'd never be able to tell. I could at least feign confidence and spin it all on him.

I walked in slowly, a lot more unnaturally than I would've liked.

"Greyson," He said in his way that screamed calm, cool, collected and powerful. I hated how he could do that. I made a mental note to learn that kind of skill.

"Connor," I tried it back, sounding a little weak if I was giving an honest rating. "Let's just get ourselves on the same page about what happened." I kept talking. I told myself to see what he'd have to say, but I couldn't help it. I was feeling awkward so my mouth just opened up.

I looked at him and he didn't say anything. I was trying again to just wait and see what he'd say again, but the short moment of silence was still too much for me to keep my mouth closed.

"It was obviously a mistake. I don't have any feelings for you. It was just a weird moment with all the emotional life talk and I haven't slept with someone in awhile so that's why I was gettin' carried away. I assume you were probably just getting carried away for similar reasons. I'm not upset with you and I'm totally okay with just carrying on like that ain't even happen. I hope you are too. I'll work with Peter today though, just to make sure things are good." The more I spoke the more embarrassing the whole deal felt. This was the worst kind of conversation to have.

Why did Connor have to go and kiss me and make things weird? I know, I know, I kind of kissed him, but I didn't actually want to! I never would've done that if he didn't look at me like he wanted it.

I was again just staring blankly at him, waiting for him to say something. He looked right back at me and my mind flashed back to how he looked at me that night. My face got so hot I thought I was sweating.

Ugh, why was that making me so anxious?

"I agree." He responded.

Wow Connor. Thanks for nothing. I couldn't read his face and his short answer didn't really make me feel confident that we wouldn't be awkward with each other. Goodness he was terrible. He goes and creates tension and then does nothing to diffuse it. And yet, they want him in charge of the business.

I was definitely annoyed. I made my way to my desk, grabbing some things so that I wouldn't have to be in his office at all. I could feel him looking at me, and that coupled with all the anxiety and the annoyance I was feeling toward him made me angry. I shoved my laptop in my bag, threw it over my shoulder and began to stomp out the door. Every step made me even more frustrated.

When I got to the door I turned around. As I guessed, he was just sitting there, staring at me. "What?" I spat. Nothing irked me more than someone who wasn't upfront about things.

He raised an eyebrow at me like he didn't know what I was referring to.

"You're staring at me like you have something to say."

"Nope." He quickly responded and I swear I wanted to punch him.

"Fuck you, Connor." I said, allowing the anger to take over, "Things were finally going well with us and then you messed everything up and made things all weird. And instead of manning up to it, you're just lettin' it get worse by not sayin' shit. Working with you is the fucking worst." I swung open the door and walked out. Midway through slamming it shut I stopped the door and closed it nicely. It wasn't even worth it.

I really shouldn't have let him get to me.

"Greyson," I saw Amanda peeking her head over her desk. I hadn't given her an update in awhile and I was sure she was curious about what was going on. But I was done talking about Connor, I just wanted to ignore it. And I knew Peter was perfect for that.

"It's a rollercoaster ride with him," I rolled my eyes. "Is Peter in?" I was already walking in the direction of his office. I knew Amanda didn't deserve to have me being so short with her. I hoped she'd understand.

"He is," She responded simply, not pushing the matter. Thank goodness.

I knocked on his door and my mood instantly lifted when I heard his voice. "Spiderman, save me." I fake pouted and he got up from his chair, smiling and pulled me into a hug. Although I was with him for most of the previous week, I did not get tired of this blond boy.

"What's going on?" He pulled back to look into my eyes. He always seemed genuinely concerned and I liked that.

"Just the usual Connor madness. What's the good word?" I didn't have the slightest desire to let Peter know the situation and thankfully I knew he wouldn't push it. I think he actually couldn't stand it when I spoke about Connor, good or bad.

"Well, you'll be excited to know I just received a call this morning," He paused, returning to his desk. He smiled at me and I started getting excited in anticipation, "It seems your crazy idea is actually going to come into fruition."

"Shut up!" I nearly yelled when I finally caught up to what he was talking about. "Don't lie to me about something like that!"

"I could hardly believe it myself, but he laughed and actually loved it. The more I think about it, the more I like it too, so I guess I should thank you for forcing me to ask." Peter was grinning very wide. There was an actual possibility that I was making this company some money.

"And you thought it was stupid. Wow... I'm actually pretty great!" I was completely inflating my ego. This was the best thing to hear about. It definitely meant my shitty morning wasn't going to ruin my whole day. Working with Peter was actually the best.

"It was a crazy thought, but I'm sorry for doubting you. You should let the boss know." Peter said and my smile faltered.

So I wasn't actually being completely honest with everyone. The initial plan was to have Peter tell Connor about what we were working on, but for some reason that Peter wouldn't tell me about, he preferred that I told him instead. And I actually did try to tell Connor, but Connor was always an ass when I tried so I never got around to it. Then when Peter once asked me if I told Connor, for some reason I just said yes even though that was a lie and had been living the lie ever since.

As far as Peter knew, Connor was somewhat on board with everything so far. Which wasn't true, which meant Connor could actually not super like what we were up to.

Peter noticed my face drop, "Well when things settle down." He added on. If only he knew that my drop in demeanor wasn't because I was upset with Connor. But like Jay once said, if you're going to lie, you better see it through until death. So I would definitely find a way to tell Connor and make him not dislike the idea as well.

Talk about impossible.

"Yeah, I'll let him know." I finally said.

Peter smiled and started typing something on his computer. "The sooner the better though, he may not agree with this specifically. Wow, I'm surprised we've gotten so far with all of this. It's such a gamble too." The smile didn't leave his face.

Yeah, I really needed to let Connor know. Being professional sucked. It was like being beat by a stick and having to endure each smack with a smile even though you could so easily stop the stick.

That wasn't my best comparison, but the moral was me quitting was the equivalent of stopping the stick. However, considering that Peter was following an idea of mine, the stick beating felt a little sweeter.

"You're right. I'm just gonna get it over with. Better to rip the bandaid right off, huh?" He shook his head in agreement, looking at me for a quick moment before returning to his busy work.

I rolled my eyes. He wasn't being much fun today.

Without another word I walked out of his office. I looked at the door to Connor's office, thinking about whether or not I wanted to walk in or wait a few hours. It wasn't very long ago that I stormed out of it. Connor was the worst.

But he had the softest lips.

What the hell? I scrunched my face in disgust. I should not have been thinking that.

Ew, Grey, don't do that ever again.

When I finally cleared my thoughts, I realized I had walked straight up to his door. I hesitated. I really should've given it more time. I turned to look at Amanda who was already watching me. "Is he still in there?" I asked.

"Hasn't left." She responded back.

I rolled my eyes. Yep, I guess I was doing it now.

I pushed through the door, "Hey Connor, I've got something important to talk..." I cut myself off when I realized he wasn't anywhere to be seen. I scanned the room again with a raised eyebrow, walking toward his desk to check if he was under it.

Maybe he was grabbing something?

He wasn't there either and my eyes went around again. "Amanda just said..." My eyes locked with the door to his little room thing. "Ah." I always wondered if he actually went in there.

I walked straight over grabbing the doorknob, "Hey Connor," I stopped dead in my tracks when I witnessed a scene I really wish I hadn't.

Connor was on all fours, on his bed, over Samantha. Her dress was hiked up above her underwear and Connor's belt was on the floor. I looked at Samantha who was trying to pull her dress back down, but still managed to smirk at me. My eyes then connected with Connor's and he looked extremely stunned, not moving in the slightest.

"Oops! I'm super sorry," I snapped out of my staring and shut my eyes, closing the door most of the way, "I just gotta talk to you when you get the chance Connor. Nothing serious." I was talking very loudly and I shut the door immediately after. My eyes were wide as I walked straight out the office.

I was sure my facial expression resembled something close to bewilderment and Amanda immediately took notice. I didn't like the way she looked at me. There was a lot of concern on her face and I couldn't stand it. I wanted to be invisible.

I took a sharp turn and made my way to the bathroom. My throat felt like it was closing up and my head was spinning. I knew what happened on Friday didn't mean anything, but was I really just someone there to just use? Was I that worthless to him?

I sped up to the bathroom, rushing through the door so I could be alone. The good aspect of not working with many girls.

Why was I trusting him with so much of my personal crap? I was opening myself up to someone who hardly liked me. Someone who would take advantage of me when I was emotional and then act like he didn't care.

I felt tears threatening to leave my eyes. I thought about seeing them together, about how they were probably having sex at the current moment. Why did I ever think for a moment that he'd care about me. There was no reason to care about me. I wasn't anything special.

My eyes connected with themselves through the bathroom mirror. I took a deep look into my own eyes, trying to quiet all the thoughts.

Keep breathing Grey. I mentally told myself and took a deep breath turning on the water. I hadn't realized I was nearly hyperventilating. Without breaking eye contact with my reflection, I ran my hands under the faucet, allowing the cold water to soak my hands and then brought them to my face. I took another breath and turned off the faucet. Grabbing some paper towels and drying off. I looked at my reflection again.

"You need to stop being stupid. You don't like this guy, so you need to stop caring so much. Stop telling him so much." I spoke to myself out loud, feeling much calmer. I knew I was strong person. I was just so busy trying to get Connor to like me that I was allowing him to take control of my happiness.

"You are gonna pick yo' ass up and work with his ass like a professional. You about to help with this merger, get yo' money, and move on with your life." I told myself in the mirror and straightened my back.

Fuck Connor Meyers.

I walked out the bathroom and started to walk back over to Peter's office. I was going to sleep with Peter. Right now. In his office. I smirked as I thought about this. He was always so nice to me and I was sure he'd release all this tension I was feeling and I'd be able to keep my strong woman mentality.

As I got to his door I saw Jackson making his way to Connor's door. He looked over at me and immediately smiled.

"Jackson!" I didn't see him too often, but seeing him was always so exciting. He gave me this fatherly look that not even Jonny could pull off.

I ran over and threw my arms around him. He just laughed. "Greyson, I was just here looking for you." He squeezed me back and then let go. Aw, he was like a sweet uncle. One that gave you the good kind of candy whenever you'd go to see him. Not like a Tootsie Roll uncle, but a Snickers bar uncle.

"Well here I am!" I couldn't stop smiling. He came around at the best times.

"Are you free to accompany me to lunch?" He had this warm vibe to him. He was literally the best.

"I'm like, always free!" I responded back and we made our way to the elevator. "Amanda, I promise I'm not ignoring you. I will talk to you this week." I told her when we walked past. She smiled in relief. She was always patient with me and listened to me. There was no reason to start shutting her out. "Where do you have in mind?" I asked once the elevator door closed.

"There's a small bagel shop down the street. Considering it rained all weekend it might be nice to walk over." He suggested, his voice as peaceful as it always was.

"You like bagels? That's great because I do too! Perfect." I hooked my arm through his, squeezing it lightly. He just chuckled.

As we walked to the shop I told Jackson a story about how I nearly got struck by lightning because I was so curious about it as a child. He just laughed along and allowed me to tell my story. The bagel shop we walked into was adorable. It was in a shared building, so not very big at all. It had a cozy feel to it and smelled like fresh baked bread. It was one of the best smells on the planet.

Jack easily walked to the front and made his order. I ignored him to look at all the different types of bagels listed on the blackboard behind the cashier. It was slightly overwhelming, but I found one that stuck out.

"Whatever flavor the rainbow bagel is, I want it! And with strawberry cream cheese please." I said and Jackson couldn't contain his laughs, handing the man his card.

"Hey, I can pay for mine if you'd like." I added.

"You're such a pleasant ray of sunshine Greyson," The man charged his card and handed it back to him. "I invited you out, so I will pay."

"Take a seat anywhere and we'll get those out to you," The counter guy said and Jackson lightly placed a hand on my back leading me toward a seat next to the window.

"Jonathan reached out to me this weekend," Jackson spoke as soon as we were sitting. "He told me things were going well." He looked at me, expectantly.

What the hell Jon. Going off and telling Jackson these things without asking first. Jackson would now be so disappointed if I told him things weren't so.

"There's ups and downs. But Peter and I have been doing some work. He's been really helpful so that's good." I didn't want to lie to my uncle Jack, but I also didn't want to tell him his nephew was the worst person on the planet.

"And with Connor?" He added. Of course he wasn't going to let me skip past this. Of course all anyone ever wondered was how I was doing with Connor.

"Well..." I trailed off. Really not sure what to say, "It has its ups and downs. Like I said. Currently a little more down, but it's fine. It's not like I'll be here for much longer anyways." I said and Jackson just looked at me, keeping a soft smile on his lips. I couldn't tell what his expression meant. The Meyers family should've been known for their unreadable faces. I wouldn't like to play poker with them.

"That's interesting to hear. Did things become more down today?" He finally spoke. He was reading me a little too well. I broke eye contact.

"You could say that. It's just that we're very different people from two completely different upbringings. We're currently stuck in this partnership, but it gets frustrating a lot. It's like forcing two positive magnets together. If someone's forcing it they can kind of connect, but they naturally want to move away from each other. I'm just gettin' ready for summer to end. But I do love working here. You and Jon are so great to me." As I spoke my thoughts found the words and I went with it.

"If Connor were sitting here with us, and I asked him, 'how do you feel about Greyson?' What do you think he would say?" Jackson asked and I was taken a little off guard. That was a question that I basically answered for myself every single day I was at work. But I never actually asked Connor it. Not like he didn't make it very clear either way.

I thought about when I first started working there and all the really mean things Connor would say. And all the angry facial expressions he would make. He definitely wasn't as quick to anger anymore, but there were always the moments where I could tell he didn't like me. I just didn't care enough to let it bring me completely down.

"I don't think he'd say he hates me. Considering how when I almost quit he apologized. I think," I tried to think deeply about what Connor might say, "Maybe that he doesn't like that I was forced on him. And he prefers me not around and can't wait until the summer ends so that he can do his life." I looked at Jackson as if searching to see if he agreed.

He actually shook his head in agreement, but it didn't make me feel better. Why would he ask me that kind of question? Now I was feeling shitty again.

"Here you both are," The cashier guy came over and handed us a tray with our bagels. I could see that Jackson got a cinnamon raisin one. I smiled wide when I saw my rainbow bagel with strawberry cream cheese. I immediately grabbed my phone to take a picture.

"I can't believe I work down the street and I never knew about this place!" The picture went straight to my Snapchat story. It was so colorful and fun. I picked it up and took a huge bite, furrowing my eyebrows. I really wanted to taste the flavor. "Hm, this is actually pretty good." I said with my mouth full. Who knew rainbow bagels would be such a cool thing.

"Unfortunately," Jackson looked at his watch, "My brother has some business he wants me to attend to." He stood up and grabbed his uneaten bagel. "No need to rush, just call up the valet and one of them will quickly pick you up when you're done."

I frowned. It didn't seem like Jackson to just leave all of a sudden.

"I'm sorry. I would rather enjoy these bagels with you." He pushed his chair in.

"You invite me on a date and then leave me? That's kind of cold. Let me tell ya Jackson, if you do this to all of your hot dates, you'll not only end up alone, but possibly dead. Killed by a woman you stood up." I added and he laughed really loud.

"I'll make it up to you," He put his hand on my shoulder and I looked up at him. I could even see Connor in him, the family genes were so strong. "You're the best thing to happen in my nephew's life. Whether you see it or not," Jackson caught me off guard again. How could he even believe that? I opened my mouth, but he cut me off before I could say anything, "When the summer is over, I hope you at least stay in touch with Jon and myself." He smiled again and I was still trying to argue his first point.

Before I could, he turned around and headed to the door. The second part of what he said finally caught up to me, "Of course I will!" I said after him. He looked at me a final time, nodded and walked out.

Jackson was insane. No wonder he thought hiring me was a good idea. Connor was just saying how he always had to clean up after a mess he made.

I was halfway through scarfing down my colorful bagel when my phone buzzed. Amanda had sent me a text. Connor would like you to come to the office. He said you had something you wanted to talk to him about.

I rolled my eyes. He was willing to face me so soon after walking in on him, yet couldn't send me a text himself.

Be there in 10! I sent back, grabbing my bagel in one hand and my purse in the other. I sped walked back to the building. I already knew the drill with Connor. If he was ready to meet with you and you weren't ready in that same exact second he'd get cranky.

Although I knew this whole situation was extremely awkward and uncomfortable, I was going to act as nonchalant as Mr. Meyers Junior was acting. I had actual business to speak with him about.

I surprisingly made it back to the building in less than ten minutes. I hurried into the elevator and once I got out I locked eyes with Amanda. "Send a prayer that it goes well," I crossed my fingers to her and kept on walking to the office. Once inside I took a final bite of my bagel and walked over to my desk to toss it in the trash.

Connor was sitting on the corner of his desk, his arms crossed.

"Okay," I tried to catch my breath, "I'm here." I swallowed down the last bit of my bagel, wishing I had water to go along with it.

"Greyson, what you walked in on earlier..." Connor started and my eyes went wide.

No no no. No no. No. We were not about to talk about it! "Connor." I stopped him before he could say more. So he was willing to clear the air about Sam, but couldn't do that about what happened with us? Not surprised. "I really don't care. I'm not about to make things awkward. I get it. You're a grown man you can do what you want. Sometimes we have to blow off steam. You have Sam, I have Peter. It's okay." I ranted, trying to make sure we would never have to come back to this.

"You have Peter?" He questioned, making a face close to disgust, "Have you slept with Peter?" He asked, frankly.

A mixture of embarrassment and anger shot through me. What gave him the right to ask me a thing like that? He didn't even hesitate. As if it was his business to know my business. "Whether I have or have not, it doesn't concern you." There was attitude dripping from my voice. How dare he.

I saw his jaw clench. I could tell he was pissed, but even he recognized that he had no right to ask me about that. He got up from his desk and paced over to his window.

Why was he even mad? For someone who considered me a child, he was really good at throwing childlike tantrums for no good reason.

"If we can put our professional pants back on, I do have some things I need to talk to you about concerning what I'm doing at the merger." I was clenching and unclenching my fist. Dealing with him should have been an olympic sport with all the energy it took.

"Honestly Greyson, why do you think you should say anything at the merger? It's not like you have any clue on what we're actually doing here." His tone was cold and mean. And although he was infamous for saying mean things to me, it particularly hurt today. I wasn't expecting to be dismissed so quickly.

Nice Connor was officially gone again and I was tired of feeling like a yoyo.

"I don't have the energy anymore. I'm not going to fight with you Connor. Forget that I mentioned anything. I'll see ya." I rolled my eyes and left. I had no desire to get sucked into his bad energy. He always brought me down.

I made my way to Peter's room and opened the door without knocking. He was still typing away at his computer. Typical Peter. I thought about how I made plans to sleep with him and how Jackson messed that up. And now Connor thought it was a possibility that we did. And I really just wanted to go to bed.

"What's up?" He smiled up at me.

"I have no idea if Connor likes the plan. I can't talk to him." I stopped myself and shrugged, pressing my lips into a tight line. I didn't know what else to say to him. I just walked on out. I went around the floor to take the stairs. I didn't want to run into Amanda for the millionth time that day. There was way too much going on and my head couldn't take it.

I really just wanted to go to sleep.

Once I finally made it down, I walked through the lobby. My eyes landed on this fiery red hair that was unmistakable. Sam was sitting on one of the couches, texting on her phone frantically. Her face was red and blotchy, her makeup starting to smudge. Her eyes were also bloodshot and swollen.

She was not a cute crier.

"Hey, what's wrong?" I walked up to her, genuinely concerned. I knew Connor was good at being a bully and I would hope he didn't treat her as rough as he did me. I could take it, but I knew Sam really couldn't. Even though she was also known for being mean.

She looked up at me and immediately stood up. "You're the reason everything has been so shitty around here!" Her voice was shaky and people in the lobby immediately got quiet to spectate the scene she was creating. "Connor was so focused and you completely messed him up. I don't know why he didn't just figure out a way to get rid of you."

I was taken by surprise. And considering how often that was happening today, I realized I really had my guard down.

More people were gathering around. One of the valet's looked at me. We had grown kind of close over the summer and he loved listening to stories of mine. He looked really concerned and motioned his mouth to what I believe was 'Connor.' He also held up his hand to his ear like a phone.

I just shook my head, no. That would've been the last thing we needed.

"You're worth less than trash. You should see some of the things people have said about you. Someone like you should've never been allowed to even step foot in a place like this." Sam ranted on and what she said really hit a nerve. I could hear the implications of her words loud and clear.

"You can kiss my ass!" I stepped up to her so that we were only a few inches apart. I had to look down because she wasn't the tallest. "You ain't even worth my breath, because I'm still here doing my fuckin' shit and you can't touch me. But you think I'm trash?" I scoffed. "Funny."

I hadn't noticed that while I was talking two security guards had come by. The one grabbed me by my arm and the other started to stand in between us, looking at me intently. I looked at where the one man had his hand on my arm and shook my head, laughing. They didn't even bat an eye when it came to Samantha.

"This fucking place," I said under my breath, "Let's go!" I told my escort and he led me to the door.

I managed to get home, shower and take an extremely long nap. I think I blacked out I was so mad. Once I was awake there was something pressing on my mind. It was Sam saying that I should've seen some of the things people said about me. I didn't even think people knew about me, let alone talked. I decided to do a Google search on my name.

It was weird to think I would be important enough to have my name bring up anything, but possibly old Myspace photos. I knew if you Googled Connor, you'd see a whole bunch of things. But then I thought about when I was introduced at Jon's dinner to all his uppity people. Maybe people were keeping tabs on me?

Greyson Lewis. I typed my name, took a deep breath and hit enter. The first thing that popped up were a few pictures of mine, some from my instagram and some of me walking places? Like paparazzi shots!

I smiled, not honestly expecting something like that.

Then I saw some news articles. "Who is Meyers Motors new COO?" I read aloud, "Jonathan Meyers. Crazy owner who hires random college girl to become COO and win Japan." I laughed at that one. Headlines were great. It seemed there were more than a few articles written, but I just clicked on the first one.

I skimmed through it, only wanting to focus on anything that was specifically about me.

So, who is Greyson Lewis? A college student from a rough neighborhood, majoring in Graphic Design. Despite this, Jonathan Meyers, owner of Meyers Motors, has entruster her with the business of a car company. A few sources have confirmed that she's rather low performing in school and struggles with different mental disorders. We still have no word from Meyers Senior regarding this risky business move.

Another source has confirmed her father died-

I shut my laptop. How the hell did they know so much about me?

Two drops of water hit my laptop and I realized I was crying. I felt like my whole world was crumbling around me. Every single bad thing that had happened today and even during the duration of working there flooded my thoughts. I was taking so much bullshit from everybody and I never felt more out of control of my own life. This job was honestly feeling like the worst decision I've ever made.

I was feeling so alone and trapped. I needed someone to vent to. I hated crying. I looked at the time on my phone. Jay would still be a few hours to get home. The tears just kept spilling from my eyes.

I couldn't believe all my personal business was a quick click away. How could Samantha be so mean to me and never even try and know me? Why was Connor constantly the worst thing about this job? Why did I keep trying to please everyone working there?

I hated all of this.

My phone lit up and I saw a message from Connor. I'm sorry.

I looked at it until my phone went black again. What in the actual hell was wrong with him? I grabbed my phone and shut it off, tossing it on the ground. I was so tired of dealing with it all. Especially him.

Chapter Twenty-Three

Chapter 23- She's ... (Connor's Perspective)

I drove home in the rain, my mind spiraling.

I nearly had sex with Greyson Lewis, for goodness sake!

How could I process that information? How could I even explain such a thing?

She wanted it too... I briefly thought to myself and tightened my grip on the steering wheel.

What in fuck's sake was actually wrong with me?!

I arrived at my building and walked straight through the rain, not even caring about how soaked I was getting. I dripped water all across the ground floor and into the elevator. Once I got to my suite, I kicked off my shoes and pulled off my suit, tossing everything directly into the washing machine. The water I brought in didn't bother me. Anyways, my housekeeper would tidy everything up.

From there I went directly into the bathroom and turned the shower on, pushing the temperature to a very high notch. I felt like I wanted to boil my skin straight off.

I just stood there, allowing the water to simply wash over me. Staring at the ground I willed myself to go over a mental checklist of things that were either done or needed to get done for Japan. The amount of things that I felt still went unchecked was unsettling.

After I exited the shower, I dried off and pulled on some boxer briefs. I grabbed my phone from the counter, not bothering to put my keys or wallet in their actual place and went over my messages.

Sam had sent me a dozen, go figure, Adam had sent one, there was also a few from Amanda and there was one from Jonathan. I opened that one first. Connor, you disappear from the office and don't tell anyone anything about it? Very unlike you. We need to meet up and talk final details about this merger. Plan a time for us this weekend, preferably tomorrow.

I gritted my teeth, out of a million things I could've done correctly, he always found a point to nitpick. Yet, he would never take criticism for the countless stupid things he did.

Stop by tomorrow morning at 9 am. I sent back.

Amanda's messages were mostly asking where I was, Sam's were similar except I could tell she was whining. Adam had checked off an item on my checklist and I was glad that he was always so reliable.

I connected my phone to its charger and shut out the lights. In bed, I kept going through my checklist and creating a mental plan of who would be dealing with certain things and what else I needed to do personally. I was not going to allow my mind to think about Greyson.

The doorbell rang at exactly ten minutes to nine. Jon was impeccable with his timing. I was already up, brewing some coffee. I was in a full suit, Jonathan's words from when I was younger always ringing in the back of my mind. He would tell me that no matter who I was meeting with, if there was business to be done, the attire must match.

I walked over to let him in, giving him a very firm handshake and keen eye contact.

He was dressed just as professionally, which was no surprise. He made his way to my kitchen, following the scent of coffee and poured himself a cup. One of his more annoying traits was acting as my superior no matter where we were. Even in my own home, he had to be the boss.

There was something off about him today though. He was being a lot more quiet than usual. Since he hired Greyson, he was always talking and smiling and putting up this persona that I decided to blame on old age. His current demeanor was one that I had known most my life. It was slightly refreshing to see it come back.

He probably got laid.

I poured some coffee for myself, adding in two spoonfuls of sugar and a little bit of cream, and followed him into my living area. With a long sip I placed the mug onto the coffee table and looked at my plant. The keeper really did a good job at keeping the plants looking healthy.

"Have you spoken with Mr. Matsumoto during these past few months at all?" Jonathan finally said.

I had to think about this. Hitomi Matsumoto was the man my father had been trying to merge businesses with for almost his entire career. Jonathan built up his company as much as he could on his own in order to make such a move that would propel us so far forward in the world of cars. He would leave behind an incredible legacy if he accomplished this and that's why he promised the company to me after this achievement.

He allowed me to take the front seat on getting materials ready for such a move to ensure that I would know how to run the company after a merger took place. His stubbornness with Matsumoto made him confident that this will go through, especially from a private conversation he had with him that allowed this meeting to even take place.

His confidence rubbed off on the company and everyone was ready for this partnership with Japan to finally happen. However, none of this was guaranteed. A lot of the pieces we spent so long putting into place could all be in vain and honestly a waste of a couple of months if Hitomi backed out.

Despite this, all of the aspects we've gone above and beyond to put together made this move the most logical for his company to jump in on as well. There are so many guaranteed benefits that I had even grown confident in my ability to secure such a deal.

"I can't say I have. Have you?" I asked back. I knew Jonathan was the point person with the Japanese. He generally gave the rest of the company any updates that could have been happening from that side. However, now that he mentioned it, I realized it had been some time since he had come to me with updates.

"I have not," He stood up and walked over to my glass wall, peering out of it. I stayed quiet. "The last few times I've reached out to Matsumoto, he spoke strangely. I'm only telling this to you because you are my successor..." He paused to look me in the eye. I nodded, acknowledging that this was a private conversation. "I am concerned that I may have been to sure about this."

Those words hit me like a brick. If I was drunk I would've sobered up instantaneously. "And you're just mentioning this now?" I responded back evenly, not trying to show the frustration that was rising within me. Leave it to Jon to keep such a secret.

"But I have not lost confidence in you. You've worked very hard and I've seen that. I'm certain you could sell a pencil to a pencil manufacturer." He made his way back over to the couch and I clenched my jaw.

"Yet, you still feel the need to tell me you are nervous about what they'll say. Which means you believe there is a chance I can't sell this company."

"Nothing in this life is guaranteed," He spoke loudly, picking up on my annoyance. "That's the unfortunate law of life. I'm telling you this because I need you to start feeling nervous and understand the gravity of this situation. I don't want you to get comfortable. Especially now that everything is almost finalized. I want you to continue to push yourself and do what I know you can." Apparently he was a motivational speaker now.

I didn't say anything. There was no use. He didn't express these concerns earlier, so I guessed it was what it was. I would simply have to accept that he decided to tell me this information now, instead of trusting me with it earlier. I couldn't wait to take this fucking company.

"You know," I opened my mouth. He was always successful in frustrating me in a way only a few people could and I couldn't help but to speak my mind. "Everything is almost done. Not everything." He was watching me patiently, "Right now, everything could be done and I could be giving you this edge you want from me. But there's a reason we aren't at that point. It's because you thought, you thought... For the most important business move of your life to hire Greyson Lewis," My voice rose slightly. "Can you finally sit here, look at me straight, and tell me the honest reason you decided to hire her?"

He smiled and relaxed in his seat, taking a sip of his coffee. That smug look was nearly enough for me to smash my mug over his head. I clenched my fist so hard I thought I drew blood.

He pulled off his jacket and loosened his tie, making himself a little too comfortable for my liking. I guess it was safe to assume the business talk was done in his mind. "I hired her because I care about you." He replied without elaborating. I was sure those simplistic answers were the icing on the cake that I hated more than anything else.

"I know everything pertaining to her is all smiles and jokes, but I'm not here to laugh." I responded and he wiped the smug look off his face.

"A man who's smart enough to know so much about people and what makes them tick, can't figure out his own damn self," Jon shook his head and I considered his words. "When I met Greyson at that event Jackson and I went to, I had some sort of epiphany. She was so friendly, so kind and had this bold, adventurous persona. I immediately thought about your mother. Of course, Ms. Lewis is a lot more extreme in every way, but those similarities she shared with your mother was impossible to miss. Jackson picked up on it as well."

Jon looked at me, as if trying to gauge my reaction. I just looked back at him, waiting for him to go on.

"Connor, when you were very young, you had a lot of similar traits with your mom. Like myself, you didn't talk very much, but you had this adventurous spirit. You were curious about everything and you came up with wild ideas," He paused, "To be honest with you Connor, I am stubborn to a fault. I was angry with her, so when I saw her traits in you, I wanted to discipline them out of you. And for the most part I succeeded. It took me over thirty years and one crazy girl to finally understand where I went wrong with both myself and you."

I don't think I ever listened to Jonathan so intently. He never truly spoke about my mother and he wasn't one to explain himself or his personal matters.

"I've never fallen in love with a woman like I did with her. She was such a free spirit and I was always stuck in my ways. Although I never admitted this, it was a mistake to let her go. This company was the only thing on my mind and as I continue getting older, I realize that this is temporary. I will retire and once I do, I will have no one to spend the rest of my time with."

He took a sip of his coffee and in that moment he looked a lot older. It was like his true self was being revealed and I had ignored just how tired he had grown to become.

"I don't want you to make the same mistakes I have. I don't want you to need thirty more years to come to the same conclusion as me. I hired Greyson in hopes that she would give you something other than work to worry about. I gave her your position so that she'd have to work in your office and with you directly. I didn't ask you because I know you are a sane person and wouldn't agree to such an idea."

I actually couldn't believe him. He literally plotted Greyson in my office to sabotage me.

"With how stressed you became, I nearly let her go in fear that you'd give yourself a brain aneurysm. However, Jackson thought I should wait awhile longer and I was surprised about how effective my plan was. You were still stressed, but not about work. Amanda could also see a difference. Whether you recognized it or not, you were talking more, leaving your office more and allowing business to come second."

I shook my head in disbelief.

"When you made that girl quit, I was so angry and disappointed with you. I came to the conclusion that you were more stubborn than I, and I truly failed as your parent. But then you went out of your way to make the girl you didn't need in your office come back and I was shocked. You have never caught me more off guard in your entire life. You truly cared about something more than work." He smiled at me and I still had no words.

Was he actually correct? Did having her in my office change me so much?

"Connor. This is long overdue, but I am truly sorry. I should've embraced your adventurous spirit and not mold you into a robot. I did you a great disservice. However, that part of you has never truly gone away. The reason I smiled when you mentioned Greyson today wasn't to mock you... We were having a conversation that had nothing to do with her, but yet you still found a way to bring her up. I smiled because, you really wanted to talk about her. She's more interesting than business for you now. Do you see that?"

I paused for a moment and relaxed into my seat, crossing my right ankle over my left knee. "If you've realized all of this a few months ago, why are you just now telling me?" I questioned back.

"You needed to be ready to listen. If I brought this up any other time you would've argued with me. Right now you are quiet, which is unlike you." He smiled again and I frowned. I didn't like him coming to so many conclusions about me. "Before I go, I have something I want to ask you, but before that, think of this. Why did I choose such a critical time to hire her? What happens to yourself or even myself if we don't get this merger? I want you to think about those things. And now this," He got up from his seat and grabbed his suit jacket, putting it back on, "Despite any external factor you can use to convince yourself otherwise, you truly like this girl, don't you?"

I could feel my face heat up slightly. My mind raced back to the previous evening and how I could not figure out the reasons for my actions. What compelled me to want to be intimate with Greyson?

I think I do... I thought to myself. I didn't reply out loud to his question. Even as I thought that, I wasn't sure if I was finally being honest with myself or not. How was it possible that I had feelings for her? It didn't make sense, yet, after thinking that I was overcome with this sense of calmness. Then, in the next moment, my mind was just as busy trying to figure out how this could be.

For the first time in my life, I truly felt like I couldn't handle everything that I was going through. Even the openness of my father was starting to overwhelm me with this odd feeling I couldn't describe.

"Don't make my mistakes." Jonathan stood up and made his way to the door.

Early Monday morning I decided to stop at the bakery near the office. Once I stepped in, my eyes shifted to where I had met with Daisy and she gave me Sam's emails. I also recalled that was the day I found out Greyson quit.

I felt silly. After speaking with Jon, I could hardly get Greyson off my mind for the rest of the weekend. A woman never occupied my mind so often and now the one who I constantly compared a child with was all I wanted to think about.

"I'll have a banana nut muffin, thank you." I pulled out my wallet and handed the smiling woman my credit card.

Knowing I was finally going to face Greyson after what happened at her apartment and the conclusion I came to with Jonathan made my stomach knot and my face heat up. The fact that I was having such a reaction made me feel absolutely ridiculous.

Greyson Lewis, some random girl in college, had me nervous.

I kept going back and forth in my mind about her possibly rejecting me, something no other girl has ever made me fearful of, and trying to counter that thought with the fact that she did kiss me back.

Ruminating about all this was sickening. It was unlike me. And everytime I reminded myself that I had work I still needed to do, I would immediately think about how I had no clue what I would even say to her when I saw her.

"Here you go!" A woman handed me a small white box, snapping me out of my endless mental debate.

"Thank you." I nodded to her and headed to the office.

After a few hours of trying to get work done and wondering when she would even show up today, Greyson finally peered her head around my door. I just looked at her, I had no idea what to say. She slowly walked in and I knew I couldn't delay it, "Greyson." I greeted her simply.

When she opened her mouth I was shocked at what she had to say. It wasn't actually all that surprising that she didn't like me. There wasn't really any reason for her to feel any interest for me, but her words stung and I turned cold. There was no way I would try now and look idiotic. She was still just some girl and I was sure I'd get over this moronic crush.

"I agree." I responded.

It didn't come to any surprise when she found a way to get upset at me and lash out before leaving the office. I decided I was going to ignore her words and go about my day.

Halfway through a very angrily typed email, I realized I was thinking about her again. Although I thought I was blocking her out, I truly couldn't. Her words came back to my mind even louder than when she said them. I don't have any feelings for you... Working with you is the fucking worst.

I slammed my fists into the table and pulled out my cell phone. Can you come to my office? I sent Samantha, really needing a distraction.

After less than two minutes, she walked in. Her red hair was pulled up into a tight bun and she had a binder in her hands. Without any words I could read her eyes loud and clear. She was still not trying to overstep her boundaries by speaking, but she gave me a look that read, there's a lot of shit you're behind on.

"Give me the more important news first. Even better if there's a problem I need to handle."

"As far as I know, things are actually going well," She opened her binder and pulled out papers, handing them to me. "I've looked over all of these, so you just need to sign the ones with an orange sticky note and go over the ones with a pink sticky note to get caught up.

We'll need to reschedule a few meetings you've missed so you can get further updates and everyone can be on the same page. I've also starred some emails that you should definitely take a look at when you have the time."

She was extremely efficient. Anytime she spoke like that it reassured me that keeping her around was the best move. I was sure I would never find another assistant who could manage to constantly be ahead of me like her.

I skimmed over the papers and then looked at her. She looked at me and then broke to look at the floor, taking a timid step back.

She lacked confidence.

"Come here," I stood up from my desk, feeling the anger from Greyson wash over me in a cold wave and I robotically made my way to my small connecting room. I hadn't spent much time in it since Greyson was hired. I was finally going to put it to good use again.

I heard Sam's heels click as she followed closely behind. Once we walked in, I closed the door behind us and Sam stood facing me, hands at her side. She didn't make any movements, just watched me carefully.

Without hesitation I closed the space between us and kissed her deeply. I didn't like something about her mouth, but I ignored those thoughts and pushed further. I roughly hiked up her dress and pushed her onto my bed. She propped herself up on her forearms and waited, watching me.

I compared the situation with Greyson. How Greyson didn't just sit there, but made a move back. Greyson had such a level of confidence and assuredness. I pulled off my belt, attempting to push those thoughts down and went over Sam. She wrapped her arms over my neck and watched me, waiting for me to make another move.

In that moment my door swung open and my heart nearly jumped out of my chest. Of course it was Greyson. "Oops! I'm super sorry," She was saying and I could feel Samantha shifting underneath me. I was just frozen. Once she finally left I sighed and looked up at the ceiling, shaking my head in frustration.

My eyes landed on a bright speck of pink. It was a small patch, but obviously the painters didn't do a great job at painting over everything completely.

I smiled slightly, I couldn't believe Greyson had the nerve to paint this room.

"Connor..." Samantha trailed off and I looked at her.

What the hell was I doing?

"I guess we were caught." I got up, grabbing my belt from the floor to loop it back through my pants.

"Why the hell do you always let that bitch dictate your actions?" Samantha sat up on the bed, eyeing me angrily.

I scrunched my eyebrows at her, "Since when do you have the nerve to talk to me like that?" I paused and waited to hear whatever reason she could even think to come up with to defend herself. Like a coward she said nothing. Her gaze shifted to an apologetic one, but I had no remorse. "I'm done listening to you talk about Greyson, how I handle my business or actually, anything at all for that matter." I felt the anger rise the more I spoke. I hesitated. A small voice in my head reminded me that she was the best assistant I ever had. So what? I thought back. "The company will be letting you go, Samantha. Effective immediately," I started saying before she cut me off.

"Connor, I'm so sorry." I could see tears threatening to leave her eyes as she stood up, not sure how to fix this.

"Expect to have your things out of the building and all my things with me by Friday afternoon." I spoke clearly, leaving no room for conversation. I was sure this was a mistake, but there was too much buzzing in my mind and I was working on auto-pilot, letting my anger control my actions.

Yep, definitely making mistakes.

I walked out and went straight to Amanda's desk.

"What is constantly going on in your office?" She asked as soon as I was in front of her.

"I'm firing Samantha. Do not let Jonathan know until I tell you it is okay to do so. I'm headed downstairs to talk to accounting, I'll be back up in about twenty minutes." I stepped away and pressed the button for the elevator.

"But the merger is coming up..." Amanda went ahead and opened her mouth again as I walked into the elevator. It honestly felt like I was going to pop a blood vessel in my brain.

"Yes, because out of everyone here I'm the one who doesn't fucking know that," My voice got loud as the elevator doors started to shut. Before the could close, I put my hand between them, opening it back up. "Another thing. The next time you go to Jonathan to tell him my business, tell him that if your job is just to watch me and report back to him, I will fire you too." I released my hand that was gripping the elevator door and pressed the ground level button.

I decided I was going to go to the gym instead. I needed to blow off some steam. It was a bad habit to let little things get me so worked up.

It didn't take very long before Greyson flooded my mind and thus the whole situation of today. Not telling her my thoughts was a coward move. Four bench presses. It was childish to try and use Samantha to get my mind off it. Five bench presses. It was an absolutely terrible situation that Greyson walked in on it. Six bench presses.

I attempted to just keep pushing through and adding more weight to my sets. At a certain point, I was feeling overwhelmed. I was not the person to ignore a situation I needed to handle.

The weights definitely calmed my anger and I knew what I needed to do to calm my thoughts. I reminded myself to stay level-headed and accept rejection if that's what it came to. Washing my face with cold water helped solidify that mentality.

I put my button-up and jacket back on and went upstairs to Amanda. She just looked at me without saying a word. "Has Sam left?" I asked.

"No, she's in her office." She replied back coldly. I knew she didn't like what I said to her.

"Text Greyson for me. Tell her to come to the office to tell me what she wanted to say." I ignored her pouting and went to the room. I paused at my door to see if I could hear Sam, but I couldn't. So I decided to ignore that as well.

When Greyson finally came in, I was sure I wanted her to know she was something special. She was occupying so much of my mind and as much as I hated it, I also didn't mind it.

Then she implied that she was sleeping with Peter and all of my meditative thinking went out the door. I couldn't fucking stand this girl.

I noticed how dejected she looked when she walked out and once the door shut I punched the top of my desk repeatedly. My knuckles were nearly bleeding when I decided to stop. I was mad at her, but I was also mad at myself.

Why was it so hard for me to control my emotions? Fucking hell, I felt like a child.

Even after understanding that, I knew I was going to speak with Peter.

I tried really hard to reconsider, but I couldn't stand the idea of him and her together in any way and even if I couldn't clear the air with Greyson, I definitely would with him.

Still mad, I found the white box on my desk that I had meant to give to Greyson. Both times I bought her a muffin she decided to mess things up. I tossed it in the trash beside my desk, promising myself not to buy her another one.

Without any further thought, I walked over to Peter's office and knocked twice before letting myself in.

"Wow it's like you read my mind. I was just needing to go over to your office to talk about the merger," Peter spoke, standing up to greet me properly. He reached his hand out to shake mine, but I ignored it, needing to make my point.

"Are you sleeping with Greyson?" The question came out quicker than I intended, but I didn't want to beat around the bush. I was mad and depending on how he answered would only make me angrier.

He squinted his eyes and looked at me inquisitively. "Unbelievable. What the hell happened to you Connor? You've been acting so unlike yourself these past few months." He crossed his arms over his chest, readying himself for an argument. That was one of the many things I respected about him, ironically. He was always deferential toward me, but saw me as his equal. If I had a point to make, he would make his point heard too.

It felt like his good qualities only bugged me more when I was angry with him.

"I know this office doesn't shun such behavior and I understand your personal affairs aren't necessarily my business. However, it is my prerogative if such a relationship is interfering with the amount of work being done." I was always able to create valid points for situations I didn't actually have valid reasons for bringing up.

"Are you going to stand there and actually tell me my work has been subpar?" He sounded a little offended.

"You have had Greyson work with you constantly and she hasn't been doing anything. I understand that she isn't so beneficial, but if you aren't actually doing work with her and just goofing off, I'd rather figure out something for her to do myself. Especially because Jonathan will have her at the merger." I retorted easily.

Peter seemed to consider my words and shook his head in agreement. He then scoffed and sat back down. "Wow," He said and continued shaking his head, nearly smiling. "You haven't talked to Greyson about the merger at all, have you? You truly don't think she has anything valuable to add here." He looked at the floor for a moment, as if in deep thought and then met eyes with me. "I get it now."

That pissed me off. He was acting as if he had me figured out. I couldn't stand his smugness.

"I'm not sure where you got the idea that I was sleeping with her, but I haven't even kissed her. But shame on you Connor, for repeating this same cycle of being such an asshole when it comes to her and undermining her ability to do anything and then when you realize you look like an ass, trying to put the blame on someone else."

It was a relief to hear Greyson wasn't being serious about them sleeping together, but I couldn't help from paying close attention to his words. If I said it once I said it a million times, but I could not ignore his opinions.

"You do realize that your actions only push her further away, right? If you want her around you need to change this bullshit you're used to. She deserves to be treated like a capable person. You'd be amazed."

It took me by surprise for a quick second that he had read me so clearly. It shouldn't have been surprising considering how great he was at reading people, however, he was implying something that I was still in the process of figuring out myself.

I felt defeated, overwhelmed and not sure what to do with myself. I sat down in a chair, exhaling fully, trying to gather some words to say. "I feel like..." I stopped myself when Peter lifted his hand.

"Connor... Listen buddy, you're a piece of shit. That's just being honest with you. I'm not going to help you figure this mess out, I have work to do." Peter looked me in the eye for a moment before placing his hands on his keyboard, shifting his focus to his computer, "I imagine you also have work to attend to." He said without missing a beat.

I got up then and left his office.

As I walked back to my office I heard Amanda speaking. I looked over to see her addressing a man standing in front of her. "I'm sorry, but you need an appointment to speak with him."

The man sighed and shook his head.

He was wearing jeans, sneakers and a baseball cap. His skin was nearly the same shade as Greyson's and that led me to walk up to them to settle the situation.

"Hi, can I help you?" I walked up, sliding my hands into my pockets. Amanda looked at me and then back at him.

He looked me up and down with bright golden brown eyes, "Only if you're Connor." He replied.

"I am," I responded back confidently, still trying to assess the situation.

"I'm Jay," He reached his hand out and I removed my hand from my pocket to shake it, "Grey's roommate. Can I talk to you for a second?"

Chapter Twenty-Four

Chapter 24 - He's Annoying (Greyson's Perspective)

I never responded to his apology text. Everything felt like shit and I woke up on the wrong side of the bed. The end of the summer was coming up and that meant the merger as well so I just needed to stop wanting to make peace with Connor. It was like a never ending ferris wheel ride and I couldn't understand why I kept myself on it.

I looked at myself in the mirror, "Girl," I said aloud at my reflection.

The good times weren't even that good and they didn't last long. And we wouldn't be friends after I finished working with him so it completely didn't matter.

"Get y'self back together." I gave myself a stern look waiting a moment, before I shook my head in agreement with myself.

When I arrived at the office, I was surprised that he wasn't around. He was almost always at his desk in the morning. It didn't really matter though, I was going to work with Peter like I usually did when I needed to get away. I grabbed some stuff, shoving them into my purse and made my way back to the door. I looked at his connecting office room, it was possible that he was in there. Which meant there was no way I was going to go in there and encounter another disgusting situation.

I walked out and smiled at Amanda, slightly off-put by how quiet everything felt. I knocked and went into Peter's office, he was just opening up his briefcase.

"Good morning," He smiled at me briefly before going back to his stuff. I could tell he was also just arriving, but getting straight to business. "Are you excited to be going to Japan?" He made small-talk with me.

"I guess we'll see. Do you think things will go well?" I asked, sitting in one of the chairs, dropping my stuff to the floor.

"No matter what happens, it will be a great situation. Don't worry about any of that." He said confidently and that made me feel a lot better.

I looked at him for a little while, watching the slight smile on his lips as he typed furiously at his computer. His blond hair looked freshly cut and he had a few really light freckles on his cheeks that had gotten slightly darker as the summer went on.

"I think we should have sex," I said to him and he didn't even flinch. He finished whatever he was typing and looked me straight in the eyes. I looked at his blue eyes that I hardly spent time noticing, waiting for him to say something. After a couple more moments of silence, I felt awkward and uncomfortable. It felt like he was looking through me.

"I've never met a woman like you. So confident and candid," I felt my face heat up as he spoke about me. It really wasn't what I was expecting. I thought he felt the sexual tension between us and was just going to say something like, oh hell yeah Grey let's do it! It became apparent that my thoughts might have been a little too hopeful. "I now have all the pieces of the puzzle." He smiled, and looked at me longer.

I finally fidgeted in my seat, not sure what he meant or how to respond to something like that.

"It's a shame, because you deserve far better..." He kept being vague.

"If you don't want to have sex, you can just say so. You won't hurt my feelings." I interjected.

He laughed once, "Greyson," His face became dead-serious, "I would fuck you here right now." He said with so much certainty, my whole body got hot. I had never in my entire life felt more embarrassed to hear anyone say any words to me ever, than in that moment. "On the condition that you weren't doing it to spite someone."

My eyebrows furrowed. "What?" My voice nearly cracked from the previous embarrassment.

"I don't think I'm the superhero you want, unfortunately." He sighed and shook his head. "Listen, I've got everything covered here, I would check in with Connor and see if there's anything he wants to go over with you." He said and I felt the full harshness of him kicking me out.

All of the confusion and embarrassment made me feel annoyed with him. So I grabbed my stuff from the floor and got up. Peter was already back to work, not looking at me anymore. With a loud humph to express my annoyance, I walked out.

I was certain I didn't want to go to Connor's office again, but Peter was my only known solace and I was sure I just made things awkward between us. I really messed things up when I was off my meds. Then Amanda popped into my head, and I decided to go to her.

She greeted me pleasantly when I walked up. I tried my best to give just as genuine a smile back, but I was sure it came across lacking a lot of enthusiasm. "I'm finally done avoiding you," I tried to laugh, but kind of chuckled instead. Peter really got to me. That was not cool.

"The week has just begun, but it's been rough on all of us," Her soft voice made me feel a lot more at peace.

"Do you think I should just not go to Japan?" I asked and before she could answer ranted on, "I honestly don't care so much about it. Not as much as everyone here does anyways. And I don't actually want to sabotage anything for Connor, which I know he thinks I'll do. Like, this job has been hella helpful with giving me a nice paycheck this summer for doing a little bit of work, but does Jon really want me to go? I feel like he kind of just gave me this job to help me and that's all been wonderful. Nobody here even likes me." I just kept going.

"Greyson, you know that's not true. You deserve to be there and it's coming up in a few days so you can't back out now." My heart dropped, was it really that soon? I had the date on my calendar, but I checked calendars very sparingly.

I ignored what she said, not actually wanting to talk about that anymore. "Where is Connor anyways?" I asked, my eyes shifting back over to the office.

"In a meeting. He's about to get a whole lot busier now that the merger is practically here. And with the way he's handling business," She shook her head, "I'm not sure what's going on in that brain of his."

"Well it's probably for the best that he's busier." I countered, hoping he'd have less time to bother me.

"When he has a lot of work to do, he can become a lot meaner." She said back.

"Sounds impossible to me." I responded and the elevator opened, revealing a group of like six men. Connor was at the front, talking to one of the men and they all looked scarily professional, like a group of top secret agents whispering to one another, making their way to Connor's office.

I locked eyes with Connor, and he managed to keep talking to the guy while staring at me hard. I broke the eye contact and saw my least favorite person in the world in the back of the group. Adam's cold blue eyes saw mine and he stopped walking to give me his signature creepy smirk.

How was he not on a registered sex offenders list?

"Good morning," He said to me, peering at a very expensive looking watch on his wrist.

Oh yeah, that's why he wasn't on a list. He could pay his way out.

"Please, just not today. Go follow them." I pointed at the group of men entering the office.

"Even if I follow them, you won't be getting rid of me anytime soon. The merger is upon us." He licked his bottom lip and I was utterly disgusted. It reminded me of when he came to my house.

"Do you even have an office here?" I asked, not sure why I was allowing the conversation to continue.

"Of course. A few floors down, I don't like to be around Connor when I'm here. He gets too needy." I actually laughed at that. I should've taken another floor when I had the chance. "Let me show it to you," He stepped in the direction of the elevators, waiting for me to come along.

"What about your meeting?" I asked, looking back at Connor's office, where the door had already been shut.

"They don't really need me." He smirked and made another step toward the elevator.

Greyson, you hate him. I tried reminding myself, but I was bored and didn't want Amanda's reassurance, Peter didn't want anything to do with me and this was someone who I was sure was distracting. Still, I was sure hanging out with him would be like dipping a foot or two into some lava.

He made another step toward the elevator.

After weighing the options, I decided I could go for a burning sensation. Ew, that sounded like STD's and I did not mean that at all.

He smiled when I followed him into it, looking at me with those pervy eyes of his and I felt like a piece of meat. It was kind of nice in a weird way. Which sounded absolutely horrible, I know, but he was giving me attention.

That still didn't sound much better, but I got bored with logical reasoning from time to time.

"I knew I'd catch your interest eventually." He whispered in my ear as the elevator went down. A chill went down my spine and I remembered why I actually hated him so much. For a moment, I had completely forgotten how terrible he was at Jonathan's house party.

Wow, I forgot about that party entirely.

We got to the floor he occupied and I vaguely remembered walking through it one day. The receptionist on the floor was a lot younger than Amanda, boobs on full display in her plunging white v-neck blouse. I could tell her full bust didn't come naturally, just like her bleach blonde hair. She smiled flirtily to Adam and then I caught a bit of a glare toward me. I could've been overanalyzing it, but if the red-headed witch of my floor taught me anything, it was that women here were far too obvious with their emotions.

He walked me over to the far side of the floor and opened a door to reveal a room that was larger than Peter's, but just a tad bit smaller than Connor's. He motioned for me to head in and followed, closing the door behind him. I flinched at that, wishing I walked in last to keep the door cracked open.

As strong as I thought I was, unfortunately, my mom had instilled this fear of the potential of being overpowered by some horny guy. I always thought that if my dad was around longer, he would've taught me more about self-defense. But, alas, he was not and I had no skills nor weapons, and I was aware that my time at the school's gym kept me toned, but didn't build any sort of muscle.

However, my dad did pass along bravery, and I would not let him know that I was nervous in the slightest. Honestly, there was no reason to be. He was creepy, but I was sure he wouldn't want to be sued. Whereas I was not afraid to go to prison.

"So how do you like it?" He asked, opening his arms to gesture to the space.

Taking myself out of my thought process, I took in his office and actually admired it. There were sketches of cars and car parts hanging as pictures along his walls. He had a very light brown desk that looked beachy and deep blue accent pieces everywhere. He had a large blue rug on the floor, a blue clock on his desk, and his pictures were all hung in blue frames.

"Wow, this is so much nicer than Connor's boring office." I said aloud.

"Yeah he likes to keep things extremely professional and old-fashioned. Strictly business. I don't hold meetings here and hardly am here, so I can keep this a lot more to my personal tastes." He spoke, obviously proud of his interior design.

Although I was facing away from him, I found myself rolling my eyes. I could probably do a better job with the space.

When I turned back around, he was partially sitting on his desk, arms crossed smugly as he watched me.

Such a creeper.

"So what? Why do you want me?" I crossed my arms to match his smugness. I wasn't as caught off guard as I was when he came to my house, and so I would show him that I could be just as professional and blunt at the same time as he could.

He cracked a smile, raising his eyebrows at me. "Always so fiery, my goodness." He licked his lips, still looking overjoyed. How he got any girls was beyond me. "Who said I wanted you?" He asked, and although I could tell he wasn't being dead serious, the fact that he was pulling that bullshit was ridiculous.

"Wow, okay." I scoffed and immediately walked to the door. I opened it without hesitation and fully planned on just leaving before he opened his mouth.

"Alright, I'll let you know." He said evenly.

I paused for a moment, considering if I should shut the door confidently when I turned around or keep it cracked open cautiously. Obviously, I went with the option that sounded more confident, even if also stupid.

Once it clicked into place I walked back over to him, and he looked a little more surprised than smug now and I loved it. Finally felt like I was getting the upper hand.

"Such a firecracker, huh?" He asked, "What makes you so curious?"

I nearly sighed. I honestly thought he had more balls than this. He had to be the one asking the questions, classic power move. Whatever, I could play along. "Well, it's interesting that a person who thinks I'm too incompetent for this job also thinks I'm in his league. Ain't it?"

He smiled again, taking a pause. "I honestly don't care that you work here. It's been hilarious hearing Connor's stories about working with you. It has made this job a lot more entertaining for me. It sounds like you enjoy making his life harder, which is difficult for anyone to do because he would have fired them by now. However, if your goal is to give him problems, I just don't want you messing up the merger, because that affects me as well. Although Connor's worked hard for it, I have as well, so you messing it up messes me up."

I was mostly paying attention to him, but my mind kept lingering on the knowledge that Connor was complaining about me to him of all people. I'd rather him complain to Samantha before this guy.

"Having heard about you and also meeting you personally made me interested. You're decently attractive and I've never actually been with your kind before. Plus, I'm sure that wild personality would be a lot of fun."

What the fuck? Decently attractive? Wild personality? My kind? He could not honestly think he was flattering me! I swore, all the people at this place grew up under a rock and were too ignorant to survive a day outside of the bubble they put themselves in.

I was pissed. If that was his way of speaking frankly, I'd do him one better.

"My personality is definitely fun, I'll tell you that," I was surprised at myself for speaking so calmly. "Alright, you gave me some good ass reasons for wantin' me and I think I'm interested in you as well. Let's see what we're workin' with. Drop your pants." I kept my expression indifferent and serious.

He chuckled once, testing my bluff, but I remained in place. He looked at me a lot more seriously now, trying to read me. "Excuse me?" He finally asked, his smug demeanor crumbling.

"Let's be honest with each other Adam. I'm sure you're lookin' for a hookup. I mean... There's no way I would date you. So, let's have some fun. But, I'm used to my kind, and my kind's average size is the only size I work with. If you fit that requirement, we can have some fun. Are you pickin' up what I'm puttin' down?"

Stunned silence followed. Checkmate motherfucker.

"Drop your pants. Let's see it." I looked down at his pants and then back up to his face. He didn't move a muscle. His face was beet red. At that moment I couldn't help it, I wish I could take a picture of his face he looked so flustered. I just started laughing. He kind of tried laughing along too, his face still bright red.

"You're pathetic," I got serious again and he looked so confused. That was fine with me. "I'm going to make this clear. I've got a cousin coming out of jail next week," I lied, "He's been in and out of the system and he would be more than happy to beat up someone like you." I knew I shouldn't reinforce stereotypes, but when someone pissed me off in that direction, I felt a need to push the boundaries. "You will not flirt with me, you will not look at me like you're undressing me with your eyes, and you will not ever come to my home for any reason whatsoever," I stared into those cold blue eyes of his, "Let me tell you somethin' else. I will be at the merger in Japan and you will simply deal with it. I'm leaving this job after that anyways."

He looked slightly pissed. Like he was trying to fight back, but really had nothing to say.

"Report me to HR if you want because, yes, this is a threat. Fuck you." I turned around and this time I actually walked out of his office.

As I made my way back to the elevator, I felt super relieved. It was like I was taking back control of all the bullshit at this office and I got the creeper off my case for good.

Today was starting to turn around.

Then I got into the elevator and realized I wasn't sure where to go. My floor would definitely bring my mood back down, but the conversation with Connor's bestie gave me confidence. I wasn't going to avoid Connor like a scared child. I'd walk in, do what I had to do and walk out, only talking to him if spoken to.

Back up to the floor, Amanda didn't even looked surprised to see me back so soon. "Are they still meeting in there?" I asked, looking at the office and back to her.

"Yes," She replied back.

"Do you know about how long that will last?" I asked, already feeling impatient.

"Not a clue." She responded and gave me a lopsided grin. I groaned. "So what happened with Adam?" She asked, pretending to be focused on her computer like she wasn't being nosy.

"That guy is an ass. Hey, so how many days away is the merger?" I asked, realizing I still wasn't completely sure.

She finally looked directly at me, blinking her eyes a few times in what I assumed was shock, "Two days." She finally responded.

My jaw dropped so wide, I was sure flies would swarm my mouth, "You're joking." I said to her and she just shook her head no. "Why did nobody tell me?! I'm not prepared in the slightest!" I started rummaging through my purse, wondering if I had enough of my things to be able to leave the office and go shop and pack and find my passport. "Shit, shit, shit!" I pushed around random papers and couldn't find my keys. I probably dropped it on my desk earlier and didn't even realize. "Fuck." I said after searching some more.

"What's wrong?" Amanda asked as I was completely freaking out.

"I am not ready for Japan." I stopped searching in my bag and started staring at the door to the office. I was biting my bottom lip and tapping my foot on the ground. It made sense that Connor was a jerk enough not tell me it was literally right around the corner, but couldn't Jonathan send a text? Or at least an email.

And then I thought about that. To be honest, it was possible that he did send an email, but I hadn't checked my email in probably a couple of weeks at the least. What an idiot I was.

"Amanda, my keys are in there and I need them," I said to her, really needing a solution. "I have to go get ready. I haven't even bought clothes for this." I was so surprised. The most exciting thing that was going to happen at this job, and I didn't even know it was coming up.

"Would you like me to call him?" She asked, and I felt some relief wash over me.

"Yes please!" I shook my head furiously in agreement. That was a good plan.

She picked up the phone and dialed his extension and I could vaguely hear it ringing through the receiver.

One ring.

Two rings.

Three rings.

Four rings.

"Pick up Connor!" I spoke up, getting antsy. It went to voicemail and she hung up.

"Sorry." She said to me.

"This boy, I swear." I rolled my eyes and pulled out my phone. I scrolled through my contact list, finding his name and hitting the call button.

It rang once, then twice, "Hello?" He picked up and my heart jumped slightly. I honestly wasn't expecting him to pick up.

"Sorry to bother you during your meeting, but I need my keys that are in there."

"We'll be done here in two minutes, that alright?" He asked.

"Yes perfect!" I responded.

"Alright, see you then." He said nicely and hung up.

I smiled, the conversation actually went well. It was proof that he usually made things more difficult than they had to be.

I looked at Amanda who was raising an eyebrow at me.

"I'm gonna go to the bathroom to pass some time. Be right back." I said and headed down the hall. Now all I would have to do is pee real quick, grab my keys, call Liz to go shopping, buy things today, pack tomorrow and then hopefully checking in with Peter wouldn't be weird, and then Japan! It was a great plan.

As I came out of the bathroom, I saw the group of men chatting near Amanda, probably waiting for the elevator. I couldn't see Connor with them which meant he was probably still in the office. And if I was playing jeopardy, I would've won some cash for that guess.

He was standing behind his desk, fixing some papers. I could tell he had a fresh haircut and just shaved. He was looking as neat as he always did. "Hi," He said to me, being way too friendly.

I rolled my eyes, "Nice Connor is back, huh?" I finally stopped staring at him and went over to my desk, "It never lasts long." I kept speaking. The situation with Adam really built my confidence. And maybe some sass as well.

"I've been unfair to you," He said and I scoffed instantly and glared at him.

"How about you tell me something I don't know," I said with a whole lot of attitude and turned to face my desk.

"I am sorry for how I've been to you, Greyson."

I shook my head, "That's honestly really great Connor, I just don't care. I promise once this Japan trip is over I'll be gone for good and you won't have to even think about me. And if this trip wasn't pretty much here, I would do you the biggest solid and not even show up. I'm not tryin' to ruin it for you. You can relax." I was rummaging through my desk drawers, not sure where the hell I placed my keys. I pulled back the chair and of course, it was on the floor.

"I didn't mean what I said yesterday. There's been a lot going on and sometimes I take out my frustration improperly. We can sit down and go over what you wanted to talk about with the merger and I'm fine with you giving your input in Japan." He walked over and was now standing next to me. How did I not notice I dropped my keys earlier?

"You are always frustrated and taking it out on me. It's like every-time I reach my hand out to you, you burn it and I just keep on stickin' it right back in. My hand's completely burnt off. So I'm done with all of this. Just talk to Peter." I stuck my keys in my purse and turned to face him. Looking into his eyes made me think about the night at my place. Some part of me was still hung up on that. "I gotta go get ready. But Connor..." I paused, still slightly mesmerized by his once very bland brown eyes, "Despite everything, I never actually hated working here. It's been stressful and annoying, and I did think about quitting, but I don't hate you. If you're truly sorry, just be nicer to the other people working here." I shrugged and went to the door.

Once I opened it I looked back at Connor to give him a half-hearted grin and I swore on the grave of my father, because I could not make something like this up...

He opened his mouth and said, "Greyson, I think I'm in love with you."

Chapter Twenty-Five

Chapter 25 - She's Intriguing (Connor's Perspective)

I took Greyson's roommate to my office, mentally going through all the possible reasons he could be looking for me. I also took note that Greyson's roommate was male, something that didn't sit well with me. I wasn't sure if she ever mentioned it or I forgot, but I did assume her roommate was female.

He was heavily built, not from fat, just pure muscle. Tattoos ran down his arms and up his neck and he was a lot shorter than me, definitely shorter than Greyson. He looked around the place, scoping it out before finding one of my chairs and sitting in it. I decided to follow his lead, sitting in the chair closest to his, instead of at my desk chair. As I sat, analyzing him and waiting for him to speak up, he met my eyes, and his were such a bright yellow/brown, it was as if he were wearing contacts. It reminded me of Greyson's eyes, so green it looked fake.

"So you the man she's workin' with." He looked me up and down, nodding his head, obviously thinking something. "You look exactly how I thought." He had a thick urban accent and something about his tone made me feel like this wasn't a friendly visit.

"What do you need?" I asked frankly, feeling my jaw clench. I would never enjoy when a person didn't make their point clear.

"Since workin' here, Grey has been so fuckin' stressed that I decided to deal with this shit myself." He sounded decently calm, but his words were so combative, I wasn't sure if he was looking for a fight or not. "I'mma be honest wit'chu. I just don't like you. I'm here as a favor to my fam."

It surprised me that we had something in common. Because I didn't like this guy either. As much as I wanted to say something, I decided to just close my mouth. Which was a really difficult thing for me to do.

"So I'm gone tell it how it is. Grey is like my sister. Her family is mine. Now uncle Tim met you at his cookout and he says you like her. I think he's buggin' but whatever. Says you a good man and likes the idea of y'all two," He paused, looking at me with his head tilted sideways. He straightened his neck and nodded again. "Ain't that some fuckin' shit."

I considered his words. It was surprising to think her uncle thought I liked her way before I thought I liked her. Especially considering I was only going to that event because I nearly made her quit beforehand.

"He really thinks you like her!" He sounded nearly incredulous, "He thinks that, when she's comin' home, every fuckin' day, stressin' because she says you hate her." He opened his arms, with the palms of his hands facing upward, shrugging to signify his confusion with this concept.

"She thinks I hate her?" I heard myself ask. I was well aware that I wasn't the kindest to her... Well, I guess if I was being fully honest, I treated her like shit. However, she would generally argue back, or come around smiles and all, talking to me like everything was fine. I knew I pushed it too far when she nearly quit because of my comment, but even then she bounced back as if it didn't truly affect her.

Then I thought about when she spoke about her mother and how quickly she brushed away those emotions although it was quite possible those things affected her. Could I have truly made every single day miserable for her?

That was sobering.

"Grey is the sweetest girl in the world. She went through so much shit, and nothin' she got makes her any less. Not no ADHD, Bipolar, anxiety, or depression shit. I never met a person, male or female, tougher than her," He paused from his rant, "If he is right, and you really like her, but you're treatin' her like shit, you betta' walk away." He pointed a finger in my face and my jaw clenched. I didn't like the way this man was talking to me, but it didn't seem smart to pick a fight with him. "I won't let any guy fuck with her. Especially not some punk ass white boy," His eyes scanned me and then he got up.

Although I didn't like what he was saying, it was rather easy to brush off his comments. He didn't mean anything to me. However, knowing that he considered himself a brother to Greyson, made me weary of how I would respond.

Even when Greyson wasn't around she managed to strike a nerve.

I stood up as well, following him back to the door, "Does she hate me?" I asked, knowing that was the most prominent thought on my mind.

"Ask her that," He stopped walking to look at me, "Every time she comes to me, she's try'na figure out how to get you to like her," He shook his head in disbelief. "Tim really thinks you like her. Listen, Grey don't know I came here. You keep it that way." He opened my door and extended his hand. I grabbed it, giving him a very firm shake. "Man up or walk away." He warned and walked out.

I watched him go to the elevator, wave at Amanda and step in. Once the doors closed behind him I walked over to Amanda, "I can't talk about it because it's personal business," I spoke, knowing what she was already thinking to ask, "And because of that, he does not want Greyson knowing he came here. Please respect that," I looked at her firmly, waiting for her to shake her head in understanding.

"Connor, the merger..." I rose my hand, stopping her from finishing whatever sentence she was about to say.

"I'm well aware Amanda. I'm going to set up all the final meetings I need for it, please, keep these next three days distraction free. Also, I need a temporary assistant, find someone internal. They'll get full rates on top of their current salary. Thank you," I walked back to my office shutting the door.

I really needed to ignore any thoughts of Greyson and get things done. The merger truly was the most important thing to worry about.

After back to back meetings with all the different departments working on the merger, I was surprised that everyone was completely prepared and ready. I hadn't realized how much I became blind to with Greyson taking up so much mental space. I had Sam keeping track of so much, I didn't have a clue about my own business.

It made me think that despite everything, Sam was exceptional. Maybe when I became CEO I'd consider rehiring her.

It was eight past ten when I was completely finished in my office. I had enough time to go over what I would be talking about and I was sure I'd get all finalized details for my presentation within the next day. When all my thoughts of work pushed itself to the back of my mind, I wasn't even surprised that Greyson came right back to the surface. Nevertheless, it pissed me off. I couldn't compartmentalize the thought of her for as long as I wanted. She just popped right back up. It ironically matched her personality.

Her roommate mentioned her mental disorders in passing, but I was floored. Was she currently struggling with depression? Or was that in the past? How often did anxiety affect her? And did she truly have bipolar disorder? I didn't actually know much about it, so I decided to google it. There were two types, and I really couldn't tell which she had. You only needed one manic episode in your entire life, but depression was the main symptom. Type two was just milder than the first.

It truly wouldn't have been surprising to learn she had the first type. The depression part was what kept throwing me off. I closed my laptop and threw my head back, relaxing into my chair. I didn't have enough of an understanding of my own thoughts to keep going through this mental cycle.

I sat up again and grabbed my phone. I went through my contacts and found Greyson's name. I clicked on the message icon and looked at my screen. I had no idea what I wanted to say to her, but I knew I couldn't talk to her through text, it needed to be face to face.

"She's so fucking hard to talk to," I said aloud to myself and typed, *I'm sorry.* I looked at the message, considering if I should send it or just wait. Compulsion got the best of me and I decided to hit send. I watched as it delivered and locked my phone, placing it back on my desk. I stared at it for a second, thinking about everything and nothing at the same time and then stood up, grabbing my things to leave.

After everything, I wasn't sure if she would respond or not, but I needed to get sleep to get through the next day and deal with my important business.

I had gotten to the office early to meet with the primary people who would be at the table in Mr. Matsumoto's office to do the deal. Almost everyone was there except for Rich who was taking a sick day and Peter who handed me his information and said he didn't need to be here for all of this. It had irritated me deeply, but I didn't fight it. I knew he was still annoyed from our conversation and his saving grace was that I knew he would be all set anyways.

After we met in the presentation room to go over the visuals, we went back to my room to talk about more private internal matters of how the meeting would be structured. Walking back I saw Greyson standing near Amanda and she looked directly at me and I met her gaze. I couldn't help the trance I felt trapped in as I walked by, she was spending so much time in my mind that it was starting to feel surreal to see her in person.

Then I thought, if I was trying to be apologetic to her, I probably should have invited her to these meetings as well.

Fuck, just another thing on the list of reasons why I was such crap to her.

Once we got in, I immediately noticed that Adam wasn't with us. "Where's Adam?" I asked, the other men looked around, shrugging. I constantly felt veins popping out of my head, "Nevermind, just shut the door, I don't have time for this."

The meeting was going great, it turned out the merger was going to be our absolute best business proposal. I was excited to let Jonathan know how well this was going to be.

"How will we celebrate Connor?" The mood had gotten incredibly light as we realized how together this was. I was proud of my team and how hard they worked. Although this meeting should've happened about two weeks ago, happening two days before put more pressure on them to get things done properly and it was nice to be on the same page. These men were great no matter what came up.

"Yeah Conn, I think we should have a lot of sushi, a lot of sake, and a lot of Japanese women," Charlie spoke up and everyone laughed, a smile formed on my lips.

"If we get Japan, yes to all of those things. You can use the company credit card for anything if we get this deal." I spoke up getting a lot of cheers in return.

My desk phone rang and I looked to see reception on the caller ID. I ignored it, listening to everyone's stories about what they wanted to do if we were successful. The positive atmosphere was something I definitely needed.

"If this deal goes through I might just volunteer to oversee Japanese business matters. I wouldn't mind moving," Someone was saying and some were laughing, others just shook their head.

"You think I trust you to be in charge of Japan?" I responded back.

My cell buzzed then and I saw Greyson's name appear. I stood up from my desk and stepped back to get away from the group, answering the call, "Hello?" I said, the men behind me immediately quieted down, whispering instead.

"Sorry to bother you during your meeting, but I need to get my keys that are in there." She sounded stressed out. Just hearing her voice made me realize how much I grew to enjoy the crazy, loud, all over the place talk of hers and how this was the last bit of business I still needed to resolve.

I became instantly determined to fix my situation with her. This time, nothing would stop me from saying what I meant.

After I hung up with her I ended our nonsense conversation and told the men to keep me informed if they needed to make any changes or realized any errors.

This was going to be my chance to truly speak with her.

After a few minutes she appeared in the office. I noticed she was wearing a long, white and olive green sundress, something I overlooked when I saw her earlier. It still wasn't proper office attire, but that was a battle I gave up on. The green in the dress highlighted the green in her eyes, and like a deer stuck in headlights, all that came out of my mouth was, "Hi."

What snapped me back to the moment and my promise to actually speak with her was her rolling her eyes and declaring that my kind persona was a temporary facade. She went over to her desk, rummaging through it haphazardly.

She told her roommate I hated her.

"I've been unfair to you," I tried and before I could continue she quickly dismissed me and stared daggers at me.

"How about you tell me something I don't know." She quickly let out and I could tell she was becoming angrier. She turned her head back around to continue her rummaging.

I was surprised. Although our bickering could go on for a few days, she usually came around, especially if I was apologizing.

"I am sorry for how I've been to you, Greyson." I pushed further. I'm sorry for every single thing, I thought to myself.

Without looking at me she completely disregarded my apology. Her comment about being gone after the merger and I wouldn't have to worry about her got to me.

She kneeled down, grabbing her keys off of the ground and I made my way over to her desk, trying to excuse my behavior instead of saying what I thought. In the past, it was easy to not think about her actually leaving for school after the merger because it was so far away. However, now...

I would lose her...

What she said rang loud in my ear. She was done putting up with me and she no longer wanted to make amends.

...but I don't hate you. She made sure to mention and her eyes seemed to glisten. She walked away from me then and I honestly panicked. I usually wasn't a person to panic, but something about how she spoke made me feel like she was truly done.

The panic came over me and before I could reason through my thoughts I told her, "Greyson, I think I'm in love with you." I wasn't sure that I meant it, and the dramatic nature of that declare made me feel like I truly wasn't in my proper state of mind, but once it was said, I could not take it back.

She was clutching the door handle, ready to step out when my words brought her to a dead halt. Her neutral expression dropped and her eyes became wide. "You..." She started but instantly stopped, her eyebrows scrunched together and she shook her head 'no' twice and promptly walked out, shutting the door.

"Fuck!" I yelled, turning to kick the chair closest to me. It was one of the chairs put into the office in front of Greyson's desk when she came. It fell to the ground and I just watched it. I ended up using the seat for my meetings more than she ever did. In fact, she never once needed it.

I absolutely hated the day Jonathan had the audacity to move this person into my office and gave her an entire desk. It not only ruined the openness of my space and made colleagues question my authority as a leader when I didn't have my own office, but it also placed the most bothersome person I had ever met, in my constant vicinity.

Now I couldn't imagine her going away. "What honestly happened to you?" I asked myself aloud. Still looking at the seat.

I really needed a cigarette. Or death, quite honestly.

It was finally the day of our flight to Japan. I was exceptionally calm because everything was exceptionally well prepared. We had all gathered at five in the afternoon to take a private jet over to Tokyo. Despite the jet, it was still going to be a decently long flight and Japan was thirteen hours ahead of us so we needed to plan enough time for jet lag and also having a full day before the meeting to get settled.

The most prominent question was how the past two days went after I ridiculously announced to Greyson that I possibly loved her. She just decided to not come to work at all. After thinking about it for almost the full first day, I asked Amanda to call her and see what was going on. Greyson ignored her calls, voicemails and texts. I thought about asking Peter, but decided that was a bad idea and as the second day came and she did not, I went to Jonathan.

I was too stubborn to call her myself, and luckily Jonathan was too nervous about his precious hiree not showing up to Japan to question my motives. She did pick up when he called and informed him that she just needed to get ready and that she would show up on time for the trip.

When I arrived, she was already there, chatting and laughing with Jackson. Jonathan was speaking with one of the pilots and most people were there except for Adam and Peter. My two most trusted employees both had a personality of showing up exactly when needed and not a moment before.

"May the merger go well," Joey said a quick prayer as he grabbed my bags from the trunk. Amanda specifically asked him to be my temporary schedule keeper because he worked in marketing, sales and services. This meant he was particularly great with understanding schedules, sticking to them, and quickly changing them when needed. Considering this was probably the most important thing I needed him for as a temporary replacement assistant, he was perfect. Thank God for Amanda.

He was also extremely excited to be going to Japan, and took the opportunity in an instant. As we approached the group, waiting to board my phone buzzed in my pocket.

Connor, I know I am extremely valuable to you and not even you know how to keep yourself organized better than me. I can be there in 15. Please, be smart about this.

I stared at the text from Sam, thinking about her words. Firing her was definitely a heat-of-the-moment move, and I wasn't sure if I should swallow my pride and bring her back. I looked at the time on my watch, she did have enough time to get here.

I looked up at Greyson, who was looking at me, but then quickly turned her head to look away.

"Joey, do you truly know my schedule?" I asked him as he came back from handing one of the flight attendants the rest of our bags.

"When I say I'm detailed oriented, that isn't just for show. Right after Amanda reached out to me, I have been studying your schedule and all of the important details nonstop. There's no way I'll let you down." He said to me and I decided to close out of my phone and ignore Sam. I liked his confidence.

He was a few years younger than myself, and was exactly what the marketing department needed to understand the current trends in social media. His resume was impressive and he was easy to get along with.

Joey was half Indian, half Caucasian and came from LA. He was incredibly short with very cropped black hair and nearly black eyes. He had a golden brown skin tone and wore these square-framed, modern glasses. His outfit consisted of black joggers and a gray t-shirt. We had told everyone to dress comfortably because it was a long flight and we wouldn't be going directly into business and he took full advantage of that.

I was obviously wearing a full suit, along with many of the older members of our group. Jackson was in shorts and I could see that

Greyson was in actual pajamas. "This girl," I mumbled under my breath taking in her long fuzzy pink pajama bottoms with white hearts all over and white tank top. She had also draped a purple blanket over her shoulders.

She truly had no shame.

We finally boarded the plane, Greyson was the first person to get on, and I tried to follow right after, but Jonathan held me up. As I entered, I could hear her loudly over everyone else, "Wow, these seats have tables! This is really nice!" She threw a bookbag in the overhead compartment and took a seat.

As I walked over to her, Jon stopped me and asked to sit with me personally. I clenched my jaw in frustration, but obliged.

We were seated diagonally from Greyson's spot, in two seats that faced each other. I made sure to sit in the seat facing Greyson as well. I saw her shaking Joey's hand and offering for him to sit across from her at the four seat conference table.

"I've never seen you before," She was saying. I couldn't hear what he responded with, but then she said, "Oh, so Sam's not here anymore? Wow." She looked out the window and then turned her head towards the entrance. Peter finally came on, sporting powder yellow shorts and a navy blue polo.

"Peter! Come sit here," She called to him and he smiled over at her before walking up. He searched the plane and spotted me, giving me a nod of acknowledgement. I nodded back, but was completely pissed off.

"Connor," Jon said, diverting my attention back to him. "Now, up until and including the merger, all of your attention is on this. Understood?"

I knew exactly what he was getting at, and I nodded in agreement. No more games, pull yourself together.

Adam finally made an appearance, looking like he recently woke up. Probably from a heavy night of drinking. He wore dress pants and a white button-up that wasn't buttoned all the way up. He had bags under his eyes and a coffee mug in his hand. He saluted me and found Greyson, throwing a briefcase in the overhead compartment, deciding to sit there as well.

The anger was just rising within me.

Merger first.

He shook hands with Greyson, who smiled in return and they all began talking to each other.

I finally looked away, it was going to be a long flight.

It was definitely a long fucking flight.

After talking to Jonathan for about a few hours and then some other men, I tried to get some sleep. However, I kept waking up, either because the merger would come to mind or I'd hear Greyson's voice.

They had all been talking nonstop, sharing stories and laughing about other nonsense. At some point Greyson learned that behind a curtain, there was a meeting table so she moved the group and a few other men came along to play card games. That became decently loud at moments and Greyson's voice rang over the others. Some of my older workers had ear plugs in as they tried to sleep through it, and surprisingly nobody seemed to truly mind the noise.

Nobody, but me.

Even when it was darker out and most people were sleeping, Greyson was generally awake, either listening to music or chatting with a flight attendant. She probably got no more than five hours of sleep the whole flight.

Once we landed, I waited until everyone walked off the plane to walk off myself. Greyson simply walked past me, she hadn't looked at me once since we boarded the plane.

It was twelve in the morning in Tokyo and very dark. I was entirely ready to actually get some sleep and hopefully sleep in. Which, for me, wouldn't be longer than eight hours. Company cars were already waiting for us, the plane attendants were packing our luggage into them.

"Greyson," I called her and watched as she looked around, trying to find me. She met my eyes and then looked down.

"Yeah?" She asked, still not looking directly at me.

"You're riding to the hotel with me." I walked over to her and pointed her to the direction of our car.

"Do I have to?" She whined quietly, pouting.

"Yes," I responded assertively. I then found Joey, "Ride with Adam and make sure he knows our schedule."

He nodded once and went over to Adam's car.

I watched as Greyson threw a small tantrum, stomping over to the car and letting herself in, shutting the door aggressively.

I smiled at that. If she was being dramatic or angry, I knew that meant I was at the very least bothering her. It was when she was indifferent or cold that worried me. In other words her tantrum proved she wasn't completely done with me.

I made my way to the other side of the car. Entering, I saw that she placed her bookbag in the middle of the seat, making sure I couldn't sit close to her at all. Even after I sat down, she kept her body facing the window, looking out it.

"Will you be facing that way the whole ride?" I asked, a smirk plastered on my face.

"Yep," She said, popping the 'p'.

"Okay, I'll just speak to your back. Jonathan made sure our hotel rooms are directly next to each other, so if you need anything I'll be easily accessible. This first day is mostly free. You can sleep in and the hotel has multiple restaurants to dine from. Feel free to use a company credit card, or keep any receipts to be reimbursed. We will have a translator meeting us at the hotel, he will be available to help whenever."

She nodded her head, signaling to me that she was at least listening.

"The hotel will definitely have people who speak English, so don't worry about that. At four p.m. we will be having one final meeting in the hotel's conference room and then the evening is free. No alcohol or late partying tonight, the meeting will be taking place at ten the following morning. Be ready by nine a.m., we are driving together."

"Okay," She responded.

After about five minutes of driving she spun her head around dramatically, causing me to meet her gaze. Her mouth was opened like she was going to speak, but after a moment she just shut her mouth and turned her head back around.

I had a good inkling as to what that moment was about. We hadn't been in the same space in over two days and the last time we were, I had confessed feelings I still wasn't sure about. I considered clearing the air, or even taking back what I said, but I decided to wait it out and let her bring it up. If she decided to never bring it up, I wasn't sure what I would do, but if I knew at least one thing about her, it was that she'd be too curious to ignore it forever.

She ended up pulling her headphones out of her bag and connecting it to her phone, bobbing her head lightly to whatever was loudly blasting in her ears.

Once we arrived, Greyson jumped out of the car in awe. "It's just like New York here!" She exclaimed, running up to the hotel and walking inside before anyone else.

"You wouldn't think she's in a foreign country." Peter came up behind me, swinging a backpack over his shoulder. "Once again Connor, good luck." He placed a hand on my shoulder, squeezing gently and looked at me for a long moment before turning to walk into the hotel with everyone else.

It felt like his good luck had a double meaning.

I walked in myself finally, following my team who quickly made their way to the front desk. Our translator was with them, Greyson was standing extremely close to him, looking at him intently as he spoke.

"You are all on the fourth floor, the rooms should be next to each other, most will be on the left when you exit the elevator." The man was saying. He handed the room keys to Jonathan, who then passed it to Jackson, who actually read the names written on them and passed them out. "My phone number is written in your booklet with the keycard, please call or text if I can be of service. My name is Tatsuo." He spoke in near perfect English and then bowed, prompting Greyson to bow back.

"Nice to meet you! I'm Greyson, you can call me Grey." She started chatting with him as everyone else made their way to the elevators, "There are a few words I want you to help me with. We can do that later though. I love Japanese culture. One Punch Man is amazing." She ranted on.

"Oh yes, yes. It's a very good anime." He responded.

"We're gonna leave you behind Grey," Peter spoke up as some men shuffled onto the first elevator. The second one opened, a young couple exited, smiling politely at us and then the rest of our group boarded on.

Greyson ran up, looking even more ridiculous in her pajama bottoms, squeezing in before the elevator doors could close. "I can't wait until it's later in the day and I get to see Japan! This is so cool." She stood, facing us, too energetic for the middle of the night. She brought out her keycard and examined it, "Peter, Joey, what's your room numbers?" She asked. They brought theirs out to show her and she eyed them and hers at the same time. "Oh Joey, you're two doors down. Great! But Peter, you're kinda far I think. Remember my number and make sure you visit me!" She smiled up at him, flashing her card number.

"Four twenty-two, got it." Peter smiled back.

I clenched my fist.

What felt like a ridiculously long elevator ride finally came to an end, I watched as Greyson immediately took a right turn. "This way," I said to her.

"Oh," She laughed, skipping over.

I walked into my room, examining the space. Jonathan took me to Japan once when I was a child and I never came back. The hotel had influences from traditional Japanese culture, with paintings of lotuses and koi fish around and there was also a bed runner that looked like it took its pattern from a Geisha. Also, as you walked in, there were slippers available and a counter with a Keurig and multiple tea cups. Everyone's room would have a queen sized bed, a fully stocked kitchenette and a bathroom with a spa tub.

Of course, so many amenities were not my idea, they were Jack's idea and as with everything else, Jon agreed. The more comfortable and relaxed everyone was meant the better the meeting would go. However, if things did not go well, then this was just a vacation our company expensed.

Either way, it was already paid for so I brewed some black tea and decided to run a bath. As I sat in the tub, it finally dawned on me just how serious this trip was. It was like myself from a few months ago finally re-entered my body, and I knew this was serious. It didn't exactly make me nervous, but becoming CEO was on the line and there was no way I was going to crack.

A knock on my door snapped my eyes open and I realized I was dozing off in the bathtub. I stood up looking at my watch that I had set on the sink counter. It was two in the morning, which meant I was out of it for about forty minutes.

I got out of the tub, pulling the plug to drain the water. I opened my suitcase that I had sitting on my bed, grabbing a pair of underwear and sliding on a robe from the bathroom.

When I finally got to the door there was another set of soft knocks coming from it. I opened it abruptly, causing Greyson to jump.

"Yes?" I asked, still trying to wake up from the incredibly deep sleep I managed to fall into.

"Why did you say that to me? Did you really mean it?" She asked and my eyebrows scrunched together for a split second until realization as to what she was talking about quickly washed over me.

She seemed decently annoyed and I nearly laughed. I knew she was probably brooding over this for the past few days and not just ignoring it like her outer persona made it seem.

"It's late and I have a busy day tomorrow. We can discuss this later." The stubborn side of me responded and I went to close the door before she stopped it with her foot.

"Did you mean it?" She asked again. She had a very stern expression and I could no longer read her emotions. I wasn't quite sure what she was hoping for.

I pondered this. It was the same question I kept asking myself since I confessed. Up until now, I was certain I'd never come to an answer. However, as she stood in front of me, finally addressing me directly, it was clear.

"Yes, I meant it."

Chapter Twenty-Six

Chapter 26 - He's Weird (Greyson's Perspective)

"Yes, I meant it." Connor said to me and my heart started to beat faster. It was the same palpitations I kept feeling the last couple of days since he literally told me he was in love with me.

Of all the things, all the bullshit, all the mean words he'd ever said to me, how could I even believe a thing like that? How was I supposed to react to a thing like that? What did it even mean?

Like, I knew what it meant but I didn't know what he meant.

I was praying nonstop that it was just a cruel, sick joke. It was hard enough to convince myself that Connor would play such a joke, but him dragging it out made even less sense. And what made least sense was believing he liked me. So could you even imagine love?

My throat felt like it was closing up and I tried to focus on breathing. "How? Why? Are you serious?" I asked aloud, still trying to figure it out myself. None of this made sense.

I even thought he might have said such a thing to scare me from coming to the merger. But I came, so there was no reason to keep pretending.

Breathe Greyson, breathe.

"I'm going to bed." He said and went to shut the door again.

This time I walked forward, grabbing it with my hand and shoving it open, making him take a step backwards.

"No. You don't get to say something like that, without any explanation, and just act..." My voice was rising and my heart was really starting to hurt. I was so confused, so annoyed and so frustrated that my composure was slipping.

Breathe.

I didn't like the way I felt. I didn't like not understanding what he was saying. I absolutely hated how much calmer he was than me. He had no idea how hard it was for me to sleep the last few nights because his words would flood my brain in such a huge wave I'd get a headache.

"Are you alright?" He asked, snapping me back to the moment.

I was looking right at him, but not saying a word. "Please, just tell me you're joking." It sounded like I was begging, which wasn't too far from the truth.

"Is it that bad?" He countered. "Am I that bad?"

I ignored his questions, "How do you even expect me to believe this? You go from tolerating me to hatin' me in the course of a few hours. Never actually seemin' like you truly enjoy my presence. And then," I paused, breathing quickly a few times, trying to calm down again.

He lightly placed his hand on my back, leading me into his room and then closing the door. It was then that I realized I was probably being way too loud for the middle of the night.

"And then, you nearly sleep with me," I just kept going, "Then you sleep with Sam the next day! And then you tell me I have no validity to speak at this meeting and then you tell me you love me?" My voice was high pitched, confusion dripping from each word. I searched his eyes, but right as he opened his mouth I cut him off, "And you're just gonna ask if you're that bad." I finalized.

"I know. I do understand exactly where you're coming from. I want you to know that I did not sleep with Samantha. Honestly, the reason I shut you out with this meeting is because you said you were doing things with Peter and I was jealous." He was speaking, but none of the words sounded like him. They sounded like they could be coming from anyone else, even Adolf Hitler, but not Connor Meyers.

"That doesn't explain all the other times!"

"It doesn't and I do recognize that. Despite it all, moving forward I am going to be a lot kinder to you. That is a promise."

I grabbed two fistfulls of my hair, nearly ripping it out in frustration, "Connor, do you realize how ridiculous this all sounds? I legitimately can't make any sense of this." I threw my hands in the air. I was feeling so angry and I wasn't even sure why.

"I know," He sympathized calmly, not helping my nerves. I wanted him to fight back, yell at me, do something I was used to. Something I could handle.

"I don't love you." My tone was very harsh and cold. I was attempting to poke the bear, get a reaction, see him act normal.

"I know." His tone was just as even.

"I can't stand you," I squinted my eyes at him and spun around, walking out.

I went back to my room, and sprawled out on my bed, face down. Talking to him didn't make things better.

How was I supposed to feel? I had convinced myself that he would never even like me as a partner and promised myself to pretty much ignore him until after this trip and then leave forever.

I grabbed my phone, wanting to call Liz. I wasn't sure what the time difference was, but I knew it was probably day time over there. I had been thinking of calling her, but didn't want to do so until I spoke with Connor first. I vaguely remembered her drunkenly saying he loved me, but that was so wild I had brushed it off.

I guess hell had froze over and pigs were flying, because the impossible was actually possible.

"Hey girl! Did you make it safely?" She picked up instantly. Her voice made me smile, I needed to hear from a level-headed female.

I flipped over on the bed to face the ceiling. "I did! Thanks for asking."

"Of course! I'm crazy jealous, but happy for ya!" Her positivity instantly put me more at ease.

"Okay, I'm just gonna say it because it's killing me inside."

"Go on," She quickly interjected.

"Remember my work partner, Connor?" I was nearly whispering, scared that he might hear because his room was on the other side of a thin wall.

"Yeah, of course, why?" She whispered back, understanding the severity instantly.

"He fuckin' told me he loves me." I quickly let out, listening as silence followed. "Liz?" I asked and immediately had to pull the phone away from my ear as she screamed.

Like, literally screamed at the top of her lungs. I kept pressing down on the volume button until it was at the last tick mark.

"Liz!" I whisper-yelled.

"Are you fuckin' with me? Grey, I can't believe it. Give me the full story." She was definitely done with whispering.

I tried to recollect my memories and gather them together in a way that made sense. However, in my adrenaline fueled mind I actually said, "So I was like, I'm tired of how mean you are to me and then I walked out of his office. But then I stopped before I actually left and I look at him, he looks at me and then he goes, I'm in love with you. Or somethin' like that. But then, today, well actually... So let me backtrack. He told me that a few days ago. I wasn't around after. But today, or, right now actually. I go, are you serious? And I don't even know, but I think he's serious. Like, what the fuck!?" My voice was rising and I shut up once I realized.

"Slow down! He said he was serious?" She asked for clarification.

"Yes!" I responded.

"I knew it! I fuckin' told you!" I could tell she was smiling from ear to ear. "So what did you say?"

"I uh," I stuttered, nearly forgetting everything that happened just a few minutes prior. "Oh, I told him I didn't love him."

"And what did he say to that?" Her questions kept coming.

"He said, I know."

"And then you said..?" She lead on.

"That was it. I left after that. I ain't got a clue on what to do. Help." I pleaded.

"Well, okay. You don't love him, but do you like him?" She asked.

Despite myself, I hesitated.

"Oh, this is great!" She quickly noticed my hesitation.

"I don't like him. He's such an asshole to me." I finally responded.

"Then why'd you pause?"

"Because I never thought I'd have this conversation about him! I still don't honestly believe this guy has feelings for me."

"Mhm." She responded simply, vexing me.

"Honestly! He's always pickin' a fight with me. Up until now, I was sure he hated me."

"Alright well now you know he's feelin' you. Do you like him?" She asked again.

"I already told you no. He ain't even my type."

"Psh! You don't go no type! And if ya did, it would certainly be men who are assholes."

"Excuse me? They ain't all assholes," I countered, thinking about this. I did date some trash men in my day, "Jay ain't one."

She laughed, "Stop playin'! He's nice now, but that nigga ain't shit when it comes to relationships. He don't know a damn thing about loyalty. Am I wrong?"

She had a point. "They weren't all bad!" I repeated, not being able to think of a person, but I knew there was one out there.

"Whether you want to admit it or not, you thrive off of men who bring drama. But I met that boy myself and I think he would treat you like a queen. And daddy thinks so too." My skin felt hot in annoyance. I shouldn't have been surprised that they were all talking about us, but of course, I was.

I just groaned, this was all too much, "Well, it's late here. I just wanted to tell you the shit goin' on in my life. I'll talk to you when I get back." I finally said.

"Okay," She sounded disappointed, "My advice to you is to give liking him a try and then tell me how that goes. Once you come back, your first call better be to me!"

I rolled my eyes, "And you say I'm the one who thrives off drama. I'll call you when I'm back, buh-bye."

"Bye girl!"

What a trip. Although it didn't feel like a very helpful conversation, content wise, it did help calm my nerves. I placed my phone on its charger and set it on the bedside table and tried my best to get some sleep.

I was in Tokyo for goodness sake.

I woke up at noon, feeling extremely groggy. Jet lag was no joke and only getting a few hours of sleep on the plane definitely took a toll.

I grabbed my phone, there were a few texts from Peter.

Are you awake? He sent at nine in the morning. I scoffed, no way.

We're all getting breakfast downstairs. Just wanted to give you a heads up. He sent around ten.

Are you dead? Lol. Was his last text at half past ten.

I smiled at the texts. I still had no idea what made him decide he didn't want to have sex with me. It made me think about what Connor had said about not sleeping with Sam. That was oddly relieving.

I decided to call Peter.

"So you're Sleeping Beauty now?" Came his voice as soon as he picked up.

I laughed, "I guess so. Where are you?" I asked.

"Connor, Adam and I are at Matsumoto's building. I knocked on your door to try and get you to come along, but after a few tries, we figured you were still recovering from the flight."

"Aw," I frowned. I couldn't stand sleeping through plans, "But how could you guys just give up? I could have actually been dead!"

He laughed, "I guess you don't remember waking up and saying, go away."

"That does sound like me. Okay, have your fun, I'm gonna figure out how to spend the day."

"Remember we have a meeting at four." He added.

"Thanks Spidey. Bye!" I hung up.

At least Connor was gone. I really didn't want to face him yet. Ignoring my problems was my favorite past-time. Adam was with them, which didn't mean anything to me. I probably wouldn't have reached out to him either way.

When he had entered the plane the previous day, he came up to me and apologized for everything saying, "I won't overstep my boundaries." He gave me his hand and I shook it. I wasn't one to hold grudges and I liked his apology. He didn't say anything that Peter or my new friend Joey could pick up on, but just enough that I understood his meaning. It was great.

I thought about finding Jon or Jack, or even Joey. Hah, another "J" name. Then remembered our translator. Whose name slipped my mind entirely. I found my room key and the little paper it was in. I plugged his number into my phone and sent a message. Hello! It's Grey. What are some good places to get noodles that's near the hotel? I sent, setting my phone down to get dresses.

I was going to enjoy every second in this place.

It turned out, Tatsuo was hired to be around all the time and he happily obliged to escort me to a ramen restaurant. Luckily it wasn't too far from the hotel so we were able to walk.

"At night, if you go down this street and turn to the left, it is a marketplace. Only open at night." He was telling me and I was trying so hard to keep the information in my mind. Tokyo was like New York, but better. There were so many electronic billboards, restaurants, Hello Kitty merchandise and there were so many arcades. We walked past one and I stared hard at some kids playing what looked like an updated version of dance dance revolution. I was definitely going to stop in there.

It was all so cool, I even saw a Japanese McDonald's and promised I'd stop in and try anything on the menu that wasn't available in the states.

"Right this way," He opened a door for me and bowed slightly. He was such a gentleman, I loved it. I looked at the title of the restaurant, I couldn't read the Japanese characters, but I was still extremely fascinated by it.

"Listen, order anything you want, I'm paying." I pulled out my company credit card.

"Oh, thank you." He smiled and then led the way to a machine. There were some people ahead of us, and I looked, eyebrows scrunched, trying to decipher what it was. "So this is where we order, I forget how you call it in English, but it has all the different options of ramen and toppings you could want. After we order we will sit down and they will deliver the food to us."

"Wow, you guys have ramen vending machines. The future is now in Japan." I said in amazement.

"Not quite, it doesn't come right away. But yes, it is similar." He was smiling at me.

I liked Katsuo. He was a few inches shorter than me with cropped black hair and he wore rectangular glasses. His voice wasn't very deep, and with his white button-up and black dress pants, he reminded me of the nerdy/analytical anime character. The one who was generally a little awkward, but also really friendly.

I was trying to figure out an exact character to match him with, but my experience with anime was unfortunately not as expansive as with something like superheros.

It was finally our turn in line and I was floored by the amount of options. I definitely went overboard, getting two full bowls of ramen, one that was spicy in a chicken broth with the works and a non-spicy beef one with the works. And by works, I meant almost every single topping. I got tofu, egg, seaweed, scallions, corn, bamboo shoots and a few other things.

There was a possibility I overdid it, but Katsuo was very supportive, so I figured this was a normal phenomenon. Well, normal to the extent that I got two bowls and they were absolutely massive when they arrived.

"Wow, this is nothing like the cups of ramen I'm used to," My eyes were bulging as I took in its beauty. Tatsuo laughed.

"Itadakimasu!" He exclaimed, grabbing his chopsticks.

"What does that mean?" I asked.

"It's like, bon appetit." He explained.

"Oh wow, say it again!"

"Ita-daki-masu," He broke it up, guessing it was because I was trying to learn. Smart man, that's exactly what I was trying to do.

"Itadakimasu," I tried and although I was sure it was rough, he shook his head in support. "So freakin' cool."

After the most fulfilling meal of my life, I had the itis and was ready for a nap. I didn't want to waste any food and I nearly ate both bowls completely, stopping with only a few bites left in the second. I learned that drinking all the soup of the first one was my biggest mistake.

"Well, I wanted to do more exploring, but I'm thinking I'll sleep before a meeting I have. What do you have going on at five?" I asked him.

"I'll be free for any of you who needs me."

"I'll definitely need you. And just so you know, hangin' with me will be a lot more fun than hangin' with any of the guys."

"I look forward to it," He smiled. He was just the friendliest.

What anime did I know that also had super friendly guys in glasses?

As we walked back to the hotel, I noticed that people would sometimes look at me for longer than a split moment. I couldn't tell if it was positive or negative, but I started to look back. Then two girls walked straight up to me, smiled and said something in Japanese.

I just looked blankly at Tatsuo, who laughed and told me, "They are asking if your hair is real."

I laughed at that myself. I washed it before the flight, but didn't do much with it since and it was definitely frizzy and all over the place. "It is real," I smiled at them and Katsuo translated.

They spoke back, directing their question to my favorite translator. "They would like to know if they can touch it."

I laughed even harder, "Yes!" I nodded and they seemed to understand, already reaching their hand up and groping at my hair. It was apparent that they didn't see too many people like me in Japan, not even in Tokyo. I had to bend slightly for them to reach comfortably,

I was a lot taller than a lot of people in general, but even more so in Japan.

"They say it's feels really cool," Tatsuo kept translating.

We finally said goodbye to them and continued to the hotel. I looked at the arcade for a moment as we passed it again, the current boys playing DDR were tapping their feet extremely fast. I was definitely looking forward to the challenge.

I woke up from my nap with just enough time to put on something kind of business-like and head to the meeting. My hotel room was now littered with clothes and toiletries, but at least the cleaning ladies came when I was still napping and I was able to shoo them away. I really didn't want anyone trying to clean with my stuff all sprawled out, they'd easily be able to steal something, or at the very least judge me for my living habits.

In my defense, I could never keep things organized at hotels. I was certain it wasn't possible.

After a decent amount of wandering, I found the meeting room. Well, I found one of Connor's goons and followed him to the room. Mostly everyone else was already there and I found a seat next to Jackson and looked around. Everyone had their laptops, notebooks and pens ready to go. I didn't know this was so formal and didn't bring a single thing beyond my phone.

Great.

Peter finally walked in with Adam, but at that point I had someone to either side of me, so I just silently watched as he sat on the other side of the table, close to Connor.

Connor, who I was still trying to avoid, was standing at the head of the table, the exact opposite of where I sat, pulling up things onto a projector. "So we're going to go through the entire presentation. Jonathan will be acting as Matsumoto, asking us any question that might catch us off guard."

My jaw nearly dropped. This was about to be so long and so boring and I was not properly prepared to sit through a full rundown.

"Okay," Connor started and I sunk in my seat.

I completely tuned him out, my thoughts on how to get out of this were screaming in my head.

As I looked around, everyone seemed to be paying attention, some guy next to me spoke up and then I saw Jon speak up, but they might as well have been the adults in Charlie Brown because I wasn't listening to any of it. I clicked on the home screen to my phone, only three minutes had passed.

My foot started tapping on the floor and I was so unsure about what to do. I forgot to ask someone how long this was going to go and I needed enough time to go back to my room, change, call Jay and then head out again with Tatsuo.

Why did people go through these things so many times? Connor was planning this for months. Couldn't he just be ready and go into this guy's office confidently tomorrow?

I sighed.

"Are you alright?" Jackson whispered to me.

"I have to go to the bathroom." I whispered back, "Can I just go?" I asked.

"Of course," He answered in a way that made me feel safe. Like nobody could complain later because he had the authority and they'd just have to take it up with him.

"Thank you so much," The chair screeched as I pushed it back. I didn't even look up at the eyes I was sure were on me. I simply grabbed my phone, spun around and left.

Time to do more exploring!

Exploring was the wrong move.

Connor called me twice, Peter once, and when Jonny appeared on my caller ID, I was sure these weren't friendly calls.

"Hello?" I picked up, timidly.

"Where are you?" His tone was not as kind and friendly as I was accustomed to.

"I, uh," I hesitated. I had just stepped out of the arcade to take his call and I was still trying to get my heart rate back to normal and my breathing steady. I lost track of how many games of Dance Dance Revolution I played. Tatsuo kept beating me, by just a little bit and I was determined to win a game.

"You left five minutes after the start of the meeting and you never came back. Are you aware that I never intended for you to come here and simply goof off?" His tone seemed to get angrier the more he spoke.

I instantly felt guilty. Disappointing him was like a low point in my life. Up until this point, it seemed impossible to get on his bad side and I missed the nice Jon.

"I'm so sorry, I'm coming back to the hotel now." I waved over Tatsuo and started speed walking back.

"I'll be waiting in the lobby," He hung up.

Oh yeah, he was pissed.

I felt my heart sink, but quickly filled that with a barrier of excuses. I've never heard Jon yell, but if he did, he would have another thing coming. I'd fight back, some way somehow.

Then I felt bad again, but I tried really hard to drown that feeling.

When we got to the hotel, Jonny was definitely waiting in the lobby. He was standing and looked right at me as I opened the door. Connor was behind him.

I looked around some more, hoping to see Jackson, but he wasn't anywhere to be seen. Which was a huge shame because I knew he'd bail me out.

"I'm going to speak candidly," Jon started and Tatsuo essentially exited stage right. "I am well aware that you two working together hasn't been calm seas this entire time," He took a step back, motioning to Connor and myself. "However, I did expect that over these past months, you would eventually have at least one point to make at this meeting."

Peter walked out of the elevator then, his laptop glued to his hands. I swore he wasn't without it since this trip started. He smiled at me, starting to walk in our direction, but I quickly shook my head, 'no', trying to telepathically let him know that this was not the time to step in.

He seemed to understand, slowing down and then just stopping, looking down at his laptop.

"Did you honestly have her working here for this long and didn't give her a single point to make at this meeting? And if you weren't doing anything, why did you not come to me and tell me this?" He was scolding both of us and that definitely made me feel better. Connor wasn't getting out of this one easily.

"To be fair, I have gone to you about Connor," I tried tossing him under the bus, really not wanting Jon to think I was a waste.

That didn't seem to make him happy with me though. He still frowned as he looked at me, opening his mouth to say more.

"May I interject?" Peter stepped forward now, cutting off Jon, "I don't mean to eavesdrop, but I'd like to clear the air. "Connor is very busy and being the one person who knows almost as much as he does with more free time, he's had Greyson work with me. Despite what's happened at this practice meeting, she knows just about everything going on and will have a few things to say, if they become necessary." He spoke and I was never more thankful for him.

He was saving my ass without lying, but definitely exaggerating the truth.

Peter was a lot more cunning than I thought.

"If they become necessary?" Jon added. It was weird to see him still angry and trying to hold on to it. I was starting to think I didn't know anyone here as well as I thought I did.

"Yes, Jon." I opened my mouth, sounding a lot sassier than I intended. Peter's input made me want to be just as cunning, "At the end of the day, you didn't hire me because of my car knowledge. You hired me because of my charm. I ain't stealing Connor's thunder for this, I'm just here to add my flare if that's needed."

To be honest with myself, it wasn't a strong point to make. However, nothing changed the fact that this whole setup never made sense to begin with. That was Jon's fault, not mine.

I think he realized it too because he stayed quiet for a moment.

"I expect nothing but perfection at the meeting tomorrow." He looked directly at Connor, basically ignoring me before walking away.

When they finally got on the elevator I threw my arms around Peter, "Thank you so much." I said to him, squeezing really tight before letting go.

"I've worked in Corporate America long enough to know how people like to hear words. But you are not off the hook, missy. You ignored my call and I need to talk to you." He shunned and I just couldn't stop smiling. He was so great.

"I'm sorry. I wasn't with my phone," I lied. I saw everytime someone called. I only picked up when Jon did. I didn't actually need to lie to him, but he brought out the devious side of me. "We can go to your room to talk, I'm free now." I said.

"Great, it shouldn't take too long." He clicked on his laptop again and headed to the elevator.

I went to follow him, but turned to look at Connor. I didn't actually want to look at him. I wanted to keep ignoring him because I was sure I'd never figure out what to do with that situation, but my curiosity got the best of me and I had to see if he looked okay. His quietness was throwing me off.

Ignoring all the talk of love, he still made a promise to be kinder to me. And yes, I knew I shouldn't have believed it, but promises were something I took extremely seriously. When he didn't blame me for my lacking knowledge of the meeting, it seemed like he was being serious.

Wow, a few days ago, I was sure I wouldn't take any of his shit, but now I was probably doing the stupid thing and essentially crawling back. Maybe it was because I took promises so seriously I felt it had to hold some weight.

Or maybe it's because he loves you. A thought resurfaced before I could shut it out.

As I looked at him, It was apparent that he was staring at me the entire time. Once our eyes met he turned around and started making his way to the door.

Ugh, why was his behavior concerning me!?

Maybe it's because you like him...

That thought stopped me dead in my tracks.

"Grey?" Peter stopped as well, holding the elevator door open.

That was impossible. I never even thought about him like that until he brought all of this up. Not even when we made out in my house did I think like that.

"Sorry," I laughed it off, skipping into the elevator beside him.

It was the day of the meeting and I was extremely nervous! This was such a huge deal and I was never involved in such an important matter.

What if everything went bad?

What if I messed up?

What if Connor froze?

There were just too many what ifs! I looked at myself in the mirror one final time. Liz and I went to the mall and picked up an expensive black business dress. I wanted something colorful, but as the photographer, Liz said we'd all look more like a unit if I matched their black business suits.

It felt slightly like a funeral dress, with the black pumps to go with it, but I really liked the way it cinched in at the waist and went to my knees. I felt so professional and grown up.

"If you could see me now," I said aloud to the mirror, thinking about my dad. I spun to check out my butt, digging the hips the dress amplified.

There was a knock at my door, "Greyson, are you ready?" I could hear Connor's voice on the other side.

I checked for any fly hairs on the meticulous bun I made that took so much conditioner and too much time to create. "Don't be nervous," I whispered at my reflection, "Coming!" I called to Connor.

We rode in the car in mostly silence. I was still so nervous, waiting for the drugs to kick in. I had taken a high dosage of both adderall and xanax, which I could hear my therapist in the back of my head shunning me for, but I needed to focus and be calm. This was my best idea to accomplish that.

"You look nice," Connor finally said and I rolled my eyes. I was far too focused to deal with his absurdity.

"Please," I rose a hand to stop him, shaking my head no. "I'm completely in professional mode right now. Good luck and just know that I'm on your side for this." I spoke and he looked deep into my soul.

He probably wasn't looking at me that deeply, but ever since his confession, I felt like every look was a soul stare.

At the building we all came together and I found my way to Peter. Tatsuo was also with us, directing us into the place.

"Pretty dress," Peter said quietly to me. Everyone else was being so quiet that it truly felt like a funeral.

"Thanks," I whispered.

We got to the front desk, Tatsuo said something in Japanese to the receptionist. She replied and Tatsuo turned to face us.

"She's letting them know we are here," He translated to us and turned back to face her.

After more speaking someone walked out of an elevator and called us in. Once we got into the meeting room, four men were already inside and seated. They were a much smaller group than I imagined, but considering we were a decent amount, it was probably the best for fitting in the space without it getting too congested.

Everyone looked so serious and intimidating. I tried to keep my expression just as grim. The Japanese men stood up to shake everyone's hands, and bow as well. I was the only female and I really wished Sam, the wicked witch, was around. I knew I would feel out of place no matter what, but this felt awkward. So I didn't shake their hands, just stood in the back, waiting for some men to sit before I did.

All the seats seemed to be meticulously chosen. Connor sat at the head, connecting his laptop to a projector. Jon was at his right followed by Jack. Adam sat to the left of him, followed by some guys whose names I did not know. Peter was next to Jack and I sat next to him, as per his plan. The men were all seated around the far side, I assumed the big boss at the head.

He was definitely an older man, with snow white hair, but didn't look any more wrinkly than Jon, so I assumed he was just a few years older.

Either way, the atmosphere started feeling like that of a mafia movie and I was ready for them to start pulling out katanas and then Connor's crew would pull out tommy guns and total mayhem would ensue.

That didn't happen, and what did happen was Connor started the meeting. I was extremely thankful for the meds because I was actually able to decipher some of the car talk he was going into. Everyone was mostly quiet, Tatsuo was quiet as well, which I was surprised because I was sure he'd be translating. Then I realized that we probably needed more knowledge in Japanese than they needed in English.

Despite how quiet everyone but the person talking was, Peter was busy typing away at his computer. It was easy to hear the clicks of his keyboard. I watched what he was doing, as he pulled up files, created many different tabs online and also texted our friend on his phone. He was working so hard and I was jealous. Although he constantly told me I was very valuable, I knew I would never come close to being able to pull things together the way he could.

Everything seemed to be going well. It was my first time watching Connor speak so professionally and he was doing such a great job. Everything was so well organized, all the numbers seemed impressive and he kept it conversational, having his men jump in seamlessly.

He would make a really great boss for the company.

"Your initial stock will see a significant jump," Connor spoke, pressing on a clicker to get to the next slide. It was a line graph and all I knew was that it had a positive slope.

Peter opened up to his one tab and started speaking, seeming unfazed by the fact that he was previously not even listening to Connor, "As you can see, your company will see an immediate jump by thirty percent with what we are offering, by year two, it'll go down, but still be fifteen percent more positive than your stocks currently, and in what we predict to be no more than five years, your new normal should be at thirty-two percent, with fluctuations, but as our resources grow we'll eventually double your current stock value." He stated.

I was amazed. I knew a little about stocks from when Peter gave me an entire week crash course on it, but didn't retain enough to understand how important such a point was.

Connor kept speaking after that and I looked at our merger buddies, watching as one man took diligent notes with paper and a pencil.

After a lot longer, Connor got to the end of his presentation and I really wanted to clap. Seeing how nobody else did, I kept my hands to my side.

We were taking a ten minute recess, the Japanese men walked out, and everyone with us started discussing how it went. Jon had a small smile on his lips. He had squeezed Connor's shoulder and I could tell he was proud of him. I couldn't stop smiling either, everyone was so excited.

Connor was now standing near a window, looking out it as Adam stood next to him, talking quietly. It made me think of Connor back at his office, always staring out of his windows.

Peter was the only one not taking a break, still typing on his computer.

"I think Connor has this," I said to him.

"The presentation was perfect," He stopped his typing to look at me. Remember, no matter what, we're okay. Are you all set though?" He asked, probably noticing my leg shaking.

"Yeah! I'm excited for anything. This is just super intense. You should really be the COO." I told him.

"You add a perspective nobody here could ever think about. Remember that." He spoke back just as the men reentered, signaling the end of the break.

The men stayed standing and Connor came back to the table, but didn't take a seat. Adam did take a seat and we all just waited.

The big boss, whose name I was only like half sure about, spoke directly to Jon, "This is the best business proposal you've brought me," His English was very broken, but still understandable. "We looked at the numbers and compared them with another offer we have gotten. Unfortunately, Jonathan, yours isn't as profitable as this one." He said, and I watched as many people's faces dropped and Jonathan's face started to get red in what I assumed was anger. "You still haven't built your company up enough Jonathan. Shame."

Connor was still just standing, his face read something of disbelief or shock.

Jonathan stood up now, "Hitomi, did you know that you had no plan to take this deal before you had us fly out here?" His tone was the harshest I had ever heard it.

Peter nudged me with his elbow, "We're up." He winked at me and I nodded, smiling in anxious anticipation.

I stood up now, along with Peter. He grabbed his laptop and phone, then made his way over to Connor's side. Big boss man looked like he was going to speak, but before he could I waved a hand in the air, breaking the tension. "Excuse me. Sumimasen," I remembered the word Tatsuo taught me. Everyone was looking at me. How cool

I felt gave me a surge of energy, "We knew something like this might happen, and we came prepared."

Peter unplugged Connor's computer, plugging his in instead.

Connor was still dumbfounded. I winked at him, trying to signal that I had his back.

"Can everyone take a seat please?"

Chapter Twenty-Seven

Chapter 27 - She's It (Connor's Perspective)

I was absolutely stunned. I realized Matsumoto completely played us. He had no desire to negotiate the terms because he was never hoping to take our case. He had us fly out just to humiliate my father, and in doing so he was humiliating our entire company.

I had no idea what to say. There was no use arguing because he knew he had no intentions to take a deal with us. I spent years waiting to have an opportunity like this and the past six months preparing our company to take on such an endeavor. All of that was in the trash.

It felt like time had slowed down. I could tell Jonathan was pissed the moment he stood up, saying exactly what I had been thinking. I watched as Hitomi smirked, readying to say something I was sure would only infuriate Jon more and further the shock felt in the room.

Then Peter and Greyson both stood up, but I was still too beyond myself to make any sense of anything.

Peter walked over with his electronics in hand and quickly whispered, "We win," before setting his stuff down beside mine on the table.

Then went Greyson, stopping everyone in their tracks saying, "We knew something like this might happen, and we came prepared."

I was so confused, but then Peter unplugged my laptop and plugged his into the projector, pulling up another PowerPoint.

I looked back at Greyson and she winked at me, a big smile plastered on her face. "Can everyone take a seat please?" She asked, and although reluctant, Jon sat and after a few moments of her staring hard at Matsumoto, he sat as well. Her eyes then found mine again, and she gestured with her hand for me to take a seat. I was far too confused and angry to want to sit down as Greyson was doing God knows what.

However, Peter grabbed my shoulder and pushed me down until I was finally sitting.

"Knowing how Mr. Meyers has been trying to get this deal with you for many years, we figured you might be dishonorably playin' us like fools," Greyson said.

I wanted to drop dead. What in the actual fuck was she doing?

"Excuse me?" Hitomi responded, not very amused.

"I suggested that you may be too stubborn to make a deal with us and so we came up with a plan B. We also have a double agent. It turns out, Mister Macchiato, that your stubbornness has made you unpopular." She nodded her head, agreeing with herself before turning to Peter and smiling at him.

"What is this?" Matsumoto asked, anger washed over his features.

"So," Peter took the stage, "You've said you received another business offer? Does the name Riku Ito ring a bell?" Peter opened to a slide with a man's face and a short description.

The description read that he had recently taken over a huge manufacturing company in Japan, that mostly dealt with planes, but his vision was to move into car manufacturing as well.

Matsumoto stood up, slamming his fists into the table, "He made a deal with me," His accent became heavy as his anger rose.

I couldn't stand how lost I was. I remembered barely catching wind of the name, Ito, and how he was the new face of this Japanese company a few years back, but I never looked further into it.

"For everyone in the room who doesn't know... As we have, Riku Ito has also attempted to make a deal with Hitomi to no avail. He first planned on buying out the entire company. Hitomi declined his offer. Riku offered more money, but Hitomi still declined. Riku finally changed his offer, trying to become partners with Hitomi instead, but again, Hitomi declined. Riku gave up, but Hitomi, probably after realizing his mistake, went back to Riku stating he would accept his business proposal. Let me show you all how much his stocks would rise with that deal." Peter clicked on his laptop, showing a bar graph of the growth.

"How do you know all this?" Hitomi asked, his men beside him just started grabbing their phones and making calls.

"We called Riku!" Greyson chimed in, "You are unpopular with a lot of people because of how stubborn you are. You can't live life thinking your way is the best all the time." She spoke.

Hitomi said something in Japanese and the man he spoke to nodded quickly and placed the phone to his ear.

"Not only are you now missing out on this deal with us, but you are also missing out with Riku who looked at our business proposal and decided to accept. It turns out his company will be more profitable with our deal than with yours. This deal has the potential to make your company obsolete, not to mention making our gain twice as much with him than with you." Peters words were shocking.

Did he truly think through this deal thoroughly and were his numbers accurate? Could he possibly make such a deal and have done it behind my back? And honestly, how could he keep this from me?

"I also have Riku here with us today," Peter pulled up his phone to show Riku on his FaceTime. Riku smiled and waved over the phone.

Hitomi, without wasting a breath started speaking rapidly in Japanese. Riku responded and I looked at Tatsuo, our translator to start doing his job.

Matsumoto asked him if this is true," Tatsuo started whispering over to me, "Ito is confirming this. Matsumoto is really upset." I looked away from him to catch my father's eyes in all of this.

He looked just as confused as I was, probably questioning if this was my doing.

"Thanks Riku, we will call you as soon as we leave here," Peter broke up the men's conversation.

"I look forward to it," Riku responded and hung up.

The room fell silent, everyone trying to process what went on.

"Jonathan," Hitomi's voice was soft, defeated. "We've known each other a very long time and I am willing to take your business proposal." He folded.

Greyson scoffed, a smile still plastered on her face as she sat down.

Jonathan was quiet for a long moment. I could tell he was trying to calculate everything in his mind.

Jackson finally leaned over and whispered something inaudible in his ear.

Jon listened and nodded in agreement. "That decision is for Greyson." He said and everyone's eyes seemed to land on her. I watched as Hitomi scanned everyone's faces, trying to find who was Greyson.

"You've lost your mind," Greyson responded, "No way. This decision is for Connor." She looked at me, her smile reaching her eyes. I could tell she was so excited and I would probably appreciate the look, if I wasn't too busy being lost as all hell.

I looked away from her, looking into the eyes of every man in the room, all of whom I had worked with for many years. Adam's eyebrows were raised, just as stunned silent as everyone else was. None of them had seen a plot twist like this, nor probably would ever see something like this again.

I then looked at Peter who was the only one, beyond Greyson, who actually knew this would happen.

He simply shrugged, signaling that this decision was my own.

My business minded persona finally resurfaced, and with strong conviction I said, "We will be going into business with Riku Ito."

Greyson laughed loudly once, standing up abruptly, "You get nothing! You lose! Good day, sir." She nodded once and grabbed her things, heading out the door.

Everyone still sat, but when Peter collected his things and began to make his way to the door as well, everyone figured it was the right move to leave and started to gather their things.

Finally Hitomi was the one stunned in silence. I saw Jonathan stay back, probably to exchange some words with what used to be his greatest endeavor. Now, in just a quick moment, that all changed.

"What just happened?" Joey asked me as soon as everyone was out of the office.

The men gathered behind Peter, who had his laptop open and was explaining the deal that was just made.

"Congratulations!" Greyson, obviously overcome with excitement, threw her arms around me in a bear hug. "This deal is gonna make your whole company a lot richer." She let go of me, a smile still on her lips and a twinkle in her eyes.

I had no words. How did this happen? When did this happen?

Without saying anything back, I turned away and went to Peter, stopping him from his glory rant, "Can we talk for a second?" I asked, and he stepped away from everyone to walk with me. "Everyone can start heading out, we'll meet at the hotel." I spoke to the group, making sure we didn't spend too much time in this building.

"Connor, what you'll be making with this deal is unheard of." He spoke up as soon as we created enough distance between us and everyone else.

"How did I not know about this?" I questioned. I honestly could not get over that tidbit. He had spent so much time around me, but never felt that this was something to, at the very least, casually mention.

"Relax, everything worked out." He responded, getting defensive.

"Relax? I had to watch silently in my meeting, my very meticulously planned meeting, as you made a deal I never even heard of. One that I'm not even sure of the details, or if it's as good as you say. Do you know how dumbfounded I looked?" I kept my tone relatively even, not trying to yell in a building I didn't own.

Peter looked fed up with me, "First, don't insult my skill level because you're mad. This is significantly more profitable than the deal with Hitomi. Second, Greyson and I both tried telling you multiple times. Maybe if you didn't keep your head shoved so far up your ass." He paused from his rant, "How about instead of scolding me, you thank me. And when you're done doing that, you can thank her as well." He started walking away, not giving me a chance to say anything.

I stared at ground, waiting for him to disappear onto the elevator.

"And by the way. I didn't need to tell you or get your approval. Greyson is COO, so going through her was completely permissible." I looked over at him as he talked on. I caught him shrugging as the elevator door closed.

So that was why he worked with her so diligently. Talk about someone who knew how to play the game.

Once outside, I was surprised to see Greyson standing beside our car. "Why are you still here?" I looked around, but every other car, besides Jonathan's and Peter's was gone. I looked at Peter's car, but it soon pulled out of the lot.

"Literally only because we share a car," She spoke frankly, "But you also lucked out because I wanted to talk about what just happened!" She hopped once, throwing her arms in the air. "Leggo!" She threw the door open and stepped in.

As soon as I got one foot in the car, she started speaking.

"Did you see the big boss's face? He had no idea that was coming! I can't believe he tried to beg for y'all to take him after that. So much for bein' so stubborn. And I can't believe I was able to speak so well! I was really nervous, but I don't think anyone could tell. Then you took the deal with Riku. Man Connor, the way you said it too," She whistled, "That was so cold. It was like you had a bucket of ice and threw it right at him! I'm so ready to party!" Her recollection was all over the place like how all of her conversations went.

This was the first time she had spoken to me so excitedly in what felt like far too long. It was refreshing to see that she could be that excited around me again.

As nice as it was, I still needed clarification, "Greyson, why didn't you tell me about this?" I could understand that Peter tried and gave up, but Greyson? It wasn't in her nature to give up. Especially if it was something she was this excited about.

"I tried! You didn't like hearing the words Japan, meeting or merger come out of my mouth so I told Peter to tell you," Her happy-go-lucky smile dropped and she became serious. "At that point it was already getting close to this trip and Peter thought I told you awhile ago. So, I suggested we ask Riku if it would be cool if we kept him on standby and have the decision made during this meeting." She was explaining like she was in trouble and needed to prove her innocence, "Peter thought that was a stupid idea and that he wouldn't go for it, but he asked him anyways. Riku is so cool, he laughed and told us about the deal he made with what's his face, and was confident he wouldn't take our deal and that it would be a funny twist. Which it was. So we decided to make it a surprise."

I considered this, still unsure about the whole ordeal.

"It's your fault," She added. "I really did want to tell you." She finalized and looked out the window.

"I know," I finally said, not wanting the atmosphere to get unpleasant again. "I'm sorry. It was my fault for never actually talking about this merger with you."

She groaned, "Is there really nothing I can do to make you angry anymore? You really aren't gonna yell at me, huh?" She turned her head back around to look at me.

I was confused. Didn't she want me to be kinder?

"Bring back the old Connor," She added.

"You want me to be angry with you?" I asked, truly trying to understand what was going on.

"Yes! Yell at me or be pissed or somethin'. Not this apologetic Connor. This isn't you."

What the fuck?

"You were literally just complaining about me being so mean to you all the time." I countered. Was she being serious? Or testing my limits, possibly?

"I know, but like..." She paused, "I don't know. I'm used to that. Not this." She sounded like she was reasoning with herself, "I just don't know how to talk to you anymore."

I scoffed, she was actually insane. "Women." I shook my head, and turned to face my window.

"Excuse me?" She spoke up. "What's that supposed to mean?

"You do realize you are making absolutely no sense?" I spun my head back around to speak to her.

"Great, now you know how I feel. You're welcome, by the way." She crossed her arms and tilted her head.

She was just far too good at getting under my skin, "For what?"

"For giving you the best deal of your life! Maybe when you're CEO, you'll think about makin' me your COO for real." She suggested.

"So you do want to keep working here?" I asked, intrigued by her proposition. It lifted a weight off my shoulders. I knew her comment about disappearing after the summer had me worried. But now, after everything that was said, she was entertaining the idea of staying longer.

"Thanks for everything Greyson! Oh, you are most certainly welcome, Connor." She mocked, rolling her eyes.

"After I look at this deal, if it is good, I'll thank you." I assured.

"I'll be waitin'." She smirked, turning to look out the window once more.

I knew somewhere deep down that this was the best outcome to happen at this meeting. Especially considering Matsumoto wasn't even planning on taking our deal.

At the hotel, we all reconvened at the meeting room and listened to Peter talk in detail about this new proposal. Everyone asked every single question they could about the specifics and any possible errors on his account, but he managed to answer every question and had looked into every detail. He truly devised this perfectly.

When it all seemed settled and Jonathan gave his stamp of approval, all the men clapped and cheered. I watched as Adam slow clapped, shock still evident on his face.

"I definitely don't deserve all the credit. I never would've looked into this if Greyson hadn't planted the seed." He motioned to Greyson and the men clapped more.

She laughed, trying to shrug it off, but I could tell she enjoyed the praise. "All I said was, this guy can't literally be the best in Japan and I wasn't sure why Jonny didn't find someone better. Peter was the one who decided to actually look into it."

"Not a single other person thought to even question Hitomi. Don't cut yourself short." Jackson added, giving her a warm smile.

"Well, we have a few more days in Japan, tonight, let's celebrate!" Charlie chimed in. I was sure this was the only reason he came along.

The men started chatting amongst themselves and filing out of the room. Peter was giving Jonathan our new business partner's information so he could start meeting with them right away. I walked out as well and pulled Adam aside.

"What are you thinking?" I asked him.

"I just," He paused shaking his head, "I've always been the one to look into loopholes and find better deals. I've know about this guy becoming CEO and wanting to move into car companies, but I never imagined it would be a much better deal than Jon's. I'm surprised at myself for shrugging it off, but even more surprised Greyson was the one who thought it was wise to look into it."

I listened to his words, it seemed everyone was surprised this came from Greyson. Although, it was definitely Peter who actually planned the deal, it wouldn't have even occured to Peter if it wasn't for her. "Believe me, I know. Just be thankful it went well and use the excuse to get drunk. It still took everyone's research and work for Peter to piece together a modified deal for Ito." I reminded him and he shook his head in understanding, walking off.

I think I owed Greyson an apology.

It didn't take too long to find her, as she was chatting with Joey and our translator. And by chatting, I meant loudly expressing herself, with arms flying out in dramatic flare.

"Greyson," I called to her as I walked over. She looked over at me and I noticed her expression fall slightly. "Can I talk with you?" I asked.

She sighed, "I suppose."

I nodded and led her in the direction of the elevator, "Are you hungry at all?"

She was quiet for a second, considering this. "Now that you mention it, yeah kinda."

"Let's grab some brunch," I said as we walked onto the elevator.

"Do you need to change first?" She asked, as I pressed on the button for the thirtieth floor.

"No," I responded.

"So then where are we going?" She said with an attitude.

"Have you not explored the hotel? There are many restaurants here." I responded back with the same amount of sass.

"Oh," Was her only response.

The restaurant I took her to was one that had a ceiling made of glass and a decent sized garden. It was like being in a greenhouse.

It was more of a place to grab tea and some small desserts, but I looked into the menu and I knew it also had a decent array of food as well.

"Wow this is so pretty! This hotel is so cool!" She looked around, walking off to look at a tree instead of following me and our hostess to our seat.

I was now used to this habit of hers and waited for her patiently at the table.

Once she seemed satisfied with her exploring she looked around for me and skipped over, a smile on her face. "I guess I need to look around this hotel more." She finally said as she settled in.

After we ordered some light snacks, Greyson spoke nonstop about Japan. She rambled on, not letting me get any words in. Even as she asked me about my opinion on the place, her questions turned rhetoric the moment she talked on.

It occured to me that she was nervous about whatever I wanted to talk about, which was hilariously adorable.

When she placed her hands on the table, I took that opportunity to place mine over hers, causing her to stop talking. She just looked at my hands as if I had pressed on her pause button, "Greyson," I said, causing her eyes to snap up to meet mine, "I want to apologize to you."

She finally pulled her hands away, taking them off the table and into her lap.

"I'm sorry that I didn't include you in the planning for this merger and dismissing you. I also apologize for truly not believing in your ability to do this job and for all of my terrible behavior towards you." I finally told her and felt this sense of relief. It was a long time coming and it definitely needed to be said properly and personally.

"Thanks Connor," She looked at the table and nodded a few times before looking back up at me. "I forgive you for that stuff. Honestly." She gave me a small smile.

Our food came then and I took that moment to truly savor her acceptance of my apology. She had such a kind and forgiving heart. I wondered if I would be so forgiving in her position.

When the waiter left, Greyson spoke up, "I know I asked this already, but did you really mean what you said to me? Y'know, about the love thing?"

"Yes," I quickly replied. It appeared this question was on her mind quite heavily.

"Why?" She quickly countered.

It was a valid question, but one I couldn't create a good enough rhyme or reason for so I decided to let it go and leave the explanation to the weird way emotions work. "I'm not completely sure," I chose to respond with.

"I don't believe you are actually in love with me," Her words caught me off guard. She spoke so evenly, like this was the simplest of statements. How could she invalidate my feelings? "Have you ever been in love before?" She asked on, as if her prior point wasn't one to discuss.

"I have not," I answered robotically, still thinking about her words. Just because she didn't want to believe it, didn't make it a lie. "Greyson, I understand that you don't think my feelings are honest, but they are."

She quickly nodded, as if agreeing with me. "Yes Connor, I know you believe you are in love with me. I'm not sayin' that you're lying. I just..." She paused, "I don't think you even know what love is, I guess."

Her words stung. Not because of her unintentional insult, but because of its truth. I wasn't sure what it meant to be in love with a woman, but nobody really did until they decided they were.

Right?

"I'm sorry," Her voice broke my inner monologue, "Connor..." She paused, pressing her lips together in uncertainty, "What exactly do you want from me? A relationship?"

Of the small ways I was recently finding to compliment Greyson on, her unpredictable questioning was certainly on the list.

Such a basic question, yet one I had not even considered.

How do you confess to someone, but have no idea how you want to proceed forward? I thought to myself.

I had spent so much time concerned that she was leaving after the merger, that I had no idea about what I wanted personally with her.

"I'm not sure," I finally said after an extremely long pause.

I knew she could tell I was unnerved. And I also knew that she was happy to have the upperhand.

"Do you just want sex?" She asked, no filter.

"No." Was my response.

"A friendship then?"

"Well yes, I definitely want that."

There was another long pause. This conversation was truly awkward in a painful way. It was outside of my area of expertise and the longer we spoke about it, the more I wanted to get up and leave.

"Well, you know," She finally started speaking again, "Once we get back I start school again in like two weeks and then after that I'm going to the military..."

I had to cut her off, "Let's not think that far ahead," I looked at her until she nodded in agreement, "I am aware you start school soon and that was originally when you and Jonathan decided you would be leaving the company, but after all you've done, I think you should consider staying and working part-time."

Her eyes lit up, "You really want me to continue working here? Or is this the emotions talkin'?" She asked, trying to push her excitement down.

"With all of your hard work, you definitely deserve it. There's going to be a lot of changes now with this merger, but I think we can find a place for you that you would enjoy. That is, if you want to stay with us."

She smiled to herself, trying to hide it.

It was definitely impossible for her to hide a smile.

"Maybe I'd like that." She finally said, still trying to pretend she was only considering this when I could tell she was definitely going to take me up on this offer.

I smiled myself. It was nice knowing she truly wanted to stay despite everything.

We finished eating and I placed a few twenties on the table before we left.

"You should get some rest. Everyone is definitely going out tonight and I'm sure the guys are planning to stay out until the bars kick them out." I told her as we headed back to our rooms.

"Yeah that's a good plan. I can't wait to party with everyone here in Japan! I think most of the guys on this trip have warmed up to me which is nice. I know a lot of them didn't like me when I first started here," She spoke, going into more detail than I believe she originally intended. "Wow, I can't believe how many people I proved wrong.

Even Miguel, my favorite company cook and my valet buddies were skeptical. But Amanda is going to be so happy!" She kept going until we reached our room doors.

"Thank you," I told her, slipping my keycard into the door.

"For what?" She asked.

"I told you that if this deal was as good as you said it was I'd thank you. So thanks. I'm proud of what you've accomplished." My door clicked open and I stepped one foot inside.

"Hey Connor?" Greyson called, causing me to step back out to look at her. "What if I like you too?" Her question, like all of her questions, floored me.

I looked at her for a moment, not quite processing her question, "Do you?" I finally asked back.

She paused as well, biting on her bottom lip, "I'm not sure."

I looked at her for a long moment, my heart was beating faster than I wanted to admit. My gut was telling me to go up to her and hold her, but my brain disagreed. "Why did you kiss me back that night at your apartment?" I asked. We had never had a true conversation about that night and I wondered if it was really just a heat of the moment thing for her.

Silence followed.

"I'm," She hesitated, "I'm not sure."

"Okay," My tone came out very flat. I wasn't sure if she was truly unsure or if she was refusing to tell me. But if she wasn't ready to talk frankly about that event, I wouldn't push it. I simply walked into my room, making sure the door closed all the way behind me.

My intention was to rest before the night out, but that didn't go as planned. The idea of Greyson possibly liking me was too much to comprehend. Even though she posed her question as a hypothetical, something about her even suggesting it, made it feel far too real.

I was trying to do some research on our new business partner, but couldn't keep my mind on that. Japan had went well. In a very strange and backwards way, no less, but it was done. I no longer had that stress on my shoulders and because Jonathan would be finalizing all the details, I truly had no work I needed to do.

It was a strange feeling for myself, the emptiness of not having any work to do, but I imagined how much greater that feeling would be if I didn't have the stress of what to do about Greyson on my mind.

Her question of what I wanted with her, her point of me not actually loving her and her hypothetical of liking me were shoved to the forefront of my mind on metaphorical large red signs with lights blaring around it.

What if I don't love her? It wasn't like me to be dramatic with my feelings. Well, that wasn't necessarily true. When I was angry, I was known to blow things out of proportions. However, with love?

I mean, I only considered the thought when Jonathan had a heart to heart with me. It was possible that I was being the one acting in the heat of the moment. This was Greyson for goodness sake! The young college girl who couldn't sit still, was far too bold and stubborn for her own good and came from a completely different world than I!

They were the same points I kept reminding myself of, but no matter how I thought about it, I truly liked it when she was around, especially when she was speaking to me.

So if she gave me the chance, what would I want with her? I pondered this point deeply. I knew I at least wanted to build a friendship, a true one, but what did that even entail? Our entire time working together started off on a bad foot. I had no idea how to start over.

And then, as if to add an ironic cherry to my elegant cake, our car conversation from earlier revisited my mind, where she was upset with me for not being mean to her.

I hadn't realized I was pacing until I sat down in my bed, placing my head in my hands. "If only this were a calculus problem." I said to myself, shaking my head in frustration.

I really needed to start getting ready. I was getting texts from the guys asking about my whereabouts. Everyone was mostly ready, but for some reason wanted to wait for me. My original theory was because there was no way they could get in trouble if I paid for the alcohol with my card.

However, Jon was also tagging along, so there was no way anyone could get in trouble.

Once we arrived, I learned the reason everyone was so concerned about me attending.

"Surprise!" Yelled Greyson, Charlie and Joey. Everyone else just laughed and patted me on the back.

"Congratulations on a successful meeting," Jackson said as we walked into the nightclub.

It wasn't actually a surprise party for me. There were already a bunch of people inside, but we did have a private section where there were balloons and a banner that said 'Congrats Connor.' It was very cheesy and unlike anyone at the job to put together.

"Do you like it?" Greyson asked.

She didn't ride in the same car as me on the way here. She had texted me saying she was already riding with the translator and Joey. Considering the awkwardness I felt between us, I didn't fight it.

"Is this your doing?" I asked her, already knowing the answer.

"Yes!" She squealed, sitting me at the table next to her. "So, I got the banner a long time ago and completely forgot about it until I was packing for the trip. Jon had a private section rented out for us anyways, so while you were resting, we were able to get the balloons and this confetti and decorate the space!" She smiled, expectantly at me.

This girl didn't dwell on anything. You'd never guess a few hours ago she told me she may like me. "This is really nice Greyson, thank you." I told her and she seemed to radiate sunlight.

"It was no big deal!" She downplayed, but I could tell she liked the praise. She always liked her efforts to be appreciated, but wanted to seem humble at the same time. It was just another adorable thing about her. "Tonight, this place has karaoke and I expect a duet!" She told me before walking off.

What a person.

Jonathan finally came up to me, a drink already in his hand. As dignified as he was, he had an immense love for parties of all kinds.

Despite how scary he could be as a boss at times, when he was having a party, he was always a lot more friendly and didn't like to let any work drama effect him. Even if he gave any of his subordinates hell at the office, that person would probably agree that he was a fun guy just from having been to one party with him.

Although I personally found certain parties unnecessary and I couldn't relax fully if work was hectic, I tried to follow his lead in allowing parties to simply be a fun event. It would have been easier to do if he didn't throw so many.

"I tried inviting our new business partner out tonight, however he could not attend. He is free tomorrow for an informal meeting with you and I. It's scheduled for four in the afternoon, so feel free to enjoy tonight to the fullest." He smiled, raising his glass as in a toast, "You and your team deserve it."

"Do you really like this deal, dad?" I asked him. With the way everything happened, I didn't have any time to talk to anyone about this.

"I do and you will too. I just can't imagine what would've happened if Jackson never proposed having this girl work here." He took a sip of his drink and walked off.

I caught on to what he was hinting at with his statement and I decided to find Jackson. Everyone else was already ordering rounds of drinks, preparing their drunk persona. Japanese pop music was also playing loudly throughout the place and it was very dark.

It seemed everyone gravitated towards Peter, allowing him to reiterate and go into more detail about his story of this merger. Peter was wallowing in his glory. Despite how he went about this, I knew he deserved his recognition and definitely a raise. I thought about our past disagreements and how I considered firing him for a short period.

And now I was thinking about giving him a better position in the company.

"Who are you?" Jackson said when I finally got to the seat he was occupying. Instead of sitting at one of the tables, he was relaxing in one of two comfortable chairs near a small table.

I took the seat next to him and signaled to Charlie, who conveniently looked over, to get me a drink. He nodded in understanding.

"I'm sorry?" I asked Jackson. One of his special characteristics involved speaking in a confusing format. It was one of the reasons I could never understand how Jon could take his advice to heart. Sitting in meetings with Jack always led me to receive a stress migraine. His personality was too eccentric and his thoughts too eclectic for such a business.

"I don't recognise you anymore," He smiled, taking a sip of what I assumed was Bourbon.

"Here ya go boss," Charlie handed me a drink. I took a sip, knowing it was Scotch. Not because it was my favorite, but because it was Charlie's, and if you ever asked him to get you a drink, it was what he'd get himself.

"Thanks," I nodded him off. I looked out past our section and saw Greyson trying to teach our translator some dance moves. She seemed to always make friends with the most unlikely people.

I finally refocused on Jack, grudgingly hoping he would elaborate on his riddle.

"I don't believe you even realize how much you have changed." He said again.

I looked at my drink for a moment, still not exactly hearing his words. "Jackson, I simply came over to express my gratitude. I know we seldom see eye to eye, but it turns out hiring Greyson was a good idea."

He smiled lightly. It was odd how much he looked like my father when he did certain gestures. "The last time you thanked me for anything, was during your thirteenth birthday when I gave you that limited edition model sports car from Germany." He spoke and my mind instantly went back to that gift. It was a shiny silver Audi Avus Quattro, and at the time I thought the design was so modern and cool. I couldn't believe Jackson surprised me with it for my birthday.

I knew I had it somewhere in Jonathan's house, still in its original box. I had collected so many model cars before that birthday, but that was the first time I kept one in the box and over the course of the next few years, I collected many more and kept them in their boxes.

"Listen Conn, I'm aware I didn't always give your father good business advice. I feel bad about the things that went terribly, but..." He paused, shifting in his seat so that he was leaning in closer to me, "Those things that you learned to fix, made you much more capable for this company. Everything was too easy for you, until my mistakes really made you think. Once Jon retires, you will be prepared for anything." He spoke, and his point didn't make me feel good at all.

Some of his mistakes almost made the entire company crash and burn. Sure I learned how to handle it, but I was confident no other issue would ever compare to his bullshit.

"About Greyson," He changed the subject and I zoned back in, "Ever since my brother gave you the title of chief operating officer, you became more and more of an asshole. No offense." He raised his hands in submission, "You had a short fuse, kept firing people for no good reason and rode on this high horse of yours." He was now speaking very offensively, which I did not appreciate.

"To be honest, I never really cared about this merger for your father. I told him she was the ticket to this because, I knew that was the best point I could make to have him agree to my idea," He shrugged, confessing to this lie I never even knew about. "I'm actually shocked things worked out because of her. I only wanted her here because the moment I saw her, I knew she'd give you hell and I had high hopes she'd be able to put you in your place." I was sure my jaw dropped, I couldn't believe it.

Did everyone think I was that bad that they teamed up behind my back to try and cause me grief?

"It turns out, she did just that and more," He laughed, leaning back in his seat once more. "So for that, your welcome Connor." He clanked his glass against mine, even though I didn't raise mine to him.

This was exactly why I didn't thank him, or talk to him often. It was aggravating. So I half-smiled at him, got up and walked back to the main group.

"What's going on over here?" I asked Joey, who was truly enjoying his time here. I thought about how I never had a male assistant. I wondered if my track record of female assistants was just for the occasional hook-ups.

"They are setting up to play a game called, 'even or odd' that I believe Tatsuo told them about. The gambling wage is a ten dollar minimum and they have to roll two dice and see whether the sum amount is even or odd. Those who picked the correct one splits the pool. I want to see how my luck is if I consistently bet odd." He explained to me.

"Connor, let's do this first round just us two," Adam called to me from across the table, "One hundred dollars, you can pick, even or odd." He winked at me, taking a drink from the bottle he was holding.

"How is he drunk already?" I asked, shaking my head. The men around him started chanting me on. Their excitement made me smile. Were they all drunk?

"So those of us who came over to help Greyson set up, decided to do a little pregaming," Joey spoke up, eyes on Adam, "Greyson took shots of water, but Adam..." He paused, looking at me, "He pulled out a bottle of absinthe. So we might have to call an ambulance by the end of the night."

I grabbed the bridge of my nose in frustration. Adam was far too reckless with alcohol.

"Connor, make this bet with me!" He called to me again.

"Make it more interesting," I countered. I wanted to teach him a lesson about his alcoholism, "If I win, I get to cut your salary by ten grand." I added. I knew it was ridiculous, and any sane person would not agree to it.

"Deal! And if I win?"

Drunk Adam was not sane. "I'll raise it ten," I said and he smiled.

"Hold on," His words were just slightly slurred. To the normal eye, it would appear he wasn't too drunk yet. However, I knew he was great at hiding his drunkenness and by the slight slur I could pick up on, I could tell he was pretty far gone, "In a year, when this deal with Japan makes you more money, I need you to raise that ten." He said.

It was his attempt at keeping his intelligence. Too bad it didn't ensure himself if he lost. "I bet even," I said and everyone cheered, watching the man with the dice place them into a cup and start shaking them around.

Adam smiled wickedly, very excited.

Long story short, he lost the bet, therefore also losing ten grand from his salary and an extra one hundred bucks from his original bet. I didn't need the hundred, but I decided to add insult to injury.

He should've known better than to make a monetary bet with me.

I finished my glass of Scotch and ordered another. I was hoping to get at least a little drunk. It would be the first time I truly let go in months, and I wanted to enjoy it. No more thinking so much about everything, only basking in the good that did happen.

A few hours passed and I was not even slightly tipsy. Adam ended up passing out halfway through my second glass and Jackson and I decided to take him back to the hotel. After angrily getting him all settled in his bed, the last thing I wanted to do was get drunk. As we were about to leave Jackson received a phone call and decided to stay in for the rest of the night.

I went back to nightclub, where everyone else seemed to be enjoying their time and decided to sit with a spaced out Jonathan. He was talking to one of his guys, but his words were slurred. The reason he was so messed up was because he also took a few shots of absinthe. Thankfully, he not as messed up as Adam, partially because he had a ridiculous tolerance level, and also heeded my warning to just drink water for the rest of the night.

I was listening in on stories of his, while also watching everyone else. Most of the men moved to the main bar, either flirting with both Japanese women and American tourists, while others were trying to learn some dance moves from Greyson. A select few, which was actually only Greyson and Charlie had done a few rounds of karaoke as well.

Apparently, I missed Greyson's first performance when I was dealing with Adam, but it was only a matter of time until she was back on the stage again. Mind you, she was completely sober as she took the stage confidently, and I learned that although she wasn't a good singer by any means, she didn't have the worst voice.

The place had a decent selection of American songs and Greyson decided on a number from Michael Jackson. I figured it was called,

Do you Remember the Time, from its repetitive chorus. It was amazing to see how into it she was and a lot of people cheered her on. If she did have proper vocals for singing, I could imagine her being a very successful musician. Despite this, she had amazing rhythm and although I didn't quite understand her dance moves, I knew she was good. It was definitely better than anyone in the club and whenever she was on the dance floor people gravitated towards her.

I enjoyed watching her have a good time. A smile never left her face as she moved and mingled with other people. She was stunning, and I wished I had the nerve to join her.

As if she read my mind, she looked up at me then and made her way to me. My demeanor dropped, I did not want to actually join her and the look on her face read a determination that I was sure wasn't good.

"Hey," She panted, her face glistening with sweat. "Why are you being a bum in the corner?" She asked me and I raised an eyebrow at her. She just laughed, "Let's do a duet! I have the perfect song in mind." "I am completely positive that I will not know any song that you recommend." I gave the first excuse that came to mind.

"Oh, but that's where you're wrong! I figured that. So, we will be doing, The Time of my Life! Don't worry, I don't expect to get all Dirty Dancing, but if you think you're strong enough to lift me, I can definitely dig doing that bit."

I looked at her, blankly, hoping she was joking, but her expression said otherwise. "Greyson, you do understand that I can't sing." I told her.

"Psh! Neither can I, that don't matter! Let's go," She grabbed my wrist, trying to pull me from my chair.

"I'm not singing with you." I told her. There was no way I was ever going to, but it was funny to see her try and get me to go along with it.

"You promised!" She whined.

"I did not," I shut her down quickly, "You decided we were singing together without asking me. You've brought your own hopes down."

She pouted, but didn't have any valid points to offer. "Okay," She finally said in defeat, "Anyways, I'm getting tired of all the movement. Let's get some fresh air?" She asked. From the way she was refusing to make eye contact with me, I could tell there was something on her mind.

"Sure," I responded, getting up from my seat.

"Actually, let's go visit a night market. Tatsuo was telling me about them and I'm kind of hungry," Greyson suggested. This girl did not enjoy staying in one place.

"So you want to leave?" I asked, just for clarification.

"Yeah, why not?"

I sighed. I couldn't tell what her intentions were. Knowing Greyson, I was probably overthinking it.

Nobody seemed to notice we left, not even Peter, who was too busy flirting with someone at the bar. We took a car over to a nearby night market, but I wasn't sure how we'd order anything without knowing any Japanese.

Greyson's eyes lit up once we arrived. She seemed to thrive in flashing lights and hordes of people. However, for me, it seemed way too cramped and there were far too many smells in the air. "Connor, do you have any yen?" She asked and ran into the midst of people before I could answer.

How she managed to not get murdered every day of her life was beyond me. I was sure in a horror movie, if there was a clearly lit sign that said, danger, do not enter, death awaits, She'd skip inside, throwing caution to the wind.

Thanks to her long curly hair and height, I managed to keep close enough to her.

Although I feared our lacking knowledge in Japanese would mean we wouldn't be able to order, I underestimated Greyson. None of that scared her and as a woman shouted words in Japanese, Greyson simply pointed at the things she want and nodded at the lady as if she understood her.

"Yes, that one!" She gave the lady a thumbs up when she picked up the item Greyson was looking at. "Two!" She signaled to her with her finger and the lady grabbed another. "Connor! Cash!" She yelled out, spinning her head to find me. When she did, she smiled. "We need money!" She squealed, extremely excited.

I handed Greyson a ten thousand yen note, who then handed it to the lady and refused the change back.

"Greyson! That was nearly one hundred dollars!" I yelled over the crowd of people, but she just waved me off, handing me the questionable meat on a stick.

"You say that like you aren't rich," She took a bite from her food. She would no longer be making any transactions herself.

"Mm, this is so good! Try yours."

"What is it?" I looked at the stick, still not sure about it.

"I have no clue! But it's hella good." Was her response.

She stopped walking to look at me expectantly and I decided to try the meat. Admittedly, it was good, but I generally liked to know what I was putting into my mouth.

"Told ya," She said, even though I didn't comment on the quality. "Sit with me," She jogged over to an empty bench, sitting in it before anyone else could.

I walked over, trying to make less of a show than she was and took a seat beside her, taking another bite from my mystery food.

"I was thinking about your question," She spared no time in getting to the point of all this. I wondered how she managed to stay quiet about it on the ride over.

"What question?" I asked, trying to think back to our conversations. I could only think about what she had said to me and not what I said to her.

"About why I kissed you..." She trailed off, looking at the ground before meeting my eyes with her astonishing green ones.

"Oh," Came my dumbstruck response. Her determined stare caught me off guard.

"I honestly don't know why. Like, I thought it was just a heat of the moment thing, but now I'm not so sure if that's true or if that's what I told myself to make me feel better about it." She explained.

I continued looking into her eyes, listening to her words.

"I've never thought about you romantically. How could I? You are from a whole different world. Like you have all this money, your family owns a successful company and culturally we're super different!" She was rambling and making motions with her hands, but I decided to simply hear her out. "Plus, we were work partners and you like, could not stand having me around. Then, I felt like I was drowning that day in my place and I guess I wanted to be comforted. I'm not sure if that meant I liked you. But then you said you loved me." Her eyes went wide, "And that was so shocking!"

I couldn't help, but smile. It was like she was trying to figure everything out now in front of me, and I was hearing a rough draft of her thoughts. However, that was always how she tried to piece things together. Out loud and all over the place.

"What?" She noticed my change of expression.

"Greyson, it's okay if you don't like me." I stopped smiling now, wanting to be serious with her. "You have many reasons not to, and that's perfectly fine. You can still continue working for the company, my offer remains."

She bit down on her bottom lip, and I raised an eyebrow. "Connor," She hesitated. "What if I want to like you? Then what?" She asked.

There she went and brought this up again. My thoughts instantly spun and I wasn't sure what I was feeling.

Why would she even want to like me? Why was she such an interestingly peculiar individual? Why did I spend so much time treating her like crap? Where did all her confidence come from?

What now?

"Then you give me the chance to show you that I'm worth liking." I finally responded to her. With the way my heart was beating, I was sure I'd have a heart attack.

"So that's it then? We're dating?" Her further questioning only made my heart hurt more.

"So you do want to like me?" I countered. My voice was slightly higher pitched and it nearly cracked. I coughed then, making sure whatever I said next didn't come out so pathetic.

Luckily she didn't seem to notice as she stared off into space. "Yeah," She finally said not looking at me.

I took a second to allow myself to process that without freaking out. "I'll take you on a proper date tomorrow night then, come on," I stood up, extending my hand to her, "It's getting late."

"What happens when we get back to Miami?" She asked again, reluctantly taking my hand and standing so that she was only a few inches away from me.

I had a beautiful gift of being able to look emotionless when I was deep in thought. Externally I seemed to have perfect control over the situation, but internally was a different story. I had no idea what to do with this situation. I wasn't sure what was in store for the future because I never predicted that she would actually go along with this so soon. Or ever to be completely honest.

This was one of those situations I never could truly piece together, because emotions didn't work like business. In business, as long as you had enough money and knew your audience, you could usually get people to go along with your ideas, but feelings...

I never really got in touch with my feelings.

"We'll just have to see," Was my response.

She nodded in understanding, "Can we kiss?" She asked.

I was certain this girl would bring me to my knees.

As if overcome by a force beyond me, my hands found her face, and I stood, in the middle of a busy night market, looking into Greyson's eyes.

As tall as she was, her lips were extremely close to mine and I could feel her heavy breathing. I cradled her head in my left hand and used my right to push away some fly hairs that had come loose from her ponytail from all the dancing.

"I'm going to do this properly," My hands released her face, wrapping around her arms in a tight hug. I buried my face into her hair and felt my body relax when she hugged me back. I kissed the side of her head lightly, before releasing the hug. "Let's go find the car." I reached my hand out to her and she grabbed it, smiling lightly as she followed me back into the mass of people.

The past few months were definitely the most different and interesting points of all my life, I could only wonder what the next few months would hold.

End.

CPSIA information can be obtained
at www.ICGtesting.com
Printed in the USA
LVHW021008211122
733502LV00008B/357

9 781837 611362